only mine

laura pavlov

Dedication…

Dear Dad,
May every little girl be as lucky as me to have a father who teaches
her to never give up. I am so lucky to call you mine.
Please do not read any further.
PUT THIS BOOK DOWN NOW! LOL!
Love you, Laura xo

one

· · ·

Dylan

I SIPPED my chai tea latte, holding it in my spare hand while my other hand rested on the steering wheel. My gaze scanned the street as people moved quickly along the sidewalk on a mission to get to wherever they were going. I loved the energy of the city. It didn't hurt that my sister, Everly, and her husband, Hawk, had an amazing penthouse here in San Francisco that I was staying at for now while they were back in Honey Mountain with my baby nephew, Jackson. I'd grown up in a small town just a few hours from here, and it was home—but I was ready to spread my wings and fly.

Duke Wayburn, the owner of the San Francisco Lions, was going to set me up in corporate housing next week, pending today's final meeting with his son, Wolfgang, went well. I couldn't believe I'd made it this far in the process of being hired as chief legal for a professional hockey team. Sure, I had my brother-in-law and sister to thank for getting me in the door, as they both worked for the organization—Hawk as the NHL superstar that he was, and Everly as the team's sports psychologist. But that connection only got me the initial meeting. After three lengthy interviews, I'd had to sell myself and convince both Duke Wayburn and his current chief legal, Roger Strafford, that I was the right candidate for the job.

A woman who was young and new to her profession, but more than qualified.

I pulled into the gas station, inching my way to the pump on my left. Thankfully, I'd allowed plenty of time this morning to fill up the tank and get my power drink. If everything went smoothly today, I'd be signing my contract before lunch, and I was more than ready. A black SUV startled me as it came from the opposite direction and just missed hitting my front fender as it slid next to the pump that I was approaching.

The freaking nerve of some people.

Chivalry is dead, my friends.

Not that I cared either way. I was not someone who needed a man to do things for me. But common decency was something altogether different. I mean, be a good human, right? Isn't that what life was all about? I'm not saying you have to open my door for me; I can open my own damn door.

But, male or female be damned, don't cut someone off at the mother freaking gas pump.

It's just bad… peopling.

My hands fisted around my steering wheel after I returned my infamous Starbucks cup to the holder in the center console. I would not allow anything to derail my mood today. I pulled around to the other side, directly next to the asshole who'd just stolen my pump, and I shot him my best death glare.

He had on dark shades and looked like some sort of bodyguard. As if he were too important to follow basic rules like the rest of us.

Nothing irritated me more than injustice.

I slid the nozzle in place, adjusting it so that it would start filling my tank automatically as I made my way around the side of the pump, pausing in front of the middle-aged man as he stood there waiting for his tank to fill up.

"Hey. You cut me off, and I don't appreciate it." I folded my arms over my chest and raised a brow. I called it like it is, and this guy wasn't getting away with his bad manners if I had anything to say about it.

"Oh, sorry about that. I didn't see you. I just do what the boss tells me to do."

"And did the boss tell you to be an asshole this morning?" I hissed.

"Is there a problem?" The back window opened, and a deep voice barked at me.

I marched around the side of the car. "I take it you're the boss?"

"That depends on who you're asking." He pulled off his glasses, and his dark blue eyes scanned my body from my toes up to my face before they locked with mine. His brown hair was slicked back, dark scruff peppered his chin, and he looked to be wearing a very expensive suit from what I could see of the top portion.

What can I say? I have an eye for good style.

That didn't deter me.

The devil never showed up in a cheap, knock-off suit—he always came clad in Armani, didn't he?

"Why don't you tell *your muscle* to wait his turn at the pump?" I said, moving closer because I wanted to get a better look.

He didn't smile. His gaze hardened as if I were some sort of mosquito pestering him. "He did. We're here. Why don't you go pump your gas, Princess."

Anyone who knew me well was aware that calling me *Princess* was a trigger, and it would get you nowhere. You'd have better luck calling me King.

"Listen, douchedick, how about you just apologize, and we'll go about our day."

"Did you forget to take your meds this morning?" He raised a brow.

A maniacal laugh escaped my lips. I could deliver sarcasm better than anyone I knew. "Of course... I call you out for being an asshole, so I must be a crazy person?"

"You can call me out however you want. We didn't see you there. Are we done?" He slipped his sunglasses back on his face, and the window moved up slowly.

Are you freaking kidding me?

I flashed him the double bird and shook my head in disgust, storming back toward my car, and the other guy winced when he saw me coming.

"I am sorry about cutting you off. I honestly didn't see you."

"Well, I appreciate you owning it. I'm sorry you have to work for a man who clearly has a small penis." I tipped up my chin, and I heard him chuckling behind me as I made my way back to my car.

My blood boiled, and I closed my eyes and counted down from ten. I'd always been a bit of a hothead, but I would not let this little encounter affect my day.

Not a chance. I pulled the nozzle from my car, placed it back where it belonged, and climbed behind the wheel.

As I pulled out on the road, my phone rang, and I answered as my twin sister Charlotte's voice came through my Bluetooth.

"Hey, big day today, right? Are you ready to meet Wolf?"

There was something about my sister that always grounded me. All four of them, actually. We always had one another's backs, and I could tell them anything.

"Yes. I just got cut off at the gas station, and this guy was such a dick!" I shouted.

She chuckled. Charlotte was the yin to my yang. The calm to my storm.

The peanut butter to my jelly.

"Did you get your gas?"

"Yes."

"Then let it go. You've got an important meeting to focus on. Although, I don't know how I feel about you actually taking this job. That would mean you'd be living in the city most of the year. It'll be just like college again, and I won't get to see you every day."

I'd attended the university here in San Francisco, so the city was definitely my second home. I sat at a red light and reached for my tea, taking a sip. The warmth of the chai relaxed me a bit.

"It's not far, and you know I'll come home often. Plus, the season runs from October to April. I can spend summers back home. Look how often Hawk and Ever are back there. He's an actual player, and she works for the team, too. So, if they can make it work, so can I."

"Touché, sissy."

"Are you on your way to school?" I asked. Charlotte taught kindergarten, and she was made for the job. She was sweet and loving and kind, and I adored her.

"Yep. They're all getting pumped up for Halloween, so that'll be fun. A boatload of sugar and five-year-olds is never a great mix. But, they're framing the house today, so that's exciting."

My sister had married her childhood crush, Ledger Dane, not too long ago. They were building a big home in Honey Mountain. I was the last Thomas girl to remain single, and I did not see that changing anytime soon.

I'd never been that girl. You know, the one caught up in the fairy tale.

The one waiting for a man to show up on a white horse and rescue me. I'd never needed rescuing. Never, ever longed for that.

I could charge the tundra on my own white horse.

That wasn't to say that I wasn't a big fan of the male species.

I was.

I loved men. I just grew bored of them quickly, which was fine by me. The thought of the white picket fence and raising a houseful of rug rats had never appealed to me. I loved my nieces and my nephew fiercely, and that was enough for me. And at the rate my sisters were getting married and knocked up, I'd have plenty of little humans to spoil.

I wanted to practice law. Challenge myself. Travel the world. Experience… life.

"That's so exciting. I can't wait to see this masterpiece all done."

"Me either. So, let's talk about this final interview. How do you feel?"

"I feel like I'm going to own it. I know they have a backup candidate, so apparently, if Wolfgang doesn't jibe with me, they may have him meet the other guy. But Duke and Roger have already told me that I'm their first choice and that I should prepare to hit the ground running tomorrow, as they have an entire itinerary lined up with agents to meet with over the next two weeks. So, I just need to woo the man's offspring. How hard can that be?"

"For Dylan Thomas? It's a piece of cake." She chuckled. "Go in there and kill it. I can't believe you're going to be jet setting all over the place. At least you brought enough clothes with you to last much longer than that."

"I plan on it. And, I have my lucky earrings." My fingers moved to my earlobe, and I twisted the gorgeous pearl stud. Charlotte knew I'd wanted pearl earrings just like our mom wore every day when we were growing up. She'd saved up and bought them for me before my first interview. I'd worn them every day since.

"Ahhh… so you've got Mama with you, too."

"Always," I said. It was true. I'd felt my mother's presence with me more than a decade after she'd passed away.

"I love you. Go kill it the way you always do."

"Love you, Charlie. I'll call you after."

I pulled into the parking garage and found the *Rocky* theme song on my playlist. It was my go-to pump-me-up music. I turned up the volume and closed my eyes as I listened. My dad and I had bonded over these movies when I was young, and this song made me feel like I could do anything I set my mind to.

Once I'd completely channeled my inner badass, I made my way inside. The security guard, whom I'd met the last few times I'd been here, smiled when he saw me.

"Well, looky here. Miss Thomas is back for more. You aren't letting those powerful men push you around, huh?" he teased and held up his hand, and I gave him a high-five.

"Good morning, Deacon," I purred. "Do I strike you as a woman who gets pushed around? Never going to happen. Today is the big day, so I'll let you know how it goes. Hopefully, you'll be seeing lots more of me."

"Only if I'm lucky," he said with a wink.

I loved a guy who had a strong flirt game but didn't come on too strong. Deacon was in his mid-thirties, friendly, and just a good guy.

I held my hand over my head and waved while making my way to the elevator.

I took a moment to gather my thoughts as I rode to the top floor. I was going to go in there and own that room. Prove to those men that I was the right person for the job.

I stepped off the elevator, and Jocelyn greeted me. She was Duke Wayburn's assistant, and she was around my age. We'd hit it off the few times I'd been here.

"Hey, you look gorgeous. Loving this look on you." She winked.

I'd worn my favorite black pencil skirt, a white silk blouse, and red heels. My hair was tied back in an elegant chignon, and I was wearing black glasses, even though they didn't have a prescription. It was all about the look.

And this look shouted: *Badass bitch, ready to conquer the world.*

"Thank you. Is everyone here?"

"Yes. Are you ready to meet Wolfgang?" she whispered and then mouthed the words, *he's so hot.*

I chuckled. Good-looking men didn't affect me all that much. Sure, I enjoyed some good eye candy, but I wasn't the girl who fell at anyone's feet.

Not now.

Not ever.

"I was born ready."

She walked me down the hallway and wished me luck as we rounded the corner to the conference room, where the door was open. I nodded my goodbye to Jocelyn and stepped inside as the men rose to their feet to greet me.

My head nearly snapped to the right when a familiar face filled my peripheral vision.

Piss on a cracker.

"Dylan, I'd like to introduce you to my son, Wolf," Duke said, as he extended his hand to me.

Wolfgang Wayburn was the douchedick from the back of the car at the gas station.

I guess I'd have to rework my plan to dazzle the man.

Either way, I wasn't leaving here without this job.

two

. . .

Wolf

WHAT ARE the fucking chances that the lunatic from the gas station was the same woman my father had been gushing about for the last two weeks over the phone? This had to be some kind of joke.

She came storming over to Gallan, my driver, shouting and outraged with her hands flailing in the air. I mean, what woman charges up to two men who happen to be more than twice her size, and throws down like that? She didn't know if we were fucking crazy or not.

I mean, I was a trained killer for God's sake.

I'd been on a call with Bullet, my SEAL brother, when she'd stormed the castle. Leaving the SEALs was not an easy choice for me, but I wasn't a man who wavered in my decisions. This had always been the plan, and I was ready to step in and take over the responsibilities for the Lions. My father gave me ten years to figure out my shit and do what I wanted to do.

And truth be told—I was ready to be done.

I'd seen things I couldn't unsee.

I'd experienced things that I'd never forget.

Good and bad.

I loved every minute of it.

But it was time for a change.

Bullet was considering leaving, as well, and he wanted to talk it through.

I cleared my throat and offered her my hand as she stood there waiting for me to say something. "My father didn't tell me that you were slightly unstable."

She made a little noise that I was fairly certain was a growl. She was trying to contain her anger, but it was impossible to miss.

The fire in her brown eyes was there earlier, and it was there now. Pops of gold and amber made them appear almost caramel colored at times.

And the way her goddamn skirt hugged her curves in all the right places made it difficult not to stare.

Luckily for Miss Thomas, I was trained to control my emotions.

"I think someone has a flair for the dramatic." She winked and chuckled before batting her lashes at my father and Roger, who were putty in her hands.

I wasn't falling for her shtick.

"Did you not just have a meltdown at a gas station? Do you really think you're fit to handle the legalities of a professional hockey team when you couldn't handle yourself when faced with the slightest bit of an obstacle?" Her small hand was in mine, and she squeezed just enough to let me know I'd pissed her off.

The way her chest rose and fell rapidly at my words, I knew she was about to lose her shit. She'd probably burst into tears and make a scene, then ask for forgiveness.

But instead, she pulled her hand away slowly and narrowed her gaze. "Hmmm... I'm guessing that's *exactly* who you want handling your legalities. Am I right, Duke?"

She turned to face my father, and I had to force myself not to roll my eyes.

My father motioned for everyone to take a seat and then turned his attention to the little minx who sat across from me.

"I take it you two have met?" My father smirked.

"Yes," we said at the same time, but she spoke louder and smiled at me like she'd won some sort of prize. "I don't think you'd be all too thrilled to know that your son cut me off at the gas station today and didn't so much as apologize when I confronted him. I'm not a woman who backs down because the *big, bad wolf*, no pun intended…" she said, pausing to chuckle, right along with Dad and Roger. "Wolf, apparently, doesn't have any manners. I won't tolerate that type of disrespect for myself, nor will I tolerate it for the people that I represent."

Well, I had to give her props. She didn't fall apart the way I'd expected. She'd actually doubled down and spun her crazy antics in her favor.

The girl had bigger balls than some of the guys I'd gone into battle with.

"Clever," I said dryly. "Sometimes, you don't pick a fight when it's not worth losing blood over."

And that was the fucking truth. She shouldn't have confronted us. She didn't know who we were. She could have been hurt.

You don't go picking fights just for kicks. There are plenty of battles that need to be fought.

"I never mind getting dirty when it comes to my integrity. If you cut me off at the gas station tomorrow, I'd do the same damn thing again."

She was reckless.

A loose cannon.

Unfortunately, I knew the other man that my father had as his second choice, Jordan Marks. He was a kiss-ass and always had been. My family had a shit ton of money, and people wanted a piece of the pie. Jordan had grown up in my neighborhood, and I'd never cared for him. He told you what you wanted to hear, what would advance his intentions—not what he actually thought.

I didn't respect that. And as the company's lawyer, I didn't think he'd do the best job representing us for that reason.

But this woman—she was a risk in a different way.

"Sometimes, we need to stop and think. Assess the situation. Not react to everything that bothers us."

"Is this an interview or a therapy session?" She raised her brow, and I leaned back in my chair.

"Miss Thomas, this position is challenging. You're newly out of law school; you have little to no experience. You lost your temper at a gas pump. How do I know you won't speak to the press and say something foolish because you can't control your temper?"

"Oh, I assure you that I can control my temper. You don't have a black eye, do you?" she said, the corners of her lips turning up, and I'll be damned if my father and Roger weren't completely dazzled by her as they both smiled.

I was not.

Sure, she was sexy as hell, and thoughts of bending her over this table were impossible to push away. But did that mean I wanted her to be the voice of reason for this team? Hell no. Hockey was a passionate sport. One I'd grown up playing before going into the Navy. The person we chose to be our chief legal needed to be someone who could handle the ups and downs of this business. Fans were outspoken. They got pissed when someone got traded. They got pissed when we lost games. Hell, they got pissed if they didn't like the style of our uniforms.

We needed a spokesperson who could handle that with the utmost control.

"So, when we go to recruit new players—and I mean, these are cocky, confident assholes most of the time—are you going to punch every dude in the face who rubs you wrong?"

"Oddly, I've never punched anyone in the face. You are the first person I've ever considered hitting."

I tipped my head back and closed my eyes for a second because I didn't have time to argue with her. My father had a list of cities he wanted me to visit, and agents to meet with, so whomever we chose for this position would be joining me. This was Roger's last year, and the season was about to kick off, so I'd be doing all the footwork for next season now.

"I'm honored." My gaze was hard, and I turned to look at my dad and Roger. "You sure about this?"

"Yes," Roger said. "You two will be working closely together these next few months. If it doesn't work out, we can always change things. But my gut tells me that she's going to be able to handle things just fine."

"Agreed. She handled you pretty well," Dad said, and he used his hand to cover his smile. "Most people would melt into a puddle on the floor when you come for them."

"That's the thing. This isn't me coming for anyone. This is me telling you that I don't think she's right for the job."

A little gasp escaped her, and she corrected herself. Her gaze locked with mine, and anger radiated from her small frame. "Who made you the judge and jury?"

"Birthright." I shrugged.

My father looked between us. "We have Roger for one more year. I say we give this a try for ninety days. We can do a short-term contract and see how you two work together."

Had he not been listening to the conversation?

"I think that's a good plan," Roger added.

"Is it wrong that I want to make sure this team is in good hands?" I asked, my voice staying completely even. I knew how to manage my anger unlike the little minx sitting across from me.

"It's not wrong," she said, tipping up her chin. "I have no problem with this plan. I'm happy to show you that I'm the right person for the job. If you don't think I'm up to it after ninety days, you won't have to ask me to leave. I'll go willingly."

"You're that confident?" I asked, intertwining my fingers and placing my hands on the table.

"I am."

"Fine. A ninety-day contract, and then we move forward with plan B." I pushed to my feet. What was the point of bringing me in for the final say if they weren't going to listen?

"So, you two will be leaving tomorrow morning for New York to meet with Braxton Jones first. He's the agent of Juan Rivera, who happens to be the best defensive player in the league. He'll be an unrestricted free agent after this season. You need to be cautious about what you say because these guys are still in season, so keep it light, but we want to get our feelers out there, and talking to an agent isn't a crime. We've got a couple of high school and college prospects that you'll be meeting with, as well, so you've got a busy lineup ahead of you.

"Accommodations are already booked, and you'll each be sent an itinerary. We're going to need to rebuild this team. Hawk is done after this season, and we've got a lot of guys down with injuries. There are going to be several positions to fill next year, so we've got a lot of work to do if we want to stay at the top as we move forward," my father said.

"Agreed. Juan has impressive stats. Since he'll be a free agent at the end of the season, I'm guessing everyone is going to want him," Dylan said, as she followed my father toward the door. "But he's going to cost an awful lot because of it. I heard he and his agent grew up together, and Juan doesn't make a move without Braxton."

"Yes. We dealt with Braxton last year when we signed Jonathan Turner. He made us jump through hoops and no-showed to more than one meeting. I don't know, maybe it's a way of getting more money out of people by not making himself easily accessible, and from what I've heard, it works. He's not your typical high-strung agent who chases the team owners down; he's laid back and takes no shit. That's apparently why so many players have signed with him. He expects people to chase him because he holds the keys to getting these guys on board. That's where your skills come into play," my father said. "Why don't you and Roger go spend some time talking about the dynamics of these early conversations. What you can say and what you can't. These are just discussions. We're not going to get any commitments right now; we just need to plant the seed. Jonathan and Juan played together in the past, and Jonathan told me privately that we should pursue him. Braxton may just shut the door in your faces like he did to us at first, so let's see what you can do. Just getting the conversation started would be a step in the right direction. The high school and college athletes will be a different experience. They want to play in the NHL, so they're going to be thrilled to meet with you."

"Got it." She glanced over at me, and all that anger was gone. She'd switched it right off.

Interesting.

I left the room and made my way to my office, and my father followed me inside and shut the door. "Listen, you are not at battle here. This is a business, not a war zone."

"You said you wanted my opinion, and I gave it to you. I don't think she's right for the job." I moved behind my desk and dropped my ass in the chair. He sat in the leather wingback chair across from me.

"You have a problem with Jordan Marks, as well. He's our second choice. Come on, Wolf. You don't need her to have your back in battle. She's an attorney, who happened to graduate first in her class. She worked as a clerk for a prominent judge who sang her praises. The guy actually said that he believed she'd make a huge difference in the world. We called a few of her law school professors, and they all believed she was the best they'd seen in several decades."

"Are these all old, horny dudes? They probably want to get in her pants."

I mean, who wouldn't?

Not me, obviously.

That would be completely inappropriate.

"Your mom would be very disappointed to hear you speak like that." He pushed to his feet, and I didn't miss the anger in his voice.

"Because I speak the truth?" I hissed.

"Because you just degraded her. I told you that several people sang her praises, and you said it must be because they want to sleep with her. How would you feel to hear someone speak about your mother or your sister like that? I know you've been through a lot, and leaving the SEALs was harder than you thought it would be, but that does not give you permission to be an asshole. I'd rather have someone lose their temper at a gas station than have someone belittle another person just because they didn't get their way. You're better than that, Wolf."

Oh, for fuck's sake. And he played the mom card?

He knew she was my weakness.

There wasn't a better human on the planet than Natalie Wayburn. The only one that came close was my sister, Sabine.

They were a big part of the reason that I'd agreed to leave the SEALs now. My mother had lost sleep over the last decade, not knowing where I was at times, what I was doing, or if I was okay.

She'd begged me to get out and start the transition for my dad to retire. Sabine constantly urged me to come back home. I'd missed a lot of the last decade of her life. She'd graduated from college a little over a year ago and had gone to work for a well-known interior designer in town.

My younger brother, Sebastian, on the other hand, had been on the six-year plan at school, which had allowed him to graduate at the same time as Sabine, even though she was two years younger than him. He'd then taken this last year to travel Europe. He'd just returned a few months ago to come to work for the Lions, as well. But Seb didn't have much of a work ethic. He was overseeing the marketing department but would only drop in one or two days a week, from what I'd heard from my father. He was a roaring good time and the life of the party, but he had no real drive professionally.

Hell, he didn't have to.

We had enough money that we didn't need to work.

I'd just always wanted things for myself. My father was a self-made man. He'd worked his ass off to make sure his family would always be taken care of. The man impressed the hell out of me.

My grandfather on my mother's side had been a SEAL. It was something I always knew I wanted to do. At least until it was time to step up for the Lions.

"Dad," I called out, as his hand wrapped around the doorknob.

"Yeah." He turned around to face me.

"You're right. I shouldn't have said that. It won't happen again." I put my hand up when he smiled as if I'd just conceded. "I still don't think she's right for the job. But I'll give her a shot."

"That's all I'm asking for. Plane leaves first thing in the morning. Touch base with Leo, and make sure your flights are all set. You're hitting ten cities over the next two weeks. Go find us some players."

Leo was one of the pilots who worked for our family, and he'd been with us for as long as I could remember. My dad found good people to employ, and he kept them around. I admired that. I was used to counting on a small group of guys to have my back. They were my brothers. My family. I didn't trust many outside of them.

And I sure as fuck didn't trust the little minx who'd be joining me on this trip.

Not a chance.

three

. . .

Dylan

DUKE HAD SENT a car to pick me up first thing this morning. I wheeled my suitcase outside of the swanky building where my sister and Hawk lived. When I returned from this trip, I'd be moving into the corporate apartment owned by the Lions. I hadn't seen it yet, but Roger assured me it was very impressive.

I was still steaming over the scene that Wolf had made yesterday. Most people would have just pretended we never met. The man completely outed me. And then continually bashed me. I'd phoned Ashlan, my baby sister, on the way home and told her what happened. That led to a sister Face-Time call with all five of us, as they gave me endless tips for how to '*let things go.*' I knew perfectly well how to let things go; I just didn't feel like I should.

But I'd be professional because I wanted this job.

I had ninety days to prove myself.

But I knew Wolf didn't want me there, so I'd keep my eye on him.

"Good morning. I'm Casper," the older man said as he stood in front of a black car and opened the back door for me.

"Good morning. Thank you for picking me up." I climbed into the car and buckled up.

As we made our way to the hangar, where a private plane would fly us to New York, I looked over my notes that Roger and I had gone over yesterday after the interview from hell. There were a lot of dynamics to consider since there were regulations in place to keep teams from contacting players during the season. The interview window was very short and ran from June 25 to June 30. Five days to meet with players to discuss general contract terms, and deals couldn't be signed until July 1. We needed several new players, and laying the groundwork now was going to be key to pulling that off. Meeting with agents, especially those who represented current athletes on our roster, wasn't breaking any rules. If we mentioned interest in other players in casual conversation, we'd at least find out if they were interested in being pursued by the Lions when the time came. I'd done my research on both Juan Rivera and his agent and followed them on social media so I could get a feel for exactly what we were walking into.

I glanced out the window as we moved down the highway toward the hangar. I wondered if it would be awkward traveling with Wolf after he'd made it clear that he didn't want to work with me.

I knew what I had to do. I had to win over Braxton Jones to prove that I deserved this opportunity. Roger had prepared me about having a thick skin because when he and Duke had flown out to meet him last year, he'd no-showed on the first meeting. Apparently, he represented some of the top guys in the league, and a man with too many options could make you chase after him. It was probably part of his game.

I'd memorized all of Juan's stats so if I had a chance to meet with Braxton, I'd at least look like I knew what I was talking about.

When we pulled up at the hangar, Casper helped me with

my bag and walked alongside me to the large plane that sat just a few feet in front of us. He climbed the steps and set my luggage inside before jogging back down toward me and motioning for me to step inside.

"Safe travels, Miss Thomas. And welcome to the team."

"Thank you." I made my way up the steps, and when I turned the corner, my gaze locked with Wolf's.

There were maybe six rows of two seats on each side of the aisle, and I scanned the area trying to decide where to sit. He was on the aisle in the second row.

"I don't bite," he said, his voice deep and void of any humor.

I fought the desire to roll my eyes or say something snide because I was here to prove that I could handle my temper.

I moved to the seat on the other side of the aisle from his and set my briefcase on the empty seat before sitting down and buckling my seat belt. "I'm not worried. We're both professionals."

"As long as I don't cut in front of you in line, right?" His jaw ticked.

"Well, you took your shot. You did what you could to make sure I didn't get this job, yet here I am, sitting beside you. I'd say that's a bit worse than cutting in front of someone in line."

Something passed in his dark blue gaze, but I couldn't read it. Maybe he felt bad? Maybe he was just trying to see how far to push me.

A man appeared in front of us. "Mr. Wayburn, we're ready for takeoff."

"Leo, you've known me since I was a kid. Please call me Wolf." He didn't chuckle, but there was the slightest bit of humor in his tone. Most people would miss it, being intimidated by this brute of a man. But I paid attention to the little things.

The pilot smiled. "You got it, Wolf. Nice to meet you, Miss Thomas."

"Oh, you can call me Dylan. It's nice to meet you, too."

"Great. Let's get this baby up in the air." He turned and disappeared behind a door just as a woman with long, dark hair stepped out from the back of the plane.

"Hi there. I'm Valentina. Once we're up in the air, I'll get your drink order and bring you some pastries." She smiled at me, and I didn't miss the way her hooded gaze took in Wolf.

The man was a sight, no doubt about it. He was tall with broad shoulders. A chiseled jaw that was sharp and distinct and peppered in just the right amount of dark scruff. His lips were plump, and he rarely smiled the few times I'd been around him, yet it was difficult not to stare at his mouth. He radiated confidence and probably intimidated most people he came into contact with.

I just wasn't most people.

Wolf Wayburn did not scare me.

Sure, he held my future in his hands. But my work ethic spoke for itself. I knew I'd do whatever it took to do this job well, and if that didn't impress him, I'd be just fine. I had several job offers; this just happened to be the one that I wanted most.

He didn't flinch at the way the gorgeous woman took him in. He just nodded, and she turned to walk to the back of the plane.

I glanced over to see him unbutton and roll up the sleeves on each arm. I was fascinated by the way his veins on his forearms bulged against his golden skin.

I forced myself to look away and pulled out the binder I got from Roger just as the plane started to move. We took off down the runway, and I clutched the binder just a little until we were up in the air. I could feel Wolf's eyes on me. I'd never flown on a private plane, so this was new. I wouldn't say that

I was nervous exactly, but I was a bit out of my element. I actually liked it. Pushing myself outside of my comfort zone was one of my favorite things to do.

"You okay?" he asked.

"Yep. Of course. I'm fine." I opened the binder as the plane bounced a little, and we continued to climb higher and higher.

"I want you to know that it wasn't personal when I said that I didn't think you were the right person for the job. I just call it as I see it."

I turned to look at him. *The arrogant prick.* He wanted me to be okay with him insisting I wasn't right for the job? "Well, we have that in common. I call it as I see it, too. And it sure sounded personal. But that's fine, Wolf. I have no problem showing everyone just how good I am at what I do. Prepare to be dazzled."

"I won't hold my breath."

The bastard was egging me on. He wanted to see if he could get a reaction out of me. I had to give him credit. He was damn good at poking the bear.

"Isn't that what you did for a living as a SEAL?" Two could play this game.

He barked out a laugh, and it managed to be completely free of humor. "I see ignorance is your superpower."

I forced the fakest smile. "Just calling it as I see it."

Valentina showed up out of nowhere and looked between us, and I swear you could cut the tension with a knife.

"May I get you something to drink?" she purred. Her eyes were on Wolf, and I wanted to wave my hand in her face and remind her that I was sitting here, too. "Orange juice, mimosa, sparkling water?"

"I'll take a whiskey, straight up." He pulled a file from his briefcase and dropped the table down in front of him.

I tried not to laugh. It was eight o'clock in the morning.

Was I already driving the man to the bottle? Good. I was irritating him as much as he was irritating me.

"I'll take an orange juice, please. Nothing like a good dose of vitamin C to get you ready for the day."

Valentina smiled at me this time and turned to get our drinks. I pulled my table down and started reading about the ten players that we'd be meeting with over the next two weeks.

"Here you are," she said, and I looked up to see her set down my orange juice along with a basket holding a few pastries in it. Wolf had the same setup, minus the juice, which was replaced by a healthy dose of whiskey.

"This looks delicious. Thank you." Valentina disappeared to the back of the plane, and I pulled out the cinnamon-covered donut and took a bite before groaning. "Oh my gosh. You have to try this. It's so freaking good."

"Do you always talk with a mouthful of cake?" He studied me.

I nodded and swallowed, reaching for my drink and taking a sip. "I don't like when people talk with their mouths full either. However, there is a gray area when it comes to pastries."

He dug into his basket and pulled out a croissant. Shocker. No sugar. The man didn't have a sweet bone in his body. Although, I'm sure he's got one impressive bone in there. The man was built like a Mack truck, so he had to be packing, right?

I digress.

What can I say?

These are the things that cross my mind.

I studied his massive hands as they held the delicate pastry, and I couldn't help but glance down at his feet.

Yep. Big hands. Big feet.

Big...

Dick.

Yep. There, I said it. I had a hunch that Wolf Wayburn had a giant penis because how else would he ever get laid? God knows it wasn't because of his charming personality. So clearly, he had to be well-endowed.

"Are you having a seizure, or are you going to finish your ridiculous statement?" he asked.

Ah... I no longer cared about the size of his... schlong. I was reminded how annoying he was just by the sound of his voice.

"Right. So, when someone's eating steak or lobster, it's good, but it's not like, *I can't wait to swallow before I tell you how good this is.* Not to mention the fact that you're eating something that was once alive. So, you need to show some respect for the deceased and swallow before you share your delight. But a cupcake or a donut, that warrants impatience, right? It's too good to wait to share. And it's not as gross to see powdered sugar or cinnamon in someone's mouth. So... you're welcome. Now you know the donut is delicious."

"Do you just make this shit up?" He looked at me, making it obvious that he was completely unimpressed with my explanation.

Well, that's a big surprise. The most miserable man on the planet is impossible to please. I wouldn't take it personally.

"You asked." I took another bite.

"No, I didn't."

"You did. You said, *do you always talk with a mouthful of cake?* I answered your question. Again. You're welcome, big, bad Wolf. You know, it wouldn't kill you to smile now and then. You might actually attract a woman if you stopped looking so broody and pissed off."

His lips pressed together in a straight line. "I assure you, that has never been a problem. Most women don't annoy me. You seem to be going for gold in that department."

"What can I say? I'm a winner." I stared back down at my

notebook. "Remember that when I get Braxton Jones to meet with us."

He barked out another laugh. But, of course, the man didn't laugh in a normal way. It was this angry, dismissive laugh—and it pissed me off. "Could you stop with the arrogant laugh? Either laugh correctly or don't laugh at all. It's very condescending, and I don't respond well to that."

"I see. You get to decide how one laughs now? Let me remind you, Miss Thomas," he hissed, turning to face me. His eyes were hard as his jaw ticked. "I am your boss. You don't call the shots here."

"You're not my boss. You don't get to tell me what to do." I met his gaze head-on. This guy did not scare me.

"You answer to me. I call the shots. My name is on your paycheck. By definition, I'm. Your. Boss." He leaned closer, his big head invading my space from across the aisle.

Angry and threatening.

And is that mint and sandalwood I smell?

Damn. I loved when a man smelled good.

And this jackass smelled like every woman's fantasy.

I brushed my hands back and forth, letting the cinnamon on my fingers fly around him. "I believe you voted me off the island yesterday, Bossman. *Yet here I am.* This is not the Navy, and I do not report to you. I came here to do a job, and I plan to do it if you'd stay out of my way."

He closed his eyes and backed away. He sat there silently for a minute. Was he meditating? Was I that hard to deal with?

"You are here because my father is a good man, and because their backup choice annoys me more than you do— which is hard to believe at the moment. But you do answer to me. And you better get that straight. I will be running this company by next year, and I will decide who works here."

"Listen, we don't need to be best friends. But we can work together and go find the best replacements for this team while we're at it. I just asked that you not laugh in a negative way when I'm trying to be positive," I said, unable to hide my irritation. He had a way of getting under my skin.

"I'll try to contain my negative laughter when I'm around you." He smirked.

But why did he have to look so sexy when he did it?

four

. . .

Wolf

"HEY, Mom. What's up? I'm just getting ready to head down to the lobby to meet Braxton Jones. If he bothers to show."

"That's what Dad said. He's hoping for a miracle. He really thinks Juan could be exactly what we need after Hawk leaves. How's Dylan Thomas doing?"

"She's a hothead. Completely unpredictable. Irrational. I don't know what Dad is thinking, pushing so hard to bring her on. Maybe it's because she's related to Hawk or because Everly has been such a good addition to the team."

"I don't think so, honey. That's not really how your father operates. He trusts his gut, and he came home after the first time he interviewed her and said he saw her as part of the future of the Lions' team."

I groaned and reached for my room key and slipped it into my back pocket. "I don't get it."

"Give her a chance. I think you two may have just gotten off on the wrong foot. Plus, Dad said it's not so bad seeing someone hold their own against you." She chuckled.

I rolled my eyes as I made my way out to the hallway. Dylan and I hadn't spoken after we'd agreed that we didn't need to be friends, but we'd still attempt to work together at least for the ninety-day sentence my father had given me. And I wouldn't laugh negatively around her.

What the fuck did that even mean? That was what I was talking about. The woman made no sense.

"All right. I'm getting on the elevator. I'll talk to you soon."

"Love you," she said.

"Love you, too." I ended the call. My mom and my sister, Sabine, were the only people I said those words to, because I'd been doing it since as early as I could remember, and apparently, old habits die hard. Not to mention, if I didn't say it to my baby sister on the phone, she would call back at least a dozen times to make sure everything was okay. I'd learned my lesson years ago, and I always made sure Sabine and my mother knew how I felt about them.

My phone vibrated when I stepped off the elevator, and I glanced down to see a message from Dylan. We'd exchanged numbers as we'd be traveling together for the next two weeks, and she'd insisted we needed to have open communication.

Minx ~ Hey, it's Dylan. Braxton Jones is not coming. He tweeted that grabbing a drink at his favorite haunt in the city was the perfect way to end the day. I used my handy-dandy detective skills after reading all the comments about the place, and I think he's at a bar a few blocks away. I'm on my way, and I'll see if I can get him to come back to the hotel for our meeting.

Yes. I put her in my phone as Minx because it fit her better than her actual name. And what the fuck was she thinking, going to a bar alone to find some jackass sports agent?

Me ~ Are you fucking crazy? You're just off on a scavenger hunt in New York City, looking for Braxton Jones?

Minx ~ Again... I don't answer to you, <Wolf emoji>! I see him. Get a table for three. I'll get him there, no matter what it takes.

Me ~ Tell me where you are. I'll meet you there. It's not safe to be doing this on your own.

Minx ~ I am not some damsel in distress. I can take care of myself just fine. I'm carrying, of course. Just get the table. He's staring at me, and let's just say, he likes what he sees. Get ready to see me work my magic.

Me ~ You're carrying? What the fuck does that mean?

Minx ~ <knife emoji>

She took a steak knife with her to a bar?

Me ~ Either tell me where you are or come back here right now.

I settled at a tall table in the bar and ordered a whiskey straight up. I wasn't a big drinker, but this woman was getting under my skin, and I needed to calm the fuck down. She couldn't have gotten that far, so I could just go walk a few blocks in each direction and look for her. My phone vibrated, and I glanced down.

Un-fucking-believable.

She'd sent a selfie of her and whom I was guessing was Braxton Jones. He had his arm around her shoulder.

Minx ~ We're both starving, so get a table, please.

What was I? Her personal fucking assistant? I polished off my drink and made my way to the hostess stand.

"Well, hello," she said flirtatiously.

"Hey. I need a table for three, please."

She reached for a few menus and glanced over her shoulder and waggled her brows at me. "Does that mean you're single?"

"Excuse me?"

"Well, there are three of you. I can only hope you're meeting a couple, and you're still on the market?"

I'd clearly been away from the real world for far too long over the last decade. I'd never hurt for female attention, but this was next level.

"Just meeting some friends," I said, as I sat down at the table.

She paused, pulled something from her pocket, and then miraculously found a pen from behind her ear and jotted something down before handing it to me. "I'm Jos, and I'm off at ten tonight. Let's meet up."

I took the card and forced a small smile. She was sexy. A little too forward for my liking. I didn't mind a woman who made me work for it. This was a little too easy, but I was on edge, thanks to my partner from hell for the next ninety days. Spending the night with a beautiful woman didn't sound like a horrible idea. I nodded. She giggled and hurried off, and I tucked her phone number into my pocket.

I glanced down to type a message to Dylan, when loud laughter drew my attention. She and Jones were walking my way, and he still had his arm around Dylan.

For whatever reason, it rubbed me wrong.

For starters, it was unprofessional.

He was a few inches shorter than me, which still had him standing quite a bit taller than her. Braxton was muscular, with a thick neck and a cocky grin that I wouldn't mind slapping off his face. Dylan looked small walking beside him. She wore dark skinny jeans that made her legs look long and lean, a black sweater that fell off one of her shoulders, exposing golden skin, and a pair of sexy-as-shit heels. Every dude in the place had his eyes on her. Her long, wavy blonde hair fell around her shoulders and down her back. I hadn't seen her hair down before, and damn if my dick didn't jump to attention at the sight of her. Thoughts of wrapping those waves around my fist and claiming her sassy mouth while she writhed beneath me filled my head. She'd clearly annoyed the fuck out of me over the last twenty-four hours, and this was just a way to shut her the hell up.

Desperate times and all that.

Her gaze locked with mine, and she raised a brow.

Told you I'd deliver.

She didn't have to speak to let me know she'd won this one.

Fuck. I'd give it to her. I wouldn't have gone searching for the asshole. Maybe she was the right person for the job.

I pushed to my feet. "Braxton. Thanks for coming."

"I wasn't going to come if I'm being honest. Hell, I didn't even remember agreeing to meet. My assistant handles my calendar, and if you knew how many people want to meet with me this time of year for a *quick conversation* about one of my guys…" he said as he shook my hand. "But how could anyone turn down Dilly?"

Dilly? What the fuck was that about? He already had a nickname for her. They'd known one another for what? Half a fucking second?

You call her Minx, asshole. You're not any better.

"I don't know," I said dryly as I studied her.

Her lips turned up in the corners, and she beamed at me. She was fucking cute when she was trying to make a point.

I pulled out her chair, and Braxton dropped into the seat beside her. He placed his elbow on the table, rested his chin in his hand, and gaped at her. Was this guy for fucking real?

Our server returned and took our drink order. I switched back to Coke because I needed to get my ass in work mode now. We had the agent for the top defender in the league at the table. This was our chance to make an impact. Plant the seed for just how good of a fit it would be for Juan Rivera to consider the Lions. Braxton ordered a mai tai. Who the fuck orders a mai tai that isn't sitting on a beach on vacation? Dylan ordered sparkling water with two limes and then proceeded to choose several appetizers for us to share. Once our server stepped away, I turned to face him.

"So, Braxton, we just wanted to let you know how pleased we are to have Jonathan on the team. The Lions have a strong lineup this season."

"Yep, I'm keeping a close eye on you guys, and Jonathan is a good man," he said. "I think you were the right fit for him. And I know there's a lot of talk about Hawk Madden retiring after this year. Jonathan seems to think Juan Rivera would be a good fit. He'd like to play for a strong team once he enters free agency after this season, and he and Jonathan played together a few years back. I figured I'd be hearing from your father and that other guy that joined him when we negotiated Jonathan's contract."

"Yes, that was our chief legal, Roger Strafford." I didn't want to remind him that he'd been an asshole to them before he finally agreed to meet.

"I thought you were chief legal for the Lions." He looked at Dylan as the server set down his cocktail, and he sucked it through a straw, nearly emptying the tall hurricane glass in one sip.

"I'm in a trial period, but I feel confident that I'll come out victorious. Roger is leaving after this year, and I'm hoping to step into the position permanently." She sipped her water and smiled.

"Well, Juan won't be coming to any meetings in June unless Dilly is part of the team. Damn. That didn't sound right. No pun intended, darling. But we won't be talking to the Lions unless she's there." He winked at her.

The cheesedick.

He's known her for all of five minutes. We hadn't discussed money or the millions of dollars we were willing to offer him. And he was going to draw a line in the sand for a person that he didn't even know?

"I assure you, whoever replaces Roger will be the best of the best, and our offer will be impressive."

"Dilly made it clear that the Lions will be competitive. I'm not worried about that. Juan's the best defensive player in the NHL, so we all know what that offer will need to look like. Obviously, you have my attention and his. Juan and I go way back, and he trusts me. And I've always been a man who trusts his gut. This girl has some giant balls, storming into a bar and telling me I missed a meeting with her. I like a person who knows what they want and isn't afraid to go after it. I don't meet a lot of genuine people these days, so I know one when I see one." He shrugged.

Our server set down several appetizers in the center of the table before handing us each a small plate. I reached for a slice of bread and some artichoke dip before turning my attention back to Braxton.

"I hope you aren't expecting some sort of sexual favor out of this. That's not what we're here for. It's not how we operate."

His eyes widened, and he smirked. Dylan shot me a warning look that almost made me laugh. If looks could kill, I'd be a dead man. Lucky for me—looks could not kill, and I'd proven over the last decade that neither could a few bullet wounds, so she'd best sharpen her steak knife, because her intimidation tactics were not working here.

"What exactly are you insinuating?" Braxton asked.

"I just find it interesting that we're discussing the possibilities of the largest package the NHL has ever seen—off the record, of course—and you're making demands about a woman you've known for five minutes. I'm wondering what that's about, Braxton, and if Juan would be okay with you making such demands on his behalf."

"Well, Wolf, as I said, I'm a man who trusts my gut. Juan pays me to do just that. You aren't going to be the only team to offer him that package. You aren't even the first. But I like her, and she's the reason I'm at this meeting. I don't take most meetings because it's just a bunch of people blowing smoke up my ass, and it's too early to make a decision now, anyway. We know he can go anywhere he wants to go, so take it however you want. But I've got to tell you, I like that you're protective of your employees. That's another point for the

Lions. Unless I'm misreading the situation. Are you two together?"

"Oh, God, no. Never. That's a negative. A hard no." Dylan rolled her eyes as if she were completely appalled by the question.

Jesus. Most women would be thrilled to be tied to me. This was a first.

"We work together. Nothing more." I shot her a look because her response was unprofessional and offensive. And it fucking pissed me off.

The next few hours were not what I'd expected. It actually wasn't all that bad. We talked shop, and Braxton asked me about playing hockey when I was a kid because, apparently, Dylan had divulged that information when she met him at that bar and said that I was a super fan of Juan's. I'd definitely have to get her back for that one. Braxton proceeded to ask me a million and one questions about being a SEAL. I gave him superficial answers because I couldn't divulge what he wanted to know. Dylan excused herself to use the restroom, leaving the two of us alone.

"Be straight with me, Braxton. Do we have a shot with him? I'd rather not waste our time or yours if he isn't truly interested. I can break it to Dylan if you don't want to let her down. But tell me what our chances are, come June."

He finished the last of his second mai tai and popped a tortilla chip into his mouth.

"The truth... I'd say the Lions are his number-one choice at this point, completely off the record, of course. This is just two friends talking right now. We've been approached by a few others who have come calling, just like you, but Juan doesn't care for the coach or the players. He's a big Hawk Madden fan, and word on the street is, Hawk might be joining the coaching staff." He shrugged. "I like you. I like Dilly. So, yeah, things are looking very strong for the Lions. You know, you'd be a fool not to hire her. I mean, the girl stormed into the bar and pulled up a chair right next to me. She acted like we were old friends and demanded I hear her out. That girl's a winner right there." He raised his chin toward Dylan, who'd just come out of the restroom and was being cornered by the hostess, Jos, who'd hit on me earlier.

There was some truth to what he'd said. Dylan had impressed the shit out of me by finding the guy and dragging him here to meet with us.

I'd give her that, even if I wasn't ready to admit it to her.

Dylan Thomas was full of surprises.

The problem was—I wasn't big on surprises.

five

. . .

Dylan

THINGS WERE GOING EVEN BETTER than expected. Braxton had been much easier to deal with than I thought he would be. He was a straight shooter who was just used to people walking on eggshells around him because he was the key to getting to his clients.

I wasn't the type of girl who walked on eggshells. I was definitely more of a bull in a china shop. But here we were, sitting at this table, talking like old friends now. Even Mr. High-Strung Navy SEAL had calmed his ass down. That is, after he insulted both Braxton and me by insinuating Braxton wanted to sleep with me as part of the deal. That was wrong for a multitude of reasons. First off, Braxton had been super cool to leave that bar and come with me to the restaurant. Sure, he was flirty, but it was all in good fun. He'd never been inappropriate. Secondly, Wolf speaking up the way he did insinuated that I couldn't handle myself.

And I didn't appreciate that, nor did I look kindly at people who underestimated me.

I'd brought the guy to the table. I did not need a babysitter or a handout.

So, I paid him back the only way I knew how. If he wanted to go low, I'd go lower. And Jos, the super cute hostess, had practically begged me for information about the big, bad Wolf. So, maybe I'd added a few minor details that had left her gasping.

Karma's a bitch, and I'm all too happy to help her out every now and then.

We'd finished eating, and Braxton had ordered one final fruity cocktail, which I found endearing for a grown man. He polished off his drink, and Wolf paid the bill before we all pushed to our feet.

"Thanks again for ditching the bar and coming here," I said, as I hugged Braxton goodbye. I'd expected to be meeting with this arrogant, hotshot agent, but Braxton Jones was just a down-to-earth, nice guy.

"I'm glad I came. I've got your numbers, and you've got mine, so let's just stay in touch. I'll be in San Francisco for a game in a few weeks to see Jonathan play, so maybe we can meet for a drink after."

"That would be great," Wolf said, extending his hand.

Wolf stood taller than Braxton; he was leaner, with broad shoulders that tapered down to a trim waist. He wore dark jeans and a black button-up, and I wasn't surprised at all that the hostess was drooling over the man. Braxton garnered his own attention, but every woman in the room had their eyes on Wolf Wayburn.

And he knew it, which annoyed me all the more.

We all walked out of the restaurant, and Jos called out to Wolf, and he let out a long breath before clapping Braxton on the shoulder. "Thanks for meeting us. I'll speak to you soon."

I couldn't help but smile as I walked with Braxton into the hotel lobby because I was giddy over the information that I'd shared with Jos. I had no idea how it would play out, but I'd enjoyed sticking it to him tonight.

"What's the story with you two?" Braxton asked.

"No story. I just started working with him. We didn't exactly get off to a fabulous start, but you don't get to pick who you work with, right?"

He chuckled. "You're a fucking rock star, Dylan Thomas. I look forward to seeing you in a couple of weeks. You stay in touch, okay?"

"I will. Looking forward to it."

His tongue dipped out to wet his bottom lip as he nodded. Classic go-to move that I was all too familiar with. But I just knew the game well, and I rarely reacted to men the way most women did. I prided myself on staying in control.

"See you soon, Dilly." He winked.

"You will." I smiled before holding up my hand and waving goodbye. I made my way toward the elevator and glanced into the restaurant to see Wolf talking with Jos. His arms were crossed over his chest, completely closed off. She was batting her lashes and giggling, giving it her best shot.

I wondered if he was a closed-off lover the way he was outside the bedroom. The man had a coolness about him—an impenetrable exterior. I wondered if that softened behind closed doors.

These were the kinds of thoughts that always crossed my mind. Trying to figure out everyone's game. Everyone's angle.

I pressed the button and waited for the elevator doors to open before stepping on. I leaned against the back wall as the doors started to close.

A large hand reached inside and pushed them open, and a brooding Wolf stepped on as the doors closed behind him.

"Oh, I figured you'd be joining the lovely Jos for a nightcap." I cleared my throat because he looked pissed.

Shocker.

The man had the worst case of resting bitch face I'd ever seen.

He just had this chronic intensity about him.

He'd lightened up with Braxton, which was a relief to see that he was capable of engaging with humans without being a complete dick.

"Did you now? You sure about that?"

"Am I sure about what?"

"That you thought I'd be having a nightcap with Jos." He raised a brow, his arms folded across his chest, his mouth in a straight line, and irritation radiating from his large frame.

"I mean, I didn't put a whole lot of thought into it, if I'm being honest. I don't really care what you do."

He moved so quickly that he caught me off guard. But studying martial arts my entire life, I quickly squared my shoulders and prepared for battle when he invaded my space.

"I think you do."

"Of course, you do. You're an arrogant prick, so you think the world revolves around you." I met his hard gaze and gave him a warning look to step back.

"What exactly did you tell her about my—er—deficiencies?"

I couldn't hide the smile spreading across my face because it had been a brilliant revenge move. "Well, the girl was on a mission. She'd grilled me about you when I came out of the bathroom. She wanted to know if you were single. I told her that you were a good guy from what I knew of you, and I assumed you were single."

"And you know this because?" He stood, crowding me, but not in a threatening way at the moment, so I wouldn't kick him in his junk just yet.

"Because you just don't scream relationship vibes." I held my hands up and smirked. "No judgment."

"Right. No judgment. However, you sure seemed to know a lot about me when you discussed the size of my dick."

I covered my mouth with my hand and looked away for a second so I could compose myself. I didn't think she'd actually tell him what I'd said so quickly. "Or lack thereof."

"Yeah. She mentioned that. She said she didn't mind that I had some limitations downstairs. What exactly did you tell her?"

"I told her that you suffered from microdick syndrome."

"What the fuck is that?"

"I don't know. I was winging it. But I think it speaks for itself." I held up my finger and my thumb about an inch apart and shrugged.

"What is your obsession with my dick?"

I rolled my eyes. "Of course, you think I'm obsessed with your schlong, but trust me, I have zero interest in what you're packing."

"Is that why you made that comment yesterday to Gallan? You're two for two. I'd say that's bordering on obsession." He raised a brow, and his tongue swiped out to wet his bottom lip, and I'll be a mother-effing flying pig if my lady bits didn't just go into overdrive.

What the hell was that about?

Braxton Jones was hot, and he'd just tried the same move, and nothing happened.

Nada.

Crickets.

Now the arrogant, pompous, annoying dick weasel licks his juicy, bitable bottom lip, and my vajazzle explodes like fireworks on the freaking Fourth of July.

"It's called revenge, genius."

"Revenge for what? You're here. I agreed to ninety days. Why in the hell are you serving me up a plate of dick insults now?"

The elevator came to a stop, and I placed my hands on his chest to push him back. His muscles bristled beneath my fingertips, and I didn't pull away as quickly as I should have.

But he took a step back as if I'd just burned him with my touch and motioned for me to step off when the doors opened.

"You slut-shamed me at dinner, and I don't appreciate it," I hissed over my shoulder as he followed behind me down the hallway.

"Slut-shamed you? What the fuck are you talking about?"

I came to a stop in front of the door outside my room, and he paused as his suite was directly across the hall from mine. "You made it sound like he wanted to sleep with me as part of the package to get Juan to come play for the Lions, which also insinuates that I would tolerate that type of behavior."

A bitter laugh left his lips, and I shot him a warning look. "Oh, yes. I almost forgot. I'm not allowed to laugh negatively. Please forgive me, *Minx.*"

I rolled my eyes, but I had to say that Minx was much more fitting than Princess, so I'd let it go. When you have four sisters, you learn to choose your battles at a young age.

He shoved his hands into his pockets. "I was defending your honor. I didn't like the way he was speaking about you, and I wanted to let him know that it wasn't okay with the owners of the team. I don't know how that was slut-shaming you."

"I'm not some helpless little girl. I can handle myself. I got him there, didn't I?"

"Yes. And I give you credit for pulling that off, but I didn't get a chance to tell you because I was too busy defending the size of my cock." He let out a long sigh. "For the record, I would defend anyone who worked for this company if I thought someone was being inappropriate. It wasn't personal. And I think he got the message."

"I think everyone got the message." I shook my head with disgust. "Don't defend me again. It makes it so we aren't on equal playing fields. How would you feel if I thought a dude was threatening you, and I stepped in?"

"I'd think you were crazy, but at this point, it wouldn't surprise me."

"I'm a black belt, jackass. Don't underestimate me."

"Are you always this exhausting?" he hissed as he pulled his hotel key from his pocket.

"I am. Get used to it. We've got eighty-nine more days together."

"Don't remind me," he said, turning his back to me and sliding the key in the door before turning back around to speak. "Get some rest. Plane leaves for Chicago at noon tomorrow. Be in the lobby at 11:00 a.m."

I turned to slip my key into the door. "I have the itinerary. I don't need reminding. I'll be there."

I shut my door and smiled because I liked how defensive he was about his micropeen. That one had just come to me on the fly, too.

I dropped onto the bed and dialed my father. I talked to my sisters often, and we had a group text going at all times. But I'd always had a close relationship with my dad.

He just got me.

Always had.

Even when I was young and a complete handful next to my sweet, easygoing twin sister, Charlotte. I was the girl who was always in timeout in school.

The principal of my elementary school felt more like a family member by the time I left for middle school.

And my father knew exactly how to handle me. He could calm me down with just a quick talk. He'd always tell me that I was brilliant and talented and that I just needed to harness all that energy for good.

He's the reason I got straight A's in school and pushed myself so hard to be the best that I could be.

It didn't mean I didn't get a shit ton of detentions in school for pushing the envelope. But I had made an effort to steer my zest for life in a positive direction.

"Hey, Dilly. How did it go? Did the hotshot agent show up for the meeting?" my dad asked.

"Not really. But long story short, we got him there. He

made it clear that Juan Rivera is genuinely interested—no thanks to Wolf, the arrogant asshole. I told you that the guy tried to get me fired before I even got the job, and now I have to travel with him."

He chuckled. "You told me, and you agreed to let it go. If you want to get this job, you're going to have to work with him."

"Ugh," I groaned as I fell back to lie on the bed. "He's just so annoying."

"You don't usually let people get under your skin this much. You had a great meeting with the agent of the hottest defensive player in the league. Why are we still talking about the Navy SEAL?"

I rolled my eyes. "He just manages to overshadow the good, I guess. But you're right. He's probably trying to derail me so I don't get the job. Tomorrow, we head to Chicago, and I will be perfectly professional."

"That's my girl."

"Where are you? Home or the firehouse?" My father was the captain of the Honey Mountain Fire Department.

"I'm at home, doing a little paperwork and watching *Rocky*."

I smiled. I loved that we shared a mutual admiration for the Italian Stallion. "That sounds pretty dreamy."

"Yeah. You're a tomato, Dilly." He chuckled. It was my favorite saying when any of us were getting kicked in the teeth and needed to channel some inner strength. "These movies never get old."

"You're right. I've totally got this. I will not allow some rich dude with an attitude to rain on my parade."

He barked out a laugh. "There she is."

We were both quiet for a minute, and I pictured him sitting alone on the couch in his den.

"Do you ever get lonely, Dad? I mean, Mom's been gone a

long time. Do you ever think about dating?" I don't know why I asked. Maybe because my sisters were all happily married now. My dad and I were the only two that were single at the moment. I worried about my father being alone.

He cleared his throat. "It's hard to be lonely when you have five daughters who never leave you alone."

"Always a jokester."

"I'm fine, Dill pickle. I was lucky to meet the love of my life and experience that. That's what I want for all of you."

I groaned. "Well, four out of five isn't a bad track record. And seeing as I'm the son you always wanted anyway, I'm doing things differently."

The ongoing joke in our family was that I was supposed to be a boy. They were told they were having one of each. So, my mother had chosen Charlotte's name because her favorite book was *Charlotte's Web*. My father had chosen my name because his favorite musician was Bob Dylan.

He barked out a laugh. "You'd put any son to shame, my badass girl. That doesn't mean you can't find the love of your life just because you're out conquering the world."

"Well, I'll let you know if anyone ever so much as knocks me on my ass and doesn't make me want to run for the hills within a week."

He barked out a laugh. "I love you, sweetheart."

"Love you, too. I'll call you from Chicago."

I ended the call and made my way to the bathroom to turn on the shower. When I stepped inside, I let the hot water beat down on my shoulders, and I pushed my long hair away from my face.

A vision of Wolf Wayburn, naked in the shower, flashed in my mind. All tanned skin and muscles rippling against the drops of water that rained down his body. I closed my eyes and pictured him. Tall and strong and sexy. And, of course, he was well-endowed.

There wasn't a micropenis in sight when I thought of him.

The man oozed BDE.

But he'd met his match.

Because we both had big dick energy.

And I would not back down, even if he was the sexiest man I'd ever laid eyes on.

six

. . .

Wolf

I MADE my way to the gym and came to a stop when I rounded the corner. The hotel gym was massive, and there was only one person in here at the moment. It wasn't even six in the morning, and there she was.

The cockblocker from hell.

Dylan Thomas was wearing black leggings that fit her like a second skin and a black sports bra, and her body was coated in a layer of sweat as she sprinted on the treadmill with perfect form. Her stomach was ripped, her arms lean and cut. Her long, blonde hair was tied back into a ponytail that swung from side to side in rhythm with the swish of her perfect, peach-shaped ass. She was laser focused as she stared ahead, headphones in her ears and pumping her arms.

She never stood still long enough for me to watch, so I took a minute to appreciate the beautiful woman in front of me.

It didn't mean I liked her.

I didn't.

She was rude and cocky and completely unprofessional.

I mean, she could be fired for her dick comments alone.

Jos had giggled and told me that we could do other things

if my *Johnson*—her words not mine—wasn't up to the task. I'd explained that Dylan was just a bitter ex whose heart I'd broken, and she'd decided to lie about the size of my *Johnson* because she couldn't stand the thought of me with anyone else.

Jos's eyes had widened as they scanned down my body and stared at my dick, and she smiled. She'd assured me she was off work in a few minutes, and she'd love to join me in my room.

But I was too pissed to agree to anything last night. Instead, I'd bowed out, aggravated with the little minx who'd inserted herself into my bootie call. So, I'd turned Jos down and hurried to the elevator so I could confront her.

She'd made no apologies, which hadn't surprised me because she was a righteous little vixen, even from the little that I knew of her.

But I didn't miss the way her chest rose and fell at my nearness in the elevator or the way her body responded when I'd closed the space between us. I couldn't tell if she was going to junk-punch me or tear off my clothes. She'd kept it together, though; I'd give her credit for that. I was hoping she'd beg me to come to her room, just so I could reject her and pay her back for that ridiculous stunt she'd pulled.

"Um, you may want to take a picture. It would be far less creepy than you staring at me," she said as she tugged the earbuds out of her ears and turned off the treadmill.

I moved toward the weight machines and shook my head as I dropped down to do some bench presses. "In your dreams. I was just thinking about the cute hostess who spent the night in my room. Let's just say, she now knows you're a complete liar. I just explained that you were a disgruntled ex who had a hard time when I broke things off."

She walked toward me, using the towel to wipe her forehead. She wore no makeup and managed to be completely fucking gorgeous with zero effort. That shit pissed me off because I didn't want to be attracted to her.

A. She worked for me.

B. She was exhausting and hotheaded.

C. She was the most aggravating woman I'd ever met.

"That's rich, even for you. And you certainly don't look like a man who got lucky last night. Resting bitch face doesn't usually follow good lovin', if you know what I mean. So, you're either lying, or you're a shitty lover." She smirked as she stood over me. "Do you want me to spot you?"

I reached for the barbell that sat above me and wrapped my hands around the cool metal bar. "That's a negative."

"Yes, sir, officer." She chuckled and reached for some hand weights and started doing lunges right beside me.

She grunted every time she dropped her knee to the floor, and my dick sprung to life. I closed my eyes and continued my up-and-down reps, trying not to catch a hint of her jasmine scent.

Fuck, even her lady stank was magnificent.

Who smells good when they're sweating?

Dylan Thomas. That's who. Of course, she does. She probably pumps some sort of pheromones into her deodorant to torture men.

I set the bar down and pushed to my feet. "Could you stop with the sound effects, please? This is my workout time, and it's very distracting."

A wide grin spread across her face as her eyes traveled down my body. I followed her gaze only to see my erection pointing right at her like he was picking her out of a lineup.

"Ah, I'm sorry to be bothering your *workout time*, especially after your fantastic romp in the hay last night." She giggled like she'd won some big prize. "At least we know the micropenis isn't true."

She walked away all cocky and proud, and I did my best to adjust myself, but my dick had a mind of his own. I ignored her the rest of the time, but I kept my eyes on her movements. I relaxed when she left the gym, and I finished my workout.

After a quick shower, I packed up my bag and made my way down to the lobby for a quick breakfast, dropping my suitcase with the concierge.

The restaurant was quiet this morning, and I was relieved that Jos wasn't working because I'd turned her down last night. I wasn't sure how she'd felt about that.

The hostess who appeared to be in her mid-seventies led me to a table, and Dylan looked up to see me walking in her direction.

"Wolf," she purred.

"Minx," I hissed, because I was still pissed that she'd given me a throbbing boner during my workout. So maybe I'd released some of that tension in the shower, and I'd tried my best to think of anything other than the woman currently gaping at me. I'd thought of my last hookup, as the woman had been sexy as hell. I tried thinking of my favorite porno from my younger years. But nope. This particular woman was invading my thoughts and had completely robbed me of getting off to anything other than her.

And that was not okay with me.

This shit would stop now.

"Oh. Do you two know one another? Do you want to sit together?" the elderly woman asked.

I was about to request a table on the other side of the restaurant just as Dylan motioned for me to join her. "Come on. We work together. We can share a meal. Look how well last night went."

I grunted and took the seat across from her as the hostess stepped away.

"Good, we can chat about Lance Waters." She reached for the file sitting beside her.

Okay. We did need to work together. Maybe we'd gotten

all the craziness out by now, and we could focus on what we came here to do. Recruit the best players and build a team that would win us a Stanley Cup in the future.

"My father wasn't sure he was ready, but I don't know. I have a feeling about him. He's young and eager, and we need another goalie. Buckley is playing too much this season because our backup is injured more than he's not. I've watched a bunch of his games, and he has the potential." Lance Waters was a college hockey player, and he was hungry to sign with a pro team. He grew up in San Francisco and would love to come and play for the Lions in his hometown.

"Agreed. I read an interview he did recently, and he was humble and anxious to prove himself. With the right team behind him, he just may surprise everyone. We don't know what he can do if he's got strong guys supporting him."

"Exactly. That's very perceptive."

"What can I say? I'm a perceptive girl." She chuckled.

We paused when our server came over and took our orders, bringing us both water and orange juice.

"Well, I don't think we'll have to hunt down Lance tonight for dinner. I think he's looking forward to meeting with us. He doesn't have an agent, but he's coming with his father and coach," I said, reaching for my glass and taking a sip of juice.

"He's young, but he sounds ready. I'm looking forward to it. And I already got a text from Braxton this morning, wishing us safe travels."

My shoulders stiffened, even though I was happy that the dude was reaching out to her. We'd need that connection if we wanted to sign Juan. But I didn't like the idea of him hitting on her. I didn't think she was a helpless woman like she believed I did; I just didn't want anyone to be disrespectful to her.

Because she worked for me.

Not because I personally cared one way or the other.

But I'd keep my thoughts to myself. If we were going to

make this work moving forward, we needed to stop talking about my dick and our sex lives. I'd need to stop thinking of her when I got off in the shower.

Period.

I wasn't proud that it had happened, but it wouldn't happen again.

Me and my dick would be moving on from all Dylan Thomas fantasies as of today.

So, instead, I nodded. "I think keeping in touch with him is a good plan."

"Was that a compliment?"

"If that's how you want to take it. I told you I was impressed you got him there, and I meant it."

"Thank you." She smiled as our server set our plates down in front of us. "Seeing as we're going to be traveling together, we may as well form a truce. Let's get to know one another, and even if we aren't best friends, we can be civil, right?"

"Says the woman who told someone I suffered from micropenis syndrome."

"You're so hung up on that." She waggled her brows, forked her sausage link, took a bite, and chewed slowly.

Was that supposed to be my dick?

Why was she waggling her eyebrows when she bit into her sausage link?

I shook it off. I would not feed this insanity.

"Fine. You're from the same town Hawk grew up in, right?"

"Yep. Honey Mountain. I lived in San Francisco and attended UCSF for undergrad, then attended law school near home so I could be close to my dad."

I narrowed my gaze. That was honorable, especially for the heartless little tyrant.

"Is he sick?"

"No. He's the captain of the Honey Mountain Fire

Department. A total badass." She beamed when she spoke of her father, and it was the first time I saw a softness in her. Her guard was down, which wasn't the norm for this woman. She always seemed to be on. Making her next move. But her father was definitely her kryptonite. We all had weaknesses, and Dylan Thomas had just shown me hers.

"You two are close? Is Everly your only sibling?" I forked some eggs and popped them into my mouth.

"No. I'm a twin." She laughed before dabbing her mouth with her napkin.

"Dear Lord. There are two of you."

She shook her head and chuckled. "No. Charlie is super sweet. And I actually have four sisters. Everly, Vivian, Charlotte, and Ashlan."

"Wow. That's a whole lot of females in one household."

"Yeah. My sisters are all amazing. And my dad manages us pretty well." She shrugged before taking a bite of her toast.

"What is your mom like?"

Her face hardened as if I'd just slapped her. I reached for my glass of juice, unsure of what to say.

"My mom lost her battle with cancer when I was in middle school." My chest squeezed at her words, and I was not a man who experienced that often. But I could see her pain as clear as day. And then she tipped up her chin and forced a smile as her dark brown gaze locked with mine. "How about you? Are there any other *charming* Wayburns running around?"

"Yes. My brother, Sebastian, is a few years younger than me, and there's my baby sister, Sabine. She recently graduated from college, and she's brilliant. Sebastian just came to work for the Lions in the marketing department. You won't see a lot of him; he's not very focused on work."

"Well, I assume he doesn't have to be. I mean, you own an NHL hockey team, and we flew here on a private jet. I'm guessing you don't have to be here either. Yet you went off and became a Navy SEAL. What's that about?"

I finished chewing. "Do *you* only work for the paycheck?"

She gazed up at the ceiling as if she were deep in thought. Her tongue peeked out and wet her plump bottom lip, and my hands fisted as I tried to keep my dick from reacting. I could fucking hold my breath underwater for longer than anyone I'd ever known. I could hike unbelievable peaks, and I'd even managed to swim almost two miles with gunshot wounds to my arm and leg. But for whatever fucking reason, I could not contain my raging boner when it came to this intoxicating, irritating, intelligent, witty-as-hell woman sitting in front of me.

It was a slap in the face to my training. I could endure unbelievable pain. Go without food and water for as long as I needed to. But I couldn't manage to control my dick around this woman.

"I do not. I mean, sure, I love making the big bucks," she said, and she did some sort of little shimmy with her shoulders. "Though I've yet to make any actual money, seeing as this is my first real paying job outside of working at Vivi's bakery part time, and I have a ton of student loans to pay. But no... If I had a million dollars in the bank today, I would still be an attorney."

"Well, there you go. You and my brother have very little in common in that area. However, I'm sure he'd appreciate your —er—*unusual personality.*"

"*Unusual* personality? Do you mean award winning? Life of the party? Dazzlingly witty?" She crossed her arms over her chest and studied me. "Tell me something about being a Navy SEAL."

"What do you want to know?"

"Tell me about a mission you went on."

I forked some potatoes and popped them into my mouth as I watched her. "Sorry. You'd have to kill me if I talked."

"I'd be all right with that," she said dryly.

"I'm sure you would. So, are we good on the small talk?"

"I think this is a decent start. Who knows, Wolf Wayburn? Maybe we'll even become friends by the end of all this."

"I wouldn't hold my breath, Minx."

"Isn't holding your breath kind of *your* thing? And what's with the nickname?"

"It suits you better than your own name. And we weren't talking about me holding my breath; we were talking about you holding yours."

"Says the big, bad Wolf. Clearly, you're a control freak if you think you've chosen a better name for me than my actual parents."

"Takes one to know one." I smirked and leaned back in my chair to let the food settle.

"So, do we agree on a truce, then? Moving forward, no more low blows or cheap shots?"

I nodded. But I was far from done after what she'd pulled last night.

Retaliation was part of war.

And the little minx had taken her shot.

It was only fair that I returned the favor.

She reached her hand over the table, and I rolled my eyes before placing my large hand over her small one. A jolt of electricity scorched through my fingertips, but I didn't let her know I felt a thing. Hell, I'd been hooked up to electrical shocks before and was trained to show no emotion.

"Pleasure doing business with you, Wolf."

I pulled my hand away. "We'll see about that, Minx."

Because this wasn't over just yet.

seven

• • •

Dylan

THE LAST FIVE days had been nonstop. We'd been to New York, Chicago, Miami, Dallas, and Denver. Five cities in seven days. And we were only halfway finished with this round. The meeting with Braxton had been a great start to the trip. Lance Waters had made it clear that he wanted to play for the Lions as he'd grown up there, and that was his team. Both Wolf and I liked him and his father, and we hoped that we could get him added to the roster. The good news was, he was open to playing for the Lions, and we knew he would be a good addition. So, we'd watch his season closely and stay in touch.

In Miami, there'd been another goalie whom we'd met with, Max Wells, who was just a senior in high school. He had the ego of a professional athlete who'd been at it for a lot longer than he had. Clearly, all the success he'd had at such a young age had stripped him of being humble in any way, shape, or form.

He was also the same guy who basically told us that he would go to the highest bidder. He was all about the money, and he didn't care where he played.

Wolf and I both found him to be uninspiring.

We'd been eating all our meals together, working out together, and traveling together. The working out together was not intentional, really; it's just that we both enjoyed morning workouts.

It was a lot.

We still argued constantly, but we'd come to some sort of truce, and we'd both held up our end of the bargain. I'd be lying if I didn't say that he was a little less annoying than he had been five days ago. But we weren't friends. We kept our conversations to business topics because getting any personal information out of Wolf Wayburn was like pulling teeth... from an alligator, who was trying to kill you.

Tonight, we were in Denver, and we were meeting with Allen Walsh, the agent of one of the best centers in the league, Donovan Brown. Allen was an old friend of Duke Wayburn's, and he had the reputation of being one of the nicest agents in the league.

Wolf and I had both gotten in a quick workout and gone to our rooms to shower before dinner. I made my way downstairs to the bar area in the lobby, where it was fairly quiet. The bartender smiled, and I pulled up a stool and sat down.

"What can I get you, beautiful?" He leaned over the dark wood bar top, and the exposed tattoos on his forearms caught my interest. Swirls of red flames and skulls meshed together into one beautiful piece of art. He had dark, shaggy hair and a whole lot of swagger.

"I'll take a glass of Chardonnay, please."

He brought over a glass of chilled white wine, and he spent the next few minutes talking to me. His name was Teak, and he was charming and funny and easy to look at.

The back of my neck prickled, and I felt his presence before I saw him.

Wolf.

He took a seat on the stool beside me and shot me a menacing look before glaring at Teak.

"Hello, boss," I groaned. "I see you're in a fabulous mood, per usual."

He turned to the bartender and ordered a whiskey straight up before looking back at me. "Must you keep analyzing my mood? And do you pick and choose when you acknowledge that I'm your boss?"

"Well, you love to remind me, so I figured I may as well throw you a bone," I hissed, just as Allen Walsh appeared at the hostess stand. I'd seen a few photos of him on social media with Donovan, which always helped when meeting people for the first time.

"Can you transfer these drinks to our dinner bill?" Wolf asked after Teak handed him his cocktail.

"Of course. Dylan, I'm off in a few hours if you want to grab a nightcap." His heated gaze locked with mine, and I was enjoying the moment until the annoying man beside me let one of his rude, condescending laughs escape.

"Seriously?" I grumped and shot him a warning look.

"Our client is here. Get your game face on, and stop flirting, Minx."

I shook my head with disgust before turning back to face Teak. "I'll be back. I want to hear about that summer you spent surfing."

"See you soon, beautiful," Teak purred.

"Wow. The dude is so original," Wolf said under his breath as we walked away.

I slammed my shoulder into his as we both beelined toward the hostess stand to greet Allen.

"You're such a pompous ass," I snarled, keeping my voice low and a fake smile plastered on my face as we approached the man who was looking down at his phone.

"Did you just check me with a shoulder bump? How very professional of you."

"It's game time. Try acting like a normal human," I said,

shoving myself in front of him. "Allen. Hello, I'm Dylan Thomas. We spoke on the phone."

"Yes. Dylan. It's great to meet you. And this must be Wolf Wayburn. Your father has spoken so highly of you over the years. My cousin is in the Navy, and when I said I was meeting with you tonight, he told me what a badass you are. Apparently, your reputation is one for the books. Did you know everyone worships this dude?" Allen asked me as we followed the hostess to the table.

Of course, I didn't. I mean, I assumed just by what I'd seen of him that he was probably great in battle because he was perpetually pissed off. But the man was buttoned so tight, I didn't have a clue what it meant to be a SEAL beyond what I'd seen in the movies.

"No. Apparently, if he tells me anything, he'd have to kill me." I sat in the chair that Wolf pulled out for me, and he narrowed his gaze.

"I said you'd have to kill *me* if I talked. I took an oath." He raised a brow. "Anyhow, thank you for meeting us, Allen. So, how do you like living here in Denver?" I asked.

Allen was very friendly, and the conversation flowed with ease. We ordered dinner and drinks, and Wolf got right down to business. The man was too damn smooth for his own good. I sipped my second glass of chardonnay when the server set down our plates and watched as he spoke to Allen about the Lions organization and what the future looked like.

"What I'm saying is, we're a family-run business. We treat our players like family. That's why we have the lowest turnover of any team in the league. Off the record, I'm sure my father has shared that we have some players that will be retiring after this year, and we need to fill those spots with guys that we think can lead us to the next Stanley Cup." He brought up Donovan Brown's name casually, as if it was just in passing and not the reason that we were here. Wolf's jaw was chiseled, and his white dress shirt strained against his muscles. He glanced over at me a few times, and I swear I had to squeeze my thighs together because he looked at me with the same hunger that I was currently feeling.

Was it the wine talking?

How could I be so attracted to a man who I couldn't stand most of the time?

But here he was, commanding the attention at the table, and Allen and I were both listening with bated breath.

"So, there it is, in a nutshell. I want you to enjoy your dinner, and I'll be happy to answer any questions or get any info over to you in the next few months if you're interested. Otherwise, just know that we are not afraid to pay for our players. We want the guys on our team to know that we want them, that we value them, and we'd prefer that they stay as part of the Lions family for the rest of their careers if they're willing. If that's a fit for any of your clients, we are open to discussions when the time comes."

"Sign me up. I'm in." The words left my mouth before I could stop them. Like I'd been in some sort of Wolf Wayburn trance and had forgotten where I was.

Allen barked out a laugh, and Wolf gaped at me like I had lost my mind.

"What? I'm just saying, that was an impressive pitch. Who wouldn't want to be part of the Lions family?" I tried to cover my outburst and act like it had been intentional.

"You know, I think we're very much on the same page. Not everyone enjoys being an unrestricted free agent, such as Donovan Brown, for example. He and his wife don't want to keep moving, so finding a place to set down roots before their daughter starts school in two years while being part of a class-act organization will be music to his ears. Raising a family and being on the move year after year isn't easy, so something long-term for their little girl would be very appealing."

Wolf smiled and nodded. "I look forward to continued conversations with you and him."

I went on to tell Allen all about my sister, Charlotte, who was a teacher, and the rest of the evening was small talk and laughter. Well, Allen and I both laughed several times. Wolf rarely allowed himself to laugh unless it was sarcastic and angry. He was a serious guy.

I could usually figure people out fairly quickly.

But this guy was a huge mystery.

Edgy and sexy and strong.

Rude and protective at the same freaking time.

The man made no sense.

Our server walked over to ask if we wanted dessert, and she set a new glass of wine down in front of me and bent down to speak close to my ear. "This is from Teak. He said he's looking forward to chatting with you some more."

Allen had to step away to take a call from his wife, and I looked up to see Wolf watching me with a murderous look on his face.

What was his deal?

I took a sip of my wine, and Allen returned to the table, telling us his son, Parker, wasn't feeling well, so he needed to get going. Wolf waved over the server and handed her his card.

"You get home. We look forward to talking to you soon." Wolf moved to his feet and shook Allen's hand. "Just know, we're hellbent on winning the Cup with the right team in place. We're holding back no expense to make it happen, and adding a bonus to the players' salaries to achieve that goal is not out of the question."

"Thanks, Wolf. I hear ya, and you're saying all the right things. I can assure you that he'll be interested in hearing more," Allen said.

"It was great to meet you. Looking forward to speaking again soon." I stood and hugged him goodbye.

"Thank you again for dinner and for taking the time to come see me. I look forward to speaking to you both soon." He held up his hand and made his way out of the restaurant.

I sat back down to sip my wine, and Wolf was quiet for a moment as he stewed in his seat.

"That went well," he said.

"Yeah. It sounds like Donovan is definitely interested."

He nodded, and the server was back with his card and a pen for him to sign.

"Okay, I'm going to use the restroom and then stop by the bar to say goodnight to Teak. I'll see you in the morning."

A wide grin spread across his handsome face, which was a rarity for Wolf Wayburn. "See you in the morning, Minx."

He pushed to his feet and strode away. I made my way to the restroom to freshen up. I wasn't super excited about heading to the bar as I was tired and ready to call it a night. But I'd stop by for a few minutes. Teak was a nice guy, and a little friendly conversation with a hot guy wouldn't kill me.

I applied some lipstick and fluffed my hair a bit. My phone had a bunch of texts from my sisters in the group chat.

Everly ~ How did the meeting go? I've heard great things about Donovan. Hawk said he'd be a score for the team.

Ashlan ~ I miss you. Come home.

Charlotte ~ How's the grumpy billionaire? <wolf emoji>

Vivian ~ You will be home for Halloween, right? Bee wants you to come trick-or-treating with us.

Me ~ Sorry. Just finished dinner. Allen is great, and I think Donovan is definitely interested. The billionaire is moody as all hell. I'm going to go have a drink with the sexy bartender, Teak. Of course, I'll be home for Halloween. I wouldn't miss it for the world.

Everly ~ Teak? That's his name? Like the wood?

Ashlan ~ That would be a good name for a hero in my book. Do you mind if I use it?

Me ~ I don't know the reasoning behind his name. I barely know the guy. And be my guest. He doesn't own the name.

Charlotte ~ I'm more interested in the billionaire. So, has he stuck to the truce? He's been nicer? And you've stopped saying he has a small peen? <eggplant emoji>

Vivian ~ <laughing emoji>

Me ~ As nice as a grumpy, broody guy can be. Okay, I've got to go. I'll text when I get to the room.

A slew of *I love you* messages came through, and I dropped my phone into my purse.

When I walked out to the bar, there were only three people lingering a few seats away. Two busboys hustled around the restaurant that was just a few steps from the bar area, as they tried to clean the tables quickly.

"Hey. Thanks for that glass of wine. That was sweet of you." I sat down and asked him for a glass of water. I hadn't finished the wine he'd sent over as I was tired, so I knew any more alcohol would put me to sleep right here at the bar.

He set a glass of water in front of me and leaned over the bar. "God, you're so fucking beautiful."

I smiled. It came a little out of left field, but I was here for a good compliment. "You're not too bad yourself."

He started asking me a bunch of questions, and we talked about where we'd grown up. He'd been to Honey Mountain a few times, so we chatted about the lake and the mountains and all there was to do back home.

He told me about his family and his little sister. About how he wanted to open a surf shop someday, and I couldn't help but wonder why he was living in Colorado if he wanted to open a surf shop.

And then my thoughts moved to Wolf.

The way he'd commanded the conversation with Allen.

How silky smooth his voice was.

The way his chiseled jaw was covered in just the right amount of scruff.

I wondered what it would feel like against my fingertips.

"And that's what brought me here," Teak said, pulling me from my daze.

"Well, this is not a bad place to be." I smiled. "I should probably call it a night. We leave first thing in the morning tomorrow."

"Don't rush off. Listen, I want you to know something."

"Okay," I said.

"I spoke to your friend. I am totally fine with your—er—special situation. So, if that's why you're running off, please don't. Hell, I think it makes you even more interesting."

"My friend? Who?"

"Your boss. He came by on his way out and gave me a nice, fat tip because he felt bad that the drinks had been transferred to the dinner bill, and he wanted to make sure I was covered. That's a stand-up dude."

Alarm bells were going off in my head. What was he up to?

"Well, that was nice of him. But I don't know what that has to do with me?"

Teak leaned forward and whispered, "He told me, Dylan. He thought you were nervous to come meet me because, well, you know? He said it was an issue for you with men, and he felt bad about it because he said you're a great girl, and you don't deserve to be judged by this."

"Judged by this?"

"My god, people are so shallow. It's a handicap, really. I would never judge you. Hell, it might be fun to explore."

My gaze narrowed, and all the hair on my arms stood on edge. I didn't know what we were talking about, but I knew it wasn't good.

"You're going to have to fill me in." I moved to my feet because I didn't like the direction this was going.

"Dylan. It's fine. It makes you even more unique. How many women can say they have two vaginas?"

That bastard.

My head tipped back, and I closed my eyes for a minute, counting down from ten to one, even though I was still freaking fuming when I got to one.

"Well, thank you, Teak, for being okay with my *extra* vagina. It means a lot to me. But I need to go right now. It takes me longer to shower than someone with just the one vagina, you know? Take care." I knocked my knuckles on the bar and stormed out of there.

Two freaking vaginas.

I opened my phone and sent a text to my sisters.

Me ~ The truce is off. The billionaire wants to keep battling, so he best buckle up.

Charlotte ~ What did he do?

Me ~ He told the bartender that I had two vaginas. <cat emoji> <cat emoji>

Vivian ~ Damn. I wouldn't mind having two vaginas after having little Bee. A spare would be nice.

Everly ~ Amen to that. <praying hands emoji>

Ashlan ~ What are you going to do?

Me ~ I don't know yet. But all bets are off. He best get ready to be penis-shamed in every state we visit.

Wolf Wayburn had no idea who he was messing with.

But he was about to find out.

eight

. . .

Wolf

A POUNDING on my door startled me as I stood over the sink, brushing my teeth. I spit, rinsed, and wiped my mouth, not taking the time to button my dress shirt that hung open as I moved to the door of my hotel suite. I looked through the peephole to see Dylan Thomas standing on the other side of the door, and I couldn't help but smirk.

Straightening my face, I pulled open the door and leaned against the door frame. Her eyes scanned my exposed abs, and I didn't mind it one bit. I couldn't have her, but it didn't mean I didn't enjoy knowing she wanted me as much as I wanted her.

"It's late. This is a little unprofessional, don't you think?" I asked.

She narrowed her gaze. "I thought we had a truce. Aren't you supposed to be a man of your word?"

"It depends on who you're asking. I never make a truce with the enemy," I teased.

"Two vaginas? Really? You just couldn't wait to go tell Teak that, could you?"

"Honestly, no. I have to admit, I enjoyed myself." I shrugged and tried hard not to laugh. Hell, it had been a long time since anyone made me laugh and smile this often. As aggravating as she was, she was also cute as hell, wittier than anyone I'd ever met before, and fucking gorgeous.

"So, what does that mean? I'm the enemy? That's why you aren't a man of your word?" she hissed before her finger shot out and stabbed me hard in the chest a couple times. I wrapped my hand around her finger and held it just an inch from my heated skin.

"You aren't the enemy. But you did tell that hostess that I had a small penis. Fair is fair."

"Please. You don't even remember her name. By the way, it was Jos. And you supposedly got together with her anyway, right? Isn't that your story? You got to show her that you don't have a small peen." She chuckled as I continued to hold her finger in my hand. The pull I felt toward this woman was indescribable. Nothing I'd ever experienced before.

"You're just so curious about my package, aren't you? It's killing you not knowing." I leaned down, my lips grazing the outside of her ear. "I have a gigantic cock, Minx."

She didn't pull away as I'd expected. Instead, she shocked the shit out of me when her hand gripped my dick which was now rock-hard. "Too bad for you that it doesn't matter how big it is. I have zero interest in it."

And then she pulled her hand away and yanked her finger free from my grip at the same time.

"Keep telling yourself that," I said, but my voice was gruff now.

Had I ever wanted a woman as badly as I wanted her?

"In your dreams, Wolf. I'm going to take my two magic vajazzles to my room now. And you best go take a cold shower because you definitely have a bad case of blue balls going on downstairs." She winked over her shoulder before slipping her key into the door and stepping inside her room.

I groaned.

The woman was going to drive me crazy.

I did exactly that.

I turned the water on as cold as it would go and let it beat down on me. But there was no relief.

So, I did the only thing I knew would work.

I gripped my dick and closed my eyes, trying desperately to think of anything other than the woman across the hall.

But all the dirty thoughts I'd ever mustered couldn't drown out this attraction. Hell, maybe giving myself the fantasy would stomp out the desire. So, I let myself have this.

Have her.

I imagined her mouth on mine.

My hands cupping her perfect tits.

Slipping my fingers beneath the lace of her panties and feeling how wet she was for me.

Tasting and exploring and making her cry out my name over and over.

And I groaned as I came hard beneath the cold water.

Fuck me.

I needed to get this girl out of my system, and it didn't help that I had to spend another fucking week with her, day in and day out.

Eating. Working out. Traveling.

Laughing. Fighting.

I turned off the water and slipped on some clean boxer briefs and climbed into bed.

But even in my sleep, the woman was there.

Taunting and teasing me like the little minx she was.

———

The next morning, we were flying out, but I made my way downstairs to grab some breakfast. Dylan was there, sitting at a table, working on her iPad. I noticed two glasses of juice on the table as I approached.

"You expecting company?" I asked, raising a brow when she looked up to meet my gaze.

The corners of her lips turned up, and she looked like she was up to something.

"Good morning, Wolf. I figured you'd want to grab a bite before we left. I ordered you a juice, but I haven't ordered breakfast yet because I wasn't sure what you'd be having."

I pulled out the chair and studied her skeptically. What the fuck was she up to? She looked far too happy to see me.

"I thought you were pissed about the two vaginas?" I asked, trying hard to remain serious because this shit was ridiculous. But this is how it was with my SEAL brothers, too. We were always pulling shit on one another. It got us through some tough times. But I didn't even know what the hell this was. It wasn't professional, that's for sure. But we were so far past being professional, I didn't really give a shit at this point.

"No. After further evaluation, I realized it's a compliment. You clearly think highly of me if the first thing you think of is to give me *two vaginas*. I mean, I gave you a small peen. *Sorry, not sorry*. But you—you gave me a superpower. Imagine what I could do with two magic vaginas versus one... Think of all the sex that I could be having. Double the pleasure, am I right?" She winked.

Did it just get fucking hot in here?

I cleared my throat and raised a brow. "So, we're even. We've got a truce."

"Sure, friend. Of course, we do." She smiled, but it was about as fake as it gets. This shit wasn't done.

The server approached, and we both ordered breakfast. I went to pick up my glass of juice and set it back down without taking a sip.

She wouldn't pull that kind of shit, would she?

Her head fell back in laughter, and then she leaned forward and whispered, "Oh, Wolf. I've really gotten into your head. You think I'd poison you? Do I remind you of the bad guys you used to go after on your missions?"

I leaned back in my chair and folded my arms over my chest. "I assure you—you don't frighten me. But I have an evil brother who likes to pull pranks, and he has put laxatives in my coffee, so I'm just being… aware of my surroundings. You can understand that, right, Minx?"

She waggled her brows. "I get it. I put down my guard last night, and I got a rude awakening. Although I have to tell you, it didn't bother Teak one bit. He was down for the challenge."

"I see. But you just couldn't wait to charge up to my room and confront me, could you?"

"Don't flatter yourself. I just wasn't feeling it with Teak. It certainly had nothing to do with you." She shrugged and looked back down at her iPad. "So, we have a busy couple of days before we go home."

There was something in her tone that caught my attention. Was that vulnerability? "You ready to get home?"

"I'm fine. I'm looking forward to getting settled in the corporate apartment. I'll go home in a few weeks for Halloween to see my nieces and my nephew trick-or-treat."

I nodded. When the server set down a piping hot mug of coffee for me, I asked her for another glass of juice, telling her that a bug had landed in my glass. Dylan rolled her eyes but seemed to be enjoying the fact that I wouldn't drink from the glass she'd ordered me.

I wouldn't put much past this woman—she was being far too friendly this morning after being so angry last night.

"I think you're going to like the apartment. It's actually right next door to mine. My father liked the building where I'd bought my apartment, and he purchased one for corporate housing at the same time. How do you like that, neighbor?"

She groaned. "It's a lot of togetherness. All the travel. Working together. And now, we're neighbors?" She actually looked disappointed, which pissed me off—don't ask me why.

Our plates were set down in front of us, and her French toast smothered in syrup with bananas piled on top looked better than my scrambled eggs and bacon.

"You can always quit, Minx."

"Not a chance. And I see you eyeing my breakfast. I'll swap you half a piece of French toast for two of your sausage links." She licked her lips, and I forced myself not to stare at her mouth.

"You have three pieces of French toast, and I have three sausage links. You're offering me half of one piece of toast for two of my links? Not a fucking chance. One link for one piece of toast. And I want a few bananas."

She narrowed her gaze before cutting a bite and popping it into her mouth. She moaned so seductively that two men sitting at a table a few feet away gaped at her as she slowly chewed and continued to sound like she were in the midst of a never-ending orgasm.

"Fine. Take the goddamn links and give me the toast. You're going to get arrested, and we don't need the company being dragged into your craziness."

She smiled and cut half a slice of toast before forking my links and dropping them onto her plate. "Pleasure doing business with you."

"So, the place is furnished and should have everything you need. My sister designed the interior, so I think you'll be pleased."

She finished chewing. "Sabine is an interior designer?"

"Yep. It's always been her passion. She had my apartment ready for me when I got back from my last mission."

"Do you miss the Navy? I'm sure it was a constant adrenaline rush. Although you are strapped to me right now, and that must be thrilling."

I rolled my eyes, even if she made a valid point. "There

are things I miss—my brothers being at the top of the list. But I was ready to leave when I did. I have no regrets. Although, being strapped to you is not what I'd bargained for."

"Well, I hadn't planned for this either, so there you go. But I'm sure it's hard to leave something that you did for a long time."

I nodded as I swallowed the best goddamn French toast I'd ever had. "Why are you being so friendly this morning?"

"We have another week together, and apparently, we're going to be neighbors. Why shouldn't I be nice?"

"Hmmm... I don't know. You looked like you wanted to kill me last night when you fisted my junk." I leaned back in my chair and crossed my arms over my chest.

"I completely forgot about that. It wasn't all that memorable." She smirked. "Clean slate. I promise."

She held her pinky up for me, and I narrowed my gaze.

"Have you never made a pinky promise? Let me guess... this isn't something you Navy SEALs do?"

I barked out a laugh because this girl was so far under my skin I could barely see straight. I leaned forward and wrapped my pinky around hers. Not because I believed for one minute that she was going to keep her word about a truce from a goddamn pinky promise. But because the urge to touch her was so fucking strong.

"What are you promising, Minx?"

"I'm agreeing to a truce. Your small peen and my magic vaginas are both off the table." She winked. "*I promise, boss.*"

I held her finger there when she tried to pull away and tugged her forward so we were both leaning over the table. "Was there something in my juice this morning?"

Her eyes were wild with excitement. She got off on this shit as much as I did.

"If I told you my secrets, I'd have to kill you."

"I'm not easy to kill. Trust me." My voice was gruff as her jasmine scent was doing a number on me.

Her nearness.

Her tongue swiped out, slowly gliding across her bottom lip.

"Neither am I. That's why we need a truce."

This pull I felt was too much.

I let her hand go and sat back in my chair.

I needed to pull my shit together.

Because this woman might just be the death of me.

And I knew better than to allow that.

nine

. . .

Dylan

WHEN WE LANDED in San Francisco, I was exhausted. Wolf had barely spoken to me on the plane. In fact, he'd been completely distracted this last week. The playful banter had all come to an end after our breakfast in Denver—when he'd thought I'd poisoned him.

I chuckled to myself at the way he'd studied me and then the glass of juice.

Of course, I hadn't put anything in his drink, but I enjoyed seeing him squirm.

That double vagina stunt was over the top.

My sisters found it to be hilarious and claimed I'd met my match.

I hadn't.

He was just a broody billionaire who happened to be sexy as hell and irritate the shit out of me.

That's not meeting your match.

It's more like meeting your nemesis.

He was unpredictable. I didn't trust him. He could easily throw me under the bus as soon as we returned to work on Monday. Who knew what this man was capable of?

Maybe that was why he was being so distant. Maybe he

was going to try to get me fired, and he didn't want me to know.

The only time we'd spent together over the last few days was when we'd met with an agent in Los Angeles, a college athlete and his coach in Seattle, and a superstar high school center from Minnesota. Otherwise, he'd been MIA. The man was so hot and cold, it was impossible to know what was going on with him.

Maybe he had a woman.

I mean... I did get a sample of his goods, and to say I'd been impressed would be a massive understatement.

And when I say massive, I mean the man had a *massive package*, and I'd even given it a good squeeze, and it had been rock-hard.

So, there you go.

He was actually a broody billionaire who happened to be sexy as hell and irritate the shit out of me... and have the most impressive penis on the planet.

We stepped off the plane and made our way to the waiting car, and I said hello to Gallan, who was waiting for us.

Wolf still hadn't spoken, but he opened the door for me, and I climbed into the back.

"Are you taking me to the new place? Or should I spend the night at Hawk and Evers's?" I was exhausted and had no time for his games.

"The apartment is ready for you. It's also been stocked with basic groceries, so we'll go there."

"Is there a reason you aren't speaking to me this week?" I didn't hide the aggravation from my voice.

"We agreed to a truce. We aren't friends. So, I think it's best we keep things professional moving forward. Especially seeing as we're going to be back in the office."

I nodded, even though I had no idea what he was talking about. We were never friends, but at least he used to talk to me, right?

"Yes, sir, boss man." I saluted him.

"This is the shit I'm talking about, Minx."

"Well, calling me Minx isn't professional either, you hypocrite," I hissed as the car came to a stop in front of the grand building.

Gallan helped me out of the car and handed me my suitcase. He smiled and winked at me as I took the handle from him.

"Thank you for being a kind gentleman." I said it loud enough for Wolf to hear as I stormed toward the building with my suitcase rocking behind me as I pulled it along. I honestly didn't even know why I was so mad. I didn't like that he wasn't speaking to me. As much as he bothered me, I looked forward to being annoyed by him each day.

And now there was just... nothing. Like he'd dismissed me. My ego didn't like that... nor did my vajazzle.

I felt his presence move beside me, and he yanked my suitcase from my hand, and I fought him as much as I could before I nearly stumbled.

"Goddamn it, Dylan. Just give me the bag!" he shouted.

I couldn't remember the last time he'd called me Dylan, but I didn't like it. There was no playfulness anymore.

I let him have the bag, and I marched beside him into the building. He introduced me to the doorman, Hugo, who was in his mid-fifties and had kind eyes.

Unlike the dark blue icicles that stared back at me when we stepped onto the elevator.

"Are you going to try to get me fired and break the ninety-day agreement? Is that what this is about? Because if so, give me a heads-up so I'm not blindsided."

He blew out a frustrated breath and shook his head. "What? No. I agreed to the ninety days. That hasn't changed."

He stalked off the elevator with my large suitcase and his small one stumbling behind him.

"How do I know you're telling the truth? You already

admitted you aren't a man of your word when it comes to the enemy. And I'm clearly the enemy," I grumped from behind him as he slipped a key into the door and pushed it open.

And, oh my gosh… This place would have taken my breath away if I wasn't so angry at the jackass in front of me. It was stunning. Marble floors and large windows over-looking the city. It was the most magnificent place I'd ever seen.

And Hawk and Everly's penthouse was dazzling, so that was saying a lot. I wandered into the modern black-and-white kitchen, which was sleek and sexy with fancy appliances. The refrigerator was all glass. I could look right into it, and there were bottles of Pellegrino and baskets with fresh fruit and vegetables. I'd never seen anything like it.

"These are your keys. We'll both use Gallan to go to and from work, seeing as we're living in the same building. I'll text you his number so that if you need anything, he'll be at your beck and call. My father had your car brought over here and parked in the garage for you, so if for any reason you need to drive somewhere, you call downstairs to the valet, and they'll pull it up front. I'll text you that number, as well. And there's also a twenty-four-hour concierge here if you need anything."

"Wow." I walked out of the kitchen and faced him as he stood in the foyer near the front door. I couldn't wait to explore this place. "This is really amazing. Thanks."

I didn't want to look at him because he was still being a jerk, but there was something about him that made it impossible to look away.

He nodded and moved toward the front door.

The man was so confusing I couldn't figure him out.

At least when we were fighting, I knew he hated me.

"For the record," I said, as his hand wrapped around the door handle. "I didn't put anything in your orange juice. It was just a joke. Clearly, I forgot that you can't take a joke because you have no sense of humor. You're all broody and pissed off and distant half the time," I said. While still mid-sentence, he stunned me by whipping around and yanking my hand toward him, spinning me so that my back was against the door.

"Stop fucking talking, Minx." His face was so close to mine, his warm breath tickled my cheek as anger radiated from his body.

"Don't tell me what to do, you pompous ass." I shoved at his chest as he crowded my space.

"I'm your fucking boss," he growled. His hand moved to my cheek, and he held it there. A soft caress that I wanted to lean into, but I couldn't trust this guy. It was such a confusing moment because his words were all angry fire, but his body was warm and comforting.

"How can I forget when you remind me every day?"

He used the pad of his thumb and traced along my bottom lip. "You're so fucking aggravating. So far under my skin, I can't fucking see straight."

I wasn't the girl who froze in these situations. I always took control. If I didn't like what he was doing, I'd have no problem shoving him off me and kicking him in the nuts.

The problem was—I liked this.

I liked *him*.

I despised him as much as I craved him.

And I wanted him more than I'd ever wanted anyone.

Or anything.

And that made zero sense.

His mouth moved closer, and his lips grazed mine. His hardness pressed against me, and I arched into him to get closer, my fingers tangling in his hair.

I didn't know what I wanted to happen next.

"Fuck!" he said, jumping back like I'd tasered him. His hands dropped to his sides, and the veins in his neck bulged.

Well, that was definitely not what I was hoping would happen next.

Now I was all hot and bothered, and the bastard was still raging.

"What is your freaking problem?" I shouted.

"You." He shrugged. "You're my fucking problem. This is not happening."

I rolled my eyes. "Don't threaten me with a good time. And don't let the door hit you in the ass."

I raised a brow and looked from him to the door as I stepped away. This guy was going to give me whiplash, and I was not having it.

"No attitude on Monday, Minx. I'm not fucking around."

Was he seriously accusing *me* of having the attitude?

Glass houses, jackass.

I stalked to the door and yanked it open. "We're not at work, so how about you get the hell out of my apartment?"

"It's technically *my* apartment." He smirked and yanked his suitcase behind him. "But I'm happy to leave."

I slammed the door closed just as he turned around, and I think it possibly hit him in the face, but I didn't even care.

The guy had me all worked up. Even after begging for a truce. Was this some kind of game for him?

The hot and cold.

The back and forth.

He'd nearly kissed me. Although I'd had a fist full of his giant schlong in my hand a week ago, so I couldn't exactly be angry.

I picked up my phone and dialed Charlotte, putting the call on speakerphone while I made my way to the kitchen to look for a snack.

She'd always been my voice of reason.

"Hey, Dilly. How's the apartment? How's the broody billionaire? Is he still giving you the silent treatment?"

There were a couple of bottles of fancy champagne, so I

reached for one. And there was also a carton of strawberries, so I started rinsing those and placed them in a bowl as I filled my sister in on my lunatic boss who currently held my future in his hands.

"I wish I had a handful of his balls right now because I'd squeeze them until he begged for mercy. And then I'd squeeze them some more. That douchedick is messing with the wrong girl."

My sister laughed hysterically on the other end of the line. "Okay. Tell me how you really feel."

I made my way into the gorgeous bedroom and into the decadent master bath.

"Well, that is exactly how I feel. And holy shit balls. This bathroom is insane." I set the bottle of Veuve Clicquot on the counter and bit off half of a strawberry before turning on the bath. "I could swim in this tub. And there's bubble bath and everything."

I dumped some powder into the steaming water and then moved back to the living room to get my suitcase.

"Did you want him to kiss you? I can't tell if you like him or hate him," she said.

"I definitely hate him. I think this is some sort of game. He clearly doesn't think I'm really going to stick to the truce, so maybe he's testing me." I marched back to the bathroom and opened my suitcase, pulling out a hair tie and piling an enormous knot on top of my head.

"But you weren't going to stick to the truce, so he's kind of right."

I popped the cork on the champagne and set the entire bottle on the side of the tub. "Whose side are you on?"

"Always yours. But I'm just trying to figure the guy out."

I stripped down and set the bowl of berries next to the tub. There were so many bubbles in the bath that I couldn't see the water. I turned off the faucet and climbed in.

"Ahhhhh. This is heaven. I'm soaking in a billionaire's

bathtub, and I've got a bottle of bubbly in here." I took a big swig from the bottle and reached for another strawberry.

"You are living the life, girl."

"Aside from this massive thorn in my side. I mean, what if he goes to work on Monday and tries to get me fired?"

"Well, he's the one who almost just kissed you. I don't think he'd have a leg to stand on."

"That's a good point. And he did tell Twork that I had two vaginas."

"Wasn't his name Tweak?" Charlotte asked.

My head fell back in laughter as I leaned back in the tub, bubbles surrounding me. "Wait. No. It was Teak, like the wood."

We both laughed hysterically, and I took another swig from the bottle. "Well, he's in for it if he thinks I'm going to cower to him on Monday. I don't cower to any man. Maybe he was trying to see if I'd want him to kiss me, you know, to exert some sort of power over me."

"Or maybe he just wanted to kiss you."

"Well, he won't get that chance again. He had me where he wanted me, and then he got all huffy and mad. No freaking way. He will not get inside my head. A Mink is more savage than a Wolf anyway, right?" I took another big swig, and the cool bubbles completely relaxed me.

"I thought he called you Minx?"

"Isn't it the same thing?" I asked over a mouthful of strawberries.

Damn. Bubble baths with berries and champagne were my new favorite things.

My sister tried to talk over her laughter. "No. A mink is part of the weasel family. I think he's been calling you a minx, which is a cunning, flirtatious girl."

My sister was a teacher and the queen of vocabulary.

"Hmmm… neither option is spectacular. But I guess I'd rather be a cunning, flirtatious girl than a weasel."

More laughter.

"I miss you," she said. "When are you coming home?"

"I'll be home soon for Halloween. I can't wait to see Little Bee, Jackson, Hadley, and Paisley in their costumes. You can come here before then if you want."

She sighed. "School's crazy busy at the moment. And Ledger and I have to be at the house so much now because it's crunch time. But I'll see you soon. Call me tomorrow." She paused and giggled when Ledger shouted hello into the phone.

"Hey there, brother-in-law."

He and I chatted for a little bit before my sister came back on the line.

"All right. I'm going to go. Love you."

"Love you."

I ended the call and took another sip as I thought about what had just happened with Wolf before setting the bottle on the side of the tub. The way he'd pressed himself against me. The way his lips had felt against mine, even if it had just been a graze. How his fingers caressed the side of my face. I'd never wanted someone more, had I? My hand slipped down my belly and settled between my legs. I let my head fall back and closed my eyes while I thought about what it would feel like to have him right here in this tub. My fingers grazed over my most sensitive area.

Desire flooded.

And I let myself go there.

Thinking of how his lips would feel on mine.

His hands on my breasts.

Pleasure was building, and I couldn't stop it if I wanted to. I could almost feel his mouth on mine. Feel his desire for me even now.

A fantasy with the enemy was fine, right?

I bit down on my bottom lip as sensation built.

A blistering orgasm ripped through my body, and my

breaths came hard and fast as I came to grips with the fact that I'd just fantasized about the man I despised.

Maybe that's all I needed to get Wolf Wayburn out of my head.

A release of sorts.

And now, I'd be ready to take on anything he wanted to throw my way.

ten

. . .

Wolf

MONDAY MORNING CAME FAST. I'd barely left the apartment on Sunday as I'd spent most of the day working. I peeked my head out a few times to see if Dylan was around, but she'd been quiet.

I'd fucked up when I'd dropped her off. I'd been putting space there because this attraction was dangerous. I'd kept my distance the last week we'd been traveling, only seeing her when I absolutely had to.

She fucking worked for me, and this would only complicate things.

It was just an attraction.

I could deal with it.

But I'd actually missed her this weekend after spending so much time together these last couple of weeks. I'd missed her annoying questions and sarcasm.

But I'd get over it.

We were quiet on the drive to work today as we had both texted Gallan within minutes of one another, so he put us on a group text. But we didn't acknowledge one another there aside from letting Gallan know we were ready to be picked up. Apparently, she was now avoiding me, too, as she'd barely said more than a short hello.

Today, we were having lunch with my father and Roger to go over everything that had happened on our trip.

Well, aside from all the sexual tension and fucked-up pranks we'd pulled.

And tonight, I was having dinner with Sabine. My sister had a way of grounding me. She was bringing takeout and wanted to fill me in on her new boyfriend.

That's the distraction that I needed.

Dylan had been given an office two doors down from mine, and I heard laughter coming from there and made my way over. I paused in the doorway to see my brother, Sebastian, in the chair across from her desk, flirting his ass off as she bellowed out in laughter.

Of course.

He was the fucking funny brother.

The life of the party.

The dude didn't have a serious bone in his body.

"Excuse me. Am I interrupting?" I said, trying to hide my irritation.

Sebastian was a player, and Dylan was a beautiful woman. He'd do what he could to take his shot.

I knew him well enough to know that.

Dylan looked up, and her shoulders stiffened when she saw me. "Hello, boss. What can I do for you?"

Such a smart-ass.

"Ah... I see someone is making sure you know that he's large and in charge. The big, hairy tuna, am I right?" Seb barked out a laugh.

"It's the big kahuna." I rolled my eyes.

"Right. Well, I just came to meet our new chief legal. I invited her to come check out the marketing department so I can introduce her to everyone."

"She's on a ninety-day trial period. I don't know that I'd

go introducing her to everyone in the office just yet." I raised a brow, and my gaze locked with hers as she shot me one of her infamous glares.

"Dad said she's all but got the job, pending your trip went well. And Dilly tells me things went great."

Oh, for fuck's sake. He was already giving her a nickname, too.

"It's yet to be decided. Don't you have some work to do?"

"Not really. It's kind of a cushy job, if you know what I'm saying. Dad wants me to learn the ropes, so I'm just sort of overseeing things. How about we go grab a coffee, and I'll show you around, Dilly?" He pushed to his feet, and my hands fisted at my sides.

"I'd like that. Thank you so much, Seb."

So, she had a nickname for him, as well.

Fucking fabulous.

"Well, I was just coming to remind you about our lunch today. Gallan will meet us downstairs a little before noon."

"Yep. I got the memo, boss. Thanks for the reminder. See you later." And she sauntered past me.

I stood there, watching them walk down the hall, chatting nonstop as my brother flirted his ass off.

I groaned and made my way back to my office.

I buried myself in work for the next few hours until my assistant, Tawny, stood in the doorway and told me it was time for my meeting.

"Shit. All right, thank you. Is Miss Thomas ready?"

"Yes. I just saw her get on the elevator to head downstairs."

I nodded and made my way to the elevators and down to the waiting car. Gallan stood at the door that he was just closing and pulled it open.

I climbed inside.

"Hey," I grumped. "How was your morning?"

"Fine. I worked on a few things that Roger requested of me and met everyone in the advertising department."

"Oh, yes. You and Seb seemed awfully cozy."

She narrowed her gaze. "I thought we were losing the attitude?"

"I said for you to lose the attitude, not me."

She rolled her eyes as we came to a stop in front of the restaurant. We were led to the table near the windows, and my father sent a text that he and Roger would be fifteen minutes late. We ordered sparkling water and sat in silence as conversation buzzed around us. This was an upscale downtown restaurant that was always packed.

She was clearly still pissed about what happened when I'd dropped her off at her apartment. When I'd nearly crossed the line. She'd practically thrown me out of the place, and thank god, because I didn't have the restraint to leave on my own.

"I—er—I wanted to…" I started to speak and stopped when I looked up.

Dylan sucked in a breath, which caught my attention, and her eyes were wide as she looked past my shoulder.

"Hey. Don't ask questions. Just follow my lead, and I'll explain later," she said, and there was a bit of desperation in her voice, which was unexpected coming from her.

Her hand was on mine, and she moved her chair closer. Her head fell back in laughter, which was clearly fake since we weren't even speaking, and then she nuzzled her face into my neck.

Her soft lips teased the sensitive area beneath my ear.

Fuck me.

This girl turned me on in ways I didn't know possible. My hand wrapped around her shoulder on instinct before tangling into her silky hair as I breathed her in.

"Dylan. What are you doing here?" The deep voice startled me.

Her head pulled back, and her fingers intertwined with

mine and settled on the table, a distinct move to make sure he saw that we were together.

The dude had to be in his forties, his silver hair a dead giveaway. He wore an expensive suit, and his eyes were drilling into her.

I didn't fucking like it.

She didn't say hello, and her voice was laced with anger. "I'm here with my boyfriend. Why don't you go find your table and move along."

Shots fired.

Damn. I'd seen this girl angry before, but this was next level.

"How long have you two been seeing each other?" he asked, and his jaw ticked, his hands fisting at his sides. I was trained to notice body posture and emotional responses during confrontation. This dude was ready to lose his shit.

Not on my fucking watch.

"I believe my girlfriend asked you to step away. I can either remove you myself, or you can choose not to make a scene and walk the fuck away."

Dylan's hand squeezed mine.

"Yeah, man. Not a problem. Just surprised to see you, Dylan, that's all. I've tried calling several times, and you've clearly blocked me."

What the fuck was happening?

She leaned into me again and nibbled on my earlobe, which nearly made me come undone right here at the table in front of this dickhead, who was seething as he watched us.

He finally got the hint, and I followed his movements as he walked to the back of the restaurant. He was sitting with a group of men, and he had his back to us. He turned around once, and his gaze locked with mine.

Yeah, I'm watching you, motherfucker.

He whipped back around, and Dylan pulled away, her

gaze moving to where he sat, and then she slid her chair over a few inches and took a sip of her water as I waited.

And I waited.

"What the fuck was that?" I whisper-hissed, and her head shot up to look at me.

"That was nothing. Don't make it a thing. Your dad and Roger will be here soon."

"I'm asking you to tell me who the fuck that was. You either tell me or I'll go over there now and ask him myself."

Her mouth fell open. "He's just a guy I went out with once. One freaking time. We'd talked on the phone for a few weeks until I agreed to go out with him, but he turned out to be a total creep. Enough said. They're here."

This was not done. I'd get to the bottom of it.

"Sorry, we're late. You know how the press gets," my father said, as he took the seat directly across from Dylan, and Roger took the last open seat.

My mind was still reeling about the asshole who was sitting across the restaurant.

"No problem at all. I'm excited to fill you in on all the amazing meetings we had over the last two weeks." Dylan paused when the server approached the table, and we all quickly placed our orders so we could get down to business.

I sat back and let her run the show, only piping in when specifically asked to. This was her moment, and she'd earned it. She'd worked her ass off on our trip, and I'd be lying if I claimed credit for half of the guys being interested in a future with the Lions.

She'd done her homework, and she'd charmed the hell out of each and every one of them.

Our food was set down, and we continued talking while enjoying lunch. But I couldn't get my mind off the fucker who had clearly left her shaken, whether she wanted to admit it or not.

Out of my peripheral, I noticed him move toward the

restroom. I made sure Dylan wasn't paying attention as my father and Roger grilled her with endless questions.

"Excuse me," I said as I pushed to my feet.

They nodded and continued with the conversation as I slipped down the hallway toward the men's bathroom. When I stepped inside, the asshole was just zipping up his pants, and I moved to the sink, turning on the water to wash my hands.

He moved to stand beside me, and my gaze locked with his in the mirror.

"Oh, hey." He cleared his throat as he scrubbed his hands together under the faucet like he was getting ready for surgery. He was nervous. "I just want to warn you, man-to-man. Don't get too invested with that one."

I turned off the water and reached for a few paper towels as I took him in. "And why is that?"

"She's a complete tease. I took her to the best restaurant in that hokey-ass town she lives in, and we go back to her place, and she shuts me down. She thought I was there for a glass of wine and some small talk. The girl is batshit crazy." He turned off the water and dried his hands.

Is that why you keep calling her, even though she blocked your number?

"So, you're the kind of dude who thinks if he buys a woman dinner, she owes him something?" I moved into his space.

He put his hands up, and a nervous laugh escaped. "It usually doesn't even take dinner, but yeah, I'm a grown-up. I'm not courting some high school girl."

My blood boiled, and my hands itched to slap the shit out of him.

"Yet, she's probably half your fucking age."

"Listen, man. I know you like her, but just a fair warning. She kicked me in the groin and then pulled a knife on me. She's fucking nuts."

A knife? Interesting.

"I wonder why she felt the need to defend herself and then use a weapon. And if she's so fucking crazy, why are you still calling her? Why'd she block you?" I moved forward, forcing his back against the wall.

"I—er—I was hoping to clear things up."

"What things are you looking to clear up exactly? That you bought her dinner so you should be allowed to fuck her? Is that what you mean?"

His eyes widened, and he looked away. The weak piece of shit.

This guy was an entitled prick.

And the only fucking way Dylan Thomas would pull a knife on him is if she felt threatened.

I wrapped my hand around his neck and pressed my thumb against his Adam's apple. "Do you know how easy it is to cut off someone's airflow? Literally, it's just all about applying pressure."

I pressed my body weight against him, and he didn't move. His words were barely audible. "I'm going to call the police."

"I don't think so, dickhead." I chuckled. "You see, I can say that you threatened me, and I was defending myself. And I highly doubt you want me to make a scene in front of those dudes you work with out there. I doubt anyone would look highly upon you for forcing yourself on a woman and then continuing to harass her."

He gasped a little bit when I applied a bit more pressure. "Okay. I'm sorry." He whimpered like a little bitch.

"Yeah. You will be. If you so much as look at Dylan Thomas again, I will hunt your ass down and fucking end you. You won't be the first one I've done it to, so don't press your luck." Sure, I was trying to scare the fuck out of the guy. I'd killed in battle, but he didn't need to know that.

He nodded, his face bright red, and the fear in his eyes told me he was scared shitless.

"Okay," he sputtered.

I lifted my hand from his throat and stepped back as he coughed a few times and leaned over, resting his hands on his knees as he calmed his breathing.

The door opened, and two of the guys from his table stepped in, and he straightened quickly and turned toward the sink.

"We were getting worried about you." One of the guys chuckled, and he nodded at me as I strode past them.

I walked toward the door and paused to see what he'd say.

"Yeah, I had to make a couple of calls. My girlfriend is flying in tonight from New York," the asshole said as I let the door close.

I was pissed that whatever had gone on had scared her to the point of her pulling a weapon. She wasn't the nervous type, and I had to admit that I found it sexy as hell that she had no problem defending herself.

Her eyes locked with mine as I approached the table, and I knew that she knew I'd confronted him just by the way that she looked at me.

She wasn't angry.

She was curious.

But if she wanted answers, she'd have to answer my questions first.

eleven

. . .

Dylan

I'D CAUGHT a ride back to the office with Roger because he wanted to discuss some contract laws with me, and Duke wanted to ride with Wolf as he said he wanted to talk about their mother's upcoming birthday.

I'd spent several hours with Roger, taking notes and asking lots of questions. He went over the contracts that they offered players and some of the language and legalities involved.

"I think you're going to catch on quick, Dylan. Did Wolf lighten up on you after a few days?" he asked, as he sat behind his grand cherrywood desk.

I finished writing from where I sat directly across from him and looked up to meet his gaze. "He was fine."

He chuckled. "I've known him his entire life. They don't make them any better than Wolf, but he can be as stubborn as they come. Did you know he has every possible accolade that the Navy gives out? He's a hero many times over. And clearly, you can see that he didn't need to be out there doing what he did—I mean, financially, none of them need to work. But it's who Wolf is. He's going to be brilliant at leading this team and this company, but it takes time for him to warm up to people. So, I hope you have a thick skin."

"Trust me. I can handle Wolf Wayburn. He doesn't scare me."

He chuckled. "You might be the first."

I shrugged. "Now, Sebastian on the other hand… he's about as easygoing as you get."

He nodded. "Yep. They've each got their strengths. Sebastian will be a valuable part of this team, as well, but in a different capacity."

"Well, thank you for taking me under your wing. I hope to make this permanent, but it sounds like the ultimate decision is up to Wolf."

"He's a smart man, Dylan. He sees your potential. He's just a cautious guy, and he doesn't trust easily. So just keep doing what you're doing, and it'll all work out. You two will be going back out on the road in a few weeks. Then everything will slow down over the holidays for a bit. So, get ready to start hitting the games."

"I'll be there." I pushed to my feet and thanked him again before leaving his office.

"Dill pickle, is that you?" Hawk's voice bellowed down the long hallway.

I hurried toward him, and he wrapped his arms around me. As much as I enjoyed being out on my own, traveling and chasing this new career path, I missed my family terribly.

They were my Achilles' heel.

The only people I truly gave my heart to.

I was still feeling a little off from seeing Anthony at lunch. The asshole had some nerve to approach me after the way we'd left things. I'd blocked him immediately and hoped I'd never run into him again.

The creeper.

"I just got a text from Ever, saying that she's here with

Jackson," I said when I pulled back. "I didn't think you guys were coming until tomorrow."

"I think she missed you. She sent me here to pick you up and bring you over to our place for dinner. Then we'll both be here tomorrow, working. My mom and dad are in the city, so they'll be watching Jackson over the next few days when Ever and I are working."

I couldn't wait for my sister to be at the office with me.

And leaving with Hawk would mean Wolf couldn't grill me any further about Anthony. Hopefully, he'd forget about the whole thing by tomorrow.

"Well, I'm starving, so I hope she's making something good." I laughed as we walked past Wolf's office.

"You heading out?" his deep voice called out, and of course, Hawk had to stop and say hello. I would have pretended I didn't hear him.

Hawk moved into the office, and Wolf pushed to his feet and extended his hand. My brother-in-law pulled him in for a bear hug because that's just who Hawk was.

"Good to see you, Wolf. Thanks for keeping an eye on Dilly for us. Ever has been miserable without her around." He chuckled this big, boisterous laugh that made me smile. Hawk Madden felt like home, and I was happy he was here.

"Not a problem. She did well." Wolf cleared his throat, his icy blue gaze landing on mine.

I didn't say anything because maybe he was just being nice in front of Hawk. He was their star player after all.

"Of course, she did. She's a badass. Always has been." Hawk wrapped an arm around my shoulder. "All right. I'm going to take her to our house before my wife comes here and does it herself. We'll see you tomorrow."

I nodded and made my way toward the door.

"Dylan. Can I have a minute? I just need to go over our meetings for tomorrow." Wolf stood beside his desk, and I could tell by his tone that he wasn't taking no for an answer.

"Sure. Hawk, give me one minute." I smiled at my brother-in-law, who was already talking about Jackson to Wolf's assistant, Tawny.

"It can't wait until tomorrow?" I asked Wolf as he moved past me and shut the door.

"If it could wait until tomorrow, would I have asked you to give me a minute now?"

I rolled my eyes. "Fine. What is it?"

"I know you're avoiding me. That won't make the question go away."

I shook my head. "And what is the question?"

"Who the fuck was that guy, and what the hell did he do to you?"

"I told you, he's just some creep I went out with," I whisper-hissed because I didn't want Hawk to know what had happened. I hadn't told my sisters. There had been no reason to worry them. I'd handled it. I didn't know why he was making it such a big deal.

"Where's the knife?"

"What? You are insane. I'm done with this conversation."

The next thing I knew, Wolf Wayburn dropped to his knees in front of me, and I found it difficult to breathe, but I composed myself.

"What do you think you're doing?"

His hands moved to my thigh, and he looked up at me. "You can either tell me where you keep your knife, or I'll find it myself. We're running a business here, and I need to know if you're carrying a weapon on you." His fingers trailed up my thigh beneath my skirt, but his eyes never left mine.

I tangled my fingers in his hair and yanked. "Stand up, you big buffoon."

"Are you going to answer the question if I get up?"

I can't say I minded seeing the man down on his knees, heated gaze, lips plump and his fingers trailing up my leg.

"Yes." The word was breathy, but I did my best not to let him know how much he affected me.

He pushed to his feet as he hovered above me and raised a brow. I reached inside my purse and pulled out my pocketknife. "Are you happy?"

"Why do you carry this? Is he following you?"

I barked out a laugh. "*No, Dad*. I've always carried it. I take it he told you about the incident when you followed him into the bathroom like a lunatic?"

"He said you pulled a knife on him. And you shouldn't call your boss a lunatic. It's unprofessional."

I fell forward in laughter. "Says the man who just dropped to his knees and patted me down."

"You left me no choice."

"It's not your business. There's no story here. I've always carried a knife. I've only used it once—on the guy you met today. He didn't like the word no, so he got a knee to the groin and a blade to the throat. I made it clear that if he didn't get the hell out of my house, I would have no problem defending myself."

His gaze narrowed. "Awfully cocky for someone who's never used a blade."

I shrugged. "I wouldn't have needed to use it. I could have kicked his ass. But I thought the knife would scare the bejesus out of him, and it did."

"Yet, he's been trying to call you."

"I wouldn't know that because I blocked him. I handled it. So, thank you for your concern, but by the looks of him when he came out of the bathroom, I have nothing to worry about now. You clearly scared him shitless."

He studied me. "Agreed. But I'd feel better if you gave me his name. I'd like to know who I threatened."

I rolled my eyes. "Anthony Glouse. Are you happy now?"

"I am. Was that so painful?" His eyes softened, and his

lips turned up in the corners just the tiniest bit. Most people wouldn't notice, but I noticed everything about him.

"Very."

He chuckled, and it wasn't even sarcastic or rude. "You'll be fine. You're off to see Ever and Jackson? So, you won't be needing a ride home?"

"Nope. I'm good. They'll give me a ride home later, or I'll take an Uber."

"You have Gallan's number for a reason. Use it," he said, his face going hard once again.

"Listen, big, bad Wolf. We aren't doing this." I motioned between us. "I can take care of myself. So go park your alpha ass elsewhere, and stop bossing me around. I don't respond well to that."

I whipped around and made my way toward the door.

"I'll check in with Gallan to make sure he texts you about what time you'd like to be picked up."

Oh my gosh. This guy had some nerve. I wrapped my hand around the knob and glared at him over my shoulder.

"Good chat." I threw open the door and stormed out to find Hawk showing Tawny pictures of Ever and Jackson.

"You ready? Ever's blowing up my phone. Dinner's ready, and she said she needs her Dilly fix." He smiled.

"Let's go, lover boy." We made our way to the elevator.

We chatted all the way home, and he told me about the new cute faces Jackson was making since I'd been gone. It was amazing that in only two weeks, they could change so much.

When we got to their place, it smelled like garlic and warm bread, which made my stomach rumble.

"Hey!" Everly charged toward me with Jackson in her arms, and I reached for him as she kissed me on the cheek. "I missed you."

"Missed you, too, sissy. But this guy..." I said as I

breathed in all his sweetness. He smelled like baby powder and sweet potatoes. "I take it he's liking the new food."

Hawk hugged Everly from behind and kissed her neck as she giggled. "Yes. He and Hawk both love sweet potatoes."

"Look how big you're getting, little man." I followed them into the kitchen as Jackson grabbed a fistful of my hair, and his eyes crossed when he did it, which made me laugh.

"Come on. Let's eat." Everly reached for Jackson and put him in his high chair, and I took the seat right beside him.

We spent the next hour eating lasagna, garlic bread, and salad while I caught them up on all that had happened. Jackson cooed and slapped his hands on his high chair as if he were taking part in the conversation.

"Well, it sounds like an amazing experience so far. Look at all you accomplished over the last two weeks. I'm sure they are going to sign you at the end of the temporary contract." My sister set the plates in the sink, and Hawk jumped to his feet and started loading them into the dishwasher.

Damn, these two were so sweet together.

"Yeah, I don't think there will be a problem. By the way he looks at you, I think you've won him over," he said.

Everly and I both whipped our heads in his direction, and she spoke first. "How does he look at her?"

"Like he wants to kill me," I said with a shrug.

"Nope. That's not what I saw. It's a dude thing. And I promise you, Wolfgang Wayburn does not want to kill you."

"Really? They sort of hate each other," Everly said over her laughter.

"I don't know what to tell you. It didn't look that way to me."

"Trust me. You're misreading it. We can't stand one another." My phone vibrated, and I moved to grab it from my purse as my sister lifted Jackson out of his chair.

Gallan ~ I'm parked outside of Hawk's building. There is no rush. But I'm here whenever you're ready.

"That bastard," I groaned.

"What?" Everly asked before making her eyes all wide as she looked between me and Jackson, reminding me that I shouldn't swear. The boy did not speak more than a few babbling words, so I highly doubted he knew what a bastard was.

"This is what I'm talking about. I told Wolf that you guys would take me home or I'd take an Uber. But he sent Gallan over to wait downstairs, even though I asked him not to. He's doing it just to bother me."

Hawk barked out a laugh. "Yeah. It sure sounds like it. How rude of him to make sure you get home safely."

"It's the point that counts. I asked him not to get involved in my business."

Everly shrugged. "I don't know. It doesn't seem like he's being rude by sending someone to pick you up."

"Of course, he finds a way to make himself look like he's being nice. Just trust me on this one. The man is crazy, and he's trying to get under my skin." I sent a quick text back to Gallan, letting him know that I was going to help my sister bathe the baby, and I'd be ready in an hour. It wasn't his fault that his boss was a domineering asshole.

"Well, he seems to be doing a pretty good job of that." Hawk winked at me.

Wolf Wayburn was used to getting his way.

But I wasn't afraid of the big, bad Wolf, so he was going to be sorely disappointed.

twelve

. . .

Wolf

"SEE, this is why having you home is so nice. I can pop over whenever I want and see you," Sabine said, as we settled onto the couch with a glass of wine.

"Lucky me."

She swatted me with the back of her hand. "You're so full of it. Deep down, you love being back. And just to see how relaxed Mom is now that you're home, makes it even better."

"Yeah. I know she's happy, and it was time."

"How about Bullet? Wasn't he thinking of leaving, too?" she asked, as she reached for her wine glass that was sitting on the coffee table beside the couch.

"Yep. He's the last one from our original team that's still in. I know Jaqueline wants him to retire. He's done his twenty years and then some. The boys are getting older, and they miss their dad." Bullet was my closest friend, and he'd been my mentor when I first joined the SEALs. Jaqueline was his wife, and he had two sons that were four and six now, so it was time to spend more time at home.

"I can't imagine how hard it is on his wife. You don't even know how many times Mom, Dad, and I sat up all night because we knew you were in danger, even though you wouldn't tell us anything. But we'd watch the news, and we knew you were on some of those missions. Even Seb worried. I mean, he'd call us and ask if we'd heard anything... even if he was out at a club when he'd call." She fell back in laughter, and I couldn't help but smile. My brother was always entertaining, to say the least. He'd need to grow up at some point, but he didn't have to do it just yet.

"Sounds about right. I'm sorry I worried you, though. But I know I was doing what I was supposed to do at the time. But it's not easy on the families, and that was definitely a motivation in my leaving when I did."

"I'm just glad you're home." She set her glass down and studied me. "I ran into Josh Landers today. He asked about you."

I pushed to my feet and took my wine glass to the kitchen and set it on the counter. Josh had been my best friend growing up. He lived down the street from us, and our parents were best friends, as well. Or, at least, they had been. Now there was a weird, fucked-up elephant in the room for everyone, and I'd been happy to be far away from it during the years I was gone.

"How's he doing?"

"He seemed okay. I think he wants to see you," she said when I sat back down on the couch beside her. I glanced out the floor-to-ceiling windows to see the lights of the city shining against the black sky.

"It's been years. It's done. There's nothing really to say at this point."

"He had Westin with him. He's so big now. I hadn't seen him in years." Westin was Josh's son.

"I saw an old Christmas card at the house with a photo of him and Westin on Mom's desk. He's a big kid now. Good for him. Glad Josh stepped up eventually. And I'm sure Kress does the best she can."

"Yeah, from what I've heard, she's a good mom. She's got

the support of her parents, which is good. And Josh has made an effort to be involved for these last few years. I think he really misses you, Wolf."

"What do you want me to say, Sabine? He fucked my girl-friend a few months after I was gone. There isn't much one can do to come back from that." Kressa and I had dated all through high school. She was the first and last girl I'd ever said I love you to, and I was just fine with that. I didn't know what would happen when I left for the Naval Academy, but I sure as fuck didn't expect her to fuck my best friend. She'd written me to let me know that she'd gotten pregnant, and they were going to give it a shot. I'd actually hate him a little less if things had worked out between them. It would have meant that it was worth fucking up all our friendships over. But, of course, Josh just took what he wanted, and then he had no use for her. He went off to college, and Kressa stayed home with their kid and lived at her parents' house. Both of them came from wealthy families, so they were lucky enough to have the emotional and financial support to afford a child at that age.

"I think they both regret it. They weren't even together by the time Westin was born, so the relationship was clearly short-lived."

"Listen, shit happens. I get it. I don't blame her for doing her thing. I wasn't sure when I was coming back. Does it suck that it was with my best friend? Hell yeah. It stung for a long time. But time heals, and I forgive her. I think he's a piece of shit because we were more like brothers. And you know Josh as well as I do. He wasn't interested in anything serious with Kressa. Everything was a game to him, and I don't have an interest in being friends with a guy like that anymore. He doesn't have a loyal fucking bone in his body."

She nodded. "I get it. But you haven't been in a serious relationship since Kressa. Not everyone is going to betray you, Wolf."

"I'm not worried about that. I've been traveling for the last decade, dealing with much bigger shit than the drama of my teenage relationship. And trust me when I tell you, I'm not suffering from a lack of female attention. But I'm not looking for anything serious. I want to focus on the team and make it so Dad can retire soon."

I kept my relationships without strings over the last decade, and that worked for me. I liked to fuck and enjoy the company of a woman, and then I liked to leave. The only expectation was to please the women I was with, and let's just say that I was an overachiever in that department. Sex was a release I'd needed during my years in combat. It was the only time I could turn my brain off from the things I'd seen and just be in the moment.

Sabine pretended to gag. "I do not want to hear about your casual relationships with women. Please spare me the details."

I rolled my eyes. "So, tell me about this new guy. What's his name?"

"Well, his real name was Todd. But he goes by Z."

"Z? Why the fuck does he go by a single letter that isn't even in his name?"

Her head tipped back in laughter. "He doesn't like labels. He's so different from anyone I've ever dated, Wolf. He cares about the environment and making the world a better place. I've been dating so many shallow guys. I think he's amazing, but I know Mom and Dad won't like him. So, I need your help at Sunday dinner when I introduce him to everyone."

"Why won't they like him?"

"He's just… unique. And special. And very opinionated. And I love it." She fell back with her hands on her chest and laughed. "Promise me you'll give him a chance."

I'd give him a chance until I thought he was an asshole, and then I'd have zero tolerance for him. It's the way I was, and she knew it. And if she was coming to me for backup, it wasn't a good situation. My parents and Seb were far more tolerant of people than I was, so this didn't make a whole lot of sense.

"I'll try. How's that?"

"It's a start." She leaned forward and kissed my cheek just as the knock on the door had us both turning away.

"Are you expecting company?" she asked as she pushed to her feet.

I knew who it was before I even opened the door. I'd always had a gift for predicting trouble before it came, so knowing Dylan Thomas was standing on the other side of the door was par for the course.

I pulled the door open, and she stormed past me. "Do you really think it's your job to decide how I get home, you arrogant, pompous, narcissistic ass—" She stopped when she spotted Sabine standing behind me. "Oh. I see you're entertaining. How convenient," she hissed.

I straightened my face because the urge to laugh was strong. Why was seeing this woman all pissed off such a turn-on?

"Hey," my sister said, looking between Dylan and me with a big smile on her face.

"Hello." Dylan bumped me with her shoulder and stalked past me to get closer to Sabine. I closed the door and leaned my back against it, knowing I was going to enjoy the show. "I'm Dylan Thomas. And I just want to warn you about this one," she said, flicking her thumb over her shoulder at me. "He's domineering and bossy and pretentious as hell."

"The list just keeps on growing. You got anything more?" I said dryly.

"Oh, yes. I hate to damper your evening, but did he tell you he has warts all over his penis?" And then she leaned forward and held her hands around her mouth and whispered loudly. "Apparently, he's been dipping into the skank pond."

Sabine's head fell back in hysterical laughter, and I crossed my arms over my chest. "Thank you for telling my baby sister that I have warts on my penis. Congratulations. You've reached an all-time low."

Dylan sunk her teeth into her bottom lip, and she winced. "Ohhhh. You must be the lovely Sabine?"

"The one and only," my sister said, extending her arm. "Nice to meet you, Dylan."

"Oh, I, um, well, your brother was on my nerves. I have no other excuse. I'm sure his penis is fine. I've never seen it personally. I've held it in my hand when I tried to squeeze the life out of his balls after he told a bartender that I had two vaginas, and it did seem impressive."

Sabine took Dylan's hand and led her to the couch as she continued to laugh her ass off at my expense. "I totally get it. Come sit. Wolfy, get your guest a glass of wine, please."

"You want me to get her a glass of wine for insulting me? If you had been a woman I was dating, this wouldn't have gone over very well."

"Well, lucky for you, I'm not a woman you're dating, and I want to meet the new chief legal for the Lions."

"She doesn't have the job yet," I said dryly, even though that wasn't true. I'd already told my father she'd be a good fit because she was damn good at her job, but she didn't need to know that just yet. I made my way to the kitchen to get the little minx a cocktail. If I had some laxatives nearby, I would seriously consider dropping a few into her glass. I couldn't believe my sister was being so friendly. Sabine always had my back. Now she was conversing with the enemy?

"My father said you have the job," my sister whispered, loud enough for me to hear.

"For fuck's sake, don't tell her that. She's already got a big head." I handed her the glass of wine and sat down in the chair beside the couch.

"Takes one to know one." Dylan took a sip of her wine

and groaned, and it went straight to my dick, which pissed me off.

"Must you always make sound effects with everything you do?"

My sister raised a brow at me before studying me for a little too long. "Don't be rude. So, tell me, Dylan, how was traveling with the broody Wayburn?"

"Well, he's not big on conversation and small talk, and he pretty much ignored me the last half of our trip, but I still managed to have a great time." Dylan plastered a fake smile on her face and glared at me.

What was she, five years old?

"Very mature. It's hard to believe that I haven't decided if you should get the job with this stellar behavior."

"*Oh, Wolfy.* Don't be so sensitive."

My sister was enjoying the conversation as she continued to laugh. Dylan went on and on about how gorgeous the apartment was, so Sabine was putty in her hands.

"I like her. She holds her own with you," Sabine said as she bumped her glass against Dylan's in cheers.

"It's great to see where your loyalty lies."

"What can I say? I'm a girls' girl." Sabine chuckled. "Hey, Dylan. Why don't you join us for Sunday dinner this weekend? You can ride over with Wolf. I'm bringing my new boyfriend to meet the family, so this would be a great distraction to have you join us, as well."

"She's got things to do," I said, my tone coming out harsher than I expected.

"I'd love to come. Thank you for the gracious offer, Sabine. What is your boyfriend's name?"

"Z."

Dylan's lips turned up in the corners, and she beamed at my sister. "Very unique."

I rolled my eyes. "Unique? It's stupid. He changed his

own name to a letter that isn't even in his name. What the fuck does that even mean?"

"Not everything has to mean something. He is taking the importance of a name out of the equation," Sabine said defensively.

"Yes. Like Wolf, for example. The name already puts people on the defensive. It's certainly not a friendly name. And then the personality that follows…" Dylan said, before shuddering dramatically as my sister fell over in a fit of laughter.

"Good. Then I'm doing my job."

"I'm so excited that you're coming. Seb will be there, too, and my brothers love to give my boyfriends a hard time. So, it would be amazing to have someone on my side."

"Hey, I'm your girl. I love disagreeing with your brother. It's one of my favorite things to do." She finished off her wine and pushed to her feet. "I really didn't mean to interrupt your evening. I was just mad that he sent Gallan over to pick me up when I already told him that I had it handled. It's so pretentious, right?"

"I can hear you. I'm sitting right here, ole wise one." I pushed to my feet and made my way to the door, yanking it open so she could make her way to the other side of it.

She chuckled. "Oh, yes. That's right. I can feel your grumpy energy sucking the life from me."

"I'll see you on Sunday. I'll get your number from Wolf and text you the details!" Sabine shouted.

"I'll be there." Dylan waved as she paused in the doorway and turned around to face me, moving close as she spewed her anger at me. "Don't go behind my back again when I tell you that I have it covered. Next time, I won't be so pleasant."

"I'm terrified," I said with zero emotion as I pushed the door closed.

When I turned around, my sister was rubbing her hands together and smiling. "I love her."

"Of course, you do. She's the most annoying woman I've ever met. Why wouldn't you adore her?" I raised a brow.

"I love how she sticks it to you. I'm used to everyone cowering in your presence. This is fucking fabulous."

"Hey, I thought you loved me?"

"I do, Navy man. But I just don't mind seeing you a little frazzled. A little more human like the rest of us." She pushed to her feet and patted me on the cheek. "I'm going to go. Jones is downstairs." He was our family driver as my sister was living back home with our parents since graduating.

"I'm hardly frazzled. I've dealt with a lot worse than the little minx. Terrorists. Taliban. Need I say more?"

She set her glass down on the kitchen counter. "This is good for you. I think you've met your match, Wolfy." She pushed up on her tiptoes and kissed my cheek.

"In her dreams. And thanks for inviting the enemy to Sunday dinner."

"You'll feel like you're back in battle." She waved as she made her way down to the elevators.

When I closed the door, my phone vibrated on the counter. There was a text from Dylan.

Minx ~ I love your sister, and your brother is so great, too. Why are you the only one with a personality disorder?

I made my way to the master bathroom and turned on the shower before responding.

Me ~ Buckle up, Minx. I'm just getting started.

Minx ~ So am I.

It should have annoyed me, but it only turned me on. Which meant another shower, fantasizing about my combative employee who also happened to be my hot-as-fuck neighbor.

And this time when I thought about going down on my knees for her, it wasn't to look for a weapon.

Unless the one between her legs counted.

thirteen

. . .

Dylan

THE REST of the week went by in a blur. I'd just arrived at the stadium with Everly to attend a home game. We had seats in the owner's box, so even though Wolf and I had kept our distance from one another most of the week—aside from a few snide comments in passing and some slightly flirtatious yet passive-aggressive texts in the evenings—I'd be seeing a whole lot of him this weekend. I assumed he'd be at the game tonight, and Sabine had sent me a reminder that her mother was looking forward to meeting me at Sunday dinner.

She was fabulous, as was Sebastian Wayburn.

The eldest brother definitely had the most flawed personality.

Seb and I had lunch together twice this week, and he was a ray of sunshine next to the dark, broody cloud that lived next door to me.

"Dilly, Everly, so glad you're here," Sebastian said as we entered the owner's box.

There were rows of chairs in the enormous suite overlooking the ice, and a buffet-style spread with a full bar when we walked in.

Bar food was my jam, and I was thrilled to see sliders, tater tots, and chicken fingers.

"Thanks for the invite." I waggled my brows as I quickly scanned the area for my nemesis.

His broad shoulders strained against his dress shirt as he stood with his back to me. I'd noticed some ink beneath his dress shirt, and I'd tried a few times to make out what it was when he wasn't looking, but I'd yet to have the chance.

He and his father were deep in conversation as they looked out at the ice. Everyone else was wearing jerseys to support their favorite players, and Wolf was the only one who was still dressed for work.

"This is one of the perks of working for the team," Sebastian said, as he guided us over to the bar. "What can I get you to drink?"

"I'm still nursing, so just water for me." Everly smiled as she cranked her neck to look out on the rink. This was a big deal for her to be up here, as she usually sat down by the ice and wasn't very social during games. I got it. She was Hawk's biggest fan, and she wanted to focus. I'd already promised her that if it was too distracting, we'd both just sneak out and go down to the seats that she and Hawk had for us.

But, I thought I should at least be seen, right? I was trying to secure a job with this organization. It had nothing to do with the fact that I knew Wolf would be here. He hadn't shared a car with me in days and had barely looked in my direction.

I didn't care at all.

And that wasn't the reason I was wearing my most fitted skinny jeans that made my ass look like I did thousands of squats a day, nor was it the reason that I'd cropped my Hawk Madden jersey at my waist to show off said ass.

"I'll take a light beer, please." I moved beside him as he handed a water to Everly, and she told me she was going to go find a seat for us. There were literally less than ten people in this suite at the moment, and there were plenty of seats for us to choose from. But I nodded and told her I'd bring some food over to her.

"My kind of girl. Beer and sliders, huh?" Seb chuckled.

"Absolutely."

"Is Everly always this nervous before games?" he asked as he handed me a beer and led me over to the buffet.

"Yep. She takes it pretty seriously, but that's what happens when you're married to the GOAT, right?"

He chuckled as someone I didn't recognize entered the suite and called his name. He didn't appear pleased, but he forced a smile and leaned close to my ear. "Excuse me for a minute. You've got to love when uninvited guests show up."

I took a swig of my beer and started piling my plate full of deliciousness.

"I see you still have the palette of a toddler." Wolf's voice was gruff, and my stomach flipped at his nearness.

What the hell was up with that? I didn't do butterflies in the belly or act giddy around a guy.

Maybe it was the combo of the sexy man and the bar food.

Yes, that had to be it.

"I see you still have your charming personality."

I tried to pile one more slider on my plate, and it wouldn't balance. He raised a brow, and I swear I saw the smallest smile trying to take over his frustratingly handsome face.

"What? It's for me and for Everly. And she's nursing, so we're basically eating for three." I shrugged, and he reached for a new plate, taking the full one from my hands. His fingers grazed mine, and it was like an electric shock straight to my vajazzle.

Holy hormones, this was not good. I squeezed my thighs together, which wasn't easy in these painted-on jeans. I needed to get my lady bits under control.

Maybe it was because I hadn't had sex in quite a while.

This must be my body telling me that I need a release.

It has nothing to do with Wolf; he just happens to be the man standing beside me.

"I've got this one. Fill another one, and I'll follow you over." His voice was even, and I glanced up to see him staring at Seb and his friend.

"Do you know that guy? I don't think he was invited." I placed a few chicken fingers on my plate before deciding to just eat one right now. Wolf seemed distracted, so I may as well eat and enjoy the show.

His jaw was peppered with a little more scruff than usual today, and my fingers itched to see what it would feel like.

"It's pretty tough to get up here without some sort of invite or clearance. But yes, I know him. He's an old friend of Seb's, who he used to get into a shit ton of trouble with, and I prefer my brother stay away from him."

Duke Wayburn glanced over, and I noticed his neck was bright red as he stared at his youngest son speaking to his friend. Seb and his friend made their way to the bar, and Sebastian ordered them each a beer, but he looked tense.

Wolf watched them as he stood beside me, a few feet from them.

"I wonder how many people wished their kids would have stayed away from me?" I asked as I took another bite of my chicken finger.

He studied me for an unusual amount of time. "I'll bet you were trouble, Minx."

"I mean, it was small-time crimes like ding-dong-ditching and toilet papering the neighbors' houses. But my sisters never met a rule they didn't follow, so I was definitely the *lone wolf* in that department—no pun intended." I laughed because the wolf jokes were just too easy.

"Why doesn't that surprise me?"

"Probably because you've been lucky enough to spend time with me and see how dazzling I am up close and person-al." I winked. "Might I add, these have to be the best chicken fingers I've ever had. They must use some sort of special, highfalutin oil."

He picked up a chicken finger and bit off the top. "It's a deep-fried, frozen, battered piece of shitty chicken. There's nothing high buck about this."

"And who do we have here?" the friend of Seb's said as they both approached. He looked me up and down like I was his next meal. I rolled my eyes because that tactic never worked on me, nor did I imagine that any woman enjoyed being ogled by a douchekabob.

"None of your fucking business, that's who," Wolf hissed, moving closer so his shoulder was in front of mine.

Of course, my only concern was the fact that the sliders were teetering on the plate that he was holding. Have I not been beyond clear that I can take care of myself?

I reached for the slider on top and took a bite as I glanced over at the asshole that Wolf was spewing his venom toward.

"I see you're as pleasant as ever, Wolf. You still with the SEALs?"

"None of your fucking business. Are you still trying to drag my brother into your bullshit?"

"Wolf," Sebastian groaned. "Can you just be nice?"

"Come on, buddy, we're old friends. Let's put that shit behind us."

"Well, Dez, the problem is that you nearly got my brother arrested with your drug-dealing bullshit. My mother lost a whole lot of sleep over that stunt, and that's not something I'm okay with."

"Wrong place. Wrong time." Dez shrugged. "Besides, your father has access to the best attorneys, and it all worked out. I got slapped with a warning, and Seb walked away clean. No harm. No foul."

"I don't live in gray areas. You had my brother in a car that you were using to move whatever the fuck product it was you were moving, and you got pulled over. If you didn't have rich parents of your own, you wouldn't be here right now, and he wouldn't have been able to finish school. So, save me the no-harm, no-foul bullshit. You fuck with my brother again and I promise you, I will fuck you up three times over. You got me?"

Holy hot Navy SEAL.

This man radiated power and strength, and I was here for it.

It didn't even matter that he was a pompous ass most of the time.

The way he stepped up for his family—I loved it.

I related to it.

I'd kill for my sisters any day of the week.

It looks like Wolf and I have something in common after all.

Sebastian's gaze softened toward his brother, and he nodded. "I love you, brother. But that was a long time ago. Dez isn't into that shit anymore. It's all good now, all right? Can we just be civil and enjoy the game?"

"Fuck yeah. Open bar and good food. Bring on the honeys, and we're all set," Dez said, his eyes landing on me, and he appeared completely unfazed that he'd just been threatened.

"Listen, Mr. No Harm, No Foul. Don't use the term 'honeys' and look at me when you do so. You need to read the room a bit better than that. Are you picking up what I'm putting down?" I raised a brow, and Wolf's hand grazed mine as he stood right beside me, and it felt like his finger was intentionally stroking the back of my hand.

"What is it you're putting down, beautiful?" He smiled like that word was going to win him some points. "Wait. Are you two together? Damn, dude. I'm sorry. I totally missed it."

"Walk away, *now*." Wolf's tone was lethal. It surprised me that he didn't deny we were together, but he'd clearly had enough.

"Yeah, yeah, yeah. I got you, man."

Sebastian shot me an apologetic look, and they moved away from us.

I reached for my plate, still sitting on the buffet table, and looked up at him. "Are you okay? He really got to you, huh?"

"I'm fine. Just stay the fuck away from him. He's trouble."

"You don't say? I couldn't tell from how friendly you just were." I chuckled as we made our way over to Everly, and I handed her a plate.

"Thank you. The game is about to start." She set the plate on the little table in front of her and rubbed her hands together.

"Enjoy the game." Wolf handed me the other plate and sauntered off.

And it pissed me off that I was sorry to see him go.

But then the buzzer rang, and I focused on hockey.

And Hawk.

And my sister squeezed my hand as we both jumped to our feet every time the Lions had the puck.

But every single time I glanced over, I found Wolf's eyes on me.

And I didn't mind it one bit.

fourteen

. . .

Wolf

AVOIDING Dylan Thomas had become more challenging than most of the torturous drills I'd been put through as a SEAL.

She was a fucking force, and the pull toward her grew stronger than ever with each passing day.

Seeing the way Dez looked at her nearly had me losing control. I was pissed at Seb for even allowing that toxic piece of shit to be near any of us. But that was my brother for you. He wanted to believe everyone was good and that everyone deserved a second chance.

I didn't buy into that bullshit.

I'd seen evil, and I knew it didn't deserve a second chance.

And Dez Lawson was not a good guy.

Not then and not now.

And seeing his eyes on Dylan left me on edge. I'd continued to track him the rest of the night, and I'd made sure there was never a moment for him to make a move on her. The Lions had dominated and won the game, so everyone was hyped up when it came to an end, and I was relieved to finally get the hell out of there.

I offered Dylan a ride home because there was no sense in

Everly and Hawk driving her when we lived in the same building.

We were quiet in the car and when my phone buzzed, I looked down to see a call from Bullet's wife, Jaqueline, and she only called me when things were bad. It was a call I always took.

"I need to take this," I said, glancing over at the beautiful woman beside me, who nodded.

"Hey, Jaqueline. Is everything okay?"

Her voice cracked, and she took a few seconds before she formed words. "He's never going to leave, Wolf."

I ran a hand down my face and cleared my throat. My loyalty was always to my brother, but Jaqueline and the boys had become family to me. "He will. I promise you, he's thinking about it. I offered him a job with the team, and I think he's seriously considering it."

She gasped a few times. "He's leaving on another mission soon, and I just don't have a good feeling."

It was fair. If she actually knew the shit that was going on, she'd never able to sleep again. My natural instinct was always to say that things weren't that bad, but the truth was, the shit we saw, the shit we faced—it was worse than most could even imagine.

A constant threat.

We weren't called out for low-risk missions.

That's not who we were.

We'd trained to be able to take on the worst of the worst.

So her fear was reasonable.

But as her friend, as Bullet's brother, my job was to comfort her.

"He'll be all right. This is Bullet we're talking about. He's the best of the best; you know that. There's no one I'd ever felt safer with than your husband."

"I know." Her words were shaky.

"I'll keep pushing for him to retire, but he's a stubborn

man, which you well know." I glanced over to see Dylan watching me, and I let out a breath. This was a side of my life I didn't share with many, but for whatever reason, I didn't mind speaking in front of her.

"Okay. You're right. It's just hard with the boys, you know?"

"How about I come see you guys in a few days? I can take the boys off your hands for a few hours and give you a break."

She hiccupped a few times, and it was fucking hard to hear how much she was suffering. It had been a driving force in me making a conscious effort not to get into anything serious over the last decade—well, that and the fact that my ex-girlfriend fucked my best friend while I was gone.

Either way, this was the shit I personally wanted to avoid.

Hurting the people you loved most.

I couldn't stop my mom and family from worrying, but I could control how many people I let into that circle.

I kept it small, and I liked it that way.

Bullet had a wife and kids whose world revolved around him—and he put his life in danger every day because it was his fucking calling.

Hell, I understood both sides. But that didn't mean it wasn't still fucked-up.

"That would be nice. I wouldn't mind getting a cup of coffee and going to sit in a bookstore for an hour." She chuckled, but it sounded forced.

"I told you and Bullet that I'm happy to get you some help," I said, because she was just as stubborn as her husband and kept turning me down.

"I can handle my own kids, but thank you. They'd love a visit from Uncle Wolfy."

"All right. I'll text you and let you know when I can sneak away. How about you get some sleep before the rug rats wake you up at the crack of dawn?"

"Okay. Thanks for picking up. I just needed someone who understands, you know?"

"You know I'll always pick up. Get some rest."

"Thank you. I will. Good night."

I ended the call just as we pulled up in front of the building. When we stepped out of the car, we both thanked Gallan for the ride and made our way inside to the elevator.

"Was that someone you worked with in the Navy?" she asked.

I nodded. "My best friend Bullet's wife, Jaqueline."

"He's still an active SEAL?"

"He is. And he and Jaqueline have two young boys, and they'd like to have their father home." I stared straight ahead because talking about that part of my life didn't come easy for me.

"Is that why you don't have a family?"

"I think it's easier not to have a lot of attachments when you're gone all the time. Just the stress it put on my mother, my sister, hell, my entire family—that was enough for me. But I also wasn't someone who'd craved having a family of their own. Bullet lives for his wife and kids, but he's a guy who loves his job, too. So, I think everyone handles that shit differently."

"Yeah, that makes sense."

"How about you?" I asked as the doors opened, and we both stepped off.

"What about me?"

"You said you're the only sister in your family that isn't married yet." I walked beside her. "What's the story there?"

She stopped in front of her door and raised a brow. "I don't know, Wolf. Maybe we have more in common than you think."

With that, she whipped around, blonde waves dancing down her back as she pushed her door open and stepped inside.

———

The following day, I'd been buried in work after I'd gotten home from the gym. I'd sent Dylan a text that we'd leave for Sunday dinner at my parents' at six sharp. I wasn't thrilled about my sister inviting her because I needed to put some distance there, and between work and home, Dylan Thomas was everywhere I turned. Having her at Sunday dinner meant we hadn't gone one day without seeing each other in quite some time.

I knocked on her door, and when she opened it, it was hard not to gawk. She had on fitted jeans, boots that came up to her knees, and a white sweater that hung slightly off one shoulder. Her long, blonde hair was pulled back into a wavy ponytail, and she looked sexy as hell. She had a bouquet of flowers and a bottle of wine in her hands.

"You ready?" I asked flatly.

"Well, hello to you, too, Sunshine. I mean, who greets someone that way? *You ready?* You're such a Neanderthal." She marched ahead of me and hit the button for the elevator no less than a dozen times because she was pissed, per usual.

We stepped onto the elevator, and I cleared my throat because her jasmine scent was doing crazy shit to me.

I needed space.

Distance.

Air.

I fantasized about her daily, and I needed to get my head on straight, which wasn't going to happen with her being around me every fucking second of the day.

"What is your problem?" she huffed. "Are you mad that I'm coming to Sunday dinner?"

"Would it matter if I was?" I moved into her space, and she glared up at me.

"Not really. Your sister invited me, so I don't need your permission. But I don't appreciate the attitude." She stormed past me as the doors opened and marched right out to the street to the waiting car.

She greeted Gallan before climbing into the car. I got in next and shot a text to Bullet to let him know I'd go see Jaqueline and the kids in a few days. And to remind him about the offer to come work for the Lions.

"Why are you being such a jerk?"

I let out a long breath. "Just because I don't feel like speaking does not make me a jerk. And let me remind you that you've called me a Neanderthal and a jerk over the course of five minutes, and you made it clear that you don't need my permission. So, I'm choosing not to engage in this conversation."

"Which only further proves my point."

I didn't like how comfortable I was with her. Even fighting with her was easy. How fucked-up was that? She was seeping under my skin with every passing day, and I didn't know how to stop it. Being a dick had always been my go-to when I had my back against the wall, but she seemed to have me figured out. She knew exactly how to press my buttons.

We sat in silence for a few minutes, and she stared down at her nails, making it clear she was done engaging with me, as well.

"My brother is going to love that you're coming to dinner." I glanced over at her. Why did she have to look so fucking good?

It pissed me off.

"Does that bother you?" She smirked. So cocky and sure of herself.

We pulled up to my parents' estate, and Gallan drove around the large circular driveway to get us close to the door.

"Don't flatter yourself, Minx."

"Just calling it as I see it. You sure seem bothered every time your brother and I speak. And don't get me started on how you reacted when Dez spoke to me."

I turned to face her, leaning in close and crowding her. "That dude is bad fucking news. I was protecting you."

She leaned in, her chin held high, letting me know I didn't intimidate her one bit. "And I told you that I don't need protecting."

"What are you going to do? Pull a knife on every asshole who crosses the line?"

"If I have to, yes. Now, if you'll excuse me, I was invited to dinner, and I don't need you buzz-killing my mood." She went to climb over me to get out of the car, and her ass hit me in the cheek when she knocked on the window for Gallan to open the door, making a scene of getting out of the car by elbowing me in the shoulder and then kicking my shin, which felt very intentional.

"Good Christ, woman," I grumped, as I stepped out of the car behind her and shook my head at my driver, who was trying hard to cover his mouth because, obviously, he found the whole thing to be hilarious.

She marched ahead of me, and I couldn't pull my eyes from her perfect, peach-shaped ass.

I reminded Gallan he was welcome to join us, but he said he had some work to do and would be in later.

Dylan stopped at the door and glanced over her shoulder. "Awfully slow for a Navy SEAL, or are you just fast in the water?"

"You do realize every time you make comments like that, you're belittling an entire profession that does a fuck ton more than spend time in the water."

"And you do realize that you're belittling my very existence with your snide comments and attitude."

I let out a long breath just as the door flew open. "Dilly, you look beautiful as always," Seb said, opening his arms for her to step in for a hug as he winked at me over her shoulder.

Dick.

Dylan walked inside, and her eyes widened as she took in

the grand foyer. The circular table held a gigantic floral arrangement, and the oversized crystal chandelier that hung above created little designs on the black-and-white marble floors.

"Hi. Thanks for having me. This place is…" She twirled around and took it in. "Gorgeous."

"It's a little pretentious, am I right?" my brother said as he flashed her his award-winning smile. "But my mother manages to make it homey."

I rolled my eyes.

Pretentious my ass.

The dude loved growing up in the grandest estate in the city.

"It's just really beautiful." Her eyes continued to move around the room.

"How's this one's mood today? Is he still pissed at me about Dez coming to the game?" He spoke to Dylan but glanced up at me and smirked.

"He's fine. You know… somewhere between broody and hateful and completely intolerable." Her gaze locked with mine.

Seb's head fell back in laughter. "Damn. This girl knows you well, brother."

I shot him a warning look. "Is the boyfriend with the initial for a name here yet?"

"Oh, yes, they just got here. And it gets even better. *Miranda's here.* She'll also be joining us." My brother could barely contain his excitement. Miranda was our cousin, and to say she was quirky was a massive understatement. But she was my mother's only sister's daughter, which made her our only cousin. Quirks be dammed. She wasn't all bad, just awkward as hell, which made the conversation a bit painful.

"Who's Miranda? Is that one of your ex-girlfriends?" Dylan quirked a brow at me, and I can't say I minded the jealousy that she didn't hide well at all.

"No." Seb barked out a laugh. "This guy only has one ex, and she would not be welcome at the Wayburn household after what she did. Miranda is our cousin."

Dylan's gaze softened, and I fought the urge to throat-punch my brother because the dude just couldn't help himself when it came to oversharing.

"Can we please drop the small talk and get this dinner over with?"

Sebastian took the bottle of wine from Dylan and hooked her hand through his elbow, waggling his brows at me.

"Yes. Here we go. May the odds be ever in your favor," my brother said in a ridiculous accent as he beamed at Dylan.

She glanced over her shoulder at me and winked.

She was enjoying herself.

At least one of us was.

fifteen

. . .

Dylan

I'D NEVER BEEN in a home like the Wayburns'. Everywhere I turned, there were fresh flowers, high ceilings, and gorgeous chandeliers. I couldn't wait to text my sisters tonight to tell them all about it. Long satin curtain panels hung beside the windows from the ceiling down to the floor, where they puddled on the marble flooring in the foyer.

When we entered the room that Sebastian called the parlor, there were turquoise velvet sofas and grand artwork hung above a gold-plated antique fireplace. Duke pushed to his feet and turned to the beautiful woman beside him. "Natalie, this is Dylan Thomas. Everly's sister."

"Oh, Dylan, I have been dying to meet you." She stood up and moved toward me, wrapping me in a warm hug. She had blonde hair like Sabine, but her dark sapphire eyes matched Wolf's.

"It's so nice to meet you," I said. When she pulled away, I handed her the floral arrangement, and she beamed. She had porcelain skin, and her daughter looked so similar as they stood beside one another that it was hard not to stare.

"I'm so glad you're here, Dylan." Sabine hugged me tightly. She and Sebastian definitely got the warm genes in the family, while their broody older brother stood behind me as his mother wrapped her arms around him.

"Okay, well, this is my boyfriend, Z. Z, you've met everyone else, but this is my brother, Wolf, and Dylan, who just started working for the Lions."

"Hi, Z. It's a pleasure to meet you," I said. He didn't shake my hand. Instead, he clapped his hands together as if he were praying and bent forward, so I did the same.

An older woman wearing an apron and holding a fancy silver tray offered me a glass of champagne, and someone else followed her in and took the flowers from Natalie to put in a vase.

"Oh, thank you so much. Don't mind if I do." I chuckled and took a sip of the bubbly, watching as she moved toward Wolf.

"There's my favorite guy," she said. It surprised me the way his gaze softened as he took her in.

"Hi, Gweny, it's nice to see you." He reached for a glass, as well, and then leaned over and kissed her cheek.

Hmmm... he clearly had a soft side for some people. It was easy to see that he and his mother were very close, and it was impossible to miss the way she beamed up at him like he set the sun.

"Dylan, this is my niece, Miranda," Natalie said.

The entire room went silent when Miranda smiled at me before belting out in song like she was in a Broadway production. "Hello, Dylan. Hello, Dylan. How are you? How are you?"

I glanced over to see Wolf watching me with a wicked smirk on his face. He didn't think I could handle an awkward greeting? He'd clearly not spent a holiday with the Thomas family.

I turned back to his cousin and cleared my throat before mimicking her gift of song. "Hello, Miranda. Hello, Miranda. I am well. I am well."

Wolf's reaction was more shocking than mine. His head fell back, and he barked out a laugh. A real laugh. "Goddamn, Minx. You just might be the least predictable person I've ever met."

Everyone laughed. Seb and Sabine smiled at one another, and Z clapped as if he'd just watched an award-winning show. Natalie was watching her son as if seeing him laugh was not the norm, and her eyes watered before she quickly blinked and turned away.

"Can we please eat? I'm starving," Duke asked, and Natalie chuckled before calling out to Gweny, informing her that we were ready to go to the table. I wasn't sure why we needed it to be announced when we could just walk to the dining room table on our own—but hey, this wasn't pasta night at my dad's with all the guys from the firehouse.

This was champagne on silver platters with a staff that hustled around as we entered the dining room. The wood-work on the walls was gorgeous with thick crown molding at the ceiling, and the table had enough seating for at least twenty people.

I paused beside Wolf, and he pulled out a chair for me, just as Seb hustled over and sat in the chair on the other side of me.

Wolf leaned close to my ear. "Are you packing your weapon tonight?"

His lips grazed the skin of my earlobe, and chill bumps spread across my skin. His breath tickled against my cheek, and I squeezed my thighs together to calm my lady bits the hell down.

"It's in my purse," I whispered as I turned to face him, not hiding my confusion.

"Well, there are two knives on the table beside your plate; feel free to use them on my brother if he tries anything," he said, before sitting down in the chair beside me.

"I can hear you, dickhead." Sebastian barked out a laugh,

and everyone else took their seats. Duke sat at the head of the table, and his wife took the seat beside him. Sabine, Z, and Miranda all sat across from us.

"Good. Protect your family jewels because she isn't afraid to use it." Wolf reached for his champagne and took a sip.

"Still trying to figure out why you're so territorial about me and our new chief legal." Seb smirked.

"It's a work thing, and it's inappropriate." Wolf stared at his brother.

I glanced across the table to see Z pushing to his feet.

"Excuse me. I'd like to say something before we eat."

"This ought to be good," Sebastian whispered.

Sabine was looking up at Z like he was a freaking rock star. "Say what you need to say, baby."

"Thank you, love." Z took his time, scanning each of us, and I tried not to chuckle at how awkward it was. Duke looked thoroughly annoyed, Natalie appeared uncomfortable, Sebastian was unable to contain his excitement, and I looked over at Wolf.

He was not pleased as he leaned back in his chair when his plate was set down in front of him. There were two people carrying out plates with dinner salads, and I quickly realized this was not a family-style dinner. This was fine dining. And I was here for it because I hadn't had a decent meal in several days.

"I just wanted to say thank you for inviting me into your home. I will not be dining with you all as I am fasting at the moment. Cleansing. Rejuvenating. So please, enjoy your meal, and I will enjoy the conversation."

"Did he say he's not eating?" Duke asked Natalie, loud enough that everyone laughed. "We can still eat, right?"

"He's cleansing. He's rejuvenating. And his name is Z. Z is for zebra." Miranda sang in a high enough pitch to make my eyes go wide.

"For fuck's sake," Wolf grumbled under his breath before

picking up his fork and diving into the medley of lettuce and colorful veggies.

"So, Z, tell me about your name. Why a letter?" Sebastian asked, and everyone started eating.

"I don't believe in labels. Names are just a form of a label. You would make judgments about me pending my name." He smiled, and his long, dirty-blonde hair fell in his face. He was tall and lanky and looked like he'd been fasting for a while if I was being honest. He and Sabine were definitely physically very different, as she was dressed to the nines in Chanel with Valentino stilettos. Trust me, I knew fashion, and Wolf's sister looked like she'd stepped off the runway. Z wore a black tee, distressed jeans, and military boots.

"And you don't think we're making judgments based on the fact that you changed your name to a letter?" Wolf asked before forking a slice of cucumber and popping it into his mouth.

Sebastian laughed at the comment, and Sabine gave her brother a warning look.

"Well, it's human nature to judge, right? So, I do my best to limit the opportunities. It's the way I live my life. The reason I chose my profession."

"What is it that you do for a living?" Natalie asked, and her smile was warm and genuine.

"I'm a spirit lifter," he said.

"You're a what?" Duke dropped his fork on his plate and stared at Z.

"I do my part to make the world a better place. I refuse to manufacture, distribute, or sell any goods or products to contribute to the capitalistic system and the destruction of society."

"This is fucking awesome," Sebastian whispered under his breath.

Wolf wiped his mouth with his napkin before dropping it into his lap again. "Yet you're dating the daughter of one of the wealthiest men in the city, the owner of an NHL team, and meeting her family members, who clearly go against everything you believe in. What's your end game?"

The table went completely still, and Sabine shot a death look at her brother.

"I have no end game. I find Sabine to be intoxicating. The heart wants what the heart wants." Z smiled, meeting Wolf's stare head-on.

"The heart wants what the heart wants," Miranda bellowed out, startling me as she continued to sing. "Through the pain, through the heartache, I shall find you. I shall find you."

No one paid her much attention as they were obviously all used to it. But I couldn't help but want to join in. This was the most entertaining dinner I'd ever been to, and trust me when I tell you, the Thomas family dinners are rarely drama free. But this was next level.

"I have to agree with my son on this," Duke said. "It doesn't sound like you and my daughter have much in common. So, am I to assume that you are offended by how we make our living?"

"I don't agree with it, but I can see past it because of my feelings for Sabine." He kissed her cheek, and I think everyone at the table thought that Z might just be a little bit full of shit, but I also saw the way she looked at him, and I empathized with the fact that she didn't have anyone on her side.

This is where sisters always came into play.

I always had them to support me.

"Well, obviously I'm new here. But, I think we're asking the wrong person all the questions. Sabine is an amazing woman, why not ask her the questions?" I said, as Gweny picked up my salad plate and winked at me.

"What would you ask her?" Z said, notably annoyed that I

was suggesting we take the attention off of him. He liked the spotlight, that much was clear.

"I'd ask Sabine if she thought there was a problem with the way Z living his life conflicts with the way she lives hers. And then I'd trust her, because she's clearly a strong, competent woman." I shrugged and then rubbed my hands together when a plate of filet mignon, mashed potatoes, and asparagus was set down in front of me.

"Thank you, Dylan. I couldn't agree more. I think that right now, our relationship is in the early stages. We don't need to decide our entire future. Z is different and fun and smart," she said, smiling up at him. "And I like him. That's all that really matters right now."

"That's all that really matters. That's all that really matters to Sabine. And to me. And to Dylan," Miranda sang out.

"Fine. Can we eat our dinner now?" Duke asked.

"I think my daughter is very wise. Thanks for pointing that out, Dylan." Natalie smiled at me. "Z, can we get you a juice or something for your fast?"

"I'm guessing you purchase your juice from the store?" he asked. "I only drink freshly squeezed juice."

"How does one afford freshly squeezed juice when he makes no money as a, what is it? A joy spreader?" Wolf hissed.

"He's a spirit lifter," Sabine and I said at the same time, and we both chuckled.

"Yes. What's the going rate for spirit lifting these days?" Wolf asked, and he didn't hide his irritation.

Classical music played through the speakers in the dining room, but it was soft enough that it didn't interrupt the conversation, yet I found it very relaxing.

"I don't work for money, Wolf." Z folded his hands together and set them on the table.

"Interesting. How do you pay the bills?"

"My parents support me. They understand my desire to give back to the world, and they cover my finances."

"Ah… What do your parents do for a living?" Sebastian asked.

"They own a production company. They are in the adult movie industry."

"I love porn!" Sebastian shouted.

"Porn isn't corn. Porn is porn. Corn is corn." Miranda looked quite pleased as she sang out the new change in conversation.

Wolf coughed hard as he appeared to choke on his last sip of bubbly, or at the fact that the nonworking Z, who didn't believe in names and the buying and selling of goods, was the son of adult movie producers. I reached for his back instinctually. It was my civic duty, right? Not the fact that I got to graze my palm along every muscle that strained against his black, fitted dress shirt. He cleared his throat, and I realized he'd stopped coughing, so I quickly pulled my hand away.

"Are you all right?" I whispered as the rest of his family was asking all sorts of questions about Z's family business. Sebastian even knew some of the stars of their shows.

Wolf leaned down and whispered in my ear again. "As all right as one can be when sitting across the table from a complete asshat. What the hell does she see in this clown?"

When he pulled back, I turned to face him. My mouth was just an inch from his, and my lips would graze his if I moved the slightest bit. I turned his head and whispered in his ear this time. "If I had to guess, I'd say she's having a little bit of a rebellious moment. And I promise you, the more you fight it, the more she'll defend him. If you say nothing, I have a feeling she'll lose interest quickly."

He nodded, and I rejoined the conversation just in time to hear Z ask Miranda if she was single. She went on to break out into my all-time favorite Beyonce song, "All the Single Ladies."

And I did what I do best.

I joined right in, and sang my ass off at the swanky table, sitting beside the big, bad Wolf as he stared at me with disbelief.

Sabine and Natalie joined in shortly after I did, and Sebastian filmed our little show.

"All the single ladies, all the single ladies," we sang.

The Wayburns were nothing like I'd expected.

Yes, they had a ridiculous amount of money.

But they were fun and silly and similar to my family, minus the sterling silver trays and the staff that waited on them.

And the cousin who should seriously take her show on the road because she was fabulous.

But there was a whole lot of love here in this house.

And that made it feel like home to me.

sixteen

. . .

Wolf

WE WERE quiet when we first slipped into the car to head home after quite possibly the craziest dinner I'd ever attended at my parents' house. Which was saying a lot, because most of our dinners were theatrical, especially once you got a few cocktails into Seb or when Miranda was invited over.

But I'd been fucking mesmerized by the woman sitting beside me the entire time. The way she handled herself. The way she managed to make everything better when she didn't even know everyone at the table. The way she made Miranda not seem like she was three sheets to crazy town. The way she took the heat off my sister when her date managed to piss off everyone in the room. The way she rubbed my back when she thought I was choking, and the way I fucking liked every second of the contact. My dick was still trying to settle his ass down.

I turned to look at her. The partition was up, so Gallan couldn't hear our conversation. The moonlight filled the cab just enough to allow me to make out her pretty features.

"Z is fucking odd. Did you see him binge-eating those nuts when we went back to the parlor to have a drink? And how many shots of tequila did his crazy ass have?" I grumped because the fact that my sister was dating that jackass was baffling to me.

"I asked him about the nuts, and he said since they grow on a tree, they wouldn't technically break his fast. But... I'm going to tell you something that you will really enjoy, but you have to promise to keep it between us."

"Why?"

"Because right now, your sister likes him. I doubt it will last, but I don't want to be gossiping about her boyfriend because I happen to like her."

"Fine. I won't say anything."

"I snuck away to thank Gweny for the great dinner before we left, and when I made my way to the kitchen, there's that hallway near the pantry. Do you know the one I'm talking about?"

"Yes. I did grow up there," I said dryly.

"Well, I saw Z in the corner near the pantry, eating a giant piece of chocolate cake with his hands. I mean, he was really going to town. So, I don't know how serious he is about his fast. I think he might have been putting on a little show for your family."

I barked out a laugh. It was the second time I'd laughed hard tonight, and it was because of this woman beside me. "He's a fucking poser. I mean, if he doesn't care about material items, and truly is appalled by the selling of goods... why the fuck is he hanging out with the daughter of a hockey team owner? I think he's a fucking gold-digging, fake-ass fraud."

"So, you don't like him, then?" she said dryly.

"Was I that obvious?"

"I mean. Your fists were gripping the table at one point, and I feared you might dive over the table and kick his ass. So, yeah, I'd say you were fairly obvious."

I leaned back against the seat. "Why is she dating him?"

"Because it's probably fun. He's completely different from the people in her world, or at least, he pretends to be. Should we look up his family's adult films?" she asked as she started typing on her phone.

"What? No."

"You afraid of a little porn, Wolf?" She smirked as she scrolled through the website.

"I don't need porn to get myself off." My voice was gruff as I took the phone from her hand and closed the website.

Her tongue swiped out to wet her plump bottom lip, and my dick was so hard it was bordering on painful.

"You're awfully confident."

"Just never been a problem for me. How about you, Minx?"

"What do you want to know?" she asked, tipping her chin up and letting me know I wasn't getting to her. At least that was what she wanted me to believe. But I noticed the way her chest rose and fell quickly when I leaned close. I noticed the way her breaths were coming faster.

I leaned closer.

I couldn't stop myself.

"Do you wonder what it would feel like to kiss me?" I whispered.

"Why do you ask? Do you wonder what it would feel like to kiss me?" Her voice was even. Completely in control.

I did my best to match her calm. "Yes. The thought has crossed my mind."

"I thought you were a badass Navy SEAL. Why don't you just find out for yourself and stop wondering?"

"Is that what you want?" I asked, my lips grazing hers, and my tongue traced along her pouty bottom lip like I'd been dying to do for weeks.

"I don't think it would hurt anything." She shocked the shit out of me by nipping at my tongue as it teased her lips.

I completely lost all control. My mouth was on hers.

Hungry.

Needy.

Desperate.

Like my life depended on it.

My hand gripped the side of her neck, tipping her head back and taking the kiss deeper, our tongues dueling for control.

She groaned into my mouth, and the next thing I knew, she was pushing me back and climbing onto my lap, straddling me.

She wanted control.

Too fucking bad.

You didn't always get what you wanted.

I gripped her hips with both of my hands, setting the pace and grinding her up against my throbbing cock as my tongue teased and taunted her sweet mouth.

We were both panting.

Moaning.

Groaning.

And I didn't fucking care.

We continued like this for what felt like hours, but, in reality, it was probably more like ten minutes.

Our heavy panting filled the car as she rocked against me faster and faster.

"Oh my god," she whispered against my mouth, and I knew she was close.

My fingers dug into her hips, knowing just what she needed. Her fingers tugged at my hair, and her head fell back. It was the sexiest thing I'd ever seen. Her eyes were closed, long waves swaying behind her as she bucked against me with need. I thrust up several times, and my mouth came down on her neck as I licked a trail down to her collarbone and back up again.

"Come for me, Minx," I whispered against her skin, and her body convulsed against me, and she cried out my name as she rode out every last bit of pleasure.

Fuck me.

If I never kissed another woman again, I'd die a happy man.

That was the hottest fucking make-out session I'd ever experienced in my life.

Unfortunately, she worked for me.

She also hated me.

And the feeling was mutual most days.

This was a recipe for disaster.

She'd want more, and that wasn't something I could give her.

I didn't do relationships.

I wasn't that guy.

What the fuck had I just done?

She sat forward, dark brown eyes sated as they took me in. "Wow. Well, that was—interesting."

I chuckled. Even in my complete state of panic, the girl could still make me laugh.

"It was sexy as fuck."

Her gaze searched mine. It started out somewhat curious, and then it turned into a glare. "Oh my god. You're freaking out, aren't you?"

She hustled off my lap and moved to sit beside me just as we pulled up in front of our building.

"I'm not freaking out. I just realized that we didn't really discuss things, and I don't want it to be awkward at the office."

She whipped around to face me. "You are such a dick sometimes."

"Why am I a dick?" I asked, as she got out of the car before it even came to a full stop.

"What the fuck are you doing?" I said, reaching for her arm, but she was already on the move.

Gallan came running around the car to help, but she was already storming toward the building, and she shouted over her shoulder to him. "Thanks for the ride, Gallan."

I shook my head and jogged after her to catch up. But she was fucking fast, and she was already stepping onto the elevator when I reached her, and I slipped in just before the doors closed. "Why are you acting like a lunatic?"

"I'm not the lunatic. That title belongs to you." She crossed her arms over her chest, and I had the sudden urge to kiss her salty mouth again. "You know what, Wolf?"

"Do tell. I'm sure there's a valuable life lesson coming my way."

"You're such a pompous ass. You immediately assume that I want something with you—because what? You gave me an orgasm? You aren't the first nor the last, so don't get a big head. Have you forgotten that I can't stand you? So, thanks for the moment of pleasure, seeing as I haven't even been able to have sex in forever because working with you has me irritated every second of the day. You've completely ruined my sex life. But if you think that means I want *you*—you are dearly mistaken." She shouted her venomous words and then marched off the elevator when the doors opened.

"I didn't say that. Don't put words in my mouth."

She whipped around, and my chest crashed into hers. "Why did you look so freaked out after? You should have been wanting to chase your own pleasure. But that wasn't what I saw when I looked at you. You looked freaking terrified. And you call yourself a Navy SEAL? Yet you're scared of a girl who's half your size. You big, dumb, arrogant—"

"Yeah, yeah, yeah. I get it. You can't stand me. You just like riding my dick in the back seat of the car, right?" I raised a brow. I knew it would piss her off, and I didn't care. I liked getting a rise out of her. God knew she got a rise out of me. *Literally and figuratively.*

"Fuck you, Wolf."

"I think you'd like to." I smirked because I couldn't help myself.

"In your dreams. And as far as your blue balls," she said,

slowly lowering her gaze to the enormous tent in my pants. "Sorry. Not sorry."

And she whipped around and pushed open her door.

"Don't worry, Minx. I have bootie calls on speed dial." I didn't, but I just wanted to piss her off. She was overreacting, per usual. Which was why it would not be a good idea to let this go any further.

But she didn't respond.

Instead, she slammed the door in my face.

Well, that went well.

Looks like I had a date with another cold shower.

Because that fucking kiss was going to haunt my dreams.

seventeen

. . .

Dylan

THE LAST WEEK and a half had been crazy. I'd worked long hours and made it a point to avoid Wolf. Even when he sent texts trying to get me to react, I hadn't taken the bait. The look I'd seen on his face after we'd made out like horny teens in the back of the car had been a warning sign.

He looked the w

ay I usually did when I thought someone might like me more than I liked them.

And I would not be playing that game.

So, I'd ignored him aside from the necessary times I'd had to see him at work. I'd acted completely professional but refused to meet his gaze when we were in the same room.

I could ice someone out with the best of them, and Wolf Wayburn would not find me chasing after him.

It was just a damn orgasm. One I'd been in desperate need of, by the way. If he wanted to make it into something more than it was, he could do that on his own.

This morning, I was surprised to find the contract for the position of chief legal on my desk. He'd texted me a few days ago to tell me he'd made the decision a while ago, and he should have been honest about it. Again, I'd ignored the message. Of course, he'd just chosen to torture me.

The bastard.

But I was thrilled to be out of the probationary period and happy to be a full-time employee with the Lions.

Today, Buckley Callahan, our goalie, was coming to the office to meet with us. Duke wanted to get a feel for where his head was at. Buck was Hawk's best friend, and there was talk that he might retire when my brother-in-law did later this year, but we were hoping he'd stay on another season. I knew him well, as he visited Honey Mountain often in the off-season, and we'd grown to become good friends.

I'd sat with Everly down by the ice last night during the game, even though Wolf had texted me and invited us up to the box.

I didn't need his fancy seats or his orgasms.

I was fine without him.

Tawny knocked on my open door, and I looked up from my computer screen. "Buckley is here, and everyone is on their way to the conference room."

"Thank you. I'll head there right now." I pushed to my feet.

"Hey," she whispered. "Do you know why Wolf has been in such a bad mood lately?"

I rolled my eyes. "Isn't he always?"

"No. The last few days have definitely been worse."

I shrugged. Probably not getting those bootie calls to come over and relieve his blue balls. "I think he's just a moody guy most of the time."

She smiled. "All right. Good luck at the meeting."

I made my way to the conference room, and when I pulled the door open, my gaze locked with Wolf's. I quickly looked away, and Buck was on his feet and hurrying toward me.

"There she is. The star of the Lions' team." He wrapped

his arms around me and hugged me tightly. He smelled like Old Spice aftershave, which is what my father still wore to this day. It made me miss home. I couldn't wait to go back this weekend for Halloween and see everyone.

"Don't be ridiculous. Great game last night," I said as I moved to sit in the open seat across from him and beside Wolf.

"Have you all signed her yet?" Buckley asked because he knew I'd been on a temporary contract.

"We did. She was given the contract this morning." Wolf folded his hands and set them on the table. "And now we'd like to keep you on the team, as well."

Buckley chuckled. "I figured that's what this was about. You know I won't play for anyone else. I'm a Lion until I leave the league. I think I've got another year in me, as long as you bring in some strong replacements, because we're going to take a hit when Hawk leaves."

The next half hour was a lot of back-and-forth between all of us about the future of the Lions, and everyone seemed to be on the same page. Buck would be a free agent at the end of the season, but we'd have first rights to match any offer, and he didn't want to play anywhere else—and we wanted to keep him.

Duke and Roger were thrilled and shook his hand before making their way out of the room. Wolf and Buck were discussing some of the prospects we were interested in signing when the time came.

"Hey now, girl. Don't you go running off. I want to take you to lunch to celebrate you becoming an official Lion today," Buckley said.

I smiled, not missing the venomous glare coming from the man beside him. The nerve of this guy. He all but runs for the hills after a make-out session, and he thinks he gets to decide who I go to lunch with?

No. He is sorely mistaken if he thinks I will cower to him.

Buck and I were just friends, but I didn't mind seeing Wolf get all worked up.

"I'd love that. Thank you." I smiled, and I could literally feel the anger radiating from the man standing next to me.

"Looks like I'm a lucky man." Buckley winked, and I didn't miss the way Wolf's hands were in fists at his sides.

Tawny appeared in the doorway and told Wolf it was time for his lunch meeting, so he hesitantly extended his arm to Buck, but his gaze never left mine.

"Glad to hear you want to stay on another year."

"Me, too. Thanks for letting me steal her away for lunch," Buckley said, his tone all teasing.

I knew Wolf well enough to know that he was pissed. The muscle in his jaw ticked. His shoulders stiffened, and he shoved his hands into his pockets before giving one curt nod and leaving the conference room.

Buck whistled once Wolf was out of sight. "I'd say someone is thoroughly pissed off."

"No. He's just in a perpetual bad mood," I said, shaking my head.

"That is not the vibe that I'm picking up on. It was kind of fun seeing him get all worked up over you." He chuckled.

"I think you're misreading the signals," I said once I was on the elevator.

"Trust me. I'm not misreading anything. I can spot a terri-torial dude a mile away. That man is losing his mind over you." He held the door open, and I stepped off. "And I'd be lying if I didn't also notice the way you seem to like getting under his skin."

"Are you a hockey player or a therapist?" I chuckled as we walked to the café next door.

A few people stared at Buckley, but for the most part, we were left alone. I liked him. He'd always been easy to talk to, and I hadn't seen him much since I'd moved to the city between my travel and his.

"I'm a little of both." He smirked as we took a seat at a table in the back of the restaurant. "So, give me the deets, girl. I can tell you're hung up on the Navy SEAL with a major attitude. He's a good guy. What's the story there?"

"I am not hung up on anyone. I like being single. I'm not looking to settle down." I paused when we both placed our orders.

"You might be the coolest girl I've ever met, Dylan Thomas."

"It's hard to argue with that," I said, and we both laughed. "So, tell me what's going on with you."

The next hour and a half was filled with good conversation, Buckley sharing the details of his last girlfriend who had not taken the breakup well. He had a large family—two sisters and two brothers—and we shared stories about growing up and all the sibling antics that came with it.

He walked me back to the building, and I gave him a hug. I needed to get back to work, and he had to get to practice. He promised to check in later in the week, and I waved goodbye.

When I stepped off the elevator to make my way to my office, Tawny stopped me. "Hey. Wolf asked me to send you in as soon as you returned. He said it was important."

"Okay. Thank you." I stopped at his door and knocked.

"Come in!" he shouted, and he didn't sound happy.

"You asked me to stop by, so I'd appreciate it if you'd lose the bark."

"Shut the door," he hissed.

"*Please.*" I raised a brow before shutting the door.

"Please what?"

"I was reminding you to say please. You don't need to be so rude."

"Jesus. I'm not going to walk on eggshells because you're sensitive. This is business. Suck it up, Minx."

I sat down in the leather chair across from him as he sat behind his desk. Everything was cherrywood with burgundy and gold décor. He had Navy medals and awards framed on the walls. There were enough to make it known that the man was highly decorated. It was impressive, especially for a guy who was only a year older than me.

"What did you need?"

"How was your lunch with Buckley? Was it business or pleasure?"

"Is that seriously what you called me in here for?" I crossed my arms over my chest and shook my head.

This guy was unbelievable.

"He's a player that we're trying to keep on the team. I know we have a verbal from him, but I need to know if he said anything. I'm not asking you if you fucked him." His fist came down on the desk, and I gaped.

"What? You are such an asshole. For your information, I don't go to business lunches and fuck people. So, fuck you, Wolf." I pushed to my feet and stormed toward the door.

But he was fast.

Faster than I anticipated.

His fingers wrapped around my arm, and he turned me. It surprised me that this brute of a man could be gentle in a heated moment.

"I just want to know what happened." His face was so close to mine that his breath tickled my cheek.

"No. You asked if I fucked him. Why do you even care?" I hissed.

"Why won't you answer the question?"

"I already told you—you've ruined my sex life. You irritate me so much that I can't seem to relax now. That must please you, huh?"

His hand moved to my hair, and he pressed closer to me, his lips on my ear. "Do you want me to make you feel good again, Minx?"

I would normally slap him in the face, but he had given me the whammy of all orgasms. And another one didn't sound like a horrible idea. Especially when I was irritated as hell.

"It doesn't mean I don't hate you." My words were strained.

"Stop talking." His hand moved down to the hem of my skirt and up my thigh before he dipped his fingers beneath my lace panties. "Are you this wet for me or for him?"

"I thought we weren't talking." I tucked my lips beneath my teeth and tried to compose myself as he continued stroking me. The sensation of his rough fingertips against my core made it difficult to stand.

And without warning, he dropped to his knees and shoved my skirt up so that it bunched at my waist. "Is this what you want?"

He looked up at me, his hair a disheveled mess from me tugging on it. Dark blue eyes burned with something I couldn't read.

Want.

Desire.

I didn't see fear this time.

I gave the slightest nod because I didn't want to give him the satisfaction of seeming too eager, but I also knew Wolf well enough to know he wouldn't continue without me giving him permission.

He was a gentleman and an asshole all at the same time.

He tugged my panties to the side and buried his face between my thighs.

Oh.

My.

God.

His tongue was working its magic, and I could barely contain myself. I bit down hard on my bottom lip to stop myself from moaning. And he took his time. Tasting and licking every inch of me.

My legs were barely holding me up when he shifted and lifted one leg at a time, resting them on his massive shoulders. My heels dug into his back as my head fell back against the door, and his lips pressed against my clit. One finger slipped inside before a second followed. Nothing had ever felt so good in my entire life. This guy was definitely proving his Navy SEAL abilities at the moment, the way he balanced me and pleasured me all at the same time. The way he took his time.

I was panting and writhing beneath him. He groaned against my most sensitive spot, and that's all it took.

Bursts of white light exploded behind my eyes.

My body shook and trembled in the most erotic way.

My fingers yanked at his hair, and he stayed right there, letting me ride out every last bit of pleasure.

Sweat covered my forehead, and my breathing finally slowed.

I glanced down to see him looking up at me with a wicked grin on his face, and he slowly licked his lips. "So sweet, Minx."

What was this guy's deal?

He'd pull me in and then distance himself.

I wasn't having it.

Not this time.

I pulled down one leg at a time from his shoulders and settled my feet on the floor before adjusting my panties and skirt.

He pushed to stand, and I patted my hair into place.

I glanced down to see the impossible-to-miss tent in his pants.

"Well, it's been a pleasure. I feel much better, and I've got a meeting in five. Good luck with that." I glanced down at his crotch and smirked.

He narrowed his gaze. "Happy to help."

"See ya." And I sauntered right out the door.

I'd just let him stew on that for a while.

Two could play this game, and he'd met his match.

eighteen

. . .

Wolf

IN ALL MY years in the Navy, missions and training and travel, I'd gone weeks without sex. But nothing had compared to the endless throbbing erection that I'd been dealing with since the day Dylan Thomas came to work here.

She'd probably cast her evil spell on my dick just to pay me back.

So maybe I hadn't reacted right the night we'd gone to Sunday dinner.

I'd freaked out a little.

I wasn't a relationship guy, and I'd just made out with our chief legal in the back of the car.

And she'd known it because the little diva didn't miss a beat.

But today... seeing her fall apart on my lips and my tongue—I was fucking done for.

I couldn't get this woman out of my head, and I didn't know what the hell that meant. Seeing Buckley Callahan flirt his ass off with her had me seeing red.

It wasn't rational.

But I never claimed to be a rational guy.

The office was quiet, and almost everyone had gone home as far as I knew. Dylan was in a meeting with Roger last I checked.

"Hey, you still here?" Roger asked as he stood in my doorway.

"Yeah. Heading home in a few. How did your meeting go?"

"Good. She signed the contract, so it looks like it's official. I'll finish the season and pass the baton to Dylan. Seems like you two have some sort of oddly close but hateful friendship?" He chuckled.

I could still taste her on my lips.

"Yep. It'll be fine."

"All right. Don't stay too late. How about you make Dylan leave here soon, too? She'll work all night if you don't stop her."

"I'll check on her."

He knocked on the door frame before leaving. I heard the elevator bell ding, and I pulled out my phone.

Me ~ Do you want a ride home? I'm leaving in five.

Minx ~ You're awfully attentive today. First the afternoon delight and now the ride home? <winky face emoji>

Me ~ What can I say? I'm very chivalrous.

Minx ~ Not bad for a Neanderthal.

Me ~ I'm leaving. Are you coming?

Minx ~ That's what she said...

Me ~ So fucking witty. You must be having flashbacks of crying out my name just a few hours ago when my head was buried between your thighs.

Minx ~ I barely remember. Was that today?

I chuckled. Damn, this girl had me on edge.

Me ~ Heading to the elevator.

Minx ~ Fine. I'll go home. I need to pack anyway.

Pack? Where the fuck was she going?

Me ~ Where are you going?

Minx ~ It's Halloween weekend. I'm going home to see my nieces and my nephew all dressed up.

I sent a text to Gallan that we'd be down soon and reached for my keys, making my way toward the elevator. I could feel her walking behind me. I turned slowly after I hit the button and took her in as she strode toward me.

Long, lean legs.

Perfect tits that I was dying to touch.

Taste.

Her hair was hanging over one shoulder, and she had this lazy, sexy smile on her face that nearly made me come apart right there at just the sight of her.

"Ah, you decided to join me," I said.

"Well, you were being so nice; how could I turn you down?"

You did it fairly easily this afternoon when you strode out of my office.

The elevator doors opened, and the building's janitors, Glen and Barney, stepped off with all of their cleaning supplies. We said a quick hello before I followed Dylan onto the elevator.

"So, how's your little situation?" she asked, glancing down at my zipper.

I raised a brow. "I think I've made it known that the word 'little' does not describe my cock, and I'd appreciate it if you would stop using that word when speaking of my dick."

"Oh, someone's a little sensitive. Is that the blue balls talking?"

"Call it what you want to. I'll be fine picturing you coming apart on my lips tonight when I get in the shower."

Her eyes locked with mine, and she took one step forward, turning to hit a button on the elevator, bringing the car to a stop. "You know, I don't normally drop to my knees for anyone, especially for someone as rude as you. But, I'm not a taker, and fair is fair. You made me feel good, and I should return the favor."

Jesus. This woman was going to be the death of me.

She slowly lowered herself to her knees, and I struggled to stay in control.

To remain calm.

To keep my breathing even.

"It's only fair," I said, my voice gruff.

"You aren't going to run off this elevator afterward because you're afraid of me, are you?" she purred, as she undid the button on my dress slacks and lowered the zipper. She tugged at the band of my boxer briefs and pulled everything down with one swift tug. Her nails grazed my skin, and my dick sprang free.

He was even more impressive than usual as if he was showing off for her.

I'd thought about this woman's mouth wrapped around my cock more times than I wanted to admit.

"I was never afraid of you." It was impossible to miss the strain in my voice.

"I guess we'll see about that, won't we?" she whispered as her tongue circled the tip of my dick.

I sucked in a harsh breath, and her eyes glanced up to meet mine. She wanted me to lose control.

Seeing Dylan Thomas on her knees for me, lips plump and eyes half-mast with desire, I was ready to snap.

I'd had a gun pointed at my head two years ago, and I'd managed to keep it together better than I was at the moment.

Her hand was wrapped around my shaft, and she looked up at me one last time, pops of gold brighter than usual— yellow like the sun—danced in her dark-eyed gaze. She smiled, and my fucking chest nearly exploded. I wanted her. Not just physically. I wanted every part of her.

But when her lips wrapped around me and she took me in, inch by inch, my hands tangled in her hair.

"You're going to kill me."

She pulled back slowly before taking me all the way in again. I'd always been impressed by my restraint, but I felt like a teenage boy getting off for the first time. I was not going to last long. Not with her sucking me in as she glided her lips up and down my erection.

My head fell back against the wall, and I tried like hell to hold on.

A little moan escaped her sweet mouth, and that was all it took. I bucked faster, and she matched me with each thrust.

"I can't wait any longer," I warned, tugging at her hair to pull her back, but she shoved my hands away and stayed right there.

It was the hottest thing I'd ever seen.

I thrust again.

And again.

Before I exploded in a way I'd never experienced.

"Fuck, Minx!" I roared.

My breathing was so erratic, it filled the space around us, and she stayed right with me as I rode out every last bit of pleasure, spilling into her mouth.

When she pulled back, she wiped her lips with the back of her hand and smiled up at me. "Looks like you're still alive."

I reached down and helped her to her feet, and I wrapped one hand around her neck before my mouth crashed into hers. I pulled back to see the surprise on her face.

"From here on out, we don't pleasure one another before my mouth is on yours." I ran the pad of my thumb over her bottom lip. "Nor do we do it with clothes on."

She raised a brow. "Really? You're not running scared this time?"

"Not even fucking close. Come home with me." I wanted her so badly I could barely see straight.

Not here in the office or in the car or in the elevator.

I wanted her in my bed. Where I could take my time. I wanted to strip the clothes from her body and taste every inch of her.

She moved around me and walked toward the panel and hit the button. The elevator immediately started moving. I tucked myself back in and zipped up my pants.

"So, you want to take me home, huh?"

"I do. Do you have a problem with that?"

The doors opened, and she stepped out, her high heels clicking against the marble flooring as I followed behind her, watching the way her ass swayed from side to side in her fitted pencil skirt.

"We can discuss my terms in the car." She didn't look back when she said it, and she pushed open the door leading out to the street.

"I was just getting worried about you," Gallan said as he pulled the back door open. "Everything all right? I feared you two might have murdered each other."

"Yes. You know the boss here." She flicked her thumb over her shoulder at me. "He's much needier than you'd guess. He just can't get me to do enough for him."

Ain't that the fucking truth.

Gallan chuckled, and I tried to look annoyed, but he knew me well enough to know that I wasn't. I climbed into the car beside her, and he closed the door.

"Such a smart fucking mouth," I said, nipping at her ear. "I want to take you home. So, let's hear the terms."

She turned to look at me, and my hand found hers, intertwining our fingers. I'd never been an affectionate guy. Even in high school with Kressa, she'd always complained about it. But here I was, sitting with this maddening woman who I wanted more than anything, and I felt a need to hold her hand. Not for her. But for me.

"Well, for starters, we'd need to go to my place."

"Why?" I raised a brow.

"Because I need to pack. I'm leaving first thing in the morning. Which also means you need to leave at a decent hour because I have to get my sleep so I can drive in the morning."

"You want a quickie?" I grumped.

"I love that you're so certain I'm going to have sex with you. Maybe I just want to chat while I pack." She smirked as we pulled in front of the building.

"Can you pick Ms. Thomas up in front of the building at nine o'clock tomorrow morning?" I asked Gallan as we stepped out of the car.

"What? No. I'm taking my car."

"You're not. I'll explain later. Nine o'clock?" I asked my driver, and he nodded.

Dylan remained quiet until we got on the elevator. "What exactly do you think you're doing? You know you're going to have to cancel him. I just didn't want to embarrass you in front of Gallan."

I moved closer, crowding her as her back pressed against the far wall of the elevator. "I'm not canceling him. I plan on taking my time tonight."

She raised a brow, but I didn't miss the way her chest rose and fell quickly at my words. "Do you, now?"

"Yes. I'm going to watch you pack and drink a glass of wine and make ridiculous small talk because that's what you want me to do. And then I'm going to fuck you until you cry out my name over and over again. And then I'll get you breakfast, and Gallan will drive you to the helicopter. That way, you won't need your sleep. I can have a car waiting at the hangar for you to use while you're there."

"Wow. Look at you. You're pulling out all the stops."

"I am. I'm tired of fighting this."

"I thought you loved to fight?" Her fingers slipped

beneath the open buttons on my dress shirt and rested against my skin.

"Well, tonight, I don't want to."

"That must have been some BJ, huh?" She waggled her brows.

"You're very good." My lips found her neck, and I moved along her jawline.

"I'm so proud. I've only done that for one other lucky bastard."

I pulled back, startled by her words, and studied her. "What? You've only been with one other guy?"

"No. I've had sex with more than one guy, obviously. I'm twenty-seven years young. But I'm not big on the blowies, if you know what I mean. That's got to be earned. I did it once in college because my boyfriend begged and pleaded, but I've never offered it up again before today." She bit down on her plump bottom lip.

"How are you so good at it?"

The doors opened, and she shoved me back before walking out in front of me. "Romance books. YouTube videos. You know, I did my homework in case I ever wanted to pull out that stunt. I wanted to be prepared."

Dylan Thomas just might be the most fascinating woman I'd ever met.

"So, why me?"

She pulled out her key and leaned against her door before opening it. "I don't know. I trust my gut. And after what you did for me earlier today, it seemed like a good call."

"So, do I get to come in for round two? Or do you need to go watch a few YouTube videos before?" I teased.

"I don't need to brush up on my skills. I'm an impressive lover, if I do say so myself."

I barked out a laugh, and the corners of her mouth turned up.

"What?"

"I like the sound of your laugh." She shrugged. "It's so much better than the sound of your voice."

I chuckled and nipped at her mouth because she was such a smart-ass.

But I liked it.

Maybe a little too much.

nineteen

. . .

Dylan

WE'D GRABBED a bottle of wine, and I pulled together a little charcuterie board, and we sat down on the couch.

"So, I know you agreed to watch me pack, but there's another thing I do every night that you'll have to sit through, as well." I piled some cheese on a cracker with a piece of salami and took a bite.

"Please tell me that it involves you stripping naked."

"Well, that would be weird, because I talk to my dad every night when I get home from work. So, there is no stripping down."

"That's cool. You're really close, huh?"

"Yeah. He's the best." I reached for my wine. "Is that going to freak you out? If I FaceTime him really quick with you here?"

He smirked. "The other night when we kissed, I'll admit, I freaked out a little. I just didn't know what it meant, and with us working together, I didn't want to complicate things unnecessarily."

I rolled my eyes. "Listen. I'm the last girl you need to worry about. I will *not* be falling in love with you, Wolf Wayburn. Hell, I can barely stand you most of the time. So, you have nothing to be concerned about. It's an attraction. We're acting on it. We spend a lot of time together. It'll fizzle out in no time, and we'll pretend it never happened. Deal?"

"Jesus. Are you always this—honest?"

"Yes. Always."

"I can't be that bad if you were willing to give me the world's best blow job."

I laughed. I'd told him the truth about that. I'd never liked the idea of getting on my knees for anyone. After trying it that one time for Matt Richards, I'd realized it would take a very special penis to get me to do it again.

And Wolf had been worth the wait.

I'd actually enjoyed it, which is how I think it was supposed to be.

At least, according to my blow job research.

So, there you go. You should learn something from every relationship that you have. No matter how short or how long. I preferred short most of the time, but this one had already lasted longer than most, and we didn't even have an actual relationship.

But whatever this was—I was good with taking it to the next level.

Then we'd get tired and bored and go our separate ways.

"You're not all bad." I reached for my wine.

"Call your dad. I can go sit in that chair so that he won't see me if you don't want him to."

"No. He knows about you."

His eyes widened. "What did you tell him?"

"Mostly all bad stuff. Like I said, I'm honest to a fault."

He shook his head, and he looked so damn sexy that thoughts of what was coming tonight had me buzzing a little.

"Please tell me you didn't tell him about the two vaginas?" He winced.

"I spared him the gory details. I just said you're usually a pompous ass but that you're funny and smart and were probably an amazing Navy SEAL because you're a hard worker and very disciplined."

"Careful, Minx. It almost sounds like you're falling for me."

"Never going to happen. I learned at a young age to stay away from the big, bad Wolf." I dialed my father and leaned back against the couch, and Wolf did the same.

"Hey, Dilly," he said, as he sat at the table at the firehouse.

"Hi, Dad. I thought you were off tonight?"

"Rusty's not feeling well, so I came in. Are you going to tell me who the large man sitting beside you is? Or are we pretending like he isn't there?"

Wolf barked out a laugh. "Well, I see where she gets her sense of humor."

"This is Wolf. The overbearing, pompous ass of a boss that I kind of work for."

"I'm not her boss. We work together."

"I thought your name was on my paycheck?" I raised a brow.

"It's my father's name. I was just showing off."

Now, it was my dad's turn to laugh. "So, what's this? Some kind of truce for the night?"

"I told you we're sometimes friends." I smiled as Wolf's cheek almost touched mine as we both tried to fit in the screen.

"It just takes my girl a few months to warm up to newcomers. She's always been cautious."

"That's not a bad thing," Wolf said.

"Well, don't go acting like you're nice in front of my dad and making me look like I exaggerated how awful you are."

"I'll try to live up to your very low expectations of me," Wolf said.

"So, you were a SEAL, huh?" my father asked.

"Yes, Sir. I spent the last ten years in that profession, and it was time to go."

"I have the utmost respect for you, stepping up for your country and putting your life at risk. Man, I thought firemen had it tough, but I've seen the training that goes into being a SEAL, and you guys are the toughest of the tough."

"Thank you. I feel the same about firemen. I'd thought about going that route for a while," Wolf said.

"I don't think there are a lot of billionaire firemen, are there, Dad?" I asked.

My father and Wolf both chuckled.

"No, but there probably aren't a ton of billionaire SEALs, either. Most people that don't need to work hard wouldn't choose such a challenging path. But that makes it even more impressive."

"Oh, for God's sake, Dad. You're going to give him such a big head." I rolled my eyes, and Wolf pinched my thigh where my dad couldn't see, and I yelped.

"You guys sure spend a lot of time together for two people that say they don't like one another." Dad raised a brow.

We did. He was right. In fact, I'd never spent so much time like this with anyone outside of my sisters. And even when he made me mad, which was often, I still couldn't wait to see him again.

Maybe Wolf did need to worry.

Maybe I *was* capable of falling for the guy.

"Okay, I need to pack. My costume should be there. Did a package arrive at the house today?"

"Yes. A package came for you this afternoon before I left."

"You're dressing up?" Wolf gaped at me.

"Yes, my nieces and my nephew will be trick-or-treating, so, of course, I'm dressing up."

"I can't wait to hear what you're going to be," he purred next to my ear, and I knew it was time to get off the phone because his nearness was doing things to me. Things that I certainly didn't need my father to be privy to.

"I'm going to be a sexy Rocky Balboa."

Wolf's mouth fell open, and his eyes widened. "Is there such a thing as a sexy Rocky?"

"I'm the female version. It's mine and Dad's favorite movie, and I'm wearing the famous white shorts with a red stripe and heels and a crop top."

"You can't make the Italian Stallion sexy. That's just wrong for a multitude of reasons." Wolf shook his head in disbelief.

My father swiped at his eyes from laughing so hard. "Remember the first time you told Mama you wanted to be Rocky for Halloween? She'd tried persuading you to be something else, but you held your ground. This girl has always had a mind of her own."

"Why doesn't that surprise me?" Wolf asked, his tone all teasing. "When all the little girls were being princesses, you were the Italian fucking Stallion?" He clapped his hands together as if it were the best thing he'd ever heard.

"Okay. I'm glad you're both enjoying this so much. Trust me, I will rock this outfit."

"No doubt," Wolf said, and I liked the way he looked so relaxed and content sitting here on my couch beside me.

"All right, sweetheart. Call or text me when you get on the road tomorrow morning so I'll know what time you left, please."

"Oh, Mr. Money Bags here is letting me take the company helicopter to save some time, apparently." I giggled when he poked me in the side.

"I see. For your enemy, he seems awfully accommodating." My father quirked his brow.

"Good night, Dad. I'll see you tomorrow."

"Be safe. I love you. Nice to meet you, Wolf. Thanks for looking out for my girl."

Wolf cleared his throat, getting a little more serious. "Always. Great to meet you as well, sir."

"Love you." I ended the call.

"I like your dad. He's a class act."

"Obviously. The apple never falls far from the tree," I said, and he flipped me onto my back and propped himself above me before I even knew what was happening.

"You told him I was the enemy?" His tongue trailed along his bottom lip, slow and deliberate.

"Well, you did tell the bartender I had two vaginas. You dangled my job over my head for weeks. You're moody and cocky and such a know-it-all most of the time."

"Yet, here we are."

"Here we are," I whispered.

Were those freaking butterflies in my belly?

Shit. Was I channeling my inner Thomas girl? My sisters got all fluttery around hot guys. I did not.

His mouth was on mine before I had another second to think about it.

My fingers tangled in his hair, and his tongue slipped in.

It was slower this time. Sweeter.

And I liked the way his lips felt against mine.

The way his body felt pressed against me.

He moaned into my mouth as we took the kiss deeper.

"Tell me what you want, Minx," he said when he pulled back.

"You."

He was on his feet and lifting me from the couch, tossing me over his shoulder like I weighed nothing. He slapped my ass, carried me to the bedroom, and dropped me onto the bed, making laughter bellow from my body.

"I'm yours for tonight." This sexy-as-sin grin spread across his face.

"I can't believe I'm going to sleep with the enemy," I said, sitting up and raising my arms for him to slip my sweater over my head.

"There will be very little sleep going on tonight. I promise you that."

"Don't threaten me with a good time." I chuckled as he

tossed my sweater on the floor, and his eyes took in the black lace bra that covered my breasts.

"I've literally fantasized about these tits for weeks. Fucking weeks, Minx."

His hands moved gently over the front of my bra, making my already hard nipples ache. He slipped one strap down my shoulder, and his mouth came down over my breast, and I yelped.

He licked and sucked and leaned me back as he tugged the other strap down. He took turns going from one breast to the other, reaching behind my back and removing my bra altogether before he chucked it across the room. He continued the slow torture for what felt like forever, until I writhed beneath him, so desperate for his mouth on mine, I nearly begged him to kiss me.

"Wolf," I whispered, not hiding the desire in my voice. His mouth found mine, and I tangled my fingers in his hair to urge him closer.

His hands moved down my stomach, and he tugged the zipper on the side of my skirt, slowly pulling it down my legs and dropping it onto the floor. His fingers teased the waistband of my black lace panties, and he pulled back to look at me.

"So fucking beautiful," he whispered.

I hadn't expected this kind of care. I thought we'd probably rip one another's clothes off, get this attraction out of our systems, and never speak of it again.

But we'd become friends somewhere along the way of hating one another.

And I didn't want to rush this either.

"You have on too many clothes." I pushed him back and moved to my knees, reaching for the buttons on his dress shirt. He clearly wasn't feeling as patient as I was at the moment, because he reached down and tore his dress shirt apart, and buttons flew in every direction, which made me laugh.

"I thought we were taking our time?" I pushed the fabric down his shoulders and gaped at the distinct six-pack of abs staring right at me. Damn. He was a chiseled god beneath his clothing. It was almost unfair how good-looking the man was. My fingers traced the gold eagle outlined in black on his shoulder. There was an anchor, a pistol, and some sort of pitchfork incorporated into it. His other arm was inked, but I was too impatient to investigate it at the moment.

"I'm taking my time with you. I don't care how my clothes come off." He yanked at his pants, along with his briefs, and had them pulled down his legs within seconds.

I gaped at his glorious body. Wide shoulders, cut muscles, black and gold ink, all leading down to a narrow waist and a gigantic package. Yes, I'd seen it earlier. I knew it was impressive. But seeing it now, as he stood there naked in front of me, had my mouth watering and my thighs trembling.

This is new.

It was probably the earlier orgasm that had me getting all worked up so quickly.

He tipped me back gently, and his mouth settled near my belly button. Warm breath tickled and teased my skin, and I nearly arched off the bed. Calloused fingers ran down my belly, and his teeth caught the band of my panties before he slowly tugged them down my legs, leaving me completely bare.

Leaving us both completely bare.

And I'd never felt more wanted in my life.

twenty

. . .

Wolf

HOLY SHIT. I'd been with my fair share of women. Especially over the last decade when I was traveling year-round and hadn't had a serious relationship.

I enjoyed sex.

I enjoyed women.

But nothing compared to this.

To Dylan Thomas lying naked on a white silk comforter with her blonde hair splayed all around her like a fucking angel.

Her body was even more impressive than the fantasy of her.

She had a lean frame with enough muscle to make it clear she was fit as fuck. I knew she was athletic, but her curves were soft and feminine at the same time.

Someone broke the fucking mold when they made this woman because I'd never seen anyone more beautiful in my life.

And she was all mine for the night.

I kissed her, my mouth trailing down her body, tasting every inch of her just as I'd promised. But she'd surprised the hell out of me when she'd made it clear that she wanted me on my back, and I'd let her roll me over so she could take control. She'd explored my body until I'd nearly embarrassed myself and blown a load just from the feel of her mouth on my chest and stomach.

She'd taken control, just as I had.

But I was not a patient man. Not when it came to this woman.

My fingers came around her upper arms, and she pulled back to look at me. A wicked grin was on her face because she knew exactly what she was doing to me.

"Have you had enough?" she asked, her voice so sexy and filled with need that I didn't bother responding.

I flipped her onto her back, and my knee moved between her legs, pushing them apart and settling between her thighs.

"Never enough, Minx. I want more."

"Me, too," she said, her fingers stroking my jawline. I closed my eyes for a brief moment to enjoy the feel of her soft skin gliding against my harsh stubble.

I leaned back and reached for my pants beside the bed, grabbing my wallet and pulling out a condom. I tore off the top with my teeth and tossed it onto the floor near the heap of clothes we'd left there. She pushed up on her elbows as if she were dying to watch as I slid the latex over my erection.

Her hands came around the back of my head, and she tugged my mouth back down to hers. I'd never been one to kiss a woman this much during sex. It wasn't like I was against it, but I'd never taken my time with anyone the way I was tonight. Never wanted it to last as long as I wanted this to last.

She settled back down on the pillow, our lips never losing contact as we continued exploring one another's mouths once again. Her hips came off the bed as if she were losing her patience, as well, and I chuckled against her mouth.

"You a little eager, Minx?"

"Yes. I want you now."

I wanted her so badly I reached for her hands with one of mine and pinned them above her head, one on top of the other, as my fingers intertwined with hers. I slid my hips forward, teasing her entrance with the tip of my cock. I moved slowly, inch by inch, looking down to make sure she was adjusting to my size. She was so fucking tight, so fucking wet, I nearly lost it. But she lifted her legs and wrapped them around my waist as if she couldn't wait another second.

Fuck me.

This woman owned me.

I thrust forward and buried myself inside her. A deep groan left my throat because nothing had ever felt this fucking good.

Not even close.

Her legs dropped back down on the bed, and I pulled out slowly before driving back in.

Over and over again.

We found our rhythm. Her body was made for mine; there was no doubt about it.

She met me thrust for thrust.

We were both covered in sweat, and when I released her hands, she nearly arched off the bed as my mouth came over her perfect tit.

She tugged at my hair, pulling my lips back to hers.

And we moved faster.

Needier.

Our breaths were the only audible sound in the room as she pushed hard at my shoulders, and I followed her lead, rolling onto my back while we never lost contact. She sat up, and my hands found hers again, and she started riding me. Slowly at first and then faster.

Her tits bounced just a little, and her blonde hair tumbled down her back as she picked up the pace. I couldn't look away. Her skin glistened as the moon shone through the windows.

Her gaze locked with mine, and it was almost like everything moved in slow motion.

Her dark brown gaze with pops of gold looked almost yellow in the moonlight.

She was fierce and sexy and fucking beautiful.

Her head fell back, and I pulled one hand away and reached between us, circling her clit just the way I knew would put her over the edge.

"Wolf," she groaned, before her body started to shake, and she came apart. I watched her with complete awe. There was no inhibition there. She was completely comfortable in her skin—the sexiest woman I'd ever seen.

I clamped both hands down on her hips before flipping her onto her back with no warning. I drove into her with a need I had never experienced.

Once.

Twice.

And I went right over the edge with her as I exploded with such a force it was startling.

The sound that left my throat was guttural, and I didn't fucking care because I'd never felt anything close to this in my entire life.

We continued to move until we both caught our breath and slowed our rhythm.

I looked down at her. A layer of sweat covered her forehead, and her eyes were sated as they searched mine.

"Impressive, sir," she whispered, which made me laugh.

"Thanks. You're not too bad yourself. That was fucking crazy, Minx."

She smiled. "Do you think we just needed to get that out of our systems?"

"I don't know. But I sure as fuck hope we can do that again and often."

She raised a brow. "You aren't freaking out right now? That didn't scare you off?"

"Are you fucking kidding me? I'm a lot of things right now, but scared is not one of them." I slowly pulled back, sliding out of her, even though every instinct I had told me to stay right where I was. I climbed to my feet and walked to the bathroom, tossing the condom into the toilet before returning to the bed. She was lying there completely relaxed, hair sprawled all over the sheets, lips plump from where I'd kissed her, and her body begging me for more.

I climbed in bed beside her, and I traced the pad of my thumb over her pert nipple. "You have the most perfect tits I've ever seen."

"Really? They aren't very big. But they are perky, right?"

I chuckled as I spread my hand over one of her breasts. "The perfect handful. And yes, they're very perky. I'd expect nothing less from you."

Her fingers ran across the tattoo on my shoulder gently, and it was soothing and sexy and sweet all at the same time. "Tell me what this means."

"It's the SEAL Trident. The anchor represents the Navy, and the other three symbols are what the SEALs protect."

"Air is the eagle?" she asked, and I nodded.

"What is the pistol?"

"That represents land."

"Ah. That makes sense. And what's the pitchfork for?"

I chuckled. "It's a trident. It represents water."

She moved her finger over to my other arm and traced over the ink there.

"A frog in scuba gear?" she asked.

"It's a frogman. We're trained for underwater tactical missions and scuba diving, so it's a common tat for SEALs." I cleared my throat. "Anything else you want to know, Minx?"

"Tell me why your ex-girlfriend isn't welcome at your parents' house."

"It's *so you* to go from explosive sex to questioning me

about my tattoos and then to something you heard over a week ago."

"Well, I'm a curious person. I make no apologies for that. But I can't imagine anyone being banned from your home unless they hurt you. And I also can't imagine anyone hurting you. You seem so…"

"Sexy? Strong?" I teased.

"Impenetrable."

The word sat between us because, in a way, I was impenetrable after my years in battle. I'd set up my life that way, not because of what had happened with Kressa, but because it worked for my lifestyle, and I'd grown comfortable keeping my relationships at a distance.

We were both quiet for a few minutes before I finally spoke. "She fucked my best friend a few months after I left for the Naval Academy."

"That bitch," she hissed, and I barked out a laugh.

"She wasn't all bad. We left things… unclear. I was the one who didn't want to stay in a committed relationship when I was going to be so far away. My ultimate goal was to become a SEAL. So, I wasn't going to give her what she wanted, and we both knew it."

"So, she went and slept with your bestie? That's freaking low. And this is coming from a woman who has no problem pulling a knife on a man, so it's not like I'm not supportive of strong women. But she could have chosen anyone; why him?"

"I don't know. I'm sure he went after her pretty hard. I don't hold any ill will toward her. I left her. She was hurt. She did what she did. He'd always wanted whatever I had, and I'm sure he made a move the minute I was gone."

"Do you guys speak anymore?"

"No. Kressa let me know that she'd slept with him and that she'd gotten pregnant. And that was basically it. He called me and apologized, and I told them both to lose my number."

Dylan sprung up to sit with her mouth gaping open. "She got pregnant? Are they together now?"

"Yes. They have a son. Apparently, they didn't stay together long. She's reached out many times to make amends. I forgive her. I just don't necessarily want to hang out with either of them." I chuckled.

"I hate shady fuckers." She shook her head, and I tugged her back down, her cheek resting on my chest.

"We were teenagers. People fuck up. My relationship with Kressa had run its course. If she'd gotten pregnant by anyone else, I would have been a friend to her, you know? It might surprise you to know that I'm not a complete dick. But the fact that it was with Josh, the dude I'd been best friends with my entire life—I couldn't get past it at the time."

"I get it. I'm sure this might surprise you… but I'm not a very forgiving person. It's something I'm working on."

I chuckled. "You don't say?"

"Yeah. Once someone crosses me, it's hard to forget it."

"I understand that. Tell me what Anthony Glouse did to you." There was a PI that worked for our family, as we'd had threats against us over the years, and I'd asked him to do a background check on the dude. He'd checked out, minus one sexual harassment case that had been filed against him at work that had miraculously been excused. Money had a way of making things go away. I knew he was an asshole the minute I laid eyes on him, but I needed to know if he tried to hurt her.

She sat back up. "You sure recalled that name quickly."

"What can I say? I'm good with names."

"You don't call me by mine, so you can't be that good." She smirked.

"Tell me what he did, Minx."

"If he did anything bad, I would have pressed charges. He

didn't. He just got handsy, and when I said no, he pushed me back onto the couch and took his shot. I kneed him in the balls and shoved him off me before grabbing my knife and kicking his ass out of my house."

"Why'd you block him? Was he harassing you?" My fingers traced between her breasts and down her stomach.

"He had stalker tendencies. I didn't give him time to try after he blew my phone up the next day. And we didn't live in the same town, so I haven't seen him in a few months."

"If he contacts you, will you let me know?"

Her head cocked to the side. "What are you going to do? Are you going to be the big, bad Wolf and scare him off?"

"I'm going to kick his fucking ass and make sure he never comes near you again." My tone was harsh, and I'd make no apologies for that. Men who didn't take no for an answer had no place in this world. The fact that he'd pushed her to the point that she'd felt the need to pull a knife—that told me that he'd gotten forceful, and that shit did not sit well with me.

"Tell me about being a SEAL. You always say that I'm belittling your career by saying you can hold your breath for a long time," she said over a laugh. "Tell me what you did on your missions."

"I'm not allowed to share any specifics. What do you want to know?" I tugged her back down. I didn't like her looking at me when she was asking these questions because it felt like she could see through me. And being vulnerable wasn't something I was ever comfortable with.

"Did you ever have to kill anyone?" she asked, her fingers tracing the SEAL trident tattoo on my upper arm.

"Yes."

"Who'd you kill?"

"Bad guys."

She laughed. "Were you ever scared that you were going to die?"

"A couple of times. But I came out the other end still breathing, so there you go."

"Are these bullet wounds?" she asked, as her fingers moved down my arm.

"They are."

She tugged me forward and crawled over me to look at the back of my arm. "They didn't come out the other side."

"Nope. They had to be taken out."

"Hmmm... that couldn't have been pleasant."

"I was out of it. I barely remember," I said, wrapping an arm around her and wanting to hold her close. This was not the norm. Not now. Not ever. I wasn't a cuddler. I wasn't an affectionate person. I wasn't a talker. But something about this woman made it impossible not to touch her. Not to want to keep her close.

"Did you sleep with that hostess in New York?" she asked, suddenly out of the blue.

"No. Did you sleep with the bartender?"

"No. Although your two vaginas plan only made him want me more. But I told you that I haven't had sex since I met you. You've irritated me too much to be in the mood." She laughed against my chest, and I stroked her hair. "Have you? You mentioned those bootie calls you have on speed dial."

"I have not had sex since that first time I saw you at the gas station. You also irritated the shit out of me."

"Well, this is certainly an interesting turn of events, isn't it?" she asked.

"If that's what you want to call it."

"What would you call it?" she asked, pushing up to look at me.

Fucking amazing.

I wouldn't say that aloud because I didn't know what the fuck would happen between us. I hadn't been in a relationship for a decade.

"I'd call it unexpected."
That was safe.
I worked with this woman.
We shouldn't go there.
But I didn't know if I could stop it now.
The train had already left the station.
And I didn't know how to turn on the brakes.
Or maybe I just didn't want to.

twenty-one

. . .

Dylan

THE SUN STREAMING in through the windows had my eyes fluttering open. Or was it the smell of bacon?

"Hello?" I shouted, wrapping a sheet around my naked body.

Thoughts of Wolf kissing me—everywhere—flooded me all at once.

So many orgasms.

I glanced at the clock to see we'd barely slept for two hours. We'd had sex again after the first time, but we'd talked for hours in between. I'd never spent so much time talking to a man. But oddly, he'd yet to bore me.

The day was young. I'd give him another hour, and I'm sure I'd be less interested in what he had to say.

"Is there a reason you're shouting?" Wolf stood in the doorway, wearing nothing but a pair of fitted boxer briefs, as he sipped his coffee and managed to look sexy as hell. My eyes scanned every single muscle on his abdomen and…

Hello, defined eight-pack.

Wolf put every underwear model I'd ever seen to shame.

I tucked my sexed-up hair behind my ears and smiled. "Yes. I assumed you left, but then I smelled bacon."

"I take it you're a fan?" He smirked.

"Of course, I'm a fan of crispy pork. I mean, I'm human, right? But I don't have any bacon here. Where'd you get it?"

His tongue peeked out to wet his lips, and my body heated as I watched. The only thing better than well-cooked bacon was Wolf Wayburn's tongue.

All of his SEAL training really paid off when it came to sex. The man was so driven and determined—he never tired. And his mission appeared to be pleasing me, and I was here for it.

I'd most definitely met my match in the bedroom, and that was a first.

"I live next door, remember?" A small, sexy smile spread across his handsome face.

"Okay, let me throw on some clothes, and we can eat all the bacon together." I pushed to my feet.

"Personally, I prefer you naked."

I raised a brow. "Save those thoughts for another time. I need to eat and then get dressed. You also did not stay true to your word because I didn't get packed last night."

I grabbed his dress shirt and slipped it on, laughing at the fact that there was only one button left on the shirt, but the smell of bacon had me in a hurry to get out there. When I started to walk past him in the doorway, he stopped me. His hands found the side of my neck, and he tilted my head back so I could look at him. "You're even fucking beautiful in the morning. How is that possible?"

I shrugged. "It's a gift."

He barked out a laugh, and I did the same because my one-liners were always spot on.

"Come on, let's eat."

I was very surprised to see the table set with napkins, silverware, and orange juice. He made his way to the kitchen before setting two plates down, one in front of me and one for himself. There were scrambled eggs, bacon, and toast on each dish.

"Wow. This looks so good," I groaned when I took a bite of bacon.

"Not much of a cook, huh?"

"Not really. I mean, I know how to. I just don't do it often."

He nodded and reached for his glass of juice.

"So, what happens now?" I asked, because we hadn't really discussed that.

"What do you want to happen?"

"Well, I wouldn't mind doing it again." I held my hands up when he started to push to his feet. "Not today. I have to leave."

"I see. You didn't get enough, huh?" He smirked.

"Don't get all cocky. You're the one who claimed you don't cuddle, yet you wrapped your body around mine for the few hours we slept. You're like a Hot Pocket, by the way. You kept me really warm and toasty."

"I run hot." He forked some eggs and popped them into his mouth.

"You sure do."

"So, we keep things going when you get back until we don't feel like it anymore. I'm fine with that if you are."

"I like that. I'm sure one more time will be all we need, and then we can go back to hating one another."

"Who said I stopped?" A wicked smile spread across his face.

"Don't worry, big, bad Wolf. I hate you, too." I didn't. And I knew he didn't hate me. But it kept things less complicated by pretending that we did.

"Maybe we should have a safe word. You know, so if one of us is over it, we can just say the word, and then we don't have to have the awkward conversation," he said.

"Yes. That's very Navy SEAL of you. It's like a covert

operation. Did you have a lot of safe words when you were with the Navy?" I spread strawberry jam on my toast.

"No. Not even one." He chuckled.

"Such a buzzkill. Fine. How about Idwy?"

"Idwy? What the hell is that?"

"It's an acronym for *I'm done with you*."

"I don't like it," he said. "It's a little harsh. I don't want to be a total dick."

I rolled my eyes. "I love that you think you'll be using the word first. I was practically over you already this morning. If you hadn't pulled out your impressive pork, I'd probably already be gone."

His laughter bellowed around the small dining space, and seeing him laugh was intoxicating. Like watching a grizzly bear surrender to a rabbit. It just didn't seem natural—yet it was a beautiful phenomenon.

"I've got some more impressive pork for you." He raised a brow.

"Yeah? We don't have time, do we?"

"You're taking a helicopter home, Minx. We can pick what time you leave."

"Look at you... You're so not ready for me to go, are you?" I teased, but I squeezed my thighs together at the thought of having him once more before I left.

"I'll survive. How about *Winx*?"

"Winx?"

"Our safe word. Wolf and Minx—Winx. When we're done, we'll just say the word. It's not too harsh, and it seems fitting."

"I'm good with it. Now take me to bed and have your way with me, you cocky bastard."

Wolf moved so fast that he startled me, even though I'd been the one to suggest it. He had me scooped into his arms, and he practically ran to the bedroom before dropping me onto the bed.

"Someone's a little eager," I said over my laughter.

He unbuttoned the lone button on his dress shirt and then stared down at my naked body beneath him. I didn't squirm. I liked the way he looked at me. It made me feel powerful and wanted.

"So, a few ground rules." His hands cupped my breasts.

"How very mature of you to get me naked, grab my knockers, and then make up the rules."

"You're fucking funny," he said as he leaned down and nipped at my earlobe.

"And you're fucking manipulative," I moaned when his lips moved down my neck. "What are your rules?"

He pulled back. "They're simple. When you're fucking me, you aren't fucking anyone else."

"Same goes for you." I reached for his hair and tugged him down to my mouth.

He kissed me hard before pulling back to look at me. "Deal. And I'm not fucking kidding, Minx. I don't share."

"Do you make all your ladies agree to this rule when you have them naked in your bed?"

His jaw ticked, and his eyes bore into mine. "No. I don't make it a habit of being with the same woman repeatedly. I had women I'd see when I'd come home from missions, but this is… different."

I nodded. "I'll bet you did. And I can get on board with these terms."

"No ex that's going to be waiting for you when you get back to Honey Mountain?" He purred as his lips moved across my shoulder bone.

"No," I whispered. "When I break up with men, I don't go back for more. When I'm done, I'm done."

His mouth claimed mine, and I couldn't think straight.

He was the only man who'd ever consumed me in this way.

So, I'd go with it while it lasted.

Being home was always the best. I'd missed my sisters so much. I'd only been home for a few hours because Wolf had managed to steal the morning by having his way with me after breakfast and then again in the shower.

The man had a ravenous appetite.

One that rivaled my own.

I couldn't get enough of him, so this break would be good for me. I needed to get my head on straight.

My Bluetooth rang in the car that Wolf had waiting for me when I landed, and Siri announced it was my cousin, Hugh. We'd gone to college together and had always been close. His dad was my mom's only brother, and we'd grown up spending summers with him and his four siblings.

"Hey, how's the restaurant going?" He'd just opened a sports bar in Cottonwood Cove, not far from San Francisco, and I owed him a visit.

"Good. Crazy busy—you know how it goes. I wanted to see if you'd be around next week. I'll be in the city for a few days, and I thought we could hit Karaoke King and get some drinks." It was our favorite bar when we were in college, and let's just say that karaoke and I were one. You put that mic in my hand, and I will deliver.

"Yes. Let's do it. I could go for a little Hammer time," I said because "U Can't Touch This" had been my go-to song back in the day.

He chuckled. "Of course, you can. You'll have everyone on their feet per usual. Congrats on signing with the Lions. Ledger told me it was official, so we can celebrate." Ledger was an architect, and he'd helped my cousin design the bar.

"Of course, and we need to celebrate your opening. I can't wait to come see it. I'm back in Honey Mountain this weekend to trick-or-treat with the kids."

"All right. Text me when you're back, and we'll meet up next week."

"I will. Love you, cuzzy."

"Love you, too." He ended the call, and I drove toward my sister's house.

I'd already been by the firehouse, which had been my first stop. I couldn't wait to see my dad. Thankfully, it had been a slow day for him, and I helped him make lunch for all the guys. My dad grilled me about Wolf, as he'd seen me pull up in the sexy black convertible my boss-slash-enemy-slash-lover had rented for me. I felt a tinge of guilt because I'd lied when he asked if anything was going on there. Because the truth was... it was temporary. There was no sense in complicating it by discussing it.

I knew better.

I'd then gone over to Charlie and Ledger's new place, and they were making huge progress on the home they were building. They were nauseatingly cute together, the way they were so invested in one another and this house, and I freaking loved it. The structure was framed, and drywall was already going up. They were hustling to get as much done as possible before the temperature dropped. It was already chilly in Honey Mountain, and I'd been grateful that I'd grabbed my favorite winter coat to bring with me, and I'd need to wear tights under my costume if I wanted to survive trick-or-treating.

We'd then gone over to Ash and Jace's new house, which they'd moved into while I was away. They'd fully renovated this old farmhouse, and it was gorgeous. Ashlan was an incredible decorator, and they were still waiting on a few final pieces, but for the most part, the house was done. She'd spent most of her energy decorating both of the girls' rooms, and I swear my baby sister was born to be a mother. They were also busy planning their wedding, and she was getting ready to release another book. I loved seeing her in her element.

Now, I was heading over to Vivi's so I could see my niece, little Bee. Her name was Beth Everly, named after both my mother and my oldest sister, and they called her Bee. It was so fitting because that little girl had a way of spreading sweetness everywhere she went. I was rarely a softy, but when it came to Bee, Jackson, Paisley, and Hadley—I was a pile of mush. My nieces and my nephew literally owned my heart. A heart I didn't even know had a soft spot until they came into the world.

Charlie and Ashlan were on their way over to Vivi's now, too, and Everly was meeting us over there as well, as she and Hawk had come home for Halloween. Hawk didn't have a game this weekend, so they were happy to have the break away from the city. We were having a little sisters' dinner, just the five of us, and, of course, Bee, Jackson, Paisley, and Hadley would be there, as well. Jace and Niko were both working, Hawk was helping his parents with some work around the house, and Ledger was having dinner with his grandmother.

I loved girls' nights with my sisters. We could say anything. We'd laugh our asses off, and it would be the perfect distraction as my mind kept wandering back to Wolf. It didn't help that we'd been texting nonstop since I'd landed. The man could *sext* with the best of them. He had a dirty mouth and a dirty mind—that is something I could appreciate in a strong man like Wolf Wayburn.

I walked up the cobblestone path to the front door and turned the knob, knowing it would be open for us. Of course, that would piss off Niko; the man was ridiculously protective over his girls, but this was Honey Mountain, and I'd never been big on locking my door either.

"Hello?" I called out, and the cutest human on the planet came waddling toward me, with brown, wild curls bouncing on her head and her chubby little arms straight out, waiting for me to scoop her up, which is exactly what I did after I dropped my purse on the floor and ran toward her. "I missed you, Bee."

Her hands tangled in my hair, and I breathed her in. She smelled like baby powder and cupcakes because she was always baking with her mama.

Vivi came running around the corner and lunged at me. "I missed you, Dilly."

"Missed you, too." The three of us stood there hugging as the door flew open, and one by one, everyone piled in, and we spent the next hour feeding the little humans and then ourselves, all while talking a mile a minute just like we always did.

We were sitting around Vivi's dining table, Paisley and Hadley were watching a Disney movie with little Bee, and Jackson had dozed off in his car seat, which was sitting on the kitchen island where Everly could keep her eyes on him.

"Spill. You were MIA last night. Did something happen after that office orgasm?" Charlie asked as she sipped her wine.

The table erupted in laughter, and I batted my lashes. I told my sisters everything, and that had most definitely surprised us all yesterday.

"Let's just say, I returned the favor in the elevator." I shrugged.

"Oh my gosh, I take Jackson in that elevator," Everly said over her laughter.

"Well, there was no one on the elevator with us, so I went for it."

"I thought you banned blow jobs?"

"I don't normally like bowing down to a man, but this was different. He had it coming." I waggled my brows. "No pun intended."

More laughter, and it felt so good to be here with them.

"And then what?" Ashlan's eyes were wide. "Did you both just go home?"

"We did. *Together*. And it was some book-worthy sex, I can promise you that."

"I'm definitely putting an elevator blow job in my next book. That's so hot." Ashlan typed into the notes app on her phone. She told us that was the life of an author, always observing and taking things in.

"It is hot," Charlotte whispered.

"It really is. And it was a good night? Were you dying to get rid of him after?" Vivian asked because she knew me well.

"Nope. It happened again this morning. And then again in the shower before I left. And we decided to continue doing it until we don't want to do it anymore. We even have a safe word, so we just say the word when we want to be done. No pressure at all."

"Wow." Everly studied me. "You like him. And there's no doubt he likes you after the way he nearly lost his mind when Seb's friend was talking to you at the game a few weeks ago. The man was so protective, I couldn't help but laugh."

"That's just who he is. It's not personal." I sipped my wine, but thoughts of how irate he'd been flooded my mind. It was sexy and hot, and I didn't mind it one bit, which surprised me. It usually annoyed me when a man tried to interfere with things that I could handle myself.

"It sure sounds personal," Ashlan said. "You already work together and text when you aren't together, and now you're sleeping together? It kind of sounds like a relationship." She chuckled.

"It's not. It's an agreement. And enough about my non-relationship. Tell me what's happening here."

"Well, we're going to take the kids trick-or-treating tomorrow night, and then we're going to go to Beer Mountain afterward. Everyone will be there."

"That sounds like a plan. I hope we don't see that ball scratcher, Tobias." I laughed, and each one of them fell back in their chair, doing the same.

"I'm glad you're home," Charlie said, wrapping an arm over my shoulder.

"Me, too. There's no place I'd rather be."

Well, maybe in Wolf's bed if I were being honest.

But I'd keep that one to myself.

twenty-two

. . .

Wolf

"THANKS FOR GOING TRICK-OR-TREATING WITH THEM," Bullet said through the speaker in my car.

"Of course. You know I'd do anything for your family."

"Yeah. Jaqueline is pissed. She's not happy that I'm heading out again soon."

I knew where he was going, and it was dangerous as hell. I understood why she was pissed, but I also understood his need to lead the guys on this mission. It was a young team, and he was training them before he officially retired. At least, that was what he kept telling me.

"She wants you home, brother. The boys want their dad home. It's time."

"I know. I swear I'm ready, Wolf. I just want to make sure these guys can handle it. Last mission. I'll be gone for a couple of weeks, and then I'll be ready to make retirement official."

It wasn't the first time I'd heard this from him, and I feared it wouldn't be the last. Being a SEAL was in his blood. The adrenaline, the rush—it could be addicting. He thrived on missions, and he was damn good at his job. The best, actually. The dude I trusted most with my own life.

"I hear you. And you'll have a job waiting for you with the Lions when you're ready."

"Thanks, brother. So, tell me about this girl you've been working with. You sounded irritated last time we spoke, but I know you well enough to know when you're into someone. Probably because it never happened in all the time that we worked together." He laughed, and Bullet's laugh was gruff and loud and boisterous and always had people turning to stare at us. "Not that you didn't pull the ladies. You just didn't ever get invested."

"She's fine. She challenges me and can be an enormous pain in the ass, but she's also fucking brilliant." I'd leave out the fact that I couldn't get her out of my fucking head. Now that I'd had a taste of her, I fucking craved her.

I'd never craved a woman—or missed a woman, for that matter. Even when I was a fucking teenager with raging hormones, I didn't miss Kressa. I'd never been that guy, so I was glad Dylan had left because that shit didn't sit well with me, and I needed to get it together.

"Oh, yeah? What the fuck does she look like? I can hear it in your voice, Wolf. You're a fucking *smitten kitten*." He laughed again, and I rolled my eyes. It was what we'd always said to him when it came to Jaqueline. We'd razzed the hell out of how whipped he was.

"Never going to happen. But sure, she's hot as hell."

"I see. Hot and brilliant. That's a deadly combination," he teased.

"Well, I told you, she's also an enormous pain in my ass."

"The good ones always are, my brother. They always are." He was still laughing when I pulled down his street.

"All right. I'm here. Give me a call before you head out, all right?"

"Yep." His tone turned serious.

"I'll make sure everyone here is okay. Don't worry about that. You just be safe. Send word when you can. Just a sign, all right?" He knew what I meant. We had codes, things only he and I understood when we'd text one another.

"Thanks, Wolf. I'll see you in a few months. You're going to see my ass in a suit, marching into your office for my interview."

"You don't need to interview; I told you that. The job is yours." I wanted to make sure he knew that the minute he was ready, I'd have his back. I always would.

"Yep. I'll see you soon. Peace out."

"Peace out, buddy."

Fuck. I had a sick feeling in my stomach, but that didn't mean shit. It could just be because I knew what he was heading out to do. I'd have to get my face straight before I saw Jaqueline and the boys. I pulled into the driveway and put the car into park just as my phone vibrated.

Dylan had sent a selfie of herself wearing her Halloween costume. How the fuck did she manage to make a Rocky Balboa costume sexy as hell? She wore tiny white shorts that looked like they barely covered her ass, and I was thankful the cold weather forced her to put tights beneath them. I couldn't stand the thought of random dudes checking her out. She had on a tank top that read, *You, me, or nobody is going to hit as hard as life,* because apparently, it was one of her favorite quotes. Her hair was in a ponytail on top of her head, and she wore a mouthpiece that boxers used and was giving me a thumbs up.

Damn, she was sexy and fierce, and my dick sprung to life.

Me ~ I want to have my way with you in those shorts. You look hot as fuck.

Minx ~ That could be arranged. But you should know, I've got a mean left hook.

Me ~ I can take a hit, Minx.

Minx ~ I'll bet you can. Are you at Jaqueline's yet? Have you seen the boys?

Me ~ Just pulled up.

Minx ~ And you have the toys?

She'd given me all these instructions because apparently, you can't go to a house with kids without presents. So, she'd sat on the phone with me last night when I ran to Target, and she told me what to get.

Me ~ Yeah. Thanks for your help with that.

Minx ~ Of course. They are going to love it. And that'll help with them missing their dad. I remember after my mom passed, everyone kept bringing us presents. It didn't stop us from being sad, but at least it was a distraction, right?

I stared at the phone for a minute and thought about how to respond to that. She'd lost her mom at a young age, and I knew that it had to be painful as hell to lose a parent like that.

Me ~ You're a strong fucking woman, Minx.

Minx ~ I'm shaking. Was that a compliment? <smirky face emoji>

Me ~ It was. Don't get used to it.

Minx ~ Never. I still hate you.

Me ~ Hate you, too. Be safe tonight. I'll text you when I leave.

What? Why did I say that? Why was I updating her every time I did anything? This was not smart. Her going away for the weekend was supposed to be a time for me to get my head on straight, not fucking text her every time I took a shit.

Minx ~ Don't blow down any houses, big, bad Wolf.

Me ~ The only thing I want blown is my <eggplant emoji> on your <lips emoji>

Minx ~ <panting emoji> <panting emoji>

I laughed as I stepped out of the car and slipped my phone into my back pocket. I grabbed the bags out of the trunk and made my way to the door.

Jaqueline pulled open the door, and the boys came flying around the corner.

"Uncle Wolfy," Drake said. He pummeled into me, and I scooped him up. His brother, Slade, was right behind him, and I reached down with my free arm and lifted him up, holding one kid on each hip. These dudes were as cool as their dad, and I didn't mind hanging out with them at all. I was happy to be living back here full time so I could see them grow up.

I wanted the same thing for their father because I knew how much he loved them.

"Hey, guys, are you ready for some trick-or-treating?" They cheered, obviously ready to get things going as I set them back down on their feet.

Jaqueline looked ready for a break as I kissed her on the cheek. Being a military wife could be a bitch, but all in all, she handled it well.

I hurried her out the door and spent the next few hours playing with the boys until Jaqueline returned, and we took them out door-to-door, collecting enough sugar to keep them going for weeks.

Dylan and I texted several times, and I sent her a photo of the boys all dressed up.

And it hit me as I stared down at my phone, smiling at the picture she'd sent of her and Bee all dressed up—I missed her.

And that, I hadn't been prepared for.

Not even fucking close.

twenty-three

. . .

Dylan

WE ALL TOOK turns going to the door with the kids, and I sent a few pictures to Wolf. He'd sent me one of the boys in their Batman and Spiderman costumes. They were cute as hell, and I had to say, thoughts of Wolf out there, trick-or-treating with two little boys while their dad was away, had my ovaries threatening to detonate.

I wasn't that girl. You know, the one who sat home planning her fairy-tale wedding and dreaming of her two-point-five kids who had names picked out since she was nine years old. I had sisters who did that. I was the girl who sat at home figuring out how she was going to make the world a better and fairer place. I daydreamed about paying off my father's house for him someday. About traveling the world and doing whatever the hell it was I wanted to do.

My ovaries had no place in my daydreams.

We'd made it around the entire neighborhood, and Bee had fallen asleep in Niko's arms, while Jackson was sound asleep in the wagon they'd brought. Hadley and Paisley were finally starting to tire, and we'd all made our way back to Vivi's house for our traditional spaghetti dinner. This is what we'd done every year of my life on Halloween. Even after our mama passed away, my father and Everly had continued the tradition, and then Vivian took over, and here we are.

Eating yummy noodles smothered in sauce and parmesan cheese and laughing about all the candy we used to hide from our parents.

"Dylan was the ringleader when it came to Operation Candy Hoarding," Everly said over her laughter.

"Why am I always the ringleader?"

"Well, I think because you always came up with these ideas and then convinced us to go along with you," Charlotte said as she reached for a piece of garlic bread.

"That's sort of the definition of a ringleader," Vivian chimed in.

"Hey, some might call that the childhood genius who guided you well."

Niko and Hawk barked out a laugh, Jace shook his head and tried to hide his smile, and Ledger raised a brow. "Is this you trying to get us all on board with the childhood genius label?"

"Whatever," I said as my phone vibrated.

I expected to see a text from Wolf because we'd been talking all day. But instead, it was Lottie, my father's best friend, big Al's wife. She was part of our "fire family" and always had been. My heart raced, just like it did every time a text came through about a fire. It never got easier, my father putting his life on the line every time he went to work. And now that Niko and Jace were also firefighters, we were always worrying about all of them. Hell, all the guys were family at this point.

"It's Lottie. There's a fire out at the apartment complex on Third Street."

Niko and Jace quickly reached for their phones and were on their feet.

"Shit. I need to go, baby. It's a big one." Niko kissed Vivian's cheek and grabbed his keys.

"Sorry, Sunshine," Jace said, doing the same to Ash.

I was already moving. I'd never been good at being patient and waiting around, and I needed to make sure my father was okay.

"I'm coming with you," I said, grabbing my purse and hugging each of my sisters goodbye. "I'll text you and let you know. Love you."

I jumped into Niko's truck, sitting in between him and Jace, and we were all a little on edge as he hauled ass down the road.

"I can't believe they didn't call us in. I just had the one text from Gramps, letting me know they were heading out there," Niko said. Gramps had been fighting fires longer than my father, and he was one of his closest friends.

"Same." Jace's voice was quiet, which made me even more nervous.

"Do they not have enough guys tonight?" I asked as my fingers drummed on my thigh, anxious to get there.

"They're a little short, but it just depends on how big the fire is. It's a huge-ass building, so if they contained it quickly, they'll be okay." Niko stopped in front of the firehouse, and they both ran inside to change into their gear while I texted more with Lottie.

Me ~ I'm on my way with Niko and Jace. How bad is it?

Lottie ~ It's just grown faster than they expected. And Brady Townsend has it all taped off already, so they won't let me in there. I can't see a damn thing with all the smoke.

Me ~ Brady Townsend used to eat paste in third grade. He will not be keeping us out of that fire. The guys are back. Be there in five minutes.

"Lottie said it's bad," I said as they both climbed into the truck.

They gave one another a look, and my head ping-ponged between them. "Oh, hell no. Do not keep a secret from me.

Start talking right now or I will twist your earlobes off your head."

"Fuck," Niko hissed under his breath. "Tell her."

"Don't call your sisters until we know more, please." Jace cleared his throat. "We only got bits and pieces off the radio, but it's a big one, and your dad went in as the lead. He fucking knows better than to do that when we aren't there to back him up."

"What? Why would he do that?"

"Because some of the new guys were probably not ready. I'm sure Rusty tried to stop him, but your dad must have insisted that he'd go in first."

"Oh my god," I whispered as we approached the building that was literally up in flames. They most definitely didn't have it contained at all. I knew quite a bit about fires from growing up in this world, and this fire was completely out of control.

"Jesus." Niko came to a halting stop and put the truck into park as we all jumped out. We were sprinting toward the building while people stood off to the side, gaping and watching and taking photos.

Brady Townsend was blocking the path, and Jace turned back to me. "He's not going to let you in. I'll come back and fill you in as soon as I can, Dilly, all right?"

No fucking way was I going along with that plan, but I nodded because the last thing I wanted to do was slow down Niko and Jace when I knew they needed to get in there.

Brady held the tape up, and Niko looked back at me and tossed me the truck keys just before he slipped under. "I'll text you as soon as I can. You can take it home if you want to leave."

Jace gave one last glance before he took off running toward the flames.

"Sorry, Dylan. I can't let you in there." Brady stood there, listening to someone telling him the fire was growing faster than they could handle.

No duh, genius.

Anyone with two eyeballs could see that.

But then the words I feared most in life came through on Brady's radio as I stood just inches from him. Lottie had made her way over to me, and we both heard it clear as day.

"Jack Thomas has taken a big fall. He's in bad shape and unconscious."

The words were still processing before I charged. Brady dove at me as I tore the tape apart, and he wrapped his arms around me tightly.

"Dylan, settle the fuck down."

I kicked him hard in the shin and broke free.

"If you want to stop me, you're going to need to shoot me." I didn't recognize my own voice. It was angry and fierce, but I knew it was fear talking.

I could not lose my father.

We could not lose my father.

We'd had enough loss in our lifetimes.

Brady held his arms up as if he was not going to fight me, and Lottie shouted for me to go. I sprinted toward the flames, seeing fire trucks and several ambulances lined up outside the building.

"Jace!" I shouted as I saw him standing near one of the paramedics, who were just lifting a man into their truck.

"Fuck, Dilly. He took a bad fall." His voice cracked, and Niko sprinted toward us.

"What the fuck happened?" he shouted.

"The floor gave out. He fell two stories," Rusty said, his face covered in soot as tears streamed down his face. "I tried to stop him from going in, Dilly."

The ground started to spin.

"Is that him?" I asked, and Jace nodded. I jumped into the

ambulance as I heard Niko shouting out orders to pull themselves together. They still had a fire to put out.

"Go with him. We'll meet you at the hospital as soon as we can," Niko said, and Jace squeezed my hand one last time before all three of them charged toward the building.

My father was hooked up to all sorts of tubes and had a mask over his face. They were cutting some of the clothing off his upper body to check for burns, I think.

I reached for his hand, and he didn't squeeze back. There was no life there. "Is he okay?"

"I don't know," the paramedic said, his gaze empathetic when he looked at me. I didn't recognize him or the other two guys that were there.

"I'm right here, Dad." I sniffled. I would not fall apart. My dad needed me. My sisters needed me. "Why isn't he moving?"

One of the guys shouted to the driver. "I called it in. We need to get him there now. His pulse is barely there."

I could literally feel my world spinning on its axis. I had no control to stop it, and my throat tightened as I tried hard to breathe because I didn't know if I could survive in a world that my father wasn't in.

"Can you drink this?" a voice said, and I blinked a couple of times and saw one of the EMT guys offering me a little container of juice.

"No. I'm okay."

"You look like you might be ready to drop. You lost all the color in your face." He glanced over his shoulders as the other two guys continued taking care of my father. But there was no sign of life. He wasn't talking. He wasn't coughing. He wasn't moving.

We pulled up at the hospital, and there were at least six or seven people waiting for us outside when we pulled up. I was shoved back as they hurried my father out of the ambulance, and I jumped down and chased after him.

"Dad!" I shouted, catching up and reaching for his hand again.

"I'm sorry, but you need to stay here. You can't go any further. We'll let you know how he is as soon as we can," the nurse said. She was tall with red hair and kind eyes, and I just stared at her, refusing to let go of his hand.

"I need him to be okay."

She reached for my hand and helped me unclench it from my father's. "I promise we will do everything we can to help him."

I nodded and dropped my hand, taking a few steps back until I hit the cool brick. I watched as they took him behind the double doors, and I reached for my phone, which was tucked inside my purse that was hanging around my neck. I looked down at my other hand, which was still clenching Niko's keys. Blood covered the silver keys that I'd obviously squeezed so tightly that it had punctured my skin in several places. I wiped the blood on my tights, and the realization that I was still dressed in my Rocky costume seemed unbelievable. It didn't even feel like it was the same day. My hands shook as I dialed the phone.

"Dylan. What's happening?" Everly did not hide the fear in her voice.

"Tell everyone to come to the hospital now." That was all I could get out without losing it. I would not fall apart right now. My sisters would lose it if they thought I was terrified.

And I was terrified.

But I wouldn't tell them that.

I swallowed hard and ended the call because if I stayed on this phone with her, I wouldn't be able to keep it together. I walked to the bathroom and locked the door before leaning against it and completely losing it.

I sobbed in a way I hadn't in many years.

I broke down in a way I hadn't allowed myself since we'd lost my mom.

In what world was it fair to lose both of your parents?

I punched the wall and kicked the toilet and wailed and cried and sobbed.

And then I pulled myself together to go out and find my sisters.

I'd spent years training myself to control my emotions.

To be strong.

And it was game time now.

twenty-four

. . .

Wolf

DYLAN HAD GONE COMPLETELY radio silent. In my world, no news usually meant that someone was hurt or dead or hiding. We'd been texting nonstop yesterday, and then she just stopped responding last night.

I felt like a desperate little pussy because I called her twice, and it went to voice mail. And now it was the next day, and she still wasn't responding.

Fuck.

This is why I didn't do this shit.

But my gut told me something was wrong.

Could that fucking asshole Anthony Glouse have gone there? I sent a quick text to my PI, who had eyes on the dude, and he wrote right back and said he was in the city and there'd been nothing out of the ordinary.

I paced for another hour before I swallowed my pride and called Hawk.

"Hey, Wolf," he said, and his voice sounded more serious than usual.

"I, um, sorry to bother you. I'm trying to reach Dylan and haven't been able to. I just wanted to make sure everything was okay."

"Jack Thomas, Dylan's father, was injured pretty badly in a fire last night. Everly and I just got home. We spent the night at the hospital. It was touch and go for a while, and we didn't know if he was going to make it. He took a bad fall and broke his arm and a few ribs, but the man is made of steel. He's going to be okay. But Dylan is still there. She refused to leave. She was the one who was there on the scene when he was taken in, and you know, that's just her. I'm guessing her phone is dead. The girls all tried to get her to leave, but she refused. She's the only one who didn't break down when things got bad last night. But it's coming. She's fighting hard to keep it together. You know how she is."

Did I? I felt like I did. I did know her. None of this surprised me. She was stoic and strong, but I saw the vulnerable person that was somewhere beneath it all. I'd seen a few glimpses over the last few weeks.

"I'm so sorry to hear that. That makes sense. Is he going to be in the hospital for a while? Expected to make a full recovery?"

"Yeah. They wanted to watch him through the night because he took a good shot to the head, but he's been alert and aware for the last few hours. They're going to keep him for a few days."

"What hospital is he at?"

"Honey Mountain Hospital. There's just the one," he said with a chuckle. "What are you up to, Wolf?"

"Not sure. But I'll keep you posted." I ended the call and texted our pilot. Honey Mountain was a quick up and down. The least I could do was make sure she was okay. We were friends—temporary lovers. Coworkers, at the very least. This is what normal people did, right? They checked on one another.

It didn't take more than an hour to get myself in that helicopter and up in the air. I landed in Honey Mountain and had a car waiting there for me just like I'd done for her.

I drove straight to the hospital.

The nurse at the front desk was friendlier than I'd expected. She didn't ask for ID or who I was, she just clapped her hands together. "Oh, yes. Jack Thomas is such a wonderful man, isn't he?"

"Yes." I shrugged because I'd heard great things about the man.

"I'll take you myself. Follow me." She led me to the elevator, and I'd never met a person who could talk that long without taking a breath. She'd probably be fabulous underwater because the woman had enough oxygen to keep her going for a long-ass time. She managed to tell me about the patient with the bee sting in the ass that came in this morning, the nurse who left with the flu, and then casually shared how her husband left her for another woman. All of this was on the elevator ride to the third floor. Imagine what this woman could share if we were going to the top floor. I nodded and cleared my throat several times because this kind of personal small talk was probably my least favorite thing to do.

"Here you are, Wolf. Stop by on your way out. We're old friends now." She patted my shoulder and smiled before turning on her heels and heading back to the elevators.

I peeked into the room and saw Dylan in bed with her father, both of them sitting up with a laptop on her lap as she fist-pumped the sky. "Get up, Rocky!"

"He's getting up. There he goes," her dad said, his voice sounding sleepy.

I knocked on the door frame, and Dylan's eyes shot up and locked with mine. She must have paused the movie because the sound stopped.

"Well, if it isn't the big, bad Wolf," she purred.

Was she ever not on her game?

She'd clearly had the scare of her life. It looked as though she'd slept in a chair since there was a blanket and pillow there, and she was still here watching movies, which meant she was going on little sleep.

Yet she was totally on.

No surprise.

No hesitation.

"Hey. How's everyone doing?"

She closed her laptop. "Dad, this is Wolf. You met him the other night on FaceTime."

"Ah, yes. The enemy has come to check on you. Interesting."

Well, at least I knew where she got her smartass comebacks. Didn't this dude just take a bad fall?

"Come in. What are you doing here? Did you miss me? I warned you this would happen." She smirked.

"Please, don't flatter yourself," I said, moving into the room and dropping into the chair beside the bed. "I was in the neighborhood."

"Clearly." She chuckled. "We're just watching *Rocky.*"

"I can see that. And you're obviously still dressed for the part."

She glanced down and sighed. "Yeah. It was a rough night. But he's doing well now."

"Wolf, you want to do me a solid?" her father asked.

"Of course. What do you need?"

"Take my girl home. She's a little clingy when she thinks you got your bell rung. But she needs sleep and so do I."

Dylan gasped and shot her father a look. "You're such a traitor."

"Dilly, I love you, sweetheart. But my ribs are broken and so is my arm, and I wouldn't mind taking a pill and getting some sleep."

"Why didn't you say something?" she asked as she climbed off the bed and set the laptop on the table beside him.

"Because you made Niko go get my computer so we could

watch *Rocky,* and after the second movie, I thought we'd call it a day, but you kept going."

She smiled. "There he is. You must be feeling better."

"I'm really feeling okay. A little sore, but nothing serious. Sleep would help, and I can't sleep with you pacing the room and hovering over me."

"Fine. I could use a shower and a good night's sleep. But you'll text me if you need anything? I'll go home and charge my phone right away."

"I'm going to sleep for a long time, so don't worry if you don't hear from me. Love you, Dilly."

"Love you," she whispered and leaned down to kiss his cheek.

"Wolf, you get my girl home, okay?"

"Yes, sir," I said.

"As if I can't get myself home? Don't offend me." She shook her head at her father, grabbed her purse, and winked at me.

I followed her into the elevator, and she stood on the opposite wall, studying me.

"Is there something I could help you with?" I asked.

"Do you have a car? Because I came by ambulance."

"I have a car."

"Good." The doors opened, and we walked through the lobby and out to the car.

She guided me to her place but was otherwise quiet.

When I pulled into the driveway on the side of the large house and put the car into park, she turned to face me. "This is Hawk and Ever's house. I live in the guest house."

"Okay…" I raised a brow, waiting for her to invite me in.

"Are you here for me?" she asked, tucking her long hair behind her ears.

"I am."

The woman hadn't slept at all and still managed to look fucking gorgeous. When she lowered her hand, I saw the gashes on her palm and wrapped my fingers around her wrist.

"What happened to your hand?"

She looked down as if she had forgotten about it. "I had Niko's keys in my hand when my father was taken on the ambulance. I must have squeezed them on the ride over."

I pushed my door open and came around to open hers. "Come on. Let's get you cleaned up."

We were quiet on the short walk to the front door, and then she pulled out her keys and pushed inside. It was small but charming, with large glass windows overlooking the lake. I reached for her hand and led her to the door on the right, which I assumed was the bedroom. Seeing as this place was pretty tiny, there weren't a lot of options. There was another door that was clearly the bathroom, and I led her straight through. Her eyes widened when I turned to face her, putting two hands on her hips and hoisting her up onto the bathroom counter. I knew the look on her face. The sadness. The fear. The worry. The shock. The adrenaline. Hell, I'd lived that life for a long time. I turned on the faucet and rinsed her hand. She didn't flinch when I used the pad of my thumb to rub away the scabs that were forming so I could clean them. I turned off the water and found some peroxide under the cabinet, and she just raised a brow when I poured it over the palm of her hand. Little bubbles formed in each of the cuts. I let the back of her hand rest on her thigh while I moved toward the shower and turned on the water.

"Lift," I said, motioning to her arms, and she did what I said. I couldn't believe she wasn't fighting me, but she was exhausted, and this is what happens when your body shuts down.

I unsnapped her bra, and even though the urge to tip her back and take her nipple into my mouth was strong, I didn't do it. I tugged my sweater over my head and dropped my jeans and briefs on the floor.

I lifted her off the counter and set her feet down on the floor before dropping to my knees and kissing her belly as I slipped her shorts and tights and panties down her legs. Her fingers gently stroked my hair, and I pushed back up.

I took her hand in mine and led her into the shower. She didn't speak, which was very out of character. I squeezed some shampoo into my hands, and she gasped when I placed them on her head and started massaging. She groaned when I turned her around and ran my hands through her long hair, covering it in bubbles as her back rested against my chest.

The first whimper came as soon as she'd turned around and had her back to me, and then the sobs followed. I just stayed right there as she fell apart. I dropped her long, soapy hair down her shoulder and wrapped my arms around her, holding her tight. We stood under the water, not saying a word as she let it all out.

Her hand came over mine on her chest, and her breathing slowed before she finally turned around. "I'm sorry."

"Don't be sorry for being scared, Minx. He's your father. That shit is terrifying. You're all right. It just makes you human like the rest of us. But don't worry, I won't tell anyone."

She smiled and pushed up on her tiptoes and kissed me. It was fast and soft, and this had quickly become the most intimate moment I'd ever shared with a woman. She was vulnerable, and I wanted to comfort her.

She turned back around and tipped her head back so I could continue rinsing her hair. I chuckled as the water poured down between us, water droplets rolling down her beautiful body. I reached for the nozzle above and pulled it down, guiding it over her long, silky hair as I washed all the soap away.

I turned off the water and pushed open the door, reaching for a towel on the rack beside the door before drying her hair and patting her down before lifting her arms so I could wrap the towel around her chest. I tucked the corner in between her breasts and then reached out for another towel, drying my hair quickly and then tying it around my waist.

I picked her up and carried her to the bedroom, and she nuzzled into my neck before I gently set her on the bed. I climbed in next to her and rolled onto my side, and she did the same. It was completely dark outside now as I gazed out the window in her bedroom.

"Thank you," she whispered.

"You're okay, Minx." I stroked her hair away from her face, and her dark brown eyes welled with emotion. There were no pops of yellow or gold today, as she was completely exhausted.

"When I was in middle school, my mom took me and Charlie and Ash to get Halloween costumes. Vivi and Ever were in high school and were too cool to be dressing up any more. All the girls my age were getting these zombie or pirate costumes. But none of those appealed to me."

"What did you want to be?" I asked.

"My dad and I had just started watching all the *Rocky* movies, and I told my mom I wanted to be Rocky Balboa. She just smiled and said we could make that costume instead. She told me to always be whatever I wanted to be." She swiped at the single tear rolling down her cheek. "So, we went home, and she went online with me, and we found everything I needed. And then Halloween came, and when I came out in my costume, my mom surprised me and came walking out in an Apollo Creed costume, and then my dad strolls out as Micky, the trainer. Because they just got me, you know? And it's the reason that I always try to be exactly who I want to be. Because they loved me for that, which is rare."

"Of course, they did," I said, tugging her closer because I wanted to comfort her.

"I'm not always easy to love. And they both did. And then we lost my mom, and last night…" Her voice cracked, and I tipped her head back so I could look at her. "I thought my dad was going to die, Wolf, and that thought just scared me and made me feel so alone." Her lip quivered, and my fucking chest seized.

I could physically feel Dylan Thomas's pain, and that was scary as shit.

And for some reason, I didn't care, because I wanted to take that from her.

Comfort her and make her feel better in any way I could.

"Hey, he's okay. I've had close calls with friends when we were on missions, and I know how fucking scary it is to see someone who looks like there's no life left in them. But guess what?"

"What?" she asked.

"He made it. Your dad's a strong man. And now I know where you get all that strength."

"He is. But he looked like he was gone in that ambulance. He wasn't moving. Wasn't talking. Wasn't even coughing."

I reached for her hand, the one that I'd just cleaned, and I kissed the palm of her hand gently, over and over. "He's okay, Minx. And so are you."

"Thank you for coming," she whispered, and her voice was sleepy. "I hate you, Wolf Wayburn."

"I hate you, too, Minx."

And just like that, sleep took us both.

We didn't have sex.

It wasn't about that.

And I didn't have a fucking clue what that even meant.

twenty-five

. . .

Dylan

WHEN I WOKE UP, I was under the covers; the towel was gone and so was Wolf. Had I dreamed that? Had he really been here?

Yes. The man had washed my hair and my body and had cleaned my hand.

He'd been so gentle.

He'd come to Honey Mountain to find me.

And the most surprising part... it didn't bother me. Normally, if a man wanted to shower with me, I would have kicked him to the curb. But with Wolf, I had thoroughly enjoyed every minute of him taking care of me.

And I'd cried in front of him.

I pulled the covers up over my face as I remembered my breakdown.

I didn't mind that he'd seen me naked or that he'd found me in a hospital bed in a day-old Halloween costume, but the fact that he'd seen me cry... I'd never cried in front of a man. Hell, I could count on my fingers the number of times I'd cried in front of my sisters. I didn't shed tears easily, and when I did, I preferred to be alone.

"Why are you under the covers?" Wolf's gruff voice said, and I knew he was standing nearby because I could feel his presence.

"Did I cry last night?"

He was silent, which answered my question for me.

"Hey," he said, and the mattress dipped as he tugged down the comforter and looked at me. "I don't care that you cried. You were worried about your dad. That doesn't make you weak."

"Yes, it does. It's the epitome of weakness. When was the last time you cried?"

"Not that long ago." He smirked, and I knew he was lying.

"Liar. I'll bet you haven't cried since you were a kid," I said, and damn, he looked good this morning. "And why do you look so good?"

"I have to admit, I like this vulnerable side of you. I do look good, don't I?"

He was wearing nothing but his boxer briefs, and his toned, tanned skin was on full display. He reached for my arm and pulled out my hand to inspect my palm. His thumb gently ran across all the little cuts that were left there. Like he was soothing my pain away.

"Listen. You have nothing to be embarrassed about. I'm the one who came here uninvited, but you don't see me hiding under the covers."

"True. That does make you a bit needy, doesn't it?" I chuckled, and he dove forward on top of me.

"No one has ever called me needy," he growled, before kissing my neck.

"Just admit that you missed me," I said.

He pulled back. "Fine. I did. And I was worried about you. I don't know what the fuck it means, but I don't live my life trying to figure it out. I trust my gut. So here I am."

"Here you are," I said.

"Do you want me to leave? I mean, you're okay now. Your dad's going to be okay. I can head home if you want your space."

"I think I actually want you to stay." A lump formed in my throat as I said the words because I couldn't even believe that I was saying them.

Even more shocking was that I meant it.

"You obviously missed me, too," he teased.

"Don't get cocky. Let me check on my dad real quick, and then we can figure out what we want to do."

He pulled back and grabbed my phone off the nightstand and handed it to me.

I dialed my father's number, and he answered on the first ring. "Hey, Dilly. Did you get some sleep?"

"Yes. I slept really well. How about you?"

"I just woke up. I'm about to have breakfast, and I'm hoping to get out of this bed and move a little bit today."

"That's great news, Dad."

"I'm going to be just fine, sweetheart. Is the enemy still in town?" he teased.

"He is."

"Why don't you show him around Honey Mountain? I'm going to eat, see the doctor, take a walk down the hallway, and hopefully, get some more sleep. Big Al said a bunch of the guys from the firehouse are coming by today, so take a break, all right?"

"Nice try. I'll be by later today to check on you. Call me if you need anything."

I ended the call and took in the man watching me like I was some sort of mystery he was trying to figure out.

"How's he doing?" he asked.

"He sounds great. It's crazy that just thirty-six hours ago, I was afraid he was going to die, and now he's anxious to get out of bed."

Wolf nodded. "I get that. I've had some pretty bad injuries

myself, and I've seen friends get wounded in a way that I didn't think they'd survive, and then a few days later, they were up and moving. The human body is pretty amazing, and your dad is clearly in good shape from fighting fires, so he will rebound pretty quickly. Although the broken ribs and arm are going to take some time."

"How long were you down from the bullet wounds?" I asked, leaning forward to trace the scars that ran along his upper arm.

"Not long. Broken bones are different. They take longer to heal. Bullet wounds are only bad if they hit you in the wrong place. I got lucky."

"Is it weird that you were away doing undercover shenanigans and now you're just here, working at a normal job?"

He barked out a laugh. "Undercover shenanigans? That's new."

"Well, you haven't told me anything specific, so let's go with that."

"Fine. No, it doesn't bother me. I knew this was the plan. I was ready to go when I left. Tired of traveling. Tired of losing friends. Tired of all of it. So, this has been a good change. And there's nothing normal about this job because I work with this little vixen, and she keeps me on my toes."

"You're sleeping with the enemy," I teased. "You found a way to make it exciting."

"I sure did." He looked away for a minute as if he were gathering his thoughts. "So, how are you feeling today?"

Now it was my turn to laugh. "Is this you trying to be thoughtful?"

His mouth fell open. "What?"

"You're acting all awkward, like you shouldn't be carrying me off to the shower and having your way with me. Do not make me regret having a very unusual meltdown in front of you. I'm not that girl. You don't have to treat me like I'm made of porcelain."

He fell back onto the bed, and I pulled my legs out just in time to keep them from being crushed. "I was trying to be a decent guy. It's okay that you were upset about your dad. I'm not treating you like you're a porcelain doll. I'm treating you like you're a human being."

I wrapped the sheet around myself and lunged forward, straddling his hips as he lay sprawled out across my bed. "Don't insult me by calling me human."

He chuckled a deep, throaty laugh, and it bellowed around the bedroom. His fingers intertwined with mine. "I didn't come here to fuck you, if that's what you're thinking. I wasn't expecting anything."

"Bummer," I whined. Something in the distance caught my eye, and I cranked my neck and gasped. "It's snowing!"

I jumped off the bed and reached for his hand, hurrying to the window.

"Where the hell did that come from?" he asked as he stared out at the flakes falling from the sky.

"Welcome to Honey Mountain. The ski resorts don't open for a few weeks, but we can get snow in October."

"Weren't you wearing short-shorts two days ago?" he teased.

"I was. And even with tights underneath them, I still froze my ass off. But beauty comes at a price, right?" I turned to face him, pulling the sheet tighter around me. "Let's get dressed and go get pancakes and hot chocolate. I'll take you to my favorite place."

"Sounds like a plan. I'm starving."

"You're always starving," I said, moving toward my dresser and pulling out some panties and a bra. I dropped the sheet and got dressed as Wolf dug into his duffle bag and pulled out a pair of dark jeans and a gray sweater. He moved to the bathroom with his toiletry bag; the guy was so effortlessly put together, it was almost comical. I pulled my favorite black turtleneck sweater from the hanger and then tugged on a pair of distressed jeans and my black booties. I stood beside him in the bathroom as we both brushed our teeth.

I found my hairbrush and caught him staring at me in the mirror as I brushed through my long hair. "Thanks for washing my hair last night."

"It wasn't a big deal, Minx." He turned so he was leaning against the counter as he watched me tie my hair up in a bun on top of my head. I rubbed some moisturizer on my face and then added some mascara to my lashes and some gloss to my lips.

"Let's go."

I could barely contain my excitement about the snow as Wolf drove us toward town. It wasn't sticking, but it was starting to come down pretty hard.

"I always loved the first snow. I used to count down the days until the ski resorts opened." I pointed toward Sunshine Coffee Shop, and he pulled in front and parked.

"Are you a skier?" he asked as he unbuckled and rubbed his hands together in front of the heater.

"Ummm... is the pope Catholic? Is the sky blue?" I raised a brow. "Are penguins the cutest animal on the planet?"

"Well, the last question is somewhat subjective. But I take it you ski." He pushed out of the car and came around to open my door. It was a gesture that normally annoyed me, but I liked seeing Wolf Wayburn hustle around the car to get my door. It worked for him.

I stepped out. "I do. How about you?"

"Yes. Never met a hill I didn't like."

Suddenly, I had thoughts of him skiing down the Honey Mountain ski slopes wearing nothing but his boxer briefs with his biceps bulging and beautiful ink on display before he gets to the bottom of the hill, then drops to his knees because he can't go a second longer without tasting me.

My face hit the restaurant's front door so hard I literally bounced back, and Wolf had both hands on my shoulders to steady me.

"Jesus, Minx. Are you okay?" He turned me to face him, and the concern in his gaze made me feel slightly guilty for my dirty thoughts.

"I'm fine. I went to dirty town." I shrugged as I rubbed my nose. "And let me tell you, that one should definitely go into Ash's next book."

"I don't know what we're talking about, but you just slammed your face into a glass door."

My head fell back in laughter. "I'll explain it over breakfast. Come on."

He pulled open the door, and we stepped inside. It smelled like cinnamon and maple and pumpkin. My stomach rumbled, and I rubbed my hands together to get warm.

"Well, looky here. My favorite Thomas sister is back in town," Dean Joybill said. He and his wife, Delilah, owned the place, and we'd been coming here since we were kids.

"You know, my sisters and I got to talking one night and realized you say that to all of us." I raised a brow and smirked.

"Hey. I never met a Thomas girl I didn't like."

"Oh, stop flirting, you dirty old man. Hi, Dylan," Delilah said. "Who do we have here? Is this a 'special friend?'" She used her pointer finger and middle finger on each hand to make air quotes.

I looked over at Wolf, who looked notably uncomfortable at the question, so I decided to shake things up a bit. "God, no. He's my enemy and my lover."

Wolf's eyes widened, and Dean clapped his hands together. "This girl is always pulling our legs."

"She sure is." Delilah batted her lashes at Wolf.

"This is Wolf Wayburn. We work together in the city," I said.

"Actually, I'm her boss." Wolf extended a hand, and they both took it before Delilah led us to a table in the back of the restaurant as she flirted shamelessly with Wolf.

"I don't know if HR would be okay with how you take care of your employees," I said close to his ear as we walked side by side through the busy café.

"It's my job to make sure you're happy." He paused at the table and waited for me to sit down, and Delilah set two menus in front of us and hurried off.

"You know, for a dirty-talking, cocky bastard, you've got awfully good manners."

"What can I say? I'm full of surprises. Tell me why you walked into the door."

"I was thinking about you servicing me on the ski slopes." I paused when the server stopped at our table, and he ordered coffee, and I got a hot chocolate. Sunshine Coffee Shop makes the best hot cocoa in the whole world. We both ordered pancakes and bacon, and Wolf moved his chair closer to me.

"You want me to service you right here?"

"You wouldn't dare! Poor Dean Joybill would be traumatized." I leaned forward, my mouth just inches from his.

"I'd climb under this table and spread your legs right now if you asked me to. I wouldn't give a fuck what Mr. Joycock thought."

"It's Joybill, and they're still recovering from me calling you my lover." I chuckled and leaned back when two piping hot mugs were set in front of us.

"Well, then I guess we better eat quickly because now that I've got my mind on dessert, I'm not as hungry for pancakes."

I smiled. "The pancakes are really something here."

"Your pussy is better."

"I can't argue with that."

He barked out a laugh, and I just watched as a wide grin spread across his handsome face.

The dirty talk. The banter. The arguing. The attraction.

The sex.

I'd never enjoyed hating someone so much.

twenty-six

. . .

Wolf

WE'D STAYED a few extra days in Honey Mountain because Dylan wanted to wait until her dad was released from the hospital.

And for whatever fucking reason... I didn't want to leave her.

And she was happy to have me stay.

We both couldn't figure it out, but I was done questioning it.

I could work from anywhere right now, and Honey Mountain with Dylan is where I wanted to be.

We'd spent a lot of time with her father. I'd met her other sisters and their husbands and all the kids, and it didn't give me hives or make me want to run for the hills.

The guys were great. Her sisters were hilarious. And her father was a guy's guy, so we got along well.

We'd gotten home last night and were both a little unsure about what we'd do when we got back to reality, so we'd agreed on the helicopter that we'd sleep at our own apartments.

Being out of town together was different.

This wasn't a relationship, and we needed to have some boundaries.

Some rules in place.

And I'd barely slept a fucking wink because now that I'd fallen asleep with her beside me, I found myself reaching for her all night. I missed the smell of jasmine wafting around me while I slept.

And the sex. Don't even get me started. We were explosive together.

In and out of the bedroom.

I'd taken a cold shower this morning—alone, because we'd come up with all these dumb fucking rules.

I got a text from her that she was already downstairs in the car when I stepped out of my apartment and made my way down the elevator and into the car.

"Hey," I said.

"Good morning. How'd you sleep?"

"Like a bag of dicks."

"How does a bag of dicks sleep?" she asked, and her tongue slipped out to wet her lips, and I groaned.

"Not well. How about you?"

"I wouldn't call it a great night either. Should we plan a sleepover tonight?" she asked. "Because I need to get some sleep, and apparently, I sleep better with you now, and the good sex helps me fall asleep."

I smiled. I thought she was going to torture me this morning and tell me she slept great without me. So this was music to my fucking ears.

And to my dick.

"Yes. I can get on board with that."

"Pleasure doing business with you, Mr. Wayburn." She smirked, and the car came to a stop, and we both climbed out when Gallan opened the door.

We rode the elevator up, and I couldn't stop myself. I pushed her up against the wall and kissed her.

I kissed her like I'd die if I didn't.

And she kissed me back with the same ferocity.

There was a ding in the elevator, and she pulled away just before the doors opened. We both stood on opposite sides of the elevator as three men stepped in.

"Have a good day," she said as she strode off in front of me. I watched her ass sway back and forth as she passed my office and went to hers.

The morning was swamped with meetings, and the knock on my door pulled me from my computer screen.

"It's open," I said.

Tawny poked her head inside. "There's someone here to see you. She doesn't have an appointment, but she said it's important."

"Who is it?"

"Kressa Mason."

I let out a long breath because I didn't feel like dealing with this. But she'd called a few times, and I hadn't answered, and she was here. I wouldn't send her away.

"It's fine. Send her in."

I pushed to my feet, and Kressa stepped through the door. It had been a while since I'd seen her. Several years, actually.

She wore some sort of black tights and a short red dress and high heels. Maybe she worked in the city.

Her dark hair was shorter than it used to be and was cut at her shoulders.

"Hi, Wolf. Thanks for giving me a few minutes."

"No problem. How are you?" I leaned over and gave her the world's most awkward hug as I patted her on the back a few times before pulling away. She was still holding on, and I had to assist her with removing her arms.

"I'm doing well. I'm working part time at a law firm up the street."

I motioned for her to take a seat in the leather chairs across from my desk, and I moved back around to sit down.

"That's great." I folded my hands together and rested them on the desk. "What can I do for you?"

She smiled, and I knew by the way she was looking at me that she was feeling nostalgic.

But I felt nothing.

There weren't any old feelings churning in me. I wasn't angry anymore.

When I looked at her, I just felt nothing.

It was a teenage relationship. It had run its course and ended in a way that didn't leave me wondering what it could have been.

"I, um, well, I heard you were back for good. And I just thought I would pop in and see you. You haven't answered any of my calls or texts. Are you still angry with me?"

"No, Kress. I'm not angry with you. I just don't really know what we'd need to call one another for. I think we can be friendly when we run into each other, but we're both busy with our own lives now." I'd been back for a few months and had saved myself from this sort of confrontation until now. I still didn't get the point of all this, anyway.

"That's the thing, Wolf. I'm not that busy. Westin is in school and sports. He's eight now, and so we've got all that. But..." She let out a breath, and her eyes were wet with emotion. "You're back now. We only broke up because you were leaving."

Fuck me.

Was she serious? Did she even hear herself? We'd ended things almost a decade ago, for God's sake.

"I'd say there was a little more to it. Listen, I don't have any hard feelings toward you. I wish you nothing but the best. I've heard that Westin is a great kid, and I'm happy for you, Kress. I really am. But there is no you and me. Not anymore."

A sob left her throat, which caught me off guard, and she

whimpered. I moved to my feet and came around the desk and bent down in front of her.

"What's this about? We haven't spoken much in almost a decade. Why are you upset about this?"

She swiped at her cheeks and got herself under control. "You're right. I don't know. I guess I just thought maybe we could try again. Are you single?"

"I'm not. I'm with someone, and I'm happy." It wasn't a complete lie. Dylan and I weren't in a normal relationship, but we were monogamous, and I was fucking happy with her.

Kressa nodded just as the door flew open, and Dylan Thomas stormed the fucking castle. Her eyes were full of fire, and she glared at me as I was bent down in front of my ex-girlfriend, which could come off as inappropriate if one didn't know the context.

I pushed to my feet, and Dylan marched toward me with a handful of files. She swatted them against my chest, and the look on her face was venomous. "Here you go. I need you to look at these as soon as possible, as they're urgent."

I opened the top folder, and there was nothing inside except for some blank paper.

"I see. Well, I appreciate how diligent you are."

"I'll bet you do. I didn't mean to interrupt your little—" She tapped her finger against her lips. "*Rendezvous*."

Kressa was on her feet and moving toward the door. I don't know if she was scared of Dylan or if she realized her intentions were not reciprocated or both—both would work. "I'm just going to head out. Thanks for your time. Take care." She pulled the door closed behind her.

I tossed the folders beside me and sat on the edge of the desk with my arms folded.

"Well, did you just have sex with her?" Her arms flailed around.

"Are you fucking kidding me right now? You walked in on us. Did it look like we were having sex?"

"I don't know, Wolf. You looked awfully comfortable down on your knees for her," she hissed and stalked toward the door, but I was on her heels. I reached for her forearm and turned her around.

"No fucking way are you going to pull that shit with me. I was not down on my fucking knees. I was bent down because she was crying, and I'm not a monster."

"Tawny told me that was Kressa. So, your ex-girlfriend just happens to stop by your office unexpectedly, and then she starts crying? Do you expect me to believe that?"

"I don't know why the fuck you wouldn't. That's exactly what happened. I haven't seen her in years, and she just showed up because she heard I was back in town."

She narrowed her gaze. "What did she want?"

"She wanted to see if I was single and if I wanted to give things a shot again. It's ridiculous."

"Sure, it is. What did you tell her?"

I moved into her space because the fact that she was riding my ass like I'd committed a crime when we weren't even in an actual relationship was madness. "Why the fuck do you care?" I raised a brow as my hands wrapped around her wrists so she wouldn't run.

"Because we had a deal, and I wanted to see if you were breaking it."

"You'd like that, wouldn't you?" I growled, my mouth moving to her ear. "So you could say I fucked you over and that all men suck, and this little... arrangement could end because it's getting fucking complicated, and you don't like that."

She whimpered this little sound, but it made my chest squeeze. "What did you tell her?"

"I told her I was in a relationship. Because whatever the fuck this is, it makes me happy. I don't want anyone else. And

I know that fucking scares you, and it scares me, too. And maybe it will end in a day or two. Who the fuck knows? But I told her I wasn't interested because I was with someone else."

I had my hand on her neck, and I pulled back to look at her. She lunged forward, her mouth colliding with mine, and I walked her backward toward the door so I could lock the handle. Our mouths never lost contact.

"Fuck, Minx. I missed you."

"I missed you, too," she said against my mouth as I reached for the hem of her skirt and tugged it up around her waist. I lifted her off the floor, and her legs wrapped around me as I walked her toward the desk and sat her ass there.

She reached for the button on my dress slacks and had my cock free in seconds before my mouth was on hers again.

"I still hate you," she said.

I pulled back and reached for my wallet in my back pocket. Our breaths were labored, and I wanted her so badly I couldn't wait another second.

"I hate you, too," I said, pulling a condom out and tossing my wallet onto the desk.

"Give it to me." She took the foil packet from me, tearing it open with her teeth and looking like a fucking goddess as she did so. She slowly rolled the latex over my throbbing cock, and I closed my eyes to stay in control. The feel of her hand on me. Her breath so close to my mouth.

She tangled her hands in my hair, pulling my mouth back to hers before I reached down and teased her entrance with the tip of my erection.

"Please, Wolf," she whispered, and that's all I needed to hear. I drove into her, over and over again, and we were both needy as hell.

She leaned back, arching her chest up, hair falling all over my desk, and I unbuttoned her blouse and tugged her lace bra down to expose her perfect tits. My mouth came over her nipple, and I pumped into her, knowing she was close. My hand came down between us, and I rubbed her clit the way I knew she wanted me to. I pulled my mouth from hers and moved to her ear.

"We have to be quiet, Minx."

"Then kiss me," she whispered, her breaths coming fast, and my mouth covered hers again as she dug her nails into the back of my neck, and she tightened around me so much I couldn't hold on. She exploded and cried into my mouth, and I went right over the fucking edge with her, and a guttural sound left my throat as I came harder than I ever had in my life.

We continued to move, riding out every last bit of pleasure, and I thrust into her over and over.

We finally slowed.

Our movements.

Our breaths.

Our need.

I pulled back to look at her, stroking the hair away from her face. Her forehead was damp with sweat, and her eyes were sated.

"Just another day at the office, huh?"

She smiled. "That was something."

I slowly pulled out of her and helped her to her feet. I pulled off the condom and grabbed some tissue from my desk, wrapping it up and tossing it into the trash can.

Dylan adjusted her bra, buttoned her blouse, and pulled her skirt down as I tucked myself back in and crossed my arms over my chest.

"Do you believe me about Kressa?"

"Yes. I overreacted." She lifted one shoulder and looked away.

I moved in closer, crowding her. I tipped up her chin. "Maybe I should punish you for that."

"What do you have in mind?" She waggled her brows.

"We can discuss it over dinner. Be ready to leave in an hour."

"I have to meet my cousin at Karaoke King later." She walked backward toward the door. "Come with me after dinner."

"What the fuck is Karaoke King?"

"Only the best place in the world. You can meet Hugh. He's a great guy. And then you can have your way with me again." She winked.

I scrubbed a hand over my face after she shut the door.

I was getting in deep with this girl, and it scared the shit out of me.

But I'd never been one to run from things that scared me.

Looks like I was going to Karaoke King.

twenty-seven

· · ·

Dylan

"THEY'RE GOING to think we're dating," I said, as we strode down the street toward Karaoke King. My happy place. It was an old college haunt that I used to frequent often, and I couldn't wait to get back up on stage.

I'd asked Gallan to drop us off two blocks back so I could show Wolf my old stomping grounds. There was the little market on the corner that I'd shopped at when I was in college, the best taco stand around, which we'd just passed, and a boutique I'd always loved. This part of town was a little more hipster than the city, and the college kids dominated this area.

"I don't give a fuck what anyone thinks. Sabine said she and Z wanted to meet for a drink, so they can just meet us there. I wasn't going to tell her we'd meet them after leaving this godforsaken karaoke bar you're dragging me to."

I chuckled. He was grumpy about the most ridiculous things. Yet the man swam in the ocean after being shot three times.

Choose your battles, dude.

It's freaking karaoke.

You've done worse.

"Why not?" My hand grazed his, and his pinky finger wrapped around mine for a brief couple of seconds before he let it go.

And a little part of me wanted him to grab my hand.

How messed up was that?

I wasn't a hand holder.

"Because I'm going to suffer through what I consider the equivalent of hell and listen to drunk assholes who think they can sing, just so I can get you home and spend the rest of the night worshipping your body. And I know you wore those leather pants just to fuck with me."

I came to a stop and turned to face him. He tugged at my dress coat, pulling it closed. That was the thing about Wolf. He worried about me being cold. He worried when my father was injured, and he'd flown there to make sure I was okay. But I couldn't read him outside of those little details. He'd made it clear he didn't do relationships, yet he also wouldn't be with me unless we'd both agreed to be monogamous.

And I wasn't pushing it because I didn't know if I was even capable of being in a serious relationship.

But I knew I missed him when he wasn't there. I loved spending time with him. He made me laugh. He challenged me.

But he was also pigheaded and bossy.

And I was just waiting to wake up and be done with this.

It just hadn't happened yet.

And I found myself thinking about him all the time. I'd never done that with anyone else. So, it was scary and exciting and mysterious all at the same time.

"These are leggings, and they are very popular right now." I glanced down at my outfit. A white blouse with the top three buttons low enough to show the lace of my bra, black leather leggings, red stilettos, and several layered gold necklaces. The camel-colored dress jacket added a little sophistication and a whole lot of warmth. "I do not choose my clothing to fuck with you." So maybe I knew he'd lose his mind over these pants, but it wasn't to mess with him; it was to make sure he was looking at me when we were out. But I'd keep that to myself.

He backed me up until I felt the brick building behind me. We were on a side street one block away from Karaoke King, so it was fairly quiet. Wolf wore an off-white fitted sweater, dark jeans, and military boots. He had on a black trench coat that he'd left open. He looked ridiculously sexy. His hands slipped inside my jacket, gliding up and down my ribs.

"You look so fucking gorgeous I can barely see straight."

My tongue dipped out to wet my lips. "Good. Then the outfit is doing its job. But, if you talk like that at the bar, your sister will definitely know something is up. And my cousin, Hugh, is very observant. I told him that you were just a guy from work. We want to keep this a secret, right?"

I wasn't sure why we were being secretive. My sisters knew we were having a little fling. I mean, the man had flown to Honey Mountain and stayed for days. I'm pretty sure Dad was onto us. But we'd kept things on the down-low at work, even when I'd had my mini meltdown this afternoon when Tawny came into the break room and told me that Wolf's ex-girlfriend had come to see him. I'd kept it together in front of her before I'd marched in there, ready to burn the place down.

I didn't think anyone suspected anything as we'd been fairly professional at the office—well, if you don't count the time he dropped to his knees and buried his face between my thighs, and the fact that he'd lifted my skirt and plopped me onto his desk today and gave me yet another office orgasm. Yikes. And there was that elevator blow job.

So, maybe we weren't being as careful as we thought we were.

"Do you want to keep it a secret?" he asked, his lips finding my neck.

"I mean, it could all end tomorrow, right? We don't want people at the office in our business," I said, but my words were breathy and full of need.

"So, this is the *friend from the office*, huh?" a deep voice said with a chuckle, and Wolf's head shot up to turn and see my cousin Hugh walking toward us.

Hugh was a big guy, tall with broad shoulders, long, dark hair, and he was one of my favorite people on the planet.

I put my hands on Wolf's chest, and he straightened. "Wolf, this is my cousin, Hugh."

"Nice to meet you. I was just—er—trying to warm her up because she was cold." He extended his arm, and they shook hands.

Hugh barked out a laugh. "Dude. That's rich. Your secrets are safe with me. Bring it in, girl."

I rolled my eyes and stepped into his arms.

"Lucy, you've got some 'splaining to do," he whispered.

"I have no idea what you're talking about." I started walking toward the bar. "Come on. I'm ready to get in there."

"Have you heard her sing yet?" Hugh asked as he strode beside Wolf. I glanced over my shoulders, and they were similar in size and both a little intimidating if you didn't know them.

"No. I'm not much of a karaoke guy," Wolf grumped.

"Yeah. I hear you, man. Dilly and I were in college together, and this was her favorite place. She'd drag me here all the time. And it kind of grows on you."

"Please. You love it here." I shook my head as we approached the big, red door.

"I've never come without you. It's just a karaoke bar with a bunch of drunk people when you aren't here."

"Do I want to know what that means?" Wolf asked as he pulled the door open for me.

The place was just how I remembered it. The last time I'd come to the city, I'd dragged Charlie here with me and Hugh. She'd sung "Tiny Dancer" by Elton John, which was a favorite of mine, too, but it didn't really bring down the house and get the crowd going.

"Just wait, Wolf. You're in for quite a show."

"Dylan!" Sabine was on her feet and waving us over. Z was sitting on the other side of the table, and he looked very intoxicated, and Seb was there, too, with a girl on each side of him.

"Hey, this is my cousin, Hugh." I introduced him to every-one, and we quickly ordered a bunch of cocktails, beers, and shots and settled around the large table.

The dim lighting, the dark red flooring, and the vintage chandeliers that dangled overhead set the mood. It smelled like nachos and tequila. Two of my favorite things.

Wolf took the seat beside me and sipped his beer, looking like he was assessing the place for exit doors.

"You look very out of place, brother," Seb said after taking a shot of tequila and biting down on the lime.

"He does not." Sabine winked at her big brother, and I'd noticed it each time I'd been around her; she adored Wolf. She definitely understood him, whereas I think most could misin-terpret the way he carried himself. "This is so fun. Thanks for inviting us."

I found his hand beneath the table and rubbed my thumb across his palm a few times. He let out a long breath. "It's not my typical hangout, but it's fine."

"So, you just come to karaoke bars with coworkers now? What's the story here?" Seb asked, with a wicked grin on his face.

"The story is, I asked him to come with me. He lives next door. We're friends. I wanted him to experience a little MC Hammer." I waggled my brows, and everyone laughed.

"Listen. This place wasn't for me either, but here I am.

Dilly has a way of making everyone have a good time," Hugh said.

"What can I say? It's a gift." I chuckled as the server put down two platters of nachos in the middle of the table, and Z was the first one to dive in. He looked like he was several cocktails in already, and Wolf glanced over at me and raised a brow. "So, what do you do?" Z directed his question toward Hugh. "These guys own a hockey team and are wealthier than sin—are you in the same boat?"

"What the fuck does that mean?" Wolf growled, and Sabine glared at her boyfriend. She didn't look like she was having a great time with him, as they weren't even sitting beside one another.

"It just means you're rich." He shrugged and glanced back over at my cousin, who was normally very chill, but he was watching Wolf, and I could tell that he liked him.

"I own a bar and restaurant in Cottonwood Cove. You'll all have to come check it out sometime."

"Dylan told me about it. I haven't been out that way in a while, but I've heard it's got a cool sports pub vibe. Ledger helped design it, right?" Wolf asked, and he'd moved my hand to his thigh beneath the table and rested his big hand on top of it.

"Yeah. You know Ledger? He's got an eye, man. You're going to have to come check out all the details."

"I met him in Honey Mountain. He showed me some of the projects he's done here in the city, and it's impressive stuff."

"That's right. You were gone for a few days. Were you in Honey Mountain?" Seb asked, and he was trying hard not to laugh. He loved to give his brother shit, and it was funny to see them go back and forth with one another.

"I had some business there, yes."

"Dilly, weren't you there, too? My dad said your father

had an accident but that he was okay," Seb asked, but he stared at his brother as he spoke.

"I was home for a few days, waiting for him to be released from the hospital."

"Uncle Jack is a badass, man. You can't keep that guy down," Hugh said as a tray of tequila shots arrived, and the server set them down beside Seb. Wolf groaned.

"What a kawinky-dink that you were both there." Seb raised a brow and handed his brother a shot glass before passing the rest out to everyone else.

"Cheers to seeing our girl on stage," Seb said, and we all tipped our heads back, letting the cool liquid slide down our throats. "I think I might have a song or two in me."

"Good god. This is going to be a long night," Wolf groaned, and Hugh patted him on the back and laughed.

The first woman to get up on stage looked like a college student and sang her best rendition of Madonna's "Like A Virgin." She slurred her words and giggled multiple times, but the crowd cheered her on. That was what I loved about this place.

"When will you be gracing us with your presence?" Wolf whispered in my ear, and his fingers traced along the back of my neck.

I'd turned down the next few rounds of shots, and so had Wolf and Hugh. But everyone else was having a good time. I noticed Sabine keeping her distance from her boyfriend, but I didn't know what that was about. Z seemed to be drinking heavily, and he'd clearly made up for his fast, as he was downing nachos like he hadn't eaten in weeks.

"I'm going to sing one for you, baby," Z slurred as he pushed to his feet.

Wolf's shoulders stiffened, and he looked between Z and Sabine, and his jaw ticked.

"She's not leaving here with him," he said against my ear.

I heard my cousin talking to Wolf on his other side, and I

knew Hugh well enough to know that he was offering any backup Wolf might need if things got messy. Seb was completely unaware as he continued to make another play with the cute waitress, who was paying him a lot of attention. The girls beside him didn't seem to mind at all.

"Hey there, karaoke peeps!" Z shouted through the microphone, and I cringed because he was talking too close to the mic, and anyone who knew karaoke etiquette knew to hold it away from your mouth a bit. "This one is for my girlfriend. I love you, baby."

"Oh, God," Sabine whispered.

Z proceeded to sing Beck's "Loser" completely off-key, and he didn't keep up with the pacing of the song, so it was a complete disaster. The crowd booed him, which was not typical. You had to be really off your game to get them that annoyed. Sabine looked mortified.

"How about I have Gallan pull up and take him home? You're not going with him, though," Wolf said.

"Trust me. You don't have to twist my arm. I broke up with him tonight. That's why I wanted you to meet me here, because I didn't know if he'd take it well."

My jaw fell open. "Oh, okay. You've had enough?"

"He admitted that he cheated on me with his ex-girlfriend last week. But he was being relentless about getting together to talk about it, so I agreed to meet him out. It's done, and I couldn't be happier about it."

Wolf was on his feet, and Hugh was right behind him as if they'd already discussed this. When Z strode off the stage, they both walked on each side of him and led him right out the door.

They weren't gone long.

When they came back in the bar, Wolf looked tense, and he paused to speak to Seb on the other side of the table.

Hugh walked over to me and bent down to speak in my

ear. "Damn, Dilly. Your boyfriend is a badass. I don't think Sabine will need to worry about Z."

I didn't know what had happened, but I got the feeling Wolf scared the life out of him. But I glanced up at my cousin and shook my head. "He's not my boyfriend."

"Sure, he isn't. Now go kick some ass on stage."

And that's exactly what I planned to do.

twenty-eight

• • •

Wolf

I WANTED TO BE AGITATED. Wanted to be pissed off after escorting Z to the car while the little shit had a meltdown, insisting that he'd only cheated on my sister once. I'd slammed his ass against the car and told him that I'd have eyes on him, and if he came anywhere near her again, I'd know it.

My hands were fisted, and I ordered a glass of whiskey to calm my nerves. And then Dylan took the stage.

Hugh clinked his glass against mine and smirked. "You're going to enjoy this."

I liked her cousin. He was a cool dude. Reminded me of the guys on my SEAL team in the Navy. I was good at reading people, and this guy was a cool cat.

I sipped my cocktail while Seb continued flirting his ass off with the three women surrounding him, completely clueless about the fact that our sister had been upset. But she'd rebounded quickly. She'd run into a few friends, and they'd come to our table to talk to her.

"Who's in the mood for a little Hammer Time?" Dylan purred into the microphone as if she were completely comfortable standing up in front of this crowd.

Every dude in the place had his eyes on her, and I wanted to start moving through the bar and beating the shit out of every last one of them. But I couldn't fault them. She was gorgeous and confident and cool.

Her long, blonde hair fell around her shoulders, and her black leggings fit her like a second skin. Her blouse dipped low, and I wanted to demand she button it all the way up, but I knew that would probably make her unbutton another button if I tried to tell her what to do. I didn't like all these guys staring at her.

Mine.

Where the fuck did that come from?

"Relax. She's just got a way of getting the crowd into it. They used to offer her money to come in on Friday nights because everyone would be on their feet. She's one of a kind, man." Hugh sipped his bourbon.

The music started, and she immediately belted out, "You can't touch this."

And the place went crazy. She repeated the words over and over along with the music and moved across the stage as she did so. Sabine and her friends were on their feet whistling, and I let out a breath, knowing I wasn't going to like all these eyes on her.

"That's the problem, isn't it?" I said, raising a brow at him and sipping my cocktail.

"You got nothing to worry about there. She's as loyal as she is stubborn." He barked out a laugh.

And then she walked down the steps off the stage, singing about the music hitting her, and then she sang out, "Oh my Lord. Thank you for blessing me."

She continued rapping like she wrote the fucking song as she walked around the bar, no longer near the screen.

"Doesn't she need to read the lyrics?" I leaned close to her cousin and asked, but my eyes never left her.

He laughed. "She's done this enough that she's got it

down. Dilly gets things quickly. And she knows how to put on a show, that's for sure."

She marched toward us and started shaking her hips and singing her ass off and stopped in front of me. "Yo, I told you," she sang. "You can't touch this."

The entire room roared and jumped to their feet as she turned her back to me and then bent all the way over, and my hands moved to her hips of their own volition. She glanced over her shoulder and smiled. "You can't touch this."

Then she started walking toward the center of the room again as she continued singing every last word, which she'd clearly memorized. She grabbed a chair at the empty table near the stage and then climbed right up onto it.

"What the fuck?" I hissed under my breath.

Hugh was on his feet, cheering her on.

She stood on the table and broke out in the chorus again before shouting, "Break it down." The crowd sang along with her, and then she yelled again. "Stop. Hammer Time."

The next thing I knew, she was saying, "Wave your hands in the air," and then something about a bump, bump, bump and then you can't touch this on repeat.

She stepped off the table and back onto the chair before stalking toward my sister, who joined right in, and they both turned around and bumped their asses together. I couldn't help but laugh, all while scanning the room to make sure no one was going to do something stupid.

She moved back onstage, and the room went crazy as she belted out the last verse, and everyone sang together, "*It's 'Hammer! Go, Hammer! MC Hammer! Yo, Hammer!' And the rest can go and play!*"

The noise was deafening, and I just stared in awe at the little minx up there, holding the attention of everyone in the room.

I couldn't blame them.

I couldn't look away even if I wanted to.

And I didn't want to.

When the song ended, she walked off the stage, and everyone was standing and cheering as she stalked toward me, her gaze locked with mine. She didn't pause or slow down; she was on a mission. One leg moved beside the chair where I was sitting, and the other moved to the opposite side so she was straddling me.

"You can touch this, big, bad Wolf."

I tangled my fingers in her hair and tugged her mouth down to mine. I kissed her like there wasn't a room full of people watching us.

Because I didn't give a fuck.

I wanted everyone to know she was mine.

I didn't know what it meant or how long it would last, but right now, I wanted her.

Needed her.

And I hadn't felt that—ever.

Hugh clapped loudly beside us and whistled. "Damn. Very smooth, Dilly."

She pulled back and studied me. "I don't care who knows tonight."

"I don't either," I said, my hands gripping her hips to keep her there.

"Uh, I don't think anyone here doesn't know you're together. The cat's out of the bag, kids," Sabine said as she smiled down at us before clinking her glass with Hugh's.

"What do you say we all get out of here?" I asked.

"I mean, the show's over, right?" Dylan teased.

"Oh, it's far from over, Minx," I whispered against her ear.

Hugh rounded up my brother like he somehow knew I wouldn't leave without him.

Sabine rolled her eyes when Seb followed us with two of the girls from the table, and we all made our way out to the street.

Elliott pulled up; he was Seb's driver and he would take

my brother and the two girls, but Sabine asked if she could ride with us instead. Obviously, whatever Seb had planned was not something she wanted to witness.

"Dude, go home. Be safe," I said, pulling him in for a half hug and clapping him on the back. He had an apartment just a few blocks from mine.

Seb didn't let go of my hand. "It's good to see you happy, brother. It's been a long time. Don't fuck it up."

I rolled my eyes. "Thanks for the vote of confidence. Go home and get some sleep. I'll see you at work tomorrow."

"I'm taking a me-day!" he shouted over his shoulder. "Hey, Dilly," he said.

"Yeah?"

"Badass, girl. MC fucking Hammer. Rolling deep in the nineties, my little hipster." Elliott helped Seb into the car, and he made eye contact with me. I gave him a nod, which was code for him to take my brother straight home. No stops.

Dylan's head tipped back in laughter as the four of us piled into the car. We told Hugh we'd drop him at the hotel. He was here in the city for a few days, looking at some possible venues to open another restaurant down the road. He didn't want to drive back and forth to Cottonwood Cove, which was only an hour away, so he thought he'd just enjoy the city for a few days.

Dylan immediately started grilling my sister. "Are you done with Z?"

"Totally. I've kind of been over him for a few weeks." Sabine shrugged. "And then I confronted him, and he really thought I'd be okay with him cheating. It was kind of a relief. I wasn't sure how to end it. That made it easy. It's nice having you home, Wolfy."

"It sure is, Wolfy," Hugh said with a chuckle as we pulled up in front of his hotel. "Thanks for a great night. I head back tomorrow, but I expect to see you guys at the restaurant soon."

"Count on it," I said, shaking his hand as Gallan opened the door. Hugh kissed Sabine on the cheek and told her not to settle for dirtbags, which made us all laugh.

Dylan jumped out of the car and hugged him goodbye, and he spun her around.

"She's really great. I hope you don't mess this up. And her cousin is sure easy on the eyes," Sabine said, falling back into a fit of giggles.

"Why does everyone think I'll fuck it up? It's not serious. But we're having a good time." Even I wasn't buying my own shit. It was serious, wasn't it?

It had been so long that I didn't even know how this worked.

I'd never considered it to be anything other than temporary.

But now I couldn't imagine not being with her.

She climbed back into the car and leaned against me.

"Your cousin is so hot," Sabine said over a hiccup.

Dylan chuckled. "He's the best."

"He's great, but he's my age, which is too old for you," I said.

"Thanks, *Dad*. Ugh. I hate boys. And I really hate Z." Sabine leaned against my other side. I looked down to see Dylan's hand wrapped around my sister's hand, and I don't know why, but it nearly undid me.

Things were getting complicated.

I didn't do complicated.

But I wasn't going to figure it all out tonight.

We pulled up to Sabine's building, and she hugged Dylan.

"Call me if you want to talk about the little rat, but remember, you don't settle. You're too good for that, okay?" Dylan told her.

"Yes. I couldn't agree more. Happy hour this week?" my sister said as she climbed out.

"Absolutely."

I moved out of the car and walked her into the building, hugging her goodbye. "You sure you're all right?"

"Yeah. I'm really happy you're home, Wolfy. I used to have nightmares that you wouldn't come home." She squeezed me even tighter.

"Not going anywhere, Sabine."

She nodded and kissed my cheek before walking toward the elevator and waving goodbye.

When I got back in the car, Dylan was talking to her father, and I said a quick hello before she ended the call.

"He's up late," I said, wrapping an arm around her and pulling her close.

"He's not used to not working. He doesn't know what to do with himself." She chuckled. "Was Sabine okay?"

"Yeah. She seems all right. I'm glad she's done with that little shithead."

"Me, too. Did you have fun tonight?" she asked, and she sounded sleepy.

"Yeah. You're a fucking rockstar, Minx. I think you singing a little Hammer time is my new favorite fantasy."

She laughed. "I can sing to you anytime you want."

"I normally wouldn't choose that song, but something about you in your hot pants, owning the room and belting out 'U Can't Touch This', was fucking sexy as hell."

"Now you have a fantasy just like I do," she said, sitting up to look at me.

"Oh, yes, the one where I service you on the slopes?"

"It was a bit more detailed than that." She chuckled.

"Tell me." I ran my fingers through her hair.

"You had just told me that you were a great skier, and I imagined you skiing down the Honey Mountain ski slopes in nothing but those fitted black boxer briefs and then dropping to your knees at my feet."

My head fell back.

This girl was fucking crazy, and I couldn't get enough of it.

"I don't see me skiing down any slopes in my underwear. But I'll happily drop to my knees anytime you want me to." I nipped at her bottom lip as we pulled up in front of our building.

"Good to know." She stepped out of the car and said goodbye to Gallan. I thanked him and clapped him on the back before following her inside.

Once we were on the elevator, we were both quiet. She stood a little bit away from me and looked deep in thought.

"What are you thinking about, Minx?"

"Just wondering if we're going to be staying at the same apartment tonight?"

"Fuck yeah, we are. I say we just stay together as long as we both want to."

She smiled. "I still hate you, big, bad Wolf."

"I hate you, too, Minx." I wrapped my arms around her as the doors opened, her back to my chest, and we stepped off together.

"My place or yours?" she asked over her shoulder.

"*Mine.*" The word had more meaning than I wanted to admit.

Because she was mine.

There was no way around it anymore.

twenty-nine

. . .

Dylan

WOLF HAD GONE to work out after we left the office, and I'd planned a FaceTime call with my sisters. The last couple of weeks had been surprising and unexpected.

I had my laptop set up at the kitchen counter, and I poured myself a glass of wine as everyone joined the chat.

"Hello," Vivian called out.

"I'm here. The girls are playing in the snow with Jace, so I have a little quiet time," Ashlan said as I settled onto the barstool.

"Sorry, you're going to get a little boob action, because someone is completely off his schedule and wants to nurse all the freaking time." Everly adjusted her blouse, and little Jackson clamped right on.

"I've seen more of your boobs than my own lately," Charlotte said over her laughter.

"I don't even live there, and I feel like I see them constantly. And might I say—they are so… voluptuous."

"It's called engorged. They are full of freaking milk because this little guy has a ravenous appetite, just like his father."

"I heard that!" Hawk shouted in the background. They were in a hotel room in Dallas for a game.

Wolf and I didn't attend all the out-of-town games, as we usually kept things together back at the office.

"Well, you're sitting right next to me, so I sort of assumed you would hear me." Everly's head fell back in laughter, and Hawk's face appeared on the screen.

"What's up, girls? Dilly, I heard you got Wolf to agree to come to Honey Mountain for Thanksgiving. Things are getting serious, huh?" He bit into an apple and managed to chew and smile at the same time.

"It's not serious. It's temporary. But yes, we are going to his house for brunch that morning and then flying home in time for dinner. It's called compromise. I'm learning how to do it. It's a new skill for me." I reached for my glass and took a sip of wine.

Did it catch me off guard that we didn't want to be apart for Thanksgiving? Sure. Had I ever spent a holiday with a man before? No.

But, we both agreed it wasn't a big deal, and this is what we wanted to do.

For now.

"Um, I don't know a lot of temporary relationships that spend the holidays together." Ashlan shrugged as she lifted an orange and white mug to her mouth.

"We're making our own rules up as we go. But I'm telling you, I'm sure one of us will be sick of this soon."

"What's your safe word again?"

I spelled it out because Wolf and I had an agreement that we would never casually use the word. When I was fuming that Kressa had stopped by to see him, I didn't toss it out as a threat like I was tempted to do—we'd agreed. It would be a one-and-done with the safe word. We would only use it when one of us wanted out, and there would be no questions asked.

So, I wasn't even comfortable saying it. "W. I. N. X. Please don't say the word in front of me. I'm superstitious."

"You know… safe words are normally for people who are kinky in the bedroom, right? I've never met anyone who had a safe word to bail on a relationship that they wouldn't even call a relationship, even though they spend every minute of the day together. This whole thing is just craziness." Everly unlatched Jackson from her breast and then covered herself up after Hawk carried him away.

Everyone burst out in laughter at her words because none of them understood this agreement that Wolf and I had. And guess what? They didn't need to.

This was our thing, and we made the rules.

"This is how people who don't want relationships date. And trust me, we're plenty adventurous in the bedroom. I just don't need a safe word because I'd never tell him to stop." I waggled my brows, and Everly groaned.

"There's a baby in the room," she whisper-hissed.

"He lives off of breast milk; he can hardly understand the meaning of good sex." I raised a brow.

"Okay, so you have a safe word for when you've had enough. But you work together. You sleep together. You travel together. You've met one another's families. You're spending the holiday together. I'm sorry, Dilly, but this sure sounds like a relationship," Vivian said.

"I agree. And it's the best one you've ever had." Ashlan clapped her hands together.

"I can't believe he doesn't annoy you. That's unheard of for you," Charlotte said over her laughter.

"Oh, he annoys me plenty. I just sort of—*like it*. I'm bothered when he *isn't* annoying me." I took another sip of wine.

"Well, I don't see anyone using the safe word any time soon," Everly said. "And don't overthink it. You're happy. This doesn't make you less independent or less driven or less anything—you can love a man and still be *you*."

My mouth fell open, and I leaned forward to whisper. "Do not use the L-word. Jeez. That's as bad as the W-word."

Everyone was laughing, per usual, but I didn't find this funny at all.

"You mean the W. I. N. X. word?" Vivian could barely get the letters out as she chuckled uncontrollably.

"There's nothing wrong with having feelings for someone," Ashlan said, her eyes full of empathy.

"Okay. I'm done talking about this. I'll see you guys in two days for Thanksgiving. I'm going to call in for some takeout for me and my non-boyfriend, who I do not love. I actually tell him that I hate him every night before bed. And he hates me, too. This is what works for us."

More laughter and a few eye rolls, and we said our goodbyes.

Did I love Wolf Wayburn? Yes.

But no one needed to know that.

Not my sisters and not Wolf.

I was still processing the fact that I was in love with this man.

Now I just had to figure out what to do about it.

———

Thanksgiving brunch at the Wayburns' was what I imagined a holiday gathering was like at Buckingham Palace. They were throwing a small, intimate brunch for forty people. In my world, that was normally called a potluck or a barbecue.

But they'd extended the table to seat forty people, and their chef was doing all the cooking.

It was colder than usual for this time of year, and I'd worn the new cream sweaterdress that Wolf had bought me. He'd surprised me yesterday with the beautiful dress and some tall, gorgeous, brown leather boots that came just past my knees and ended at the bottom of my thighs, to go with it.

The gesture had been unexpected. Apparently, he'd gone shopping with Sabine, and he claimed he saw the dress and the boots and thought of me, and he knew I'd been working long hours and wouldn't have time to shop. He then followed that by saying it was no big deal at all.

It didn't mean anything.

Brenton, a man who worked for the Wayburns, whom I'd met when we'd come by for lunch last weekend, was greeting people at the door, and he took our coats.

There was a large Christmas tree in the entryway, and it was covered in white and silver ornaments with white twinkle lights.

Gweny appeared with her silver tray filled with glasses of what looked like champagne and orange juice.

Wolf kissed her cheek, and she smiled at me. "I'm so happy to see you two spending the holidays together."

"It's no big deal. We've all got to eat turkey, right?" Wolf said, his voice even, but his finger wrapped around mine for a brief couple of seconds as the words left his mouth.

The man was so confusing, and the mixed messages were starting to bother me.

He was attentive and thoughtful most days, but he also always made it clear that none of it meant anything.

And normally, I wouldn't care.

But for whatever reason, I cared.

I cared a lot.

And I hated it.

Because what we shared—it meant something to me.

And that pissed me off.

I reached for a glass and took a sip. "Thank you so much, Gweny. I hope you get to spend some time with your family today."

"Ah, yes. I'm heading home at two o'clock, and we'll be eating turkey and stuffing shortly after." She smiled before walking away.

"I'm so happy to see you, Dylan. My friend, Dylan, who I like so much," Miranda sang out, appearing out of nowhere and startling me a bit.

"Hey, Miranda. Happy Thanksgiving." I hugged her tight. The girl was quirky, but I liked her so much. I appreciated people who marched to the beat of their own drums, and Miranda did exactly that. She hugged Wolf, and he had a genuine smile on his face while she held the hug with him a little longer than most would. I noticed that when Wolf smiled and laughed, it was usually when we were alone or when he was around his family. I got it. I was the most comfortable in my own skin when I was with my family. The most at peace.

We clearly had that in common.

We were chatting with Miranda when Wolf's mom, Natalie, came around the corner. "Dylan, I'm so thrilled you could join us."

When she hugged me, it reminded me of the way my mom used to hug me. I felt all that warmth and love. This woman didn't know me all that well, but she acted like she'd known me my entire life. And I liked it.

A lump formed in my throat when I pulled away, and I found Wolf watching me. His gaze narrowed, and he looked concerned.

I forced a smile. "I'm so happy to be here. Thank you for having me."

She moved toward her son, but his gaze never left mine as he hugged her. Gweny called Natalie away, and she told us she'd be back shortly, and Miranda excused herself to use the restroom.

The front door flew open, and Jaqueline, Drake, and Slade walked in. Wolf had told me he'd invited them today, and I was looking forward to meeting them in person. He was worried about Bullet but wouldn't talk about it much with me. He'd just say that Bullet had left on a mission, and he hadn't heard from him and neither had Jaqueline.

Wolf tried to be there for them as much as he could. He'd taken the boys out trick-or-treating and called them several times a week. I'd been in the room on a couple of their Face-Time calls and had met Jaqueline and the boys. She was always so kind, but I saw the sadness in her eyes when we spoke.

"Uncle Wolfy!" Slade shouted and jumped into his arms.

"Hey." He bent down and scooped him up before Drake dove at him, as well. He held them both in his arms when he pushed to stand. He leaned over and kissed Jaqueline on the cheek as she slipped out of her coat. "I know you've all met on FaceTime, but now you can finally meet in person."

"You're pretty," Drake said as he squirmed out of Wolf's arms, and his brother did the same as he gaped up at me and nodded.

I chuckled and bent down to hug them before pushing to my feet.

Jaqueline pulled me in for a hug. I felt like I knew her better than I actually did because I knew about her husband being gone and Wolf spoke to her often.

"It's so nice to finally meet you in person, Dylan. And thank you so much for getting that book signed for me by your sister." She reached for my hands and didn't let them go. "I think you might be responsible for this one being a little less grumpy than usual."

Wolf grunted. "Please. I'm still grumpy."

"I can vouch for that," Seb said as he came around the corner. He took his turn hugging everyone, and Jaqueline dropped my hands, but every time I looked over, she was smiling at me.

Classical music was playing throughout the house, and Sabine came around the corner to greet us.

"Who wants to see all the holiday trees?" she asked, reaching for my hand.

Jaqueline and I both said we'd like to see them, and Wolf, Seb, Drake, and Slade all grumbled and made their way toward the parlor.

"Mom has twelve trees this year. Each one has a different theme," Sabine said as she led us through the grand estate. The formal living room had a tall white tree covered in angel ornaments. The family room donned a green pine that had to be at least twenty-five feet tall, drawing the eyes up to the vaulted ceilings. It was covered in Santa and snowmen ornaments with red-and-black plaid ribbon draping around it, layer by layer. I'd never seen anything more extravagant in my life. This house was decorated for the holidays, no matter which way you looked. We made our way to the library, which was filled with floor-to-ceiling cherrywood bookcases, and a dark leather couch sat in the center. In the corner, there was a pine tree that was a few feet taller than me, covered in Navy ornaments. I moved closer, inspecting them, as I'd never seen a tree like this. There were medals hung from the branches, as well, and when I turned them around, they were engraved on the back.

Wolfgang Wayburn.

Some were awards he'd earned for courage and leadership, and some were for specific achievements in battle and training. There were ornaments that were both the Navy and the SEAL logos, and there were ornaments of different countries. When I looked up, I saw Sabine and Jaqueline watching me.

"Those are for every country that Wolf has been to in his travels with the Navy. And then all his awards. Mom does a tree for each of us in different parts of the house, but Wolf's is definitely the best one. Mine and Seb's are just filled with silly things like the first car I drove and Seb's short-term interest in playing tennis. Wolf's tree really shows you all that he's accomplished."

I nodded.

It made me want to know even more about his life before I met him.

But he shared little bits and pieces each time we were together, and I wouldn't push, which was very out of character for me—but I respected that he protected his former life.

"That's amazing. He's quite the decorated officer."

"My husband says that Wolf is the best he's ever worked with. And Bullet is tough to get a compliment out of—unless you're his wife and kids, then he gushes all over you." Jaqueline chuckled.

I liked that I was learning more about this man every day.

And I only wanted more.

thirty

. . .

Wolf

WE'D TAKEN the helicopter to Honey Mountain after brunch with my family, and we were heading straight to Ashlan and Jace's house, as they were hosting this year. Apparently, the Thomas family switched off every year, and Dylan couldn't wait to get here.

She and Jaqueline had hit it off, which I'd expected. Sabine and Seb were crazy about her, and my mother pulled me aside to ask if we were officially dating today, and my father appeared to like her more than he liked me.

I hadn't prepared for this.

Hadn't seen her coming.

She'd weaned her way into my heart, one I didn't even know was still capable of feeling anything like this.

But I'd fucking fallen into the abyss with this woman.

When I'd get back from a mission, I'd let numbness overtake me. The things I saw. The things I'd done. The things that I'd experienced—they'd required compartmentalization. I'd learned to justify the things that I'd done, knowing they were for my country. There could be no second-guessing, no guilt. All of that curbing of emotions built a bastion inside of me that few could squeeze through. My family, of course, was welcomed in easily, though my mom thought I was closed off my first months back. But somehow, Dylan wormed her way in, and I know I didn't make it easy for her. And now, I know just how special she is.

I know that we belong together.

We'd set up all these fucking rules, and I didn't want to follow a single one of them anymore.

I wasn't an easy man. I was moody and grumpy most of the time. I focused on work, and I'd never had to make room for anyone. I'd kind of always been a bit of a loner, and the military enhanced that even more. It's how you stayed alive. Never trust anyone except your immediate team.

Dylan was part of my team now, and I didn't want to fuck that up.

Everyone wanted to know if we were dating. Of course, we were fucking dating. We spent the majority of our days together—every single day.

Every single night.

Now, I didn't know how to sleep *without* Dylan Thomas in my bed.

The sex was out of this world, and I fucking loved her.

That crazy, possessive, I-can't-live-without-you kind of love I'd always thought was foolish.

It was dangerous. And reckless.

Not something I ever craved or wanted.

So, I needed to think this through.

She and I never stopped reminding one another about the rules of this arrangement, and I wasn't sure how she really felt.

"Take a right at the corner," she said, pulling the mirrored visor down and applying some lipstick. "So, Jaqueline said she still hasn't heard from Bullet. Are you worried?"

"I don't know. No word doesn't necessarily mean anything is wrong. He could just be unable to reach out." I cleared my throat because I was fucking worried. My gut told me something wasn't right. I'd reached out to a few of my contacts at the Navy but hadn't heard anything back yet.

"That has to be hard, not hearing from her husband on the holidays," she said, as I pulled into the long, circular driveway and put the car into park.

"It's not an easy career path for families. It's why I kept my attachments light. Aside from my family, of which my mother and sister lost sleep when I was gone for weeks at a time, I didn't have anyone else."

She turned to face me. "Do you like it that way, Wolf?"

"I used to, for a long time."

"But now?" she asked, a wicked little grin on her pretty face.

"Things are—a little different now."

She rolled her eyes and smiled. "You're so stubborn. Come on. Let's get inside."

I held her hand but let her walk a little ahead of me so I could check out her ass in this dress. She looked fucking gorgeous.

I wanted to buy things for Dylan. Spoil her. Pamper her.

Take care of her.

But she was a strong woman, and I didn't want to scare her away.

Or maybe I was protecting myself, using that as an excuse not to go all in.

"I know you're watching my ass, you perv." She pushed open the door, and it was like walking into something straight out of a movie.

It was loud as conversation and laughter floated around the house. Ashlan came running over and lunged at her sister, while Jace extended his hand.

"Glad you could be here, Wolf. I think her sisters would have lost it if she wasn't here." He clapped a hand around my shoulder as his daughters raced toward Dylan, and she bent down to give them each a hug.

"You're handsome, and I'm Paisley. Are you Aunt Dilly's boyfriend?"

I glanced over at Dylan, and she smirked before leaning down. "Remember? I told you that no man was going to steal my heart. Wolf is my friend. But he is handsome."

Ouch.

Well, this was exactly why I needed to tread lightly.

"Pick me up, please," the smaller one said to me, holding her little arms up.

Jace chuckled. "That's Hadley. She'd have you carry her all around if you were willing."

She was freaking adorable. Her pudgy little hand landed on my cheek, and then she leaned her head on my shoulder.

We walked into the crowd and made our rounds, saying hello to everyone. This was normally not my thing. But I didn't mind it here.

There was so much love in the room, you couldn't miss it.

And everyone treated me like I was part of the family, whether we were dating or not.

I sipped my beer and settled beside Jack Thomas on the couch. The man had finally made a full recovery and was back to work full time, but that didn't stop Dylan from worrying about her dad. Ledger sat on the other side of him, and Niko sat in the chair across from me while Hawk stood, screaming at the TV as we watched the football game. Jace kept sneaking away to the kitchen to help Ashlan, but then he'd run back in to see what the score was.

My stomach rumbled because it smelled the turkey and pumpkin pie.

"Thanks for bringing her home in time for dinner," Jack said, turning to face me.

"Of course. Happy to be here."

"Spending the holidays together seems like a... thing... Am I right?" he asked, looking completely awkward, and I felt the way he looked.

"Shit. Are you trying to give him the birds and the bees talk?" Niko barked out a laugh. "He's here. She's here. They'll figure their shit out. Don't worry about it."

"This is my poetic son-in-law." Jack chuckled.

"I'll tell you what. As soon as we figure it out, you'll be the first to know." I felt like I should give him something more. He was her father. He loved her, and he was just looking out for her. "But—er—it's new for me, and I'm trying."

"You're good for her," Ledger said. "Charlie said she's never seemed happier."

"You're doing great, my brother. This is a good man right here." Hawk walked behind the couch and clapped me on the shoulder.

I couldn't help but laugh. "What is this? Some sort of induction?"

"Listen, if you can get past that one"—Jack flicked his thumb at Dylan—"you're already in. She's the toughest one to win over in this group."

"Tell me about it," I said, taking a long pull as they all covered their mouths to hide their smiles.

"Are you talking smack over there, big, bad Wolf?" Dylan shouted and came running over with her arms crossed over her chest.

"How did you possibly hear that over there?" Hawk's laughter bellowed around the room.

"My bat senses were going off." She raised a brow, and it took every bit of restraint I had not to yank her over to me and settle her onto my lap so I could kiss her senseless. This was a family gathering with kids running around, and I was fantasizing about her while I was sitting next to her father.

What kind of sick fucker does that?

This was what I was worried about. I'd killed people in battle. I had a temper and hadn't had a decent relationship since high school—and I wouldn't exactly call that one decent, anyway. And if Dylan Thomas wanted to leave right now and have sex before we ate turkey, I would run right out the door with her.

I was not boyfriend material.

"Hey, can you come help me with something?" She raised a brow. Everyone's attention was back on the TV, as the game was close.

I moved to my feet and followed her down the hallway to a bathroom. She closed the door and turned around to look at me. "What's going on? You looked like you were thinking really hard, sitting on that couch next to my father."

"How the fuck do you know me so well?"

She shrugged. "I'm very observant. What can I say? You look all perplexed."

"Did you bring me in here to have sex before turkey?"

Her eyes widened, and she chuckled. "No. Did you want sex before turkey? I mean, if it's important to you, we can sneak away to my house, but it's not happening in here. It's too small." That's my girl.

"I'm fine. But if you asked me to have sex with you, I'd always say yes." I shoved my hands into my pockets.

"So would I. Why are you saying this?"

"I'm just—fuck, Minx. I just don't think I'm what you need sometimes."

"Family gatherings can be a lot. You're exactly what I need right now, Wolf Wayburn. And I'm a fabulous lover, so don't beat yourself up for thinking about having sex with me all the time. Who could blame you?" She moved closer and tipped her head back so she could look at me. "Why are you over-thinking this? Nothing's changed since this morning."

"I don't know. Just thinking. I grew up with a lot of money, and it always bothered me a little bit." I shrugged. Which was a big part of why the military seemed the route to go. I wanted to give back.

"Why did it bother you?"

"Because everyone always assumes that everything you have is handed to you because you have more money than God. Big houses and all the toys and even a family that loves one another. But I never liked that people assumed everything that I achieved had been handed to me. It wasn't. It was probably a big reason I wanted to become a SEAL."

"Because you couldn't buy your way into it. You had to earn it, right?" she asked, her gaze empathetic and understanding.

"Yeah. The military has nothing to do with your social status or socioeconomic standing. You only make it if you earn your way there with hard work and discipline."

"I get that." Her fingers grazed mine as if she wanted to comfort me but wasn't sure she should. I intertwined my fingers with hers. I liked holding her hand.

"Being here—no one treats me like a spoiled rich kid. They aren't pretentious or judgmental, and I like them."

"And that freaks you out?" she asked. "Because you like my family, and you like me."

"No. I'm fine. I still hate you, Minx," I whispered, running the pad of my thumb over her pouty bottom lip.

"I hate you, too. And later tonight, we'll be alone, okay? Just you and me."

Someone shouted that dinner was ready, and she pushed up and kissed my cheek before leading me out of the bathroom.

We all gathered around the big table. The kids had a small table nearby, and I ate more food than I'd ever consumed in my life, and that was saying something because I'd always had a hearty appetite.

There were multiple conversations going on at the table as we passed the dishes around, and everyone was laughing and chatting and having a good time.

Dylan got up to get some more rolls for the table, and

Everly turned toward me as she was sitting on the other side of me.

"You're good for her, you know? I've never seen her this happy." She kept her voice low, looking around to make sure no one was listening.

I didn't feel the need to make something up and tell her it wasn't anything serious for some reason. Everly and I had become friends since working together for the Lions, and she loved her sister fiercely.

I leaned close to her. "I don't know about that, Ever. But I do know she's good for me. And that scares the shit out of me."

When I pulled back, she was smiling at me, her eyes wet with emotion. "I know you are. And so is she. But neither of you are people who run from their fears. Love is scary. But it's also amazing."

"Okay, more rolls so we can all carbo load," Dylan said, handing the basket to her father and sitting back down beside me.

Everly winked before turning her attention back to little Jackson, who was sitting on Hawk's lap beside her.

They all proceeded to tell stories, and most of them revolved around Dylan, the beautiful woman sitting beside me. How, when she was young, she'd once taken a frozen turkey their mom had been thawing in the sink and hidden it in the garage because she didn't want them to eat it.

"Hey! I was six years old. I didn't know it was already dead. I thought cooking him would kill him." She threw her hands in the air, and everyone burst out into a fit of laughter.

"Yeah, well, you refused to tell me where you hid him, and my entire garage stunk until I found him buried under a bunch of towels in my cleaning bucket," Jack said, swiping at the tear running down his face from laughing so hard.

"Rest in Peace, Joshua the turkey." Dylan put her hands together as if she were praying.

There was so much more to this woman than most people knew. She was sexy and sassy and smart as hell. But she was also tenderhearted and would do anything for the people she loved. She was fierce and strong but also guarded and cautious.

Dylan Thomas was what had been missing from my life.

This wasn't temporary—this was forever.

After a lot of laughs, way too much food, and a few intense rounds of board games with her sisters and their husbands after the kids went to bed, we headed back to Dylan's place.

We didn't have sex. We were both exhausted and full, and she'd fallen asleep on me two minutes after we'd slipped into bed.

I watched her sleep and stroked her hair, and she moaned a little bit as she curled into me.

"I fucking love you, Dylan Thomas," I whispered and closed my eyes.

I felt a weight lift off my shoulders once I said it. Words I never thought I'd say to a woman that wasn't my mother or sister.

Even though she hadn't heard me say it, I had.

And it felt good to say it out loud.

thirty-one

. . .

Dylan

WE'D JUST RETURNED to the city after we'd spent the weekend in Honey Mountain. I'd taken Wolf out to the ski slopes a few times, and he was as competitive as I was. We'd raced down the hills over and over, and neither of us had ever gotten ahead of the other.

We'd hung out with my family every night. Having Wolf around the people I loved most in the world—it meant something to me.

He means something to me.

I wanted to tell him that I loved him, but I was fairly certain he would freak out and run for the door.

We could take our time.

We'd eventually get there, right?

A large hand wrapped around my stomach and pulled me closer. "Why are you up so early, Minx? What time is it?"

"I don't know. I couldn't sleep, I guess. It's almost six o'clock."

His hand moved lower, settling between my legs. "Tell me what you're thinking about."

"I must have been dreaming about you on that ski slope,

practically naked," I said with a moan as he stroked me slowly.

"Mmmmm, I see. Well, I'm naked right now."

"Yes, you are. What should we do about that?"

"I don't know. You're awfully wet for six o'clock in the morning." His voice was gruff as he continued to stroke me. He nipped on my earlobe before flipping on top of me, the sheet draped over his head as he moved down and pushed my legs apart.

"This isn't a bad way to start the day," I groaned as his tongue swiped along my most sensitive area, waking up every nerve ending in my body as my eyes rolled closed.

"This is my favorite way to start the day." He looked up at me with this sleepy, sexy smile, the white sheet forming a hood around his face. I shoved him back down, and he chuckled as his lips covered my clit, and I gasped.

He licked and nibbled and took his sweet time.

He'd bring me close to the edge and then slow things down.

My fingers yanked at his hair, my forehead covered in a layer of sweat, as I bucked against his mouth, desperate for release.

"Please," I begged, and I tugged hard on his hair because I was frustrated.

He looked up, his mouth glossy, and his tongue swiped out along his bottom lip, and a sexy moan escaped his mouth.

"I don't want to stop. You have the sweetest pussy. I could die a happy man right here." He raised a brow.

"You will die an unhappy man if you don't let me finish," I panted.

He chuckled and dove back down. And this time, he didn't slow down.

His tongue slipped inside, and I nearly came off the bed as I arched and bucked and writhed beneath him.

His hands gripped my hips firmly, and his tongue continued to slide in and out until I couldn't see straight.

"Oh my god," I cried out as little bursts of light exploded behind my eyes. My hands fell from his head and gripped the sheets as the most powerful orgasm I'd ever experienced exploded through my body.

I shook and whimpered, and he didn't let up. He held me there as I rode out every last bit of pleasure.

When my body stopped shaking, and my breathing slowed, he raised his head from between my legs, which made me laugh.

"Better?" He quirked a brow.

"I mean... I guess. I barely noticed." I laughed, and he pulled himself up and tickled me until I couldn't take it. "Fine. Yes. It was life changing. You're the best lover I've ever had, Wolf Wayburn."

"Damn straight. And don't you forget it." His dark blue eyes locked with mine, and his head moved when his phone vibrated on the nightstand.

"Who would be calling you this early?" I asked.

He shifted off me like he couldn't get to the phone fast enough, and he looked down at the screen. "Fuck."

I pushed to sit up. "What is it?"

He stormed through his bedroom, dialing a number and pulling on his briefs before he held the phone to his ear. "Tell me."

Tell him what?

I hurried to my feet and pulled on my panties and found Wolf's big Navy sweatshirt and slipped it over my head before padding out to the living room. He was pacing in front of the window, his muscles straining as his fist clenched on his free hand. I put on some coffee, figuring he'd need it for whatever he was dealing with.

"How long?" he growled, and he looked up when I

offered him a cup of coffee, but he shook his head, his gaze locked with mine.

This was bad. I knew it in my gut.

"Of course, I'll be there. I'll be on the next flight." He moved toward the laptop sitting on the kitchen island and pulled up an airline and typed in Quetta International Airport while listening intently to the person on the phone.

"You waited too fucking long," he hissed and ran a hand through his hair before slamming his laptop closed.

"Yes. I can do it. I'll leave shortly and see you tomorrow. Get the team ready." He ended the call and stormed toward his bedroom.

"Wolf." I walked behind him and almost had to jog to keep up. "What's going on?"

He pulled a duffle bag from his closet and tossed a few items of clothing into it before turning to face me. "I have to leave. I can't tell you much more than I'm going to Pakistan to find Bullet."

"What? You can tell me more because you aren't in the Navy anymore."

He moved to the built-in drawers in his closet and pulled out some briefs and socks and added them to the bag along with a pair of boots. "I'm going as an independent contractor."

"Wait." I reached for his arm and forced him to stop moving. "Where is he? Please tell me what's going on."

Was I breathing heavily?

Why were my hands tingling?

"Bullet has been fucking taken prisoner. He's being held somewhere in Afghanistan." His gaze locked with mine, and his jaw ticked.

"Why do you need to go? They already have people there. It's dangerous." My voice cracked, and a large lump formed in the back of my throat.

"Because I've trained to do this. Because I'm his best shot.

They aren't searching for him. We're going to put together a small team of our own, and I'll go in. He's got a wife and kids, Dylan. I can't leave him there. I can't."

"You've got me," I croaked, sounding so pathetic and desperate I barely recognized my own voice. Even as I said it, I thought of Jaqueline and the boys and knew he needed to go if he thought he could make a difference. But I was scared to death.

"I've already told you more than I should. Do not tell anyone where I'm going. Say that you don't know, and I didn't tell you anything when my family hounds you. You need to just trust me, okay?" He squeezed my hand before turning around and bending down to zip up his bag. "I have to go now. I'll be in touch when I can."

When he walked out of the closet, his long strides moved down the hallway, and I chased after him. "I'm coming with you. Give me five minutes."

He whipped around, and my chest crashed into his. "No fucking way. Don't even think about it."

"I can just be there waiting, so at least I'll be there if anything happens and you need me."

He put his hand on my cheek, and I could see the struggle in his dark blue gaze. He was conflicted. He knew this was dangerous. Would this be the last time I'd see him?

"That's not how this works, Minx. You can't help me with this. You aren't trained, and it isn't safe. I'll contact you as soon as I can. Stay. Fucking. Put. Do you hear me?"

Tears were streaming down my face now, and I didn't care. "You can't tell me what to do. I know you're flying into Quetta International Airport. I saw you book the flight, and I'm quite capable of booking my own flight, too."

"Do you know how fucking dangerous that would be?" he shouted, and he pulled his hand away like I'd just threatened his life. "Do not fucking leave this country. Do you hear me?"

"I—I." I swallowed the lump in my throat and swiped at my face. "I love you. I'm coming with you."

His eyes softened for a brief second, but they hardened just as quickly. He moved close to me and bent down so his face was right in front of mine. "Winx."

"What?" I gasped.

"You heard me. This is done. It ends now. Do not fucking follow me." He stormed out the door, and I stood there in complete shock.

What just happened?

I raced toward the door and yanked it open just as he stepped into the elevator.

"If you leave now, don't even think about coming back," I sobbed hysterically as he just stared at me without saying a word. "Fuck you, Wolf."

The elevator closed, and I slammed the door and marched to the bedroom, dropping down to sit on the bed.

Oh my gosh. Was I actually crying?

I'd fucking lost it.

He was the big, bad Wolf.

But why did it hurt so much?

My chest ached.

I picked up my phone and did the only thing I knew would help.

I sent a text in my sisters' group chat.

Me ~ I told him I loved him, and he said WINX! He ended it. And I'm crying real tears. I really do hate him now. He ruined me.

I couldn't stop the tears from falling as I gathered up all my stuff and made my way back to my apartment. I dropped everything on the floor and climbed into my bed and turned off my phone. I didn't want to talk about it. My sisters would know that I wanted to be alone. Everything ached, and that pissed me off. I didn't want to think anymore. I didn't want to hurt anymore.

I squeezed my eyes closed until sleep finally took me.

A loud banging on the door woke me, and I startled. I glanced around the room, and it was gray outside, which made it impossible to know what time it was or how long I'd slept, but I guessed that it had been several hours. I pulled on a pair of leggings beneath Wolf's sweatshirt.

I closed my eyes and sniffed it because it smelled like him.

And apparently, I loved the smell of the devil.

Because I was a masochist. I'd fallen in love with a man who wasn't capable of loving anyone but himself.

And his family.

And obviously Bullet.

I'd fallen in love with a man who wasn't capable of loving me.

He didn't love me.

And I'd put myself out there.

I hated him for that.

I whipped open the door to find Everly, Vivian, Charlotte, and Ashlan standing there.

"Well, you look like hell," Everly said as she raised a brow.

"Come here." Charlotte wrapped her arms around me.

"What are you doing here?" I asked, as the tears started to fall again. "Oh my god. I'm crying again. Real human tears. That fucker has me all messed up. I can't even channel my inner bitch long enough to hate him. But I do hate him. I hate him so much." I sobbed as Charlotte pulled back to look at me.

Vivian's eyes were wide as she wrapped her arms around me. "You're just sad. It's okay to be sad."

They all stepped inside my apartment, and Everly closed the door. Ashlan reached for my hand and walked us toward the couch, where we sat, and I wiped away my tears again with the sleeve of Wolf's hoodie.

"Tell us what happened," Everly said.

And I told them everything. Well, not the part about me waking up to him between my legs or the most powerful orgasm of my life. I started with the phone call. I couldn't tell them where he'd gone because apparently, I still felt the need to protect the bastard. I told them that it was a very dangerous country and that he was going to help a friend, and the situation was bad. Really bad. And the tears came again. And I let it all out.

"Wait. You told him you were going to book a flight to the…" Everly used two fingers on each hand with dramatic effect. "'Dangerous country' and then said I love you after?"

"You know I hate when you do air quotes. It's very annoying."

"It looks like you're channeling your inner bitch just fine." She raised a brow. "Answer the question," Charlotte said.

"Does it matter when I said it? I put myself out there. I tried to go with him and then threatened to go on my own because I freaking loved him. I made a fool of myself."

"Ummm, it kind of matters. I mean, clearly, he wanted to protect you," Ashlan said, looking at me like I had three heads. "You left out a pretty important piece of information in your text."

"I think he loves you, too, and that's why he said W.I.N.X.," Charlotte said, wrapping an arm around my shoulder and kissing my cheek.

"You don't have to spell it anymore. He already said it. It's done. He does not love me. I told him that I loved him, and he used the safe word. Not that we were even really dating. It was a fling. A fling that I fell for," I groaned. "Why did the first man that I've ever loved have to be the big, bad Wolf?"

Vivian started laughing first, and then the other three followed.

"This is funny to you? My sadness is humorous?" I hissed as a knock on my door had us all straightening.

"Are you expecting company?" Ashlan asked.

"Maybe he sent someone to evict me. Nothing would surprise me at this moment." I moved to my feet and yanked the door open to find a very upset Sabine and Sebastian.

Sabine's eyes were all puffy and red as she lunged into my arms. "Please tell us you know where he is."

Sebastian stepped inside and closed the door behind him. "He sent a text to all of us saying he had to go away but couldn't say where or why. Our parents are an absolute mess. My mom is losing it. Please tell us he told you where he was going."

And even though I hated him at the moment, all that worry was still there.

I couldn't break his trust.

"I'm sorry. I can't tell you where he went, but just know it's to help someone in need. Because that's the kind of man he is. He protects the ones he loves."

And apparently, so do I.

thirty-two

. . .

Wolf

FOUR DAYS.

Four fucking days we'd been camped out, waiting for the right moment to go in.

Six fucking days since I'd left Dylan.

Life was all about choices, and loving her meant protecting her. When she'd threatened to come after me, I saw the look in her eyes. She'd meant it.

She'd be crazy enough to fly to Pakistan alone and try to find my ass.

I was on edge over Bullet being missing, but I couldn't fucking fathom the thought of anyone hurting her.

I'd burn down the whole fucking city.

No. I'd done the right thing.

I'd get Bullet out safely, threaten his ass to retire and be with his family, and I'd go home to my girl.

Thinking about her was not wise. This is why I'd never allowed myself to have attachments. They were dangerous in war.

I'd tried hard to get my head on straight, but I couldn't get the thought of her with tears streaming down her face out of my head.

I love you.

The words played over and over in my mind.

I'd said them to her just days before, but she hadn't heard me. It was probably for the best. The more she hated me right now, the less risk I had of her doing something crazy, like getting on a plane and heading into a fucking war zone.

I'd called my PI and had him follow her, with strict instructions to stop her from getting on a plane. I'd sent a cryptic text to Hawk, asking for his help. I couldn't say much, but I'd said I needed him to make sure he kept her safe, which meant her staying in the US, and that was all I could share.

The man hadn't asked one question. He'd understood and responded with a message letting me know that he'd make sure she didn't leave the country and he'd keep her safe. He'd told me to be careful and get home safely.

Why couldn't she have made things easy?

Why couldn't she have trusted me enough to just say goodbye and remain calm?

That wasn't who she was, and I couldn't fault her for it because that was what I fucking loved about her.

She was passionate and strong and stoic.

"Wolf. Today's the day. They're down two guys. This is our chance to strike. As soon as it's dark, we're going. Are you ready?" Birddog asked. He'd been my captain for the last five years that I'd been a SEAL. I trusted him with my life.

"Fuck yeah. It's about time."

This was somewhat of a covert operation with just our team. Bullet had been taken because he had special missile training, and al-Qaeda thought he was more valuable to the US than he actually was. They wanted money for him, and the US wasn't about to shell out that kind of money to terrorists, not even for one of their own.

We'd received proof of life three days ago and were fairly certain he was being held in a cave on the border of Pakistan and Afghanistan. We'd hiked in and set up camp a few miles away, where we'd taken turns going in and watching their patterns.

"First, we get him out. Then we figure out how to get the fuck out of here. I've got Scotty One nearby, and if all goes smoothly, they will be here for us when we're ready. I'll make the call when you go in, and I'll have them here when you come out." He clapped me on the shoulder. Scotty One was what he called the team in the air. The helicopter would come in, and we'd be ready.

If all went well.

Which didn't always happen.

We didn't know what condition Bullet was in or if he was still alive, as we hadn't heard anything in forty-eight hours.

But I knew in my gut that he was alive.

He'd been there for me when I thought I'd seen my last day on this earth.

He'd saved my life.

And it was time for me to return the favor.

I huddled the guys around me. Three I'd worked with before, and two that were new on the team. Birddog assured me they were the best, and I knew they wouldn't be here if that wasn't true. But they were still green. They were young. And going into battle the first few times could fuck with your head, no matter how much training you'd had.

"Dagger and Bear, you're going to go out first. Take out the two dudes guarding the cave. Clark, Stealth, and Limbs, you move forward and guard the cave. There should only be two men inside with Bullet, so if you don't hear from me, I've either got them or I'm dead." I paused, and Dagger's eyes were wide.

"How will we know?" he asked.

"Oh, you'll fucking know," Stealth said with a chuckle. "Wolf wouldn't go down quietly. If you hear a fight, we're moving in. We'll give you three minutes to either get in and get it done or give us word you're okay, or we're coming in."

"They aren't deep in the cave. I better have my ass out of there with Bullet by then. If not, it's all hands on deck. Go in blazing and get our brother out of there."

"I'll be nearby with the chopper, waiting for you. If you have Bullet, get the fuck out of there and get your asses on it so we can get out of here before they realize we were here." Birddog handed me some beef jerky. "Eat. You're going to need your fuel because you may need to carry his ass out of there."

I took the stick of beef and ate it quickly.

I was ready.

We were ready.

The next two hours were brutal. We went over our plan several times, and then we waited. I thought of Dylan. I wrote her a note just in case something happened to me and I didn't get out of here. I needed her to know the truth. I made my way over to Birddog and handed it to him.

"Anything happens to me, you get this to my family and ask them to give this to Dylan Thomas, okay?"

"You going soft on me, Wolf?" He smirked.

"Never soft. Just a dude who loves a girl."

"Fuck me. I never thought I'd see the day. But don't you fucking make me deliver this letter. Get Bullet and get the fuck out of there. You got it?"

"That's the plan."

He tucked the note into his back pocket and studied me. "You sure you don't want to have Stealth go in? You can stay outside the cave."

He was giving me the safer path. Not that we weren't all at risk, because we were. But going into a dark cave with armed terrorists was definitely not the least risky position. I've got the skill set and experience—it was my job.

"I've got this. I'll bring him out if it's the last thing I do."

"That's what fucking worries me, brother."

We all got quiet, which meant we were getting ready. Dagger walked over, as he'd been on the final watch, making sure no one else showed up to guard Bullet. Surprises were never good, and we were fairly certain we now outnumbered them. They also weren't expecting us, so we had the element of surprise. It could work both ways, though, because we had no way of knowing if there was another way into or out of the cave from the other side, or if a crew had been inside before we arrived that we weren't aware of.

Surprises could cost you your life.

You prepared for every scenario and always had an exit strategy.

Aside from things like this today.

There was no exit strategy without Bullet. I was going in regardless if there were two or ten men guarding him. I wasn't going to leave my brother there alone.

It wasn't happening.

This is why I needed to say goodbye to Dylan quickly. If she'd asked me too much. If she'd pushed me—I wouldn't lie to her.

Hell, I hadn't told my own family about where I was going and what I was doing. I'd told her because I fucking trusted her.

But for all I knew, she could tell my family, who could make calls to the Navy and blow things up. Hell, my father would send a team of men here to get me out if he knew where I was.

But I'd learned a long time ago that you have to have faith in something if you want to survive. And for whatever reason, I had faith in Dylan Thomas.

Not that she wouldn't try something crazy like get on a plane and fly her ass to Pakistan. But for whatever reason, I believed that she wouldn't tell anyone where I was, no matter how hurt or pissed she was.

I'd said the one thing that I thought would keep her safe.

But that could backfire on me, too.

She had a temper, and that made telling her where I was going very dangerous.

Yet I'd done it without hesitation.

"Okay, boys, it's time. Scotty One is nearby and ready to go. The minute Wolf goes in, he's in the air. In and out. Clean and easy. Let's do this."

We all huddled together one last time and slapped each other's backs, then I turned to Dagger and Bear. "You've got this. We're right behind you."

"We got you, Wolf," Bear said, giving me a quick nod.

"In and out." Dagger cleared his throat, and they both took off jogging as we tucked behind.

Once we were close enough, they both held up a hand to let us know they were going in. I let out one last breath when they took off. We wouldn't hear gunshots because the last thing we needed was to warn the guys inside that we were here. That we were coming for Bullet.

We gave them a thirty-second lead, and then I signaled for Clark, Stealth, and Limbs to fall behind me.

Adrenaline pumped as my eyes scanned left to right in my night vision goggles, which allowed me to see in the dark. I looked for movement in the grass or in the trees around us. The weather was chilly, but it didn't bother me. The cold had never been a problem for me. I'd always adjusted easily to different climates both in and out of the water.

Bear and Dagger stood in front of the cave and gave me a thumbs-up, letting me know they'd taken care of the two men guarding the cave.

It was game time.

I moved inside, my guys remaining outside the cave just in case things went sideways. It would allow time for them to get away. All of us storming the castle could be catastrophic. Two lives lost would be better than seven.

That's just the brutal truth of it.

I moved in slowly, and I heard voices that sounded like they were only a few feet away. I rounded the corner, and a light hung from above where I saw Bullet strapped to a chair, his head hanging forward, which had my blood pumping. I couldn't tell if he was alive.

I couldn't think about it.

I had to move.

React.

I took my first shot when I realized there were three guys there. The first two dropped to the ground, and Bullet's head shot up just as another guy pointed a gun at Bullet. I shot him without hesitation, and he dropped just as his gun fired up at the ceiling.

Fuck.

If their camp was close, they'd just gotten warning that we were here.

I unstrapped Bullet from the chair. "Can you walk?"

"I don't think so. My legs are broken," Bullet said, and I knew by his voice that he was wounded pretty badly.

I glanced at the other two bodies on the ground. They were grown men still holding their weapons. This was battle, and they were prepared to kill both Bullet and me. War was ugly and unfair and inhumane all at the same time.

But it was the name of the game.

"Wolf!" Clark shouted. "You guys whole?"

"Yep. We're coming out. Is the chopper here?"

"It is!" he hollered. "But that gunshot was loud. I'm guessing we're going to have company soon."

I lifted Bullet's giant fucking body and tossed him over my shoulder. The dude was definitely down a good twenty pounds, but he was still a big guy. None of that mattered. I wasn't leaving here without him.

"Go!" I shouted as I ran toward the exit.

Bullet didn't make a sound, and his body was limp as I

hauled ass out of the cave with him hanging over my shoulder. I heard shouting in the distance.

"Let's go!" Birddog shouted from the other direction, where he called from the helicopter, as a sharp pain hit me in the calf.

I didn't look back, and I didn't stop running.

Whatever the fuck it was—it was going to take a hell of a lot more to stop me.

Everything moved in slow motion, and all of our guys stood in the helicopter and started firing their weapons, which meant I had guys right behind me. Stealth and Bear dropped their weapons and yanked Bullet from my shoulder as I dove into the helicopter, my legs still hanging out as we took off. Gunshots filled the air around us as Birddog pulled me in. Our guys continued shooting as did the men from the ground.

Once we were up in the air, everyone lowered their weapons, and we made our way back to Pakistan where we'd go to the safe house and check on Bullet's wounds before getting the fuck out of there.

"How is he?" I asked as I tossed my goggles beside me and pushed to sit up, leaning against Bear's legs as he sat in the seat.

"Well, it took you guys long enough," Bullet said and then groaned.

"Shut up, fucker. We got you out," Birddog said, but I heard the concern in his voice. "You've got a few broken bones, I think, but it's this nasty infection on your leg I'm worried about. We'll get you checked out as soon as we're on the ground."

"Did any of those bullets hit you, Wolf?" Dagger asked as the wind whipped around us.

"I may have taken one to my leg. We'll see when we land."

"You're bleeding pretty heavily on your arm," Stealth said, bending down to assess me with a flashlight.

I glanced down. "Nah. I think it just grazed me."

"You don't bleed like that from getting grazed, brother." Birddog's tone was harsh.

I closed my eyes and listened to the sound of the propeller and the whistling of the wind and the voices of my brothers.

They moved around me, wrapping something tightly around my arm and leg.

Whatever it was, we'd deal with it.

Both me and Bullet.

We were both breathing and whole, and that's all that mattered.

"Wolf, I knew you'd come," Bullet said, and he reached for my hand. "My brother."

"Always." I squeezed his hand, and the further we moved from the cave, the more my shoulders relaxed.

I thought of Dylan. Imagined her scowling at me and angry that I'd been shot.

That I'd left her.

I thought of those dark brown eyes—which were always more yellow than brown when she was angry—as she glared at me the last time that I saw her when she'd told me to fuck off.

And then I remembered what she'd said before that.

I love you.

I love you, too.

And everything went dark.

thirty-three

. . .

Dylan

WOLF HAD BEEN GONE for nine days, and I hadn't heard from him. His family called to tell me they'd gotten word from someone at the Navy three days ago that he and Bullet were both okay, and they would return home soon. They hadn't heard anything from him either.

I didn't get the call from the Navy because I wasn't his wife or even his girlfriend, for that matter.

Hell, I didn't even know if I was his friend anymore.

But I did know one thing. Those six days without a word had been excruciating. I hadn't slept and had barely eaten as worry had taken over. Even though I'd been angry at him, I'd been overcome with fear once the realization had settled in that first night that I might never see him again. My father had showed up on my doorstep the day my sisters left to go back home, and he'd slept on my couch for the last few days. I'd been like a zombie at work, but I'd forced myself to carry on. Everyone at the office was somber, but no one talked about the fact that we didn't know where Wolf was.

Well, they didn't know where Wolf was.

They knew he was on a mission and that it was dangerous.

But I knew where he was. I knew what he was doing.

Duke had tried every tactic in the book to get me to talk, and honestly, I'd almost spilled the beans a few times because a part of me worried that my keeping quiet could cost Wolf his life.

But the other part of me, the part of me that knew this man so well, knew that he'd want me to respect his oath.

So, I'd refused to speak.

And I'd carried that weight with me for six long days before we'd heard anything.

And now I was angrier than ever that he was okay and hadn't even bothered to pick up the phone and call anyone.

The bastard.

It was easier to hate Wolf Wayburn than to love him.

But I didn't know how to stop loving him.

I'd gone my whole damn life without loving anyone but my family, and now I'd fallen in love with a man that was making me insane, and I couldn't stop.

My father and I had driven back to Honey Mountain for the weekend yesterday. He thought being home would do me some good.

But it had been more of the same misery, just with different scenery.

Sabine and Seb and I had been texting multiple times a day.

We'd all check on one another.

Natalie phoned me daily, even though I'd told her that Wolf had ended things with me the day that he left. She didn't seem deterred. She told me I was an important part of her son's life, which made me an important part of her life.

I sat on my bed in my guest cottage at Everly and Hawk's place, wearing my long underwear and a heavy sweater because it was so freaking cold outside, and I couldn't shake this sadness that had consumed me in a way that was so unfamiliar I didn't know how to pivot.

The last time that I felt a deep sadness in my life was when my mother passed. It was this heavy weight that sat on my chest for such a long time. An emptiness that couldn't be filled. But time had healed my wounds slowly—not completely—but I didn't wake up feeling that weight of it every day anymore. And I'd made a conscious effort not to ever go there again if I could control it. I already loved my dad and my sisters and their kids and their husbands, and I couldn't change that. But I was careful who I gave a piece of my heart to. I always had been.

But I'd let my guard down with Wolf.

I remembered one of the last conversations I'd had with my mama before her body couldn't fight the cancer any longer. My sisters were all crying as we sat around her bed in our living room. Vivian had sobbed that she wouldn't be at our graduations or at our weddings and all that hoopla. Everly had yelled at her for saying it and making our mom feel bad. Charlotte had cried because they were fighting. Ashlan was too young to understand what was happening, and she just sat there crying because she was scared.

But I didn't cry that day.

And that's the day that our mother decided who would be the maid of honor for each of us at our weddings, and I think it was her way of being there before everyone even walked down the aisle.

When they'd all left the room and it was just me and my mother there, she asked me why that hadn't made me sad. I remember the conversation so clearly; it felt like it had happened yesterday.

"You know it's okay to be sad, right? This isn't fair, and you're allowed to be angry and sad and confused and all those things. But don't hold that all in, okay? Will you promise me that?"

"Yes. But that's not why it didn't bother me."

"What is it, then?"

"I'm never getting married, Mama. I don't need a man to rescue me. I'm going to change the world all by myself."

She chuckled. Her lips were dry, and her hand was limp when it covered mine. "Oh, no doubt about it. You certainly will. But don't run from love, okay? You have such a big heart, my Dilly girl. And one day, someone is going to come into your life, and you'll just know. You'll know that's your person." Her voice was weak.

"Well, they'll have to find me because I won't be looking."

She smiled. Her skin was so pale she was barely recognizable. "They will. Trust me."

"Well, you were right, Mama. He found me. He stomped on my heart. And then he fled the country. I sure can pick 'em, right?" I said to no one, but I did this often with my mother. I'd always felt her presence.

There was a knock on my door, and I startled before moving to my feet and padding through the tiny guest house to the door. Everly stood on the other side, wearing a white snowsuit with fur all around the hood. She had on a white beanie, and her dark hair hung down to her shoulders.

"Hey. Where are you going?" I glanced outside to see the snow coming down again. We had gotten a few feet of snow this week, and Honey Mountain looked like a winter wonderland.

"Hawk's parents are watching Jackson so we can hit the slopes. Come with us?"

I shook my head. "I'm not feeling it today."

"Dylan, listen to me. Hawk has been working so much with all the games they've had. He wants to ski, but I'm so freaking tired between work and the baby. I have my Kindle hidden in my coat, and I'd love to sneak away and drink hot chocolate and read Ash's new book. But you know how Hawk is. He wants to be challenged on the mountain, and I —" She shrugged.

"You suck at skiing. You're too cautious."

She laughed. "Well, thank you for that. And you're the

only one who can give the man a run for his money. Please. It'll do you good to get outside, and the slopes have always been your happy place." She put her hands together like she was praying, and I rolled my eyes.

But she was right. I wasn't this girl. I didn't sit inside sulking over a man who'd kicked my ass to the curb.

Hells to the no.

"Fine. Give me five minutes," I said, and she jumped up and down a few times and followed me inside.

I pulled out my black ski pants and matching jacket. A black turtleneck. A black beanie. Black gloves. Black goggles.

"Wow. You're really going for the all-black look, I see. Like a cloud of darkness on the white snow." Everly raised a brow.

Yeah. My outfit matches my black, jaded heart.

"Hey, if you want me to come, you don't get to judge the outfit." I brushed my hair into a low ponytail so I could pull on my beanie easily. I slipped on my ski pants and jacket and grabbed my ski boots to bring with me.

"Deal. And Hawk has already loaded your skis from the garage."

I quirked a brow as we walked toward the door. "Someone was feeling awfully confident that I would come."

"I wasn't going without you, so I planned to drag you out that door if I had to."

When we stepped outside, I looked up and let the snow hit me in the face. I loved winter in Honey Mountain. The downtown area was decorated with white lights zigzagging back and forth across Main Street. Large baskets with poinsettias hung from all the streetlights. Holiday music was piped through the speakers, and everyone was in the spirit.

I would most likely be the only person in this town dressed in all black, channeling my inner Johnny Cash, and I was just fine with it.

I'd never been good at faking my feelings, so I wouldn't start now.

"There's our little princess of darkness." Hawk's laughter bellowed around the large driveway. He picked me up and spun me around. "You're going to be all right, Dilly. I need you to trust me on that."

I nodded when he set me down because that was just who Hawk was. He wanted everyone he loved to be happy. He couldn't stand to see anyone upset.

The drive to the lodge was as entertaining as a ride could be when you felt like you just wanted to go back home and climb under the covers.

Everly was going to stop nursing this week, and she'd read everything under the sun about weaning baby Jackson off her breast milk.

"What if he's upset, though?" she said, and Hawk reached for her hand beside him.

"Baby, he's going to be just fine."

"You can't keep him on the tit forever," I said dryly because I was annoyed that I was even here.

This is the last place I wanted to be. I wanted to wallow in my own little private pity party, but Everly had dragged me out here to ski, not to talk about her engorged bosoms.

She sighed and turned around in her seat to look at me. "I'm glad you came."

That was not the typical response from her after what I'd just said, and I narrowed my gaze.

"Do not feel sorry for me. I just said something rude. The least you could do is bite back. Don't be nice; it only makes me feel like a loser."

Hawk laughed, and Everly shook her head and reached for my hand. "Is it so awful that your family loves you and wants to be there for you?"

I closed my eyes when we pulled into the ski resort parking lot, and I counted down from ten. "No one needs to be there for me. I'm fine. You're the one who constantly has milk leaking from your breasts—let's focus on that."

Everly chuckled, and Hawk put the truck into park. I jumped out and made my way to the back, anxious to hit the slopes now that I was here.

"So, I'm going to go to the lodge and have some hot chocolate and read for a bit. You go race Dilly down that mountain, okay?" She pushed up on her tiptoes and kissed his cheek before doing the same to me. "I love you, sissy. Even when you're grumpy."

She was acting a little strange. A bit too chipper. But maybe this was just her hormones reacting to all the changes in her body as she weaned little Jackson off her breast milk. We both waved goodbye and slipped into our ski boots, tucking our shoes back into the truck. Hawk grabbed my skis and poles for me, and we walked toward the hill.

"I know it's hard for her to stop nursing. I shouldn't have joked about it."

Hawk tossed our ski equipment over his shoulder and glanced at me. "You going soft on me, Dilly?"

"Never."

He came to a stop in the snow and set down the skis for us. I stepped onto mine, my boots clamping in with a snap.

"It's okay to be sad, Dilly. You love him. You're worried about him. I've been there, and I get it." He handed me my poles and pulled his beanie over his head.

"I hate him for making me love him," I whispered, surprised by my own words. But Hawk was that guy... He had a huge heart and would never share what I told him with anyone else. He never judged or made you feel stupid for saying what you felt.

He nodded. "Listen, it's never easy. The question is, is it worth fighting for?"

"Worth fighting for? There's nothing to fight for. He's gone. He ended it. He left me."

"Do you really believe that?" he asked before letting out a long breath. "Everly and I went through a whole lot before we found our way back to one another. And sometimes, people leave because they think they're protecting the people they love. So don't jump to conclusions. He'll be back, and I'm sure he'll explain what happened to you then. Give it time."

A lump formed in my throat. "I told him I loved him, and he ended it. He doesn't love me."

"Are you kidding me? You're Dylan freaking Thomas. Who wouldn't love you? I don't buy it."

"I'm hard to love," I finally said, holding my poles out to the sides. "I'm snarky and untrusting and difficult."

He barked out a laugh, and it echoed all around us. "What are you talking about? You're honest and funny and strong. You're one of the most caring people I know. Come on, now. This isn't you."

I nodded. He was right. This wasn't me.

Wolf Wayburn had ruined me.

And I didn't know how to get myself back.

"I'm done talking about it. I want to ski." I took off for the chairlift, and Hawk followed.

This had always been my happy place.

But I felt anything but happy.

thirty-four

. . .

Wolf

"SHE'S BEEN in a mood since the day you left. It's a good thing you're a Navy SEAL because I think it's going to take some work to get her back," Everly said with a shrug.

"Work has never scared me. Your sister on the other hand —she terrifies me."

I knew better than to call Dylan because this needed to happen face-to-face. I'd had a hellish last few days and had just gotten back to the States a few hours ago. Bullet had flown back with me, and he was with Jaqueline and the kids now. We'd both spent a little time in the hospital before we could get the hell out of there and head home. He'd officially let the Navy know that he was retiring, and he'd accepted a full-time security position with the Lions.

Hawk had helped me set this up, and I was preparing to grovel.

She chuckled. "You're a brave man, Wolf. It took a lot for me to get her to come out here today. Let's get you out on the mountain."

The snow was coming down hard now, and I grabbed my boots and skis before we made our way outside. I had a backpack on my back, which I'd be giving to Hawk up on the hill. We'd come up with this grand plan that Everly would say she wanted to stay in the clubhouse, and Hawk would ski with Dylan—until he found a way to ditch her at the top of the hill so he could help me.

Everly walked with me until we were a few feet away from the chairlift, and she looked down at her phone. "Okay. They just got to the top, and he's going to tell her that his mom is calling about Jackson as soon as you get on that chairlift. Then he'll tell her to go down the hill on her own. You ready?"

"I am. Thanks for your help, Ever."

She smiled. "Nothing I wouldn't do for Dilly. Just don't break her heart again, or I will hunt you down and torture you slowly."

I chuckled as I stepped into my skis and held up my hand before making my way to the chairlift. When I got to the top, I looked around to make sure she wasn't there. I spotted Hawk, and he waved me over.

"Did she go?"

"She's being a stubborn ass. She wanted to wait for me. I kept telling her to go, so she just took off thirty seconds ago. You've got your work cut out for you."

I nodded and dropped my poles before handing him my backpack, pulling off my coat and then my sweater. Hawk shoved them into my backpack as he stood there, laughing his ass off.

I covered my mouth with my hands and blew into them for some heat one last time before stepping out of my skis to pull off my jeans, and then I slipped the boots back on and stepped into the skis once again.

"Is this funny to you?" I asked, standing there in a pair of black boxer briefs and nothing else but a beanie and some gloves. I reached for the front pocket of the backpack and pulled out the letter I'd written Dylan before I'd gone in that tunnel, then looked down for a place to tuck it before sticking it inside my boxer briefs.

"It's fucking funny. And you are definitely getting some looks." He whistled.

I glanced over to see a group of women staring and smiling at me.

"All right. I need to go. You'll have my clothes down at the bottom?"

"I've got you, brother. I'll take the small hill down, and Ever and I will be waiting for you. She's wearing all black, so you'll find her pretty easily. Go get your girl." He clapped me on the shoulder, and I used my poles to take off.

"You're crazy. It's freezing out here. Why aren't you wearing any clothes?" a dude around my age shouted as I paused at the top of the hill.

"I'm eating crow, brother."

"Ahhh... it's always about a girl, isn't it?"

"Never has been before now." I pulled my goggles down over my eyes and spotted her about halfway down the hill. There were only a few people on this run right now, so I'd be able to keep my eye on her. "But there's a first for everything."

He held up his fist, and I gave him a pound.

"Go get her!" he shouted as I took off.

I intend to.

It was cold as a horse's balls in the winter, but I'd been through worse. I didn't even care because I just wanted to see her. Talk to her.

Explain myself.

Tell her why I did what I did.

I'd had a few days to think since I'd last seen her.

Days outside of that cave before we got Bullet out, wondering if we were going to get home alive.

Days after wondering if Bullet was going to make it.

Time to think.

And every thought I had, had been about this girl.

Dylan Thomas.

The most stubborn, strong, infuriating, beautiful woman I'd ever met.

The missing piece I didn't even know I needed.

It's like the first time you come up for air after being underwater for a long time, and you suck in that first long breath.

It's your lifeline.

She'd become my lifeline.

I closed the distance as she stormed down the hill.

She was fast.

I was faster.

Because I was now on a mission to catch her. The snow had stopped falling briefly, giving me a clear view down the mountain.

She skidded to a stop at the bottom of the hill as I swerved around and circled her before snowplowing and coming to a complete stop right in front of her.

She lifted her goggles from her face, and her eyes widened as she took me in. Her gaze moved down my body before moving back up to meet mine.

Her dark brown eyes were wet with emotion before they hardened, and she glared.

That was her. Hot and cold. Ice and fire. Love and hate.

"What are you doing here?" she hissed, before her hand reached out to touch the large bandage over my chest. "Oh my god. Were you shot?"

I moved forward and dropped my poles before reaching for her gloved hands. "No. Well, yes. But not in the chest."

"Are you okay?" Her voice wobbled.

"I'm fine. Better now that I'm here with you."

She shivered and I tugged her jacket together and pulled the zipper all the way up, just beneath her chin.

"You're practically naked and you're worried about my neck being cold?" She shook her head with disbelief.

"Yep."

"I hate you so much," she said, and the tears started to fall. "Look at what you've done to me. *I cry now.* All the freaking time." She yanked out of my grip and held her chin high.

"Minx," I said, tugging off my gloves so I could touch her. I used the pads of my thumbs and wiped the tears from her cheeks. "No more crying."

"You don't get to decide when I cry and when I don't. We're not together. Remember? You ended it." She crossed her arms over her chest.

"I did that to keep you safe because I know you. You'd have gone there, thinking you could help me. But you couldn't. You aren't trained to help me. So, I did what I did to keep you safe. And you did what you did to keep me safe, right?"

Her nose was red, and her gaze watched me cautiously.

"How did I keep you safe? You didn't allow me to do anything to help you." She rolled her eyes.

"You didn't tell anyone where I was. You could have caused a whole lot of shit for me, but you chose not to."

She shrugged. "I heard Bullet is going to be okay. It would have been nice for you to call and tell me."

"Dylan." My voice was firm, and she straightened.

"What?"

"I love you. I told you a few nights before I left, but you were sleeping." I reached into my briefs, and her jaw fell open as I pulled out the folded-up piece of paper. "I wrote this to you before I went into that cave to get Bullet. I didn't know if I'd be coming out."

Her eyes softened, and another tear rolled down her cheek as I handed her the note.

"You wrote me a letter?" She tugged off her gloves and dropped them in the snow and held out her hand.

"I did. You know I'm a man of few words, but when it comes to you—I'll always break the rules."

She unfolded the paper and read it aloud, probably just to torture me.

"Minx. I love you in a way I didn't know was possible. My life doesn't work now without you, and I want you to know that if I don't make it home, you were my last thought. My only thought. I know you're pissed because you're always pissed at me, right?" Her words broke on a sob, and she smiled up at me, tears streaming down her pretty face before she looked back down at the paper. *"I left you because I would die before I'd let anyone, or anything, hurt you. This is what I know. My need to protect you is innate. And if I survive this, I'm coming for you. I'll always come for you, Minx. You're mine, and I'm yours. No more secrets. No more exit strategy. And if I don't come back, I hope that you won't date anyone else because I will hunt that fucker down from the grave. I love you. The big, bad Wolf."* Her voice shook, and she broke down right in front of me.

This strong, stoic woman was making herself vulnerable for me.

I wrapped my arms around her and pulled her against my chest.

"I love you. I love you so fucking much," I said again, making sure she knew it. Moving forward, I planned to tell her often. Because the way I felt about this girl had been what I thought of when those two bullets pierced my skin before I dove into that helicopter.

"Did you really come out here in your underwear to tell me this?" she croaked as she pulled back to look at me.

I nodded. "It's your fantasy, right?"

"This is better than the fantasy." She placed a hand on each of my cheeks. "I love you."

"Love you, too." I kissed the tip of her nose.

"You must be freezing," she said, her voice laced with concern. She ran her hands up and down my chest, trying to warm my skin. But I was fine now that I was with her. Hell, I'd spend the night out here if she wanted me to prove my point. "Why do you have a bandage over your chest? And what are those bandages?" She pointed at my arm and my leg, where two small bandages covered my wounds. "Were you stabbed? Burned?" Her eyes were panicked as they searched mine.

"I'm fine. This one is the only one that matters. It's my reminder." I stepped back and reached for the edge of the large bandage that covered my chest and tore it away from my skin, exposing the tattoo that now covered my chest. My heart specifically.

Minx.

Her fingers gently traced over the black script, and she raised a brow.

"Damn. This is some serious groveling. I hated you so much just an hour ago, and now—"

"Now, you love me. Which means you'll hate me again in another hour. It's what we do." I chuckled and reached for her hand. "I'm not a man who gives my heart away, Dylan. And maybe that's because it always belonged to you, even before I met you. But it's yours. Love me. Hate me. It doesn't matter. We belong together."

"We do, don't we?" She pushed up on her tiptoes and kissed me. "But you said you weren't shot in your chest? Did you get shot somewhere else?"

"I took a bullet to the calf and one to the arm." I shrugged.

"You could have been killed," Dylan said as she took in the bandages.

"But I wasn't."

She ran her hands over my chest. "Fair point. Let's get some clothes on you so you don't get pneumonia and die just when you finally confessed your undying love for me."

I glanced around and waved as Hawk and Everly hurried toward us.

"Well, looky here. Looks like someone is out of the doghouse," Hawk said as he wrapped a red-and-black wool blanket around me.

"Where did this come from?" I asked as I reached for Dylan's hand.

"Everly brought it in the car because we knew you'd be freezing."

"I've been telling him to run over here and give it to you. You've been standing out here in the cold for thirty minutes," Everly said.

"My boyfriend is a Navy SEAL. This is nothing for him." Dylan chuckled as she leaned against me.

Hawk grabbed our skis, and we made our way toward the lodge.

"Your boyfriend, huh?" Everly teased. "Wow. Dilly usually holds a grudge for a good week. This is impressive work."

"What can I say… she loves me." I waggled my brows.

"Well, you are half-naked, looking like every woman's fantasy, with a tattoo of my nickname across your chest. You brought your A-game."

"As long as I'm your fantasy, that's all that matters," I said, leaning down close to her ear as Hawk and Everly walked in front of us.

"You always have been." She shrugged.

"Even when you said I had a micropenis?" I pulled her closer and wrapped the blanket around us both.

I wanted her closer.

Needed her closer.

"Yep. Even then."

"Even when I said you had two vaginas?"

She chuckled. "Even then."

"Same, Minx. Same."

Because it was the truth. She'd been it for me since the day I met her. She'd wormed her way into my cold, jaded heart, and she'd never left.

And I planned to keep her there forever.

thirty-five

· · ·

Dylan

WE'D BEEN BACK in the city for a week, and we couldn't get enough of one another.

Christmas was around the corner, and Wolf and I were lying in bed, sipping hot chocolate, arguing, per usual.

"Those are your two choices. You pick which you want to do."

"That's how you ask a woman to live with you? By threatening to knock the wall down between our apartments?"

"No," he said, setting down his mug before reaching for mine and putting it on the nightstand. He yanked me down so I was lying flat on my back and moved so quickly, I gasped as he propped himself above me. "I gave you two choices. Knock the fucking wall down or find a new place together. That's called compromise."

I chuckled. "That's called being a Neanderthal."

He rolled his beautiful blue eyes. "Time's ticking, Minx."

"You sure you can handle being with me all the time? That's a big commitment."

"I'm sure. How about you?" His lips teased my ear, and I nearly arched off the bed.

"I'm sure. I told you I was all-in."

"So, what do you want to do?" he asked as he kissed his way down my neck.

"Well, I think it would be nice to stay here because we already have this place. But we don't need both places. Your apartment is plenty big enough for both of us." I was panting now as his lips moved to my collarbone, and he pushed up to look at me.

"You want to just live in this apartment together? I thought we'd make it our own by finding a new place or tearing down the walls."

"What if we stay in this apartment in the city and get our own place in Honey Mountain? We both love getting away from the hustle and bustle here. We could spend our weekends there."

"Ahhhh… I like the sound of that. We could ski naked on the slopes in the winter and skinny dip in the lake in the summer." His mouth was back on me as he pulled down the sheet and covered my breast with his lips. His tongue was warm and silky as he circled my nipple.

"I will never ski naked," I groaned, my fingers tangling in his hair.

"Never say never, Minx."

"I'll go in the lake naked with you, but not in the snow."

He moved to the other breast, and my eyes fell closed. His hand trailed down my belly and stopped between my legs, and he stroked me a few times.

"What else won't you do?" he asked as he lifted his head to look at me again. His fingers were still moving between my legs, and I was so turned on, I couldn't think straight.

"There's nothing else I wouldn't do," I whispered.

"Me either. I want to do everything with you." He reached for the nightstand, and I wrapped my fingers around his forearm.

"I've never been with anyone without protection, and I'm on the pill now."

"I haven't either. I'd fucking love to feel you wrapped around my cock with nothing between us."

"Me, too."

He was fast, but I was ready. He flipped us over and settled me above him, as he was now flat on his back, and I was straddling his waist. His hands were on my hips as I shifted, centering myself just above his erection. I wrapped my hand around his shaft and teased my entrance.

"Is this what you want, big, bad Wolf?"

"You're what I fucking want," he growled.

"I'm yours." I slowly moved down, taking him in, inch by inch. My head fell back at the feel of him bare inside me.

"Fuck," he hissed. His hand came up to the side of my neck, his thumb gently tracing my jawline. "You feel so fucking good."

"You do, too," I groaned as I started to move. Up and down. Slowly at first. He tugged me closer so my mouth was on his. My lips parted, allowing his tongue inside as he kissed me deeper. His fingers tangled in my hair as we found our rhythm.

We kissed, and we moved together for so long that my entire body was tingling. A layer of sweat covered my back and neck, but I didn't want to stop.

I never wanted to stop.

This man had made me want things I never thought I'd want.

A commitment.

A future.

A home.

And so much more.

"I love you, baby," he said when I lifted my lips from his and started to move faster. My head fell back, and my hair trailed behind me, grazing the tops of his thighs. One of his hands moved to my hip, controlling the pace, as the other covered my breast, and he tweaked my nipple.

Faster.

Needier.

Our breaths were frantic and labored.

Our bodies crashed into one another over and over.

Again and again.

"Come for me, Minx." His voice was so sexy, and his hand moved between us, knowing just what I needed. And that was all it took.

I exploded.

The brightest colors lit behind my eyes as an overwhelming orgasm ripped through my body. Wolf didn't miss a beat. He pumped harder and faster.

He shouted my name as he went over the edge right along with me, and we both continued to move together.

Riding out every last bit of pleasure.

"I love you," I said as I fell forward, and he wrapped his arms around me.

I'd never thought I'd be a woman who would tell a man I loved him every day, least of all during sex.

But I'd felt it.

Oh, man, had I felt it.

And I wasn't afraid of it. I wasn't afraid of falling hard for this man because I knew, without a shadow of a doubt, he would always catch me.

He was the big, bad Wolf to the rest of the world.

But to me, he was just—everything.

My lover.

My best friend.

And my heart.

When our breathing settled, he rolled me to the side and smiled before pulling out slowly. He pushed to his feet.

"You don't need to dispose of a condom," I reminded him.

"I know." He walked into the bathroom, and I heard the water turn on before he came striding toward me with a towel. He gently pushed my legs apart, and the warmth of the towel hit my center.

He took his time cleaning me up, and it might have just been the sexiest thing I'd ever seen.

And keep in mind, the man had just skied down a mountain wearing nothing but a pair of boxer briefs a week ago, so topping that was no easy feat.

But this kind of care, coming from this gruff, tough man—it did something to me.

"That was sexy," I said, as he continued to move the towel between my legs.

"You're sexy." He dropped it onto the floor and then moved to sit beside me, pulling me back into his arms.

"Do you ever think about getting married? Having kids?" he asked.

"I never used to. But I think about it sometimes now."

He stroked my hair away from my face. "Yeah?"

"Yep. How about you?"

"I never used to, either. When I was a SEAL, my job was dangerous. I didn't know how Bullet was able to separate that part of his life. You know, going into missions knowing he might not come out. Knowing those boys and Jaqueline were waiting for him."

I rolled on my stomach so I could see him. "Maybe it gave him something to fight for."

"Yeah. When I was heading into that cave, I didn't know what I was walking into. And it was your face that I saw. I realized I had something bigger than myself to fight for. Sure, I'd always thought of my family, but for the first time, Minx, I saw a future. A future with you. And I knew I had to get out of there."

I ran my fingers over the scar from the bullet wound on his upper arm.

"What did you see in that future?"

"Nothing specific. My adrenaline was pumping. But it was your face. It was you. The rest of my life was with you."

I sighed. "I guess I'm sort of like a bullet. The kind that gets in there but doesn't come out the other side."

"Those are the kind that kill you," he said as he barked out a laugh.

"I'm not going to kill you. But I am going to keep you."

He smiled this wide grin on his handsome face. Just enough gruff peppered along his jaw to make him look sexy as hell. "Good. Because I'm not going anywhere."

I settled my head on his chest and listened to the sound of his heart as I dozed off.

And there was nowhere else in the world I'd rather be.

————

Christmas Eve at the Wayburns' was about as entertaining as Christmas would be at my dad's tomorrow morning.

I loved Wolf's family.

The house looked like something out of a magazine, but it still managed to be homey at the same time. Holiday music piped through the surround-sound speakers as Seb and Sabine met us at the door, and we all found a quiet place to chat in the library, where we sat down on the couch with a glass of champagne. There were about thirty-five people meandering around from the parlor to the formal living room.

"So, you're finally admitting that you're together. This is a very exciting change of events, brother dearest." Seb chuckled.

"Shut the fuck up. And that drug-dealing friend of yours better not show his face here tonight," Wolf grumbled.

"Nope. He actually left the country. Possibly on the run. I haven't heard from him since he showed up uninvited to the game, but Mom heard about it from the neighbors." He laughed.

"Good. I hope he stays away."

"Should you really be acting like I'm the one to be worried about? I mean, you left the fucking country, had Dilly here all upset, and then you got shot twice. Glass houses, brother."

"Touché." Wolf raised his glass to Seb's, and Sabine rolled her eyes.

"So, what did you decide? Are you knocking down a wall between the two apartments?" Sabine asked, leaning her head on my shoulder. We'd grown close since Wolf had scared the hell out of all of us.

"We're going to move into his place and find a place of our own in Honey Mountain, as well," I said, and she squealed.

"I love Honey Mountain. Let's all get houses there."

Wolf groaned. "Why is everyone so fucking clingy now?"

"Because we love you," his sister said, blowing him a kiss just as Miranda walked in.

"There you are, there you are," she sang out, and we all chuckled as she dropped down on the couch beside Wolf.

"No more hiding in here." Natalie appeared in the doorway. "It's time for dinner."

She waited for us all to stand and hooked her arm through mine. "I'm so glad you're here."

"Me, too." I kissed her cheek, grateful for this family and how, in so many ways, they felt like my own.

It had always been that way with Wolf.

And his family was no different.

We spent the rest of the night eating and visiting with Wolf's family and friends. We snuck out because we were heading to Honey Mountain tonight so that we could wake up there to see the kids on Christmas morning.

"I love your family," I said as Gallan drove us toward the helicopter.

"They love you. In fact, my father told me they like me a whole hell of a lot more now that we're together."

We pulled into the gas station, and Wolf shifted me off his lap and pushed the button to lower the partition just a little bit. "I've got it, Gallan."

He stepped out of the car, and I glanced out the window and chuckled when I realized it was the gas station where we'd met for the very first time. I leaned over to roll down the window to tell him, and he was standing there.

"Hey, this is the place where we met." I waggled my brows.

"Is it?" he asked. His voice was all tease as he leaned forward, his forearms resting on the window. "Is this where you insulted me and called me all sorts of names?"

"Well, you did cut me off." I smirked.

"I remember every detail of that day. The way your dark brown eyes were full of golden fire. The way your hips moved in that sexy-as-fuck pencil skirt. The way that smart mouth of yours frustrated the hell out of me."

"Ahhh... such sweet memories."

Before I realized what he was doing, he dropped to his knee. "We don't do anything conventional, Minx. But you're it for me. I already know you're my forever, so I thought we could make it official. We love big. We fight hard. And we just work. I'm not certain about a lot of things in this life, but I'm certain about you. About us."

Tears were streaming down my face as I had half of my body hanging out the window, watching him. "And look at you, making me cry again. You've ruined me, Wolf Wayburn. You've made me a big sap."

I was so far out the window now that he pushed to stand and pulled me all the way through, and my legs wrapped around his waist.

"What do you say, Minx... You want to get hitched?" He held a black velvet box in his hand and flipped the top open with his thumb.

The man was too smooth for his own good.

My eyes bulged at the sight of the gigantic yellow diamond with pavé diamonds around it, all set on a platinum band.

"Oh my god," I whispered as he slipped it out of the box with one hand, still holding me with the other. "It's the most beautiful ring I've ever seen."

"I chose the yellow diamond because it's the same color as the pops of yellow in your eyes when you're turned on."

My head fell back in laughter. "Is that so?"

"I know every fleck of yellow and gold and amber. When you're happy, when you're angry, and when you're pretending you aren't stewing." His tongue swiped out to wet his bottom lip. "So, is that a yes?"

"You had me at *turned on*. It's a big, fat yes." I kissed his forehead, his cheeks, his nose, and then his lips.

He chuckled and slipped the ring onto my finger. "Nothing like a gas station proposal, huh?"

"It's so us."

"I wanted to do this with just you and me before we went to Honey Mountain."

"My family is going to freak," I said as my hands tangled in his hair. The streetlights shone down on us as we stood in the parking lot with cars driving by around us. Nothing else mattered but us in that moment.

I'd shut out the rest of the world.

Just like I always did when I was with him.

"Remember when I came to the slopes in my underwear for you?" he purred as he pulled open the car door and settled me on the seat.

"Yes."

"I asked your dad for his blessing that weekend. I knew if I survived getting Bullet out of there, I was going to do this. I don't think he's told your sisters, but he knows."

"What did he say?" I asked.

"He said it was about time we both came to our senses

and that when you know, you know. Then he went on to do a few Rocky Balboa quotes." He chuckled.

Gallan put the window down briefly and congratulated us before honking the horn a few times in celebration.

"Thanks for asking my dad first."

"Thanks for marrying me." He nipped at my ear.

"I never thought I was the marrying type, and then I met you."

"I'm pretty irresistible," he said, his voice laced with humor.

"So cocky. But so true."

"And you are the most irresistible woman I've ever met. Even with just the one vagina."

I laughed as I tipped my head back to look at him.

"Well, it's pretty magical as is, right?"

"It is. The best around." He smirked.

"I never thought I'd want forever with anyone, but I want it with you."

"That's a good thing because I'm all yours. No getting rid of me now."

"I promise to still hate you sometimes," I said.

"I promise to hate you, too. But I'll always love you more."

We pulled up to the hangar, and the car came to a stop.

"I love you," I said as he opened the door.

"Of course, you do." He winked over his shoulder, and I laughed as he helped me out of the car.

"Come on. We've got Christmas and then a wedding to plan. Forever starts right now, Minx."

"Forever started the day I met you, Wolf Wayburn."

And that was the truth.

I'd found my forever when I wasn't even looking for it.

And now I couldn't live without it.

epilogue

. . .

Wolf

FOUR MONTHS LATER

"I'm excited to see the restaurant," Dylan said as I helped her out of the car. I paused to speak to Gallan, letting him know I'd text him when we were ready to go. Dylan waved at our driver before he pulled away from the curb.

I looked up to see a tall brick building with rustic wood accents. We'd come out to Cottonwood Cove to see Hugh's restaurant, Reynold's Bar & Grill, that he'd recently opened. The place was packed, and the energy was high. Country music played through the speakers, and it was impossible to miss the cool vibe as we stood on the sidewalk, taking it in. The bar was hopping, and the restaurant was packed, as well.

"This is nice. And it looks like business is booming." My fingers intertwined with Dylan's, and I led her to the large dark wood doors, which were propped open. The weather was finally warming up after a brutal winter, but it was still breezy and cool in the evenings, but today was particularly warm outside.

The hostess greeted us, and when Dylan gave our name, she clapped her hands together once.

"Oh, yes. You're Hugh's cousin. He's expecting you. Let me take you to the table that he set aside for you." She motioned for us to follow her, and she continued chatting as we walked through the restaurant. "He's been so excited for you guys to get here. Don't tell him I said that; he'd probably be embarrassed." She giggled and fanned her face.

We arrived at the table, and Dylan thanked her as I pulled her chair out for her. Once we were both seated, she leaned close to me, her jasmine scent making it hard to concentrate. Damn, I couldn't get enough of this woman. Never thought I'd be engaged, but even more surprising was that I couldn't wait to walk down that aisle and make it official.

I wanted the whole fucking world to know she was mine.

"Clearly, she has a crush on Hugh." She smirked.

"Who?"

"The hostess. Did you see how red her face was when she was talking about him?"

"No. I was too busy looking at your perfect ass sway in those jeans," I said.

She chuckled. "Baby. Focus. The poor girl was all worked up. This is how it was when we were in college. Girls would fall all over the guy. Hugh's always been a bit of a playboy, and women eat that up."

"Funny, he told me that he was practically your body-guard in college because all those lame-ass college dudes were all over you."

"We did make quite a pair." She waggled her brows. "And then I met this gorgeous, infuriating, broody Navy SEAL, and that's all she wrote."

I leaned forward and nipped at her bottom lip just as a hand came down on my shoulder.

"Do you need a room?" Hugh said as he pulled out the chair beside us and sat down.

"Always," I admitted.

Dylan smiled and shook her head. "Hugh, this place is amazing. I'm so proud of you. You always said you would follow in Uncle Bradford's footsteps, and look at you now."

I'd met his family at Ashlan and Jace's wedding a few months ago, and I'd learned that Hugh's parents had been in the restaurant business, as well. Hugh had taken over their burger place and their small pub a few years ago, and he'd finally opened his own place now.

"It's got a great vibe. And the place is jam-packed, so you're clearly doing something right." I leaned back in my chair and glanced around again.

"Yeah. It's been really good so far. I can't complain. I got your wedding invitation the other day. Who'd have thought Dilly girl would ever be such a swanky bride?"

"Me," she said. "I've always had an inner swanky side. I just saved it for my special day."

We were getting married in a few weeks, and we were having the wedding at my parents' home in the city. My mother, of course, was over the moon, and she and Dylan were planning the whole thing together. As far as our big day went, I cared about two things.

The bride having everything she wanted.

And getting her out of her dress as soon as possible after the wedding.

We had a lot to look forward to between the wedding and my father's retirement party shortly after the wedding. I'd be stepping into his shoes at work, and I'd have my wife by my side, so it didn't get much better than that.

"I'm really happy for you guys. It's going to be a gorgeous day. Damn, we just had Ashlan and Jace's wedding not that long ago, and now, here we are again. You Thomas girls sure are busy." Our server arrived at the table with a bottle of wine and three glasses, even though we hadn't ordered anything yet. "I have our best bottle of wine to celebrate you being here and your upcoming nuptials."

Once the glasses were filled about halfway, we each held up our glasses and clinked them together before taking a sip.

"Yeah, I've heard from everyone in the family, and they'll all be there." Dylan set down her glass.

"They wouldn't miss it for the world."

Apparently, all the cousins had spent summers together growing up, and they'd always been close.

"Hey, boss," the hostess said as she waggled her brows, and this time, I noticed that her face was bright red. I'll be damned. My future wife was the most observant person I'd ever known. "There's someone here to see you."

"I didn't think you'd make me stand at the entrance and wait for her to come call for you," a voice said from behind the hostess before a woman with dark hair jumped out.

"Oh. I asked her to wait," the hostess grumped.

Hugh was on his feet and wrapping his arms around the other woman, which appeared to upset the employee who'd come to get him. On further inspection, the hostess couldn't be more than sixteen or seventeen years old. I glanced up to see Dylan raise a brow at me.

I told you so.

I raised one back.

You did, but you don't need to be so cocky about it.

We had a way of communicating without words. It was similar to my relationships with my SEAL brothers, but then you throw in the fact that she was the most beautiful woman I'd ever laid eyes on, we had explosive sex—a lot of it—and I was madly fucking in love with her.

Dylan was standing now after Hugh set the stranger down on her feet and told the hostess it was all good, and she could get back to work. I almost laughed at the way she sulked and walked away.

"Lila, right? You're Travis's little sister? We met a couple of times when we came for the summer, but it's been years." Dylan hugged her.

"Yes. It's so good to see you, Dylan."

"Wolf, this is Lila James. She's my best friend's little sister. You're looking at the NCAA cross-country champion right here."

Lila's cheeks pinked before extending her hand to me when I pushed to stand.

"Hi, Wolf. Nice to meet you. You can stop bragging now," she said, smiling up at Hugh.

Hugh's gaze moved from Lila's feet to her face. She may be his best friend's little sister—or whatever the fuck you wanted to call it—but the dude was checking her out.

"Glad you're coming home for a little bit, Snow," Hugh said, as Dylan and I returned to our seats.

I wasn't sure what the situation was between them, or why he called her Snow, but I could tell that he was happy to see her.

"Me too. It feels good to be back. Travis thinks it's a mistake, but he doesn't get to boss me around anymore." She shrugged. "All right, well, I don't want to interrupt your dinner. I'm meeting some friends in the bar, and we're going to have a drink and some appetizers. I'll see you later this week to talk about the new job?"

Hugh nodded. "Yeah. Looking forward to getting you started."

"Me too." She smiled and held up her hand. "Good to see you, too, Dylan. And nice to meet you, Wolf." She started to walk away and then turned back. "Oh, and, Bear, your teenage hostess practically gouged my eyes out when I asked for you. I guess you're still breaking all the girls' hearts." She smirked.

Interesting. They both have nicknames for one another.

Hugh gave her a slow nod, but he stood there watching

her walk away for so long that Dylan finally had to clear her throat to get his attention.

"I haven't seen Lila since we left for college," she said, as Hugh sat back down in his chair. "Wow. She's all grown up, and she's absolutely stunning."

"Did she move away?" I asked.

"Yep. She went to run for Northwestern University in Chicago on a full ride scholarship," Hugh said.

Dylan studied her cousin. "You sure seemed happy to see her."

"Yeah, it's nice to have her back but she won't be staying long. Travis doesn't want her to give up all the good things she's got going for herself by coming back here." Hugh reached for his wine glass, appearing to be a million miles away. "All right, tell me more about this wedding."

"Well, it's going to be fancy, but with an edge. Imagine the most beautiful wedding gown you've ever seen, and then put a pair of cowboy boots underneath it." Dylan chuckled, and we spent the next few hours talking about the wedding and eating some of the best food I'd ever had.

When we finally said our goodbyes and headed out to the car, Dylan rested her head on my chest as we headed home.

"Hugh said he knows where you're taking me on the honeymoon. Why won't you tell me?"

"Because I want to surprise you. You've asked a couple hundred times. The answer is still the same. No. You have to wait."

She chuckled and tipped her head back to look at me before she jumped up and wrapped one leg around each side of me, straddling me. Her hands rested on each side of my face.

"I have my ways of getting things out of you, Wolf Wayburn," she purred as she ground up against me, knowing I was already hard as a rock.

"I can't wait for you to try again. Remember, I'm a trained

SEAL. I'm trained not to speak, even when you're grinding that sweet pussy of yours against my cock."

"Ohhhh… we're bringing out the dirty talk, I see," she groaned, and I tangled one hand in her long hair that ran down almost to her waist, and the other hand rested on the side of her neck, my thumb tracing her jaw.

"I never said I played fair, Mrs. Wayburn."

"I like the sound of that," she whispered as her lips moved closer.

"Me, too. Love you, Minx." I tugged her closer.

"I love you, big, bad Wolf."

The End

Do you want to see Dylan tell her sisters that she's engaged? Click the link for a special bonus scene https://dl. bookfunnel.com/5nwcg1z08h

Did you enjoy your journey with the Thomas sisters? How would you like to meet their cousins (and see glimpses of Honey Mountain) in my new interconnected Cottonwood Cove series…

Pre-Order book 1, Into the Tide HERE https:// geni.us/intothetide

Do you want to see Hugh Reynolds meet his match with his best friend's little sister? Keep reading for a sneak peek of Chapter One from Into the Tide!

into the tide

Chapter One

Hugh

I planted my ass on a stool at the bar at Reynold's, the restaurant I'd opened a few months back. Business was booming, and between opening this place and running my parent's pub and diner for them, I was existing on very little sleep. I hadn't expected business to be as busy as it had been since the day we'd opened the doors. We were understaffed at the moment, and I needed help.

The door swung open, and sunlight flooded the space, highlighting the marble bar top and the rustic wood flooring. My two best friends, Travis and Brax, walked in, letting the door fall closed behind them.

"Hey, sorry we're late. I've got sandwiches." Travis held up a bag and walked toward me.

"Thanks for picking those up." I pushed to my feet and made my way around the bar to grab us each a drink. "You guys want a beer?"

"Hell, yeah." Brax pulled up a barstool and sat down. The guy was always down for a good time.

"Nah. I've got to go back to work, so I'll just stick to water for now. Those fuckers on the site can't figure out how to hammer a nail unless I'm standing right over them," Travis grumped.

I laughed and handed them their drinks, grabbing a Coke for myself. Travis was a contractor and was responsible for most of the new builds in town. He'd worked on this restaurant for months, and the dude never let up. But he was a grumpy motherfucker, and most people pissed him off. Luckily for me and Brax, we'd been his best friends since preschool, so we usually got a pass.

"Are you sure you aren't just micromanaging them again?" I raised a brow and unwrapped my sandwich.

"Right? You're a bit of a dick when it comes to working. Are you sure this isn't you being a control freak?" Brax asked over a mouthful of food.

Brax owned the largest real estate company in Cottonwood Cove, and he was about as relaxed as you get when it comes to running a business. Those two were night and day with how seriously they took things, and I fell somewhere in between.

"Pfft... please. I have no choice when, every time I look over, they're fucking around." He shook his head before narrowing his gaze at me. "You look tired. I'm sure you're ready for Lila to start helping out." Travis's little sister was going to be home for a few months, and she'd agreed to come work with me at the restaurant.

"Yeah. You're giving me Trav-vibes over here, and I can't deal with two damn control freaks in my life." Brax reached for his beer.

"Yeah, I'm fucking drowning, man. The timing couldn't be better with her coming on board, even if it's just temporary." I took a bite of my turkey on rye and shrugged.

Travis studied me. "This place is a huge undertaking, and you're still trying to run Burgers and Brews and Garrity's.

You can't be in three places at once, brother. And you're talking about expanding to the city? You need to figure out how to manage all this shit. Lila's brilliant, so hopefully, she can help you get things figured out and running smoothly over the next few months."

He was right. I'd taken over our family restaurants when my father retired, and since opening my own place, I was stretched too thin.

"I can't believe I'm going to say this, but I actually agree. And you know it kills me to agree with this one," Brax said, as he flicked his thumb at Travis. "But you need help, or you're going to burn out."

"Agreed. And you know I don't like people in my business, but I obviously trust Snow," I said after I finished chewing, referencing the nickname I'd always called Lila.

My siblings were all busy with their own careers, and my youngest sister, Georgia, was taking summer school classes and would be graduating from college in December. I sure as hell wasn't going to burden any of them with my shit.

"Yeah, I think she'll help out a lot, and then you can figure out if you need to bring on more people full time when she leaves. She'll definitely get your ass organized." Travis reached for his chips and tore open the bag.

"Aside from work, you look like you're wound awfully tight, so I'm guessing you haven't been laid in a bit either." Brax barked out a laugh. The dude was too loud for his own good. And of course, the asshole found it hilarious that I was in a bit of a rut in that department. I hadn't been out in two months, and I slept every free minute I had, but it still wasn't enough.

"Thanks for pointing that out, dickhead."

"You're a lover, man, so you're always moodier when you aren't getting female attention. No shame in needing a release, brother."

"Oh, for fuck's sake. He gets laid plenty. That's hardly been a problem for him." Travis rolled his eyes.

"Hey, maybe I'm tired of the game. I'm getting older. And not all of us are so lucky to marry our fucking high school sweetheart," I said, shooting Travis a look.

He nodded over a mouthful of food and reached for his water. "Cry me a river. I'm not Hugh fucking Reynold's, Cottonwood Cove's biggest player."

"Don't be humble, you broody bastard. It doesn't suit you," I said.

"Please. This fucker doesn't have a humble bone in his body." Brax smirked. "Still not sure why Shay agreed to marry you and carry your moody-ass spawn… but I wouldn't look a gift horse in the mouth."

"You and me both, brother," Travis said.

"She's the best. Don't fuck it up." I reached for my glass and took a sip. They'd just recently found out that Shay was pregnant, and he was still processing the fact that he was going to be a father soon. "Anyway, Snow was in here last night with Delilah, Sloane, and Rina. Are you still pissed about her being back here?"

Travis's shoulders stiffened at the mention of his little sister's decision to come back home for a few months. I wouldn't bring up the fact that my dick had also stiffened at the sight of her last night. She'd always been gorgeous and sweet, but hell, when she left Cottonwood Cove four years ago, I'd looked at her more like a kid. But Lila fucking James wasn't a kid anymore. She'd just graduated from college and returned home. I'd called her Snow for as long as I could remember because the girl had watched *Snow White* more times than any one kid should, and her dark hair and all that sweetness made it an easy nickname to hold on to.

Travis loved the shit out of his wife, Shay, but anyone that knew him well knew that his kryptonite was Lila. They'd been through a shit ton at a young age, and he'd been looking out for her our entire lives. The number of dudes the three of us had threatened on her behalf over the years was countless. And when she'd left for Northwestern in Chicago on a full cross-country scholarship, he'd been proud as hell. But I knew that it was tough for him having her so far away, as it had always been the two of them against the world.

"She's refusing to stay with me and Shay because she says we're newlyweds and are expecting our first baby, so she thinks we deserve some kind of bullshit privacy. My dad is a fucking train wreck, but that doesn't stop Lila from wanting to fix him. She's too fucking loyal. Too fucking stubborn. And too fucking good to be dealing with his shit. I'm sure it's a big adjustment. She's been racing and competing for so long, and now that part of her life is over. As much as I want her to come back home, I don't want her to get sucked into my dad's bullshit. She deserves better. She deserves more." He shook his head.

"Fuck, Trav. You've got to chill out. She's a grown-ass woman. I say this because I also ran into her last night when I stopped by to have a beer with this fucker," Brax said, raising a brow at me as if I didn't remember. "She was just leaving, and damn, your baby sister has grown up into a fine woman." He whistled, knowing it would get under Travis's skin. We'd seen her over the years since she'd gone away to school, and we'd always given him a hard time about how pretty she was.

"Fuck you. Don't be looking at Lila like that. She's still young. Far from a grown woman." Travis shot Brax a warning look. "She got offered a job at that big, fancy company she interned with this past year. She's so damn smart. They agreed to hold the position for her until the beginning of September so she could come home for a while and make sure Dad was okay. The man isn't going to change, so I don't know why she's insisting on putting her life on hold."

I understood his need to protect her because I had two sisters my brothers and I were protective of. But this was different. My siblings and I had two parents who worried about all of us plenty. But Travis was all Lila had unless you counted their father, who had checked out years ago.

"Let her come back for a little bit and spend some time with you and Shay. Maybe your dad will clean up his act while she's here, and then she'll head back to Chicago. She said the job is waiting for her, so let her take a few months and just relax."

"Jeez, man. I agree. The girl has worked her ass off. When we were younger, I can't remember a time when she wasn't out on a run or training. It took her to college, where she spent four years going to class and racing. Let her have a break." Brax shook his head, and I chuckled because the dude was rarely logical, but this was the wisest thing he'd said in a while.

"She seems happy to be home. She's probably exhausted," I said.

"That's true. But I don't like her living at Dad's house. He runs with some shitty people, per usual. I don't want her around all that, you know?" Travis balled up the paper that had been wrapped around his sandwich and set it on the bar.

I understood his concern. We'd always looked out for her. There were a few years between us in age, and at times, I knew she resented the way Travis, Brax, and I treated her like she was a little kid. And if I were being honest, I didn't particularly like the idea of her staying at her father's house, either.

"You know, I've got the casita at my place. I'll offer it to her when she comes in this week to talk about the job and what she'll be doing. Georgia plans on moving in there after she graduates, but that won't be until after Snow heads back to Chicago." Georgia was my baby sister, the youngest of us Reynolds kids. We were close, and she had already called dibs on the casita after I bought the run-down cabin two years ago and completely renovated it.

He was nodding around a mouthful of food. His shoulders had completely relaxed.

"Thanks, brother. I owe you one for this."

"Should I be offended that you didn't ask me to hire her? We can always use an extra hand at the office, and I'll bet there'd be a lot of dudes in Cottonwood Cove buying homes if Lila was working there," Brax said as he waggled his brows mischievously.

"Fuck you, dickhead. Not a chance. Hugh would never cross that line, but *you* think with your dick too much."

I barked out a laugh when Brax gaped as if he'd just been slapped in the face.

"Hugh thinks with his dick, too. Just ask Tory Hopkins. She drunk-cried to me last week about the way you rocked her world and then left her high and dry." Brax finished off the last pull from his beer.

I shook my head. "You asshole. Why are you even talking to her about that? We dated in high school, and, if you recall, I found her under the bleachers, giving Tony Randall a blowie. So she can spin that shit however she wants, but I didn't leave her high and dry. I left her with Tony's dick in her mouth. It's not my problem that she still misses mine all these years later."

"And this is exactly why neither of you fuckers is allowed near Lila. But at least I know this one is loyal as hell, and he'd never make that mistake. You, on the other hand… I'm not sure you wouldn't cross that line."

"Fuck off. Have I ever crossed the line?" Brax held his hands up as if he were completely offended.

"You did fuck my high school girlfriend," Travis reminded him.

"You were on a break!" Brax shouted. "And no offense, but everyone fucked Donna. She was a busy girl."

"Hugh didn't, and if you'll recall... *neither did I.*" Travis tried to hide his smile. It was an ongoing joke between the three of us. Donna had strung him along for a year and a half, which was a lifetime for a teenage boy. She'd claimed she was saving herself for marriage. And then she'd dumped him and proceeded to get busy with everyone he knew.

But not me.

I wasn't that guy.

I loved women and enjoyed sex. I dated plenty, but I preferred to keep things casual. Hadn't found any reason not to yet. And I respected bro code and took that shit seriously.

Brax did, too; he just talked a big game.

"All right, I need to get back to work." Travis grabbed his wrapper and dropped it in the bag before pushing to his feet and clapping me on the shoulder. "Thanks for helping out Lila."

"Of course. You know I'd do anything for her."

He saluted me and Brax before making his way out the door.

"I guess I better get going too. We're busier than usual lately," Brax said. "So, you sure you can handle having Lila working here?"

His tone was all teasing, but I knew what he was insinuating.

"Of course. I've known her my entire life, and she's Travis's sister. No problem. Some of us can control our dicks." I raised a brow and gave him a hard look. I'd always looked at Lila like a little sister. And sure—I wasn't blind—she was fucking gorgeous now.

But unlike Brax, I knew when someone was off-limits.

And I didn't appreciate the way he was talking about her.

"Yeah, yeah, yeah. But damn, she looks good, man. She's smart and has her shit together. It might not be as easy as you think, brother." He smirked before clapping me on the shoulder. "But I'll be here to talk some sense into you when you waver."

"Never going to happen. Get to work, jackass."

He raised his hand over his head and walked out the door.

I chuckled at the fact that Brax was worried. I'd never had a problem controlling myself around women.

I wasn't that guy.

This would be a piece of a cake.

Pre-Order Into the Tide HERE https:// geni.us/intothetide

acknowledgments

Greg, Chase & Hannah...You are the reason that I chase my dreams every day! My forever loves!

Willow, I am forever grateful for you. Thanks for being such a bright light in my life. Your friendship means the world to me! Love you!

Catherine, thank you for being YOU! For the talks and the laughs and all the love! (And the peppermint bark which got me through these last few days!) Love you!

Nina, thank you for being the best gift of 2022! Cheers to many more years together! Love you!!

Valentine Grinstead, I absolutely adore you! You made this year extra fun, and I look forward to many more trips together next year! Love you forever!

Kim Cermak, I would absolutely be lost without you! Thank you for keeping me on track and staying on top of everything. I am FOREVER grateful for you!!

Christine Miller, I can't begin to thank you for all that you do for me from giveaways to releases...and all the things. I am SO THANKFUL for you!

Sarah Norris, thank you for the gorgeous graphics and for

staying on top of all the things this year! It's been a lot and I am incredibly grateful for YOU!

Debra Akins, thank you for the amazing reels and TikToks and for helping to get my books out there! Your support means the world to me!! Thank you so much!!

Kelley Beckham, thank you for setting up all the "lives" with people who have now become forever friends! Thank you so much for all that you do to help me get my books out there! I am truly so grateful!

Annette, Jennifer, Abi, Pathi, Natalie, Doo and Caroline, thank you for being the BEST beta readers EVER! Your feedback means the world to me. I am so thankful for you!!

Hang Le, thank you for bringing Dylan and Wolf's story to life and capturing them so beautifully in this cover. I am so grateful for YOU and can't wait to see what you come up with for the next series!!

Sue Grimshaw (Edits by Sue), I would be completely lost without you and I am so grateful to be on this journey with you. I love your feedback and talking through all the things with you!! Thank you for always making time for me, and being so supportive and encouraging.

Ellie (My Brothers Editor), I love being on this journey with you, and I am beyond grateful for your friendship and for all of your encouragement and support. Love you!

Julie Deaton, thank you for working with my crazy schedule and for all that you do to make sure I put the best book out there that I can. It means the world to me!

Jamie Ryter, I am so thankful for your feedback (and yes... your comments continue to be the best part of my day and so entertaining!) Thank you for loving Dylan and Wolf and for your help making Only Mine the best it could be. I am so grateful for you and so happy to be working together!!

Christine Estevez, thank you for all that you do to support me! It truly means the world to me! Love you!

Crystal Eacker, thank you for always being there to jump

in and help me with everything from forms to sign up's to formatting checks! You are the absolute best! Xoxo

Jennifer, there are people who come along in your life who you just know are so special—and that is YOU! I am endlessly thankful for you and all that you do to support me every day! Love you my sweet friend!

Paige Bode, I mean, does anyone have your dance moves? I think not! Thank you for all of your support and for helping spread the word about my books! I am forever grateful for your book recs, for our decorating chats and most of all...for your friendship!! Love you!

Rachel Parker and Sarah Sentz, your support means the absolute world to me. Thank you for taking the time to chat with me for every release!! You are my good luck charms!! I am so grateful for your friendship and your kindness!

Mom, thank you for reading all of my words, and for the feedback and the love! I am so thankful that we share this love of books with one another! Ride or die!! Love you!

Dad, you really are the reason that I keep chasing my dreams!! Thank you for teaching me to never give up. Love you!

Sandy, thank you for reading and supporting me throughout this journey! Love you!

Pathi, I can't put into words how thankful I am for YOU! Thank you for believing in me and encouraging me to chase my dreams!! I love and appreciate you more than I can say!! Thank you for your friendship!! Love you FOREVER!

Natalie (Head in the Clouds, Nose in a Book), Thank you for all the support this year and always! I can't wait to see what the future holds, and I am so grateful to be on this journey with you! Love you!

Sammi, I am so thankful for your support and your friendship!! Love you!

Marni, I love you forever, my little Stormi, and I am endlessly thankful for your friendship!! Xo

Acknowledgments

To the JKL WILLOWS… I am forever grateful to you for your support and encouragement! I can't wait for us to all be together in 2023!! Love you!

To all the bloggers and bookstagrammers who have posted, shared, and supported me—I can't begin to tell you how much it means to me. I love seeing the graphics that you make and the gorgeous posts that you share. I am forever grateful for your support!

To all the readers who take the time to pick up my books and take a chance on my words…THANK YOU for helping to make my dreams come true!!

keep up on new releases

Linktree Laurapavlovauthor
Newsletter laurapavlov.com

other books by laura

Cottonwood Cove Series
Into the Tide
Under the Stars
On the Shore
Before the Sunset
After the Storm

Honey Mountain Series
Always Mine
Ever Mine
Make You Mine
Simply Mine
Only Mine

The Willow Springs Series
Frayed
Tangled
Charmed
Sealed
Claimed

Montgomery Brothers Series
Legacy
Peacekeeper
Rebel

A Love You More Rock Star Romance
More Jade
More of You
More of Us

The Shine Design Series
Beautifully Damaged
Beautifully Flawed

The G.D. Taylors Series with Willow Aster
Wanted Wed or Alive
The Bold and the Bullheaded
Another Motherfaker
Don't Cry Spilled MILF
Friends with Benefactors

follow me...

Follow Me...
Website laurapavlov.com
Goodreads @laurapavlov
Instagram @laurapavlovauthor
Facebook @laurapavlovauthor
Pav-Love's Readers @pav-love's readers
Amazon @laurapavlov
BookBub @laurapavlov
TikTok @laurapavlovauthor